DESCENT

The Inferno Trilogy
Book One

DESCENT

A. R. Nicole

Published by

PINECONE PUBLISHING
PineConePublishing.com
ARNicole.com
AR@ARNicole.com
Follow on Twitter @ARNicoleBooks, Pinterest, and Facebook

Cover and Interior Design: Nick Zelinger, NZGraphics.com
Editor: Barb Wilson, EditPartner.com
Book Shepherd: Judith Briles, TheBookShepherd.com

ISBN: 978-1-7320699-0-9 (print)
ISBN: 978-1-7320699-1-6 (e-book)
Library of Congress Control Number: 2018949933

First Edition

Printed in the United States of America

For my father,
who told me I could be anything and
never let me believe otherwise.

I love you.

Books by A. R. Nicole

The Inferno Trilogy
Book One: Descent (2108)
Book Two: Torment (Spring 2019)
Book Three: Ascent (Summer 2019)

Watch for The Aftershock Series
Coming in 2020

BOOK ONE

DESCENT

PROLOGUE

THE ECHOING *CLICK* of the lock broke the quiet serenity of the room, ricocheting violently down the hall and across the vaulted ceilings. The large wooden door swung open, gracefully gliding against the marble floor. Moonlight filtered down through the intricate stained glass windows, throwing eerily dark and distorted figures onto the eastern wall. The lights were off. The pews were empty. A few burned-down candles flickered in the sanctuary.

Perfect.

A lone dark figure strode silently between the polished wooden benches, carrying a bundle wrapped in white. The thin fabric billowed out around him like gossamer wings on the breeze. He paused at the steps leading up to the sanctuary, bowed his head to pray, then stepped up to the glistening marble altar and placed his bundle down upon it. The meager candlelight reflected off of the gold flecks in the stone and through her bright red hair. He gently pulled the fabric aside to reveal a woman's face. Bowed, long fingers passed through the autumn curls and down the side of her cheek. She wasn't perfect, but she was close, and still so beautiful.

The figure circled the altar, lighting a single ivory pillar candle and placing it at the top of the sanctuary stairs. He descended the steps lightly, the soles of his shoes barely making a sound on the marble floor. He paused at the second pew, his arm outstretched and his fingers resting on the polished wood.

"Per me si va ne l'etterno dolore. Per me si va la perduta gente. E io etterno duro. Lasciate ogne speranza, voi ch'entrate."

Through me, you go to everlasting pain. Through me, you go to pass among lost souls. And I endure eternally. Abandon all hope, ye who enter here.

The words faded off into the night air. He retreated into the dark, his long nimble fingers caressing the edge of each pew as he went.

The door closed silently behind him. The oppressive silence of the night descended from its hiding place in the corners of the ceiling.

It was as if he'd never been there at all.

1

THE FIRST PINK streaks of daylight had just started to extend over the eastern horizon when Andrew Freedman set his feet on the cool stone floor. Despite recent renovations, the dorm rooms on his side of the hallway still ran cool at night, and with fall approaching, it was getting harder and harder to walk around barefoot first thing in the morning. And he hated slippers.

He reached for a worn-out Notre Dame hoodie at the foot of his bed, shoved it awkwardly over his head, and stared out his window toward the mountains. They were still black against an inky blue sky. He glanced at his alarm clock. 06:18. He'd beaten his alarm by twelve minutes.

"If we were meant to get up this early, you'd think *He* would've made it a bit easier to handle," he mumbled grouchily.

He ran his fingers through his floppy hair and sighed.

There's beauty in the world, even this early in the morning… Aw, who am I kidding? I really just wanna go back to sleep.

He pressed his palms against his eyes, banishing the remaining haziness of sleep. When he felt awake enough to stand without falling over, he stood up, found his much-hated slippers, and made his way into the main hallway.

A scant amount of illumination emanated up from the small safety lights on the floor. They gave off just enough light to show any wandering night-owl students safely back to their rooms. Nobody else was awake. The hallway was completely still.

Andrew shuffled down the stairs at the far end of the hall, winding slowly around and down to the main floor. It was equally as dark and silent and undisturbed. He mentally fought back against the hair starting to stand up on the back of his neck. As serene and comforting as the main halls were during the day, they took on a life of their own at night.

Same goes for early morning.

He still wasn't quite used to the place.

Rounding the last corner, he stopped outside the doors to the chapel. Two massive slabs of dark polished wood embellished with roughened iron stood before him. He walked through them every day with the other seminary students, but only the first person to the chapel every morning got to actually open them.

For whatever reason, Andrew had been getting up early to be that person since his first few weeks at the seminary, even though it meant getting up two hours before the other students. He had to beat the fathers, too. It had been easy to do when the sun had come up before six a.m. It was getting harder and harder with every day closer to winter.

He twisted the old lock and with one click, it opened. He pulled on the left side first, the old hinges softly creaking under the weight, then the right. The chapel was just starting to lighten up. The eastern windows were filtering the pink rays of the sunrise. The rosy color sharply contrasted with the darkness penetrating through the western glass.

Darkness and light, he mused.

Andrew started toward the front of the nave on autopilot, brushing his fingers along the sides of the pews. His gaze strayed to the sanctuary, focusing on the wooden cross hanging from the ceiling, Christ himself displayed from its beams. Everything was in its proper place, exactly like last night after they'd filed out of evening prayer.

Wait, what the heck is that?

There was something on top of the altar, wrapped up in what looked like a white bedsheet. He slowly moved closer, looking at both sides of the aisle, narrowing his eyes to try to get a better look.

The chapel doors were "locked" at night, but anyone could just flip the lock to gain access. Every now and again, a homeless man named Kevin would come into the chapel after a rough night, but the man was harmless. He always slept in a back pew. And he definitely didn't have curly red hair.

Andrew hesitantly stepped up to the altar, avoiding a half-burned ivory candle, and gently peeled back the edge of the thin fabric. His fingertips made contact with skin. Ice-cold skin. He frantically tugged harder and the cloth fell away, revealing a ghostly white face and black eyes. Milky, black eyes.

"Oh, my God..."

He turned away, his hands flying to his mouth to stifle a scream.

She's not moving. She's not breathing. What am I supposed to do?

He flew down the stairs and started running toward the door, his pulse pounding.

The fathers. I have to wake up the fathers!

He was halfway down the aisle when he stopped abruptly and turned back around. She was just lying there. Alone. Scared. Abandoned. He breathed deeply and wiped the cold sweat from his forehead.

Enough. Get over yourself. Someone left her here. You're responsible for her now.

He gripped the side of a pew until his knuckles were white from the pressure. He slowed his breathing, then started walking back toward the sanctuary as steadily as his legs would carry him. His voice was shaking, but the early morning sunshine didn't seem to mind.

"Per istam sanctan unctionem et suam plissimam misericordiam, indulgeat tibi dominus..."

And that's how Father Dominic found Andy Freedman at a quarter 'til seven, shaking and stumbling over his Latin, giving the last rites to a Jane Doe in the chapel of St. Vianney Seminary, the Sunday morning sunlight streaming in warm and inviting from the east.

2

EARLY WEEKEND MORNINGS were by far the best time to run. The streets were always deserted, except for the occasional homeless man doubled over in an alley or a scantily-clad college girl on an early walk of shame. The Sunday air was crisp and cool, with just enough bite to merit sweatpants and a long-sleeved shirt. The chill would burn off in an hour, he knew, but right now, fall was decidedly in the air. Some of the leaves by the river trail had started to turn. Patches of bright red and orange were already visible amidst the green leaves.

Detective Gabriel Ryder glanced down at his watch. 06:57 flashed back at him against a fluorescent green background. The rhythmic pounding of his sneakers on the pavement echoed up the sides of the skyscrapers. He'd been out for almost forty minutes. His breathing was even. His muscles were warm, but far from fatigued. Sweat was beading on the back of his neck, but there wasn't much of it.

Damn it. This isn't supposed to be a fucking jog in the park.

He hadn't been able to sleep, despite the better half of a bottle of scotch. At a quarter to six, he'd hauled himself out of bed, thrown on his gear, and gone for a run. It should have calmed him down, allowed his brain to focus on something other than the job.

Instead, it had just given him more time to think.

His last case had ended over a month ago, but it hadn't ended well. One little girl was still in the hospital, unresponsive and on a ventilator. There was talk from the district attorney's office that the sick son of a bitch responsible was going to claim insanity. Insanity … for serially stalking and raping seven-year-old girls across three states and down in Mexico.

Fuck him.

Gabriel growled in frustration and picked up his pace, his muscles finally starting to protest against the lack of oxygen.

He was about to cross over 19th Street, intent on keeping on Larimer Street for a few blocks until he could pick up the river trail and head north when he felt his phone vibrate in his right pocket. He swore under his breath, slowed to a jog, and answered.

"Yeah, what?"

"Well, you sound cheerful this morning," came the voice on the other end.

"Don't I always?"

"It's an improvement from a month ago, I'll give you that."

"Gee, thanks."

"Why are you breathing so fast?"

Gabriel rubbed the fingers of his free hand on his temples and rolled his eyes. He came to a stop at a crosswalk.

"Do you need something, Blake, or are you just calling to fucking chat on a Sunday morning?" he snapped back.

There was a pause on the other end of the line, followed by a long sigh.

"You're a pain in the ass, Gabe."

Ryder mentally cursed and forced himself to soften his tone. He'd given his partner enough hell to deal with over the last couple of months. The least he could do was rein in his anger and give Nolan a break, just this once.

"Yeah, sorry. I know. What is it?"

"I thought I'd give you fair warning. Captain'll be calling you in a few minutes."

"About what?" He stiffened.

"Don't worry, you're not in trouble this time. We've got a new case."

Thank fucking Christ. For once it isn't ... wait a minute, what?

"I thought Robinson and Terry were on call this weekend."

"Yeah, me too, but I guess we're still the lucky ones that get it."

"Great. What is it?"

"Dunno. He didn't tell me. Probably some Cherry Creek socialite found her husband in bed with the nanny, and the gun under the mattress just happened to go off. You know, our specialty."

"What a way to start a Sunday." Ryder groaned.

"That's what I said. So, whatever you're doing now, you'd better stop and go make yourself pretty. I'll be outside your place in fifteen minutes."

"Better make it twenty, Nolan."

"Why? You need time to make yourself some egg white and kale monstrosity?"

That drew a hint of a smile and a soft chuckle.

"No, but you've got to give me enough time to get home and shower."

"Get home? Why aren't you at home? Wait ... are you seriously out running right now? Fuck me, Ryder. You realize normal people are sleeping at this hour, right?"

"Bye, Nolan."

Gabriel ended the call, placed the phone back in his pocket and shook his head.

The first six-and-a-half miles may not have done the trick, but the last half mile home was going to kick him in the ass.

3

DETECTIVE BLAKE NOLAN took a hard left onto 14th and maneuvered his Subaru Forrester up to the curb. He was late. He knew it. He looked like he'd just rolled out of bed, and he wasn't wearing matching socks. He hadn't stopped for his usual gas station cup of coffee either, and the lack of caffeine was starting to have painful consequences.

He scanned the sidewalk, looking for his partner. Nowhere to be seen.

Phew … dodged a bullet there.

Maybe, just maybe, it had taken his partner longer to sprint back from whatever corner of the city he'd been running in this morning and get a shower.

Nolan smirked. He had to give it to his partner. He was dedicated to staying in shape, even with their crazy work hours. The women in the department certainly seemed to appreciate the effort. When Gabe actually found time to sleep was still up for debate, but today wasn't the first time he'd called with a case and interrupted a run or training session or … what was that Jewish Army defense-fighting thing again?

Nolan himself wasn't so dedicated. At 5'10", he wasn't the biggest guy on the squad, but he could tangle with the best of them. A few too many late-night pizzas and a recent divorce had wreaked havoc on his midsection, and the NFL schedule was definitely winning out over trips to the gym.

Oh well. I still have my farm-boy good looks. Thanks, Mom.

Mrs. Deborah Nolan called once a week to remind her son of his humble beginnings behind a tractor.

A sharp double-tap at the passenger-side window startled him. He twisted in his seat to see immaculate black slacks, a drink caddy, and a rolled-up white paper bag waiting impatiently for him to open the door. He leaned across the console, popped the lock, and pushed the passenger door open.

"You know, most people would get that fixed at some point."

Gabriel slid into the passenger seat, handing over one of the large white travel cups from the drink caddy. Nolan scowled. His partner was immaculate, like always. Black suit, crisp white shirt, ice-blue tie, and freshly shaved.

And I look like Mr. Magoo. Fucking GQ jackass.

Nolan shrugged and took a long drink of strong black coffee. "Yeah, but what's the point? It'll just break again, and I can't have the damned thing in the shop forever. Last time, it took two weeks just to get the part in. What am I going to do? Call you if I need a ride?"

"You could always try your luck."

"I'll pass, Ryder. I know how you fucking drive."

Nolan took another long drink from his cup. "Ahh, black coffee straight up. Breakfast of champions." He eyed his partner's cup suspiciously. "And just what is that? A mocha triple-shot Frappuccino with extra sunshine and sprinkles?"

Ryder wrinkled his forehead. "Don't be ridiculous, Blake."

"So? Like I would have any idea. What is it?"

"Coffee," he huffed impatiently. "Can we go?"

"Only after I get whatever is in that bag."

"Here." Ryder dropped the bag in Nolan's lap and sat back in the passenger seat. He took a drink from his own cup and stared out the window impatiently.

Blake opened the bag and grinned. "Two bear claws, huh? You buttering me up for something?"

"Not a chance."

"You want one?"

"Christ, no."

"Too many carbs for your girlish figure?"

Gabriel shook his head, his leg tapping impatiently up and down against his forearm. "Sure. Go with that."

"Good. That's the right answer. Now we can go."

Nolan grabbed one of the pastries out of the bag and shifted the car into drive. There was hardly any traffic on the road. It was easy to pull out into the light flow on 14th and head south.

They drove in comfortable silence for a few minutes, but Nolan knew it wouldn't last long. His partner had been fidgeting since he'd handed over breakfast. An agitated Gabriel Ryder never kept quiet for long.

"Where exactly are we going?" he asked, looking out the passenger window.

"Captain didn't tell you?"

"No. He just called to tell me to wake up and get my shit together. That you were headed over to come get me."

"That's it?"

"The call lasted all of thirty seconds, Blake."

"Yikes. He must've been pissed."

"Yeah. So, where are we going?"

"The seminary."

"Which one?"

Nolan pulled up to a red light and glanced over at his partner. "There's more than one?" he asked sheepishly.

"Of course."

"You say that like I should know that, Ryder."

"No, I…well, I…guess not. Look, would it make sense for a Baptist priest to train with a bunch of Presbyterians?"

"No."

"No. Exactly. The different branches of Christianity and even branches of other religions each school their own priests, or the equivalent. The first seminary was started by the Roman Catholic Church, but since then there have been…"

Blake waved his hands in front of his partner, signaling his surrender. "Okay, okay, I get it. Relax."

"So, which one are we going to?"

Nolan hoisted himself awkwardly off his seat and pulled a scrap of paper out of his front pocket.

"St. John Vianney Theological Seminary."

"They're Catholic."

"Of course you would know that. Can you save the rest of your brainpower for later, please? I haven't had all my coffee yet, and I need at least this whole cup before I try to keep up with you at eight a.m. on a Sunday."

Ryder nodded his assent and went back to staring out the window.

The car fell back into silence. Nolan narrowed his eyes at his partner. Soon enough, they'd be going on four years together. It hadn't been a smooth start, and more than once he'd thought about just what an odd couple they made. But for whatever reason, they worked well together. Who would've guessed they'd become one of the powerhouses of the department?

Blake had been loaned out to the Major Crimes Division of the Denver Police Department temporarily just over four years ago, supposedly only long enough to help bridge the squad when they'd been short-staffed. Weeks turned into months, and before he knew it, Captain McCallister had called him over to meet Gabriel Michael Ryder, the department's golden boy and his new permanent partner in Major Crimes.

Surprise, surprise.

At the light, Blake turned south onto University Avenue. Soccer moms and the few socialites who hadn't had too much to drink last night were slowly making their way outside in coordinated tracksuits and Chanel sunglasses. He elbowed his partner in the ribs.

"So, is that why you get up so early and go running?" he grinned, pointing at a particular woman on the sidewalk.

She was platinum blonde, decked out in pink velour, and clearly had a standing appointment with the plastic surgeon.

Gabriel smirked and shook his head. "I get up early to avoid running into that."

"Ha! I dunno, man. A woman like that, with all that money. She's gotta take care of herself."

"A doctor takes care of nipping and tucking and peeling on a regular basis, Blake. An overworked aesthetician and a maxed-out credit card do the rest." Ryder scowled into his coffee cup.

"Looks great in a dress though, right?"

"Until you get it off, feel the silicone, and see all the scars. Then it's a bit of a let-down, don't you think?"

Nolan nearly shot coffee out of his nose. "How in the hell do you come up with that crap?" he choked out, laughing in between sputtering attempts to clear the coffee out of his lungs.

"Tell me you weren't thinking the same thing."

"Well, now I am. All right, fine. If you don't want that—" he pointed to another similarly dressed woman pushing an expensive stroller, "—then what do you want?"

Ryder stayed quiet and turned to look out the window. "You're exceptionally interested in my personal life this morning, Nolan," he said.

"I've gotta figure you out sometime, buddy. There has to be something that makes you tick."

Gabriel shook his head. "It's not that."

His tone was enough to shut his partner up. Blake could feel the anger slowly seeping across the car from the passenger seat.

Why the hell did that set him off?

Blake shrugged to himself and turned onto a side road.

Nothing like an unexplainable Ryder mood swing to top off a Sunday morning.

Nolan pulled off to the side of the curb and shut the engine off.

"Well, we're here."

No response. He snapped his fingers twice in the direction of the passenger seat.

"Hey, Ryder! Buddy, we're here. Wake up."

Gabriel looked blankly over at his partner, his eyes unfocused. He registered Nolan's lips moving, then rubbed his fingers over his eyes, blinking rapidly to bring his partner's face into focus.

"Sorry."

Nolan shrugged. "Keep yourself shut up in that head of yours all day, and I might be able to run a lap or two around you. Show the captain I'm worth the salary he signs off on." He opened the driver's side door. "Shall we?"

Gabriel opened the passenger door and stepped into the morning sun.

It had finally started to warm up. The birds that hadn't already migrated south for the winter were waking up, singing in the trees in the morning sunshine. The seminary building was visible on the other side of the street, the bell tower reflecting the light back up into billowing white clouds overhead.

"Where are we going?" Ryder asked.

"The chapel."

"I hope you know where that is, Blake."

"I'm going to follow the flashing blue lights. Besides," he smirked over his shoulder, "I'm sure you'll tell me if I get it wrong."

4

THE TWO DETECTIVES crossed quickly over the well-manicured lawn, weaving in between pairs of uniformed officers, toward a side entrance blocked off by crime scene tape. Ryder held the tape up for Nolan, then ducked under himself a few beats behind his partner. There was one cop on duty outside the main door. Nolan waved, and the officer immediately waved back.

Ryder ignored them both.

The building's entryway was modest: two-story vaulted stone ceilings, muted walls, and appropriate Catholic artwork adorning just enough wall space to be considered tasteful, not overdone. Several well-cared-for potted plants were scattered about in corners and on side tables. Overall, it was a quaint and likely rather peaceful place on a normal day.

At present, however, it was bursting at the seams with uniformed police officers and crime scene techs. The cacophony of witness statements and evidence collection echoed sharply off the walls. At the far left of the room were two larger wooden doors, hanging wide open with crime scene tape crisscrossing the opening between them.

Nolan took the lead. He walked over to the closest uniform and flashed his badge. "Who's in charge here, bud?"

The officer nonchalantly pointed toward a short, stocky man, also in uniform, who was standing under a rather impressive oil painting of the Virgin Mary.

"That would be Officer Gavin, sir. He's my partner."

"Who's that he's talking to?" Nolan asked, pointing toward a portly man sitting to Gavin's right, his head held in his hands.

"Father Dominic. He's one of the priests here at the seminary. I think he called it in, but don't quote me."

"Okay, thanks."

Nolan glanced back at his partner, who was clearly focused on peering through that second set of doors. He rolled his eyes and snapped his fingers twice in front of Ryder's face.

"Hey. Am I boring you already this morning?" *God, he acts like an impatient kid sometimes.*

Ryder blinked hard several times, clearly having a hard time tearing his eyes away from the chapel. "Uh, sorry."

"C'mon. Let's go meet the priest."

"The who?"

"See that guy over there? The one that looks like a fat Antonio Banderas?" Nolan pointed across the entryway. "That's the guy who called it in. He's a priest."

Nolan led the way across the foyer and tapped Officer Gavin on the shoulder, once again flashing his badge. "Thanks, officer. We'll be able to take it from here. We'll take a copy of your notes when you get a minute."

The cop nodded without argument and peeled off toward one of the back corners where the crime lab techs had gathered.

Blake turned his attention to the man sitting with his head hung in his hands, dressed in burgundy pajamas and a blue bathrobe that had clearly seen better days.

He must have gotten dressed in a hurry.

The poor guy didn't even have socks on.

"Father?"

The man raised his face to look at Nolan, who smiled and raised his badge for the third time in as many minutes.

"I'm Detective Nolan. This is my partner, Detective Ryder. We're from Major Crimes."

The man extended his hand and shook Nolan's. Ryder's stayed in his pockets. The priest didn't seem to mind.

"Good to meet you, son. I'm Father Dominic, one of the priests here at the seminary. Thank you for coming so quickly. I… I'm sorry for disturbing your Sunday morning."

"Don't worry about it. You only interrupted this one's morning run around the greater metro area."

He gave Ryder a wink. Father Dominic looked toward the young man, clearly interested.

"Where do you run, detective?"

Gabriel's eyes narrowed. So did his partner's.

What the fuck?

"Downtown. Along the canal trail."

"Always in the morning?"

The scowl deepened on the detective's face.

Why do you give a damn when he runs?

"Sometimes."

"I've never been much of a runner myself, but I can understand the joy in it. Alone, at your own pace, a clear mind. In the early mornings, one is closer to God."

Ryder nodded stiffly, shifting uncomfortably from one foot to the other.

"But you didn't come down here for me to ask about your running habits, did you?" The priest smiled wearily.

"No, Father, we didn't," Nolan replied, stepping in front of his now clearly agitated partner. "Why don't you tell us what happened this morning."

The man sighed and closed his eyes briefly before answering.

"I turned in last night around ten, after prayer. I slept through the night and woke up around six, well before my usual alarm. I don't know what woke me up, but whatever it was, it gave me an unsettling feeling. I tried to go back to sleep, but my mind wouldn't have it. Have either of you ever experienced that?"

Ryder nodded. "Frequently."

"Well, I threw on my robe and headed down here. The chapel is quiet in the morning. It's a good place to refocus a troubled mind. And you hardly ever even notice that Andy's there."

"I'm sorry, who?" Nolan interrupted.

"Oh. Andrew Freedman. He's one of our newest students here. He's only been with us for the past few months. Very smart young man. We got him from Notre Dame." He smiled proudly.

Nolan looked up from his notepad. "And he's usually wandering around your chapel in the early morning because…?"

Father Dominic shrugged. "I'm not sure. I don't think he's too sure, either. The poor boy is not, shall we say, a morning person. I think he would sleep until three in the afternoon. After the first couple of weeks, I started finding him in the chapel in the morning. Just sitting in one of the pews, picking up, taking care of some of the homeless who find their way in. We didn't question it, and it seemed to bring him peace. Well, until today."

Ryder, who had been pacing close to the entrance to the chapel again, looked up. "So, this Andrew kid found the body?"

Father Dominic nodded.

"Yes. I came down to the chapel, and as usual, found it already open. Andy was up at the altar. I honestly didn't think anything of it at first. I walked in and was about to say my usual good morning to him."

"Something stopped you?"

"He was speaking in Latin. I recognized the viaticum."

It took a moment, but the priest recognized the confusion on the detective's face. "Oh, I'm sorry. Viaticum, it's…it's part of the last rites."

Nolan's eyebrows rose at that. "The last rites? Like, for dead people?"

The priest nodded. "I knew something was wrong, so I hurried up to where he was standing, and sure enough, there he was, giving the last rites to that poor girl."

The father shook his head. "To take the life of someone so young…what a horrible thing."

"What else?" Blake pressed.

"There's not much else to tell. The poor boy was pretty shaken up. He kept fumbling his Latin. I tried to get him out of there, but he wouldn't budge. Kept muttering about someone needing to stay with her. So, I threw a blanket around his shoulders and went to the office, called our rector, Reverend McCoy, and came straight back. I sat with Andrew until you all showed up."

"Why call someone else before calling the police?" Ryder asked, not bothering to hide the suspicion in his voice.

"Ryder…" Nolan warned.

"No, no, it's all right," Father Dominic waived his hand dismissively in the air. "I know we're all taught to call the police the second we see something like this. But you must understand that, perhaps as awful as this may sound, I was concerned more for Andrew than that young girl. He had seen to her well-being, detectives. I had to see to his."

Nolan glanced toward the corner to look at his partner, expecting a sarcastic remark and preparing a glare of his own. Instead, Gabriel was staring at a painting of an angel on the far wall and slowly nodding his head in understanding.

Another mood swing.

Nolan shook his head in his partner's direction, then spoke. "Thanks, Father. I think that's all we have for now."

The priest stood, rubbing his hand over the back of his neck. "Then if you don't mind, I think I will head back to the office to update the rector and the rest of the staff. Nothing detailed, of course. Just that we won't be using the chapel for a while."

"Sure thing."

The two men shook hands, and Father Dominic headed down the hallway. He stopped next to Ryder and looked up at the painting on the wall.

"Guido Reni painted that in 1636. Sadly, I have never seen the original. We make due with a printed reproduction."

Ryder nodded. "For the Santa Maria della Concezione in Rome. There's a similar mosaic in St. Peter's Basilica."

"Very good, detective. I assume then you know the story behind that painting?"

He nodded.

"It has some personal significance for you, then?"

The young man nodded again. Father Dominic recognized the look in his eyes. He looked to be in pain.

"Sicut Michael et tu vincere malum, detective."

Father Dominic smiled, patted the young man on the shoulder, and disappeared down the hall.

Ryder turned away from the painting and found his partner leaning against the wall, his left eyebrow raised.

"You wanna fill me in on your little bonding moment there?"

"Don't worry about it."

"Ryder..."

"I said don't worry about it," he growled.

Nolan sighed. There was that tone again. He wasn't going to get the answer he wanted. So, he tried for halfway. "Will you at least explain the art history lesson you two had over there?"

His partner smirked.

That means he's going to lecture me about something. Great.

"That's a reproduction of a painting on the wall of a church in Rome. It depicts the Archangel Michael defeating Satan during the war in Heaven."

"I wasn't aware there was a war in Heaven."

Gabriel nodded. "Satan and his followers were cast into Hell after they were defeated. Did you know that Satan was an angel before he was cast down?"

"Fascinating," Nolan replied sarcastically. "Now can we go talk to the freaked-out seminary student or do you need more time pretending to be the Encyclopedia Brittanica, Catholic Edition?"

"I thought I was supposed to be the cranky one this morning."

"Yeah, well, if I don't get you moving, you're going to spend the day lecturing me on the fucking archangels. I'd like to eat lunch today."

"We're in a church, Blake."

It took a moment, but realization quickly dawned on the detective's horrified face. "Oh, shit! I just swore in a goddamned church."

Ryder smiled and laughed. "Look, why don't you go talk to the kid while I look around? We'll get done faster, and you probably won't swear as much if I'm on the other side of the room."

"All right. Just please don't do anything weird in there," Nolan begged, ducking under the crime scene tape. "I don't think I can handle any of that this morning."

"I bought you coffee. Quit whining."

"There's never enough coffee for some of the crap you pull, Ryder," he said as he pinched the bridge of his nose.

Gabriel waved him off without another word.

Nolan headed down the center aisle toward a pathetic-looking figure sitting in the front pew, draped in a well-worn gray flannel blanket. The poor kid looked like a complete mess. He was staring blankly at the body draped out over the altar, barely registering the crime scene team scuttling about bagging and tagging evidence.

Nolan walked up behind him slowly, not wanting to scare him. Out of the corner of his eye, he registered his partner stalking down one of the side aisles, heading toward the altar and pulling on a pair of latex gloves as he went.

"Andrew Freedman?"

The kid turned his head. "Yeah?"

"I'm Detective Nolan," he said softly, with a flash of the badge. "I want to ask you a few questions about what happened this morning."

"Didn't Father Dominic tell you everything?" he asked, clearly exhausted.

"Sure. But I still need to hear it from you."

"All right," he sighed, spinning sideways in his seat. "Where do you want me to start?"

5

THREE HOURS LATER, the two detectives were sitting in a small restaurant midway between the seminary and police headquarters downtown. They had managed to snag a table on the patio, sandwiched between an elderly couple out for a post-church brunch and a young family with an unhappy newborn.

Nolan was digging into the second half of a pastrami sandwich like a man who hadn't eaten in a week, while Gabriel's turkey club was being eyed with a look of disinterested disgust.

"You know, most humans eat their food at lunch," Nolan said between bites.

"Huh? Oh, yeah, sorry. Not hungry."

"Oh, bullshit. Even you don't run on coffee alone for more than a few hours. C'mon, eat up."

"What are you, my mother?" Ryder bristled, pushing the plate farther away.

"I'm starting to feel like it."

Blake could see his partner's growing agitation from across the table. The stress was already radiating off of him in waves.

"Fine."

Nolan started stealing fries from Ryder's untouched plate and motioned for a refill on his Diet Coke while his partner pulled out the leather binder he always carried with him. Every note, every lead, every interview; it all ended up in that binder. Cases had been cracked at three a.m. by the information contained within it. Ryder never went to a scene without it.

"All right, so what's got you wound up so tight this time, Gabe? It's barely noon."

He shook his head and started tapping his pen rhythmically against the leather. "I don't know. It all looks like a simple dump job, but something's not right. Why dump her in a church? Alleyways and street corners are easier. Hell, it's easier to dump her on the front lawn of the church. But he took her inside and all the way up to the altar. He left a candle burning..."

Ryder's voice was pressured, tense. He was talking a mile a minute. Blake held up his hands, trying to get him to slow down and take a breath.

"Whoa, whoa, back up. I agree, it's weird she was found in the church, but who knows? Maybe she has some connection there."

Gabriel shook his head. "According to the staff, including Father Dominic, nobody knew her. What did Freedman tell you?"

"Same thing. He has no idea who she is. And he was shaken up enough that I believe him. The kid's only been in Denver for a few months and never set foot in Colorado before he transferred to the seminary. Squeaky-clean record here and from Notre Dame from what I can see. Didn't even have a parking ticket as a teenager. And it seems like these guys stick to campus. They're not out picking up girls on the weekends."

"They're training to be Catholic priests, Blake," Ryder hissed, annoyed.

"Still, though." He shrugged.

"Did he tell you anything useful?"

Nolan shook his head. "Not really, no. He got up like usual, came downstairs from the dorms, opened up the chapel, and found her. I think he was still half-asleep. He thought she was one of the regular homeless guys passed out before he noticed the red hair."

"Regular homeless guys?"

"Yeah. The most frequent is some war vet named Kevin. No last name that anybody knows of. Shows up once or twice a month, usually when it gets cold. Sleeps it off, has breakfast, and then is on his way."

"We need to talk to him."

"Already got people looking for him and told Dominic to call if he shows up. You know I take care of that stuff."

Ryder nodded. Nolan always took care of the nonsense details, the grunt paperwork. It gave him the extra time to think, and between the two of them, nothing ever got missed. For all his laid-back demeanor, Blake Nolan was exceptionally detail-oriented. He crossed every 't' and dotted every 'i'. At least, at the office. His personal life was a different story.

"What else?"

"Not much. Once he figured out she was dead, he gave her the last rites. He felt like he should be the one to do it since he found her. That famous Catholic guilt at work?"

"Not quite."

"Whatever. He was halfway done when Dominic came downstairs and found him. And you know the rest. We got called in because the rector is golfing buddies with the chief of detectives and has his cell phone on speed dial. Nobody likes finding a dead Jane Doe in a church, especially in the middle of Cherry Creek on a Sunday. What'd you find on her?"

Ryder leaned back and propped his binder up on one knee, his usual posture when running through his notes. He ran a shaky hand through his hair. Nolan knew the move well. It helped him think and thankfully controlled the fidgeting. Ryder's face relaxed, the lines fading from his forehead.

"I'd put her at mid-twenties, but she looks younger than that. Red hair, brown eyes. Not a mark on her body. No tattoos or scars. Pierced ears, of course. No bruises, ligature marks, burns, tape residue, nothing. There's no sign that this girl was restrained or abused. M.E.'s office is going to run a rape kit, but I'm not holding my breath."

He turned over a few pages.

"I...I don't think...she wasn't just dumped in that church. She was placed there. Deliberately. And posed. She was on her side, hands under her face like she was sleeping. Her eyes were closed. She was wrapped up in white linen. I couldn't smell any alcohol on her..."

"Oh God, you didn't, did you?" Blake grimaced.

"I didn't what?" Ryder looked up from his binder and stopped tapping his pen against the table.

"Please tell me you didn't smell the body again, Gabe."

His partner shrugged.

"Great. Well, I'll be getting another call from the crime scene guys about you."

Nolan shook his head, exasperated.

My goddamned weird-ass partner had to go and smell the goddamned body. Again. Damn it.

"No, you won't."

"Of course I will. Every time we get called out to a homicide, you go around smelling corpses and freaking out the junior crime techs. They go home, have nightmares, and I get called into the captain's office because you're creating a 'stressful work environment,'" he shot back, folding his arms over his chest.

"That's only happened twice in the last year, and Cristoff was working today. He's seen me do it before."

"Doesn't mean it's any less creepy, Gabe."

"Doesn't mean it doesn't work, Blake," he fired back.

Nolan huffed under his breath and folded his arms across his chest. "All right, fine. So, she wasn't drunk off her ass the night she died. We don't have much to work with here."

Gabriel shrugged again.

"We've started out with less. They're running her prints through the system, and in the meantime, we have security footage to sort through."

"From where?"

"From St. Vianney. They do have security cameras there, Blake."

"Where do they put them? Inside the gargoyles?"

"On the corners of the buildings, just like everybody else. They have air conditioning and electricity, too, you know."

"It's a miracle…" was the sarcastic reply.

Nolan grinned, turned sideways over the back of his chair, and motioned for the check.

6

THE MAJOR CRIMES Division occupied the fourth floor of the police headquarters building in downtown Denver. The building itself was cold and functional, an imposing combination of brick and concrete built in the 1970s. A recent tax hike had given the department enough money to remodel the interior and bring the building, at least aesthetically, into the twenty-first century.

Nolan pulled up outside the front entrance, hung his police placard on the rearview mirror, and grabbed his bag from the backseat. Ryder followed him up the front steps, through the lobby, and into the elevator without saying a word.

The ride back had been uneventful, except for a call from the captain demanding to know where the hell they were and when he was going to get an update on the case. He'd given them a full six hours before curiosity—and probably pressure from the chief of detectives—had gotten the best of him.

Blake glanced over nervously at his partner. Something had Ryder agitated again. His right foot was furiously tapping against the elevator floor, and he had a death grip on his binder. That combination was never good.

Early on in their partnership, Nolan had taken the silence, fidgeting, and especially the mood swings, personally. It took one particularly bad case for him to blow up in Ryder's face, and it had quickly become obvious that the young man had been completely clueless about his behavior.

Blake had tried to apologize, but Gabriel had stormed out of the squad room without a word. When he'd resurfaced two hours later, the two cups of coffee and a warm doughnut he'd brought with him had substituted for the apology they were both too embarrassed to say aloud.

Affectionately and sarcastically referred to as The Talk, it hadn't solved everything, but the bumps in the road since then had been child's play. Nolan now knew his partner had more than a few quirks, most of which he wasn't consciously aware of. Almost four years in, he was able to read his partner's body language and run interference, which Gabriel seemed to appreciate more than anything else he did on a daily basis. But the agitation usually didn't start this early in a case, and it definitely wasn't this intense.

It's a dump job, Ryder. Plain and simple. What's got you so fucking riled up?

The elevator dinged and the doors opened, snapping Nolan back into reality. They stepped out into the squad room and made their way over to their desks on the south side of the floor. The unit was quiet, even for a weekend. Paulson and Avery were the only other detectives in the office, and they looked like they were about ready to leave for the day. Closing a case at Major Crimes usually meant weekend overtime for the paperwork. The pair was halfway across the bullpen when a voice snapped from the far corner.

"Nolan! Ryder!"

Captain Carrick McCallister motioned his two detectives toward his office. He wasn't happy about being called away from his day watching football and drinking beer with his sons. He couldn't imagine his detectives were any happier about catching a case when they hadn't been on call. But the chief of detectives had requested the best team he had, and he'd known who to wake up without thinking twice.

Ryder and Nolan had the best solve rate on the squad. Blake was a good cop. He worked hard, kept his head on straight, and never backed down from a fight. The squad had gotten lucky when they'd kept him after his brief loan from homicide.

And just a few months later, I found him a partner.

During his thirty-five-year career in law enforcement, six of those as Captain of Major Crimes, McCallister had never seen anything or anyone quite like Gabriel Ryder. He was only twenty-nine when they'd first crossed paths. By then, he'd had thirty-two major busts in just under three years with the narcotics squad. He'd already had a reputation for being unorthodox and difficult to work with, but his solve rate was impressive, and whatever feathers he had ruffled along the way had been minor. Once Ryder had a few more years in narcotics under his belt, McCallister had started maneuvering for the transfer. It had been a done deal the day after Nolan had been officially transferred to Major Crimes.

McCallister shook his head as they both walked into his office. Even on a Sunday, they looked like an odd couple. Nolan was in khakis, a wrinkled button-down, and his well-worn Broncos cap. Ryder wore an immaculate two-piece suit and tie.

The Gap meets GQ.

The captain sat down behind his desk and motioned for the detectives to take a seat. Nolan did. Ryder leaned against the back wall with his binder open against his thigh, his usual perch. He never sat down in the captain's office if he could help it.

"Well? Start talking. What do you have so far?"

Nolan looked back toward his partner, who was suddenly fascinated by something in his binder. He shrugged.

I guess I'll answer since you're too busy.

"Not much yet, captain. One of the newer student priests found a girl in the chapel. That kid's superior found him, called the rector, who called the chief of detectives, and here we all are. Nobody knows her. No ID. Doesn't look like she had a scratch on her. We have nothing."

The captain looked over Nolan's shoulder at his partner, who was pacing the length of his office floor.

"And you?"

Nolan followed his captain's gaze back to Ryder. The "what the hell do you want me to say?" was etched plain as day across his face.

"I...I don't have anything more than he does, sir."

"You've got to be kidding me," McCallister replied, dead-pan and clearly annoyed.

They both shook their heads.

"You both realize you're not helping my headache," he muttered.

"Mine either," Ryder snarled under his breath.

"Well, find something. The chief is already breathing down my neck to get this solved."

"Six hours in? C'mon, captain. You've gotta be kidding me. Pretty boy here needs at least a full eight," Nolan scoffed.

"Gee, thanks, asshole," Ryder spat from across the room.

Blake grinned at him over his left shoulder. "Seriously, captain, I know a phone tree got us called in on this, but how do you expect us to have something this soon on a Jane Doe dump job? We don't even have the security tapes yet. It's Sunday, for heaven's sake."

McCallister rested his head in his hands. "Where the hell is that aspirin?" He began rummaging through his top desk drawer. "Both of you, out of my office. Get something done."

"Yes, sir."

Ryder had the door open and was through it before Nolan had even had a chance to stand up. Blake was almost out of the office himself before his captain's voice called him back.

"Hang on, Nolan."

The detective visibly cringed. His fist tightened on the doorknob.

"Yup?" He closed the door. Damn it.

"Is your partner okay?"

"Why wouldn't he be?" he asked, feigning ignorance. He knew what his captain was getting at.

"You know why. That last case took a lot out of him."

"You should be asking him, captain, not me."

"And what do you think the chances are he'll answer me, Nolan?"

"You don't know until you try."

McCallister scowled at his detective from across his desk. Blake shrugged and plopped himself back down in the chair.

"Stop playing games with me, detective. How is he?"

"Look, captain, I'm not trying to be difficult here. Our last case was fucking awful. Everybody knows that. The one girl is still in the hospital and probably won't ever wake up. Ryder thinks it's his fault we didn't get to the guy sooner. That's common knowledge, even though it's bullshit. He was fine today. He did his job. Nothing jumped out at me. If he starts speaking in tongues or levitating off the floor, I'll let you know."

"All right," the older man conceded. "Just don't let anything get out of control."

"It never does, captain."

Nolan stepped out of the office and closed the door behind him. Gabriel was already at his desk, his back to the captain's office, phone balanced in between his right ear and his right shoulder.

Blake walked over to his own desk, sat down, and waited. His partner gave him a curious look out of the corner of his eye, but Nolan let it go. He knew he was in for an inquisition worthy of medieval Spain later today, anyway. Might as well not fight it.

"Uh-huh…spell that for me…department? No local family? Wyoming…okay. Yeah, okay. Thanks. Bye."

Gabriel put the phone back into the cradle and continued scribbling a few notes into his binder without looking up.

"So, the captain's worried I'm going to need a psych ward, is he?"

Blake smirked. "No, but I promised to let him know if I need to call in an exorcist. That okay with you?" he said with a grin.

"Yeah, that's fine."

"Good."

"He's having you keep tabs on me, isn't he?"

"I've been keeping tabs on you for almost four years, Gabe. Nothing's changed."

"You've never had to stay late in the principal's office before."

"That you know of."

That quip pulled his partner's eyes up off of his binder. "Excuse me?"

"I'm kidding, moron. Who was on the phone?"

Jesus, Gabe, relax.

"I'm serious, Blake."

"So am I. Calm down. You know I'd tell you if something was up. Now, who was on the phone?"

Ryder flipped back a page in his binder. "Olivia."

"Olivia…as in our crime lab's Olivia?"

"Yeah."

"Why the hell is she here on a Sunday?"

"Same reason we are. Captain called her in. She got a hit on our victim's prints."

Nolan raised his eyebrows. "Seriously? That cute little redhead's got a record?"

"Not the kind you're thinking of." Ryder shook his head. "She's registered with the State Medical Board."

"Which means…she's a doctor?"

"Yeah, well, kind of. She's a resident."

"Oh…like *Grey's Anatomy.*"

Gabe quirked his eyebrow at his partner and smirked. "Yeah, I suppose. She's in her first year of training at Saint Joseph Hospital. General surgery."

"Okay, so definitely like *Grey's Anatomy.*"

"I'm not going to ask why you know so much about *Grey's Anatomy,*" Ryder said, shaking his head and looking back down at his notes.

"Hey! Not by choice. I used to be married, remember? I had to go as McDreamy for Halloween one year."

Gabriel winced. "Sorry. I didn't mean to bring up Miranda."

Nolan waved his partner off, quickly changing the subject. "It's been over a year, buddy. It's fine. So, what else do we know about her? I'm assuming you've got a name."

"Lisa Maria Oakes. Twenty-seven. Originally from backwoods Wyoming. Went to college in Cheyenne, one year of research there, then on to Seattle for medical school. Ended up at St. Joe's for her residency program."

"We have an address for her?"

Gabriel shook his head. "Olivia said no. The information we have is from the application for her training medical license here in Colorado. She must not have had a place to live in the city when she applied, because she listed her parents' address in Wyoming. Olivia said that's pretty common."

"How would she know?"

"Her husband's a neurologist at University Hospital."

"I didn't know Kyle worked at the University."

His partner quirked an eyebrow. "What exactly do you do at the Christmas party, Blake?"

"Drink good beer and try not to be the guy wearing the lampshade at the end of the night. You're apparently off profiling the staff."

Ryder smiled.

Nolan scowled at him across the desk, his forehead wrinkling in disapproval. "I don't want to even know what profile of me you have in that head of yours."

"Who said it's in my head?" He chuckled.

"It had better not be in that damned binder, Gabe."

"Who said this is my only binder?"

"You're an ass."

"So you've told me."

"So, what do we do now?"

Gabriel sighed. "Call her family. Have them come down from Wyoming to identify the body. And first thing tomorrow, we go to St. Joseph's."

Nolan noticed McCallister eyeing them from his office.

"Well, who gets to call the family and who gets to update El Capitan?"

Ryder picked up his binder. "I'll talk to the captain and make arrangements at the hospital. You call the family."

"I'm getting the short straw here."

Ryder glanced down at his partner, who was feigning pouting at his desk. His tone softened.

"Blake, you're good with people. You know I'm not. These people are going to be burying their daughter in a few days. They're not going to know what hit them. Please do this. Their number is on my desk."

Nolan nodded. "I hate it when you're right."

Ryder walked into the captain's office.

Blake cleared his throat and picked up the phone.

7

HAVING THE ENTIRE weekend off was both a blessing and a curse. On the one hand, it meant two whole days out of the hospital. Forty-eight hours with no charts, no rounding, no pagers, nothing. It was a blessing that came around once, maybe twice a month maximum, to a chief resident. Sometimes, not at all.

On the other hand, it meant one of the other residents had been in charge of her service over the weekend, and every single patient had to be double- and triple-checked come Monday morning. Even if her own junior residents had been on call over the weekend, she would've been rechecking everything. As luck would have it, both of them had been on vacation. So, everyone was coming onto the service essentially blind.

Great.

The list was in chaos. Patients didn't have management plans. They didn't have OR dates. Lab work wasn't done. Consultants hadn't been called.

Shit.

Grayson looked up at the wall clock over the ICU nursing station. Four a.m. They had forty one patients to see before six, and most of them were new since Friday.

Her junior residents were hunched over in front of their computers, scribbling down vital signs onto progress notes as quickly as they could. They'd both been in the hospital since 3:30. She'd been reviewing x-rays and double-checking their work since 3:00, which put her wake-up time in the 2:30 area. She had two femoral shaft fractures, three tibial plateaus, and an APC-III pelvis, all without OR dates.

This morning is not going to be pleasant.

"Dr. Carter?" A timid voice piped up from the neighboring computer.

"Yes?"

"Mrs. Hernandez in 322 has a hemoglobin of 6.3 this morning…"

"Transfuse her."

"Shouldn't we…"

"Transfuse two units now. Put the order in STAT. Check a hemoglobin one hour after the second unit. If it's still low, give another two units. You follow up on that this morning, okay, Thompson?"

She glanced sideways at the computer to her left. The frightened intern looked back at his computer screen and nodded.

"S…sure," he said meekly.

Grayson shook her head and added the lab draw to her own to-do list. Chances were, even with her busy schedule in the operating room today, she would end up checking that hemoglobin value hours before her intern would. She made a note to put additional units of blood on hold, just in case.

Ugh, this is going to be a long day.

Hastily, she twisted her hair up into a messy bun and secured it with a raggedy elastic band.

"All right. Thompson, why don't you start on the third floor? Adams, you take seven and six. I'll take all the ICU patients and meet you all on four to finish up. Sound good? Does that give you both an equal number of people to see?"

Let's try for upbeat and peppy today, guys. We're gonna need it.

The two residents nodded and quickly headed toward the elevators. Thompson violently yanked up his scrub pants mid-stride. Grayson smiled, stifling a laugh.

Martin Thompson was a good kid. He was an emergency medicine intern rotating through the orthopedic trauma service for the month of October. He'd never lost his freshman fifteen from college and had, in fact, added to it every year since then. He was unsure of himself most of the time. Exceptionally timid. The rumor was that he'd bumbled his way through a couple of near-miss cases in the ER since he'd started residency in July. Grayson hoped he'd come around, but in the meantime, she knew she'd have to keep a close watch on all of his work. She'd given him the easier patients on the third floor for a reason.

Ethan Adams was another story. He was a second-year resident from her own department. His intern jitters were gone, and he was ecstatic to be back working on bones instead of colons and hearts with the general surgeons. He was calm, efficient, and a charmer, which meant he could manipulate the nurses into doing pretty much whatever he wanted, whenever he wanted. It was a bit cringe-worthy to watch, but if it meant their patients were well taken care of, then so be it. He could flirt with the 85-year-old volunteers who brought up the morning coffee for all she cared, as long as his work didn't suffer.

Grayson stopped outside the first room on her list and peeked through the large glass door. Typical ICU room, typical bed, typical beeping of ten different machines, and not a family member to be found. She flipped open the chart and looked at the most recent entries.

...Martin Oliver, 36, found down, taken for ex-fix and fasciotomies of lower extremities...multiple comminuted fractures, rhabdomyolysis and renal failure...ventilator-dependent respiratory failure...unable to find family locally...

Grayson shook her head. She walked into the room, pulled a pair of purple exam gloves out of the box on the wall, and approached the bed. Mr. Oliver didn't move. She moved on autopilot, taking off the sheets to expose his legs.

The external fixators were normal to her, but she knew they looked barbaric. Two large silver pins the thickness of drill bits stuck out from each thigh, another two from each tibia, a third from each heel, and another from the outside of each foot. Each pin was wrapped in blood-soaked gauze and then all connected together by long gray bars. The sides of the legs were flayed open and covered with black blood-soaked sponges hooked up to suction tubing.

If Mr. Oliver was lucky, the muscle underneath those sponges would be pink and healthy when they took him back to the operating room today, but if not...he might just end up losing both of his legs instead.

Grayson took off her gloves, threw them in the trash, and exited the room. She was scribbling a progress note in the chart when she felt someone tap her on the shoulder.

"Knock, knock, kiddo," came a very familiar British accent.

She smiled and turned toward the shoulder that hadn't been tapped, knowing the trick by heart.

"Dr. Mason," she nodded mockingly.

"Dr. Carter," he mocked back.

"I didn't know you knew the hospital was open this early. You medicine guys usually stroll in about nine, don't you?"

"And I'm sure you've already been here five hours, love," he teased.

Noah Mason was one of her closest friends. They had started residency together. After his four years were up, he'd chosen to stay on as head of the medicine residents for a year. He was slated to start his fellowship in pulmonology and critical care medicine at University Hospital next August.

At 6'3", slim, with sandy-brown hair and a British accent, he gave off much more of a male model vibe than an incredibly smart doctor. He'd had more than one indecent proposal during his tenure as a resident, from patients and staff alike. Unfortunately, they had all been from the wrong sex.

"So, what do you think of our Mr. Oliver here?"

"Not much, really." She sighed. "He'll be lucky if he keeps his legs."

"What makes you say that? I thought the surgery Saturday went well."

Mason frowned.

"Well, yeah, it did. I wasn't there, so I can't give you details, but this guy was down for a while. His compartments are released, but his CK isn't coming down. His renal function is worse today. I think he's going to have a lot more muscle necrosis death than we initially gave him credit for. My guess is we're going to have to take a lot of it today in the OR."

"Really? He's not gonna be able to use his legs much."

She shook her head. "It's not just that. If there's dead muscle in there, it's a great place for infection to set in. He's been running fevers. Not sky-high ones, but they're there. I can't just chalk that up to pneumonia from being on the ventilator until we take those dressings down."

"You're taking him today?"

"Yeah, as long as you guys are okay with that."

Mason nodded. "He's medically stable and already has a tube down his throat. That's the best we're going to get for now."

"Have you guys had him on antibiotics?"

"No. He wasn't spiking fevers…until you told me about it just now."

"I love it when I can do your job for you."

"Hey, give me a break. The coffee cart isn't open yet."

"Like that's an excuse…"

The two residents smiled at each other, and Mason bent down to wrap Grayson in a bear hug.

"I'm so glad you're back, Gray," he said. "I've missed you. Your co-resident is a total arse, you know that?"

She smiled. "Yeah, I know. And I've only been gone for two days, Noah."

He released her. "You need anything from me?"

"Can you figure out what antibiotic dose we should give him with his kidney failure? I want to switch him to vancomycin and zosyn, but at least one of those can kill his kidneys, right?"

"I'll take care of it. You want it scheduled round the clock?"

"Please."

"Don't worry about it."

"Thanks."

The shrill beeping of her pager drew their conversation to a close. She grabbed the black box off of her scrub pants, clicked a few buttons, and smirked.

"Well, wouldn't you know? That's my intern. One of my patients on the floor is coding. And he had all this spare time to page me about it. Hopefully, someone else is doing compressions. Care to join me?"

The intercom system suddenly chimed above their heads, and a robotic female voice started droning over the static of the loudspeaker.

...Code blue, team one, 3rd floor...Code blue, team one, 3rd floor...Code blue, team one, 3rd floor...

"You just take care of the bones, love. I'll try to get the patient's heart beating again."

"Gee, thanks."

"At least you animals are strong enough to do decent chest compressions."

The two doctors smiled at each other before sprinting off toward the elevators.

8

AT EIGHT A.M. Monday morning, Nolan and Ryder pulled up in front of Saint Joseph Hospital in a department-issued SUV. Nolan parallel parked the behemoth with ease. He always drove. Ryder always took the time in the passenger seat to think.

And he drives like a fighter pilot with a death wish. God-damned GQ jackass.

Blake stepped out of the car, walked around the front hood, and met his partner on the other side.

Ryder was restless again, tapping his foot against the pavement and looking up at the main entrance with anticipation. They'd stopped for coffee on the way, and now Nolan wasn't so sure that had been a good idea. His partner clearly didn't need the caffeine.

"Well, you know where we're going in here, buddy?"

Gabriel shook himself out of his head and nodded. "Annex Two, fifth floor. Department of General Surgery. That's the department Lisa belonged to. The head of the department is supposed to meet us in fifteen minutes."

"That's Colonel Sanders?" Blake joked.

"Dr. Sanders, yes. He's a cardiothoracic surgeon."

"Which means he does what?"

"He cuts people open and operates on beating hearts, Blake."

"Gross."

"Maybe don't tell him that the minute you meet him."

"I'm sure it wouldn't be the first time he's heard it."

"Blake…"

"All right, all right!" he said, throwing his hands up in mock surrender. "I won't embarrass you. I'll just let you two talk about scalpels and beating hearts and all that. If anybody yells STAT, I'm leaving. Fair warning."

Gabriel shook his head. "Will you just go?" He motioned across the street toward the double doors, exasperation thick in his voice.

"I don't know where I'm going," Blake muttered.

"In the door, take the second bank of elevators to the fifth floor."

Nolan lumbered across the street without looking. Gabriel followed closely behind him.

The main lobby of Saint Joseph Hospital was a three-story spiral of sunlight, steel, and blue-tinted glass. The floors were made of pristine white marble. The modern waterfall fixture on the far-right wall provided relaxing, soft background noise against the usual din of ringing phones, patients' families, and the front-door coffee cart.

The detectives followed a strip of blue and green patterned carpet around the corner to a bank of elevators marked Annex Two and rode them in silence to the fifth floor. The doors opened onto a smaller lobby. Large, frosted glass walls loomed in front of them. *Department of General Surgery* was scrawled across them in black looped script.

"Well, that was painless." Blake grinned.

He opened the door for Ryder, who stepped up to the secretary's desk. A middle-aged bottle-blonde wearing a low-cut blouse looked up at him through mascara-laden eyelashes.

"Can I help you?" she cooed, giving Gabriel a rather blatant once-over.

"Yes. Detectives Ryder—" he held out his badge, "—and Nolan, Denver Major Crimes. We have an appointment to see Dr. Sanders."

She rifled through the sticky notes stuck to her computer screen.

"Oh, yes! You're the nice young man I talked to on the phone. Didn't know you were so handsome, though…"

Nolan coughed. "Any idea when the doctor will be in?" he asked sarcastically, eyeing Ryder over his shoulder.

"He should be coming back from morning conference in a sec. You two feel free to take a seat. I'll come get you when he's ready."

Gabriel backed away from the desk as the secretary sauntered off down the back hall.

Nolan smirked in the corner and pretended to read the cover of one of the medical journals. "So, you get yourself a new girlfriend?" he scoffed.

"Shut up, Blake."

"Seriously, I wanna know. What is it? Is it the suits? Your cologne? Do you stage this ahead of time? Because there isn't a secretary that we've ever come across that hasn't wanted to bang your brains out."

"Just drop it."

"At least give me a hint. I've had to endure four years of this."

"Drop. It. NOW."

"I'm gonna figure it out one of these days." Nolan shrugged, lifting the journal back up to his face.

Ryder whipped around to silence his partner, but a whistle from across the office lobby cut him short. "Okay, cuties, follow me. Dr. Sanders is ready to see you."

Gabriel smirked and followed Nolan down the hallway after her.

"See? You get yours, too, Blake."

Nolan glared at his partner as the secretary opened a set of large mahogany doors and motioned them into the office. He passed in front of the fawning woman and winked at her.

"Thanks, honey."

She made an overly demonstrative effort of fanning herself and shut the door behind them.

The office itself was classic, full of dark woods, large bookcases, and two plush wingback chairs facing an intricate wooden desk, behind which sat a portly older gentleman with a poorly done comb-over and a handlebar mustache. He stood when the detectives entered the room.

"Detectives, detectives, please come in and sit down."

His voice was warm and boisterous, with just the slightest hint of a drawl. He grasped each of their outstretched hands in both of his in turn, then motioned toward the chairs.

"Can I get either of you some coffee this morning? If you're like me, you can't start a morning without a cup or two."

"Um, sure, thank you. We can get our own…" Nolan started.

The man waved him off. He was already halfway toward a sideboard that had a large pot of coffee warming with cream and sugar hidden off to one side.

"Oh, nonsense. Take a seat. I get my own coffee every day. I can sure as shit get y'all some. Cream or sugar?"

Both detectives shook their heads.

"Alrighty then. I take too much sugar myself. Wasn't ever able to kick the habit. But my wife tells me that's what celery's for."

He turned back to them with two full cups, handed them over, and returned to his desk.

"I'm Marshall Sanders, head of the general surgery department. Shelly tells me you're from the Denver PD, Major Crimes. So, what can I do for ya?"

Nolan shifted forward on his chair. He could tell Gabriel was about two seconds from jumping out of his and beginning to pace.

Oh, yup, there he goes.

Dr. Sanders' eyes shot up at the sudden movement. The old surgeon looked as though he wanted to ask Ryder if he was all right.

Blake shook his head and held up his hand to stop him. "Don't mind him. Dr. Sanders, do you know a Lisa Oakes?"

"Well, yes I do. She's one of our new interns. Been here a few months."

"How much do you know about her?"

"A little. I know what's in the application she submitted to the department. She's a Wyoming girl. Spunky. Always a happy little spitfire at work. Had a bit of a rough start in her first few months."

"Rough start? In what way?"

"Oh, the usual."

Both detectives looked at each other, then back at the older man.

"Oh, I'm sorry. You both aren't familiar with 'the usual'. Let me explain. Surgery has been a man's game for a long time. Still is. Some of us have figured out that the young ladies are stronger and smarter than us, but there's still an old guard that doesn't like change. Some of our girls have an easier time coming to terms with that than others. Oakes is a gem, but she thinks too highly of people. There are attendings here that aren't going to like her as much as they like the boys, no matter how great a resident she is."

"Anyone in particular cause her trouble?" Nolan asked, sipping his coffee.

"I don't have any formal complaints from her, if that's what you're asking," Sanders replied, shaking his head. "But I know she was having a hard time, especially the first two months. Mentioned to a few people about quitting the program. When I got wind of that, I hooked her up with our unofficial mentoring program. Seemed to turn her around. She's one I don't want to lose."

Ryder stopped pacing momentarily. "Mentoring program?" he asked.

Sanders nodded. "Every year, somebody has an intern that struggles. Me, urology, ortho, whoever. Guys and gals. People just have a hard time transitioning to residency. We keep an unofficial list of rock-star residents who've had problems in the past, and we put the two of them together. Residents bond together in the trenches, but you don't show weakness in your own department. It shows you're breakable."

"And she responded well to it?"

"Seemed to. She perked up on service. She and her mentor got together outside the hospital, too, from what I hear. Good match, all around."

"Who was she assigned to?"

"Carter. One of the chiefs."

"One of the what?" Nolan asked.

"Oh, Christ, sorry…one of the final year residents. Fifth-year orthopedics."

Ryder looked over to Nolan, scribbling in his binder. "We'll need to talk to this Carter, Blake." He turned back to Sanders. "Any romantic involvement between Lisa and Carter?"

"Ha! No, not that I'm aware of." Sanders laughed hard, grabbing his belly as it shook underneath his white coat. "That would've made the hospital gossip for sure."

When he noticed the detectives not sharing in the laughter, his expression darkened.

"Now, not to be rude, detectives, but do you mind telling me what this is about? Did Oakes get herself into some kind of trouble? She's a good kid. I'd hate to see her mixed up in something. "

"It's more complicated than that, sir," Nolan said steadily. "Lisa Oakes was found dead yesterday morning."

Sanders squinted and brought his left hand up to his forehead, resting the weight of his head in his palm.

"Well, shit. What happened to her?"

"We don't know yet. We were hoping to learn more about her. See if she had any enemies here, or if someone knew she was getting into trouble."

Sanders nodded, his head still resting in his hand. The jolliness had been sucked right out of his voice.

"I wish I had something for you, detectives, but I don't. Lisa was a good kid. We had high hopes for her. Your best bet would be to talk to the residents who knew her. Talk to Carter, maybe. If Lisa was having problems, hopefully she talked to somebody."

"Apart from this Carter guy, do you have any idea…?"

Sanders nodded, raising his hand up from the desk.

"I can start you off with a decent list. The residents will probably add to it." He wrote several names down onto a sheet of paper and handed it across the desk to Nolan.

"Thanks. Any chance we can talk to these residents today?" Sanders nodded again.

"You'd better believe it. I'll make a few phone calls to the other department heads and have Shelly send out pages. I'll get 'em corralled for you."

He stood and walked across the room to the large mahogany door, leaned out of it, and hollered, "Shelly! In here, please," before glancing back at the detectives. "You can use one of the department's conference rooms if you'd like. It'd be easier than trying to get these guys to you downtown."

"That would be great, sir. Thank you."

The secretary appeared at the doorway, with a little extra blush and eyeliner smeared across her face.

"Yes, Dr. Sanders?"

"Shelly, give these detectives conference room three for the day."

The woman opened her mouth to protest, but Sanders shook his head and held up his hand to silence her.

"I don't care who has it booked, just move them somewhere else. I need the heads of all the surgery departments on the phone and a list of pager numbers for all the residents. Right now."

"Yes, sir. Follow me, detectives."

Nolan followed her out the door. Ryder trailed behind.

"Dr. Sanders?"

The physician looked up from his desk at the man standing in the doorway.

"Yes?"

"West Virginia? Just across the river from Marietta?"

The director looked surprised. "Well...yes, that's right. Born and raised. How did you...?"

"I spent a few summers at a camp not far from there. Your accent was familiar." Gabriel nodded and closed the door behind him.

Doctor Sanders looked back down at his desk and smiled.

9

SHE WAS ONLY two cases in, and the day was already plunging into chaos.

I seriously hate Mondays.

The first case hadn't been bad. A forty-something construction worker had fallen off of a ladder and broken his ankle. In and out in under an hour.

The second case, however, was not going well. Bilateral femur fractures in a housebound, four-hundred-pound woman who'd fallen down her stairs trying to get the door when the pizza delivery guy showed up. She'd gone into kidney failure and had a heart attack when she'd hit the hospital door, just to complicate things, so she'd been laying around in the intensive care unit for almost two weeks. Her cardiologist, Dr. Nelson, had finally given the all-clear to operate this morning, so they'd added her to the schedule last minute.

The first side had been a breeze, fixed quickly and easily. The second side…well…her attending was in the corner, swearing at both the x-rays on the screen and the OR coordinator. Grayson was sweating through her scrubs and the lead apron under her surgical gown.

No one could find the sterile trays with the equipment they needed. They'd broken two guide wires and couldn't get the reduction to hold. Oh, and they had four more cases booked after this.

"It's Monday…" she sighed under her breath.

The shrill beeping of her pager broke through the John

Mayer ballad playing over the speaker system. Her attending glared in the direction of the noise and swore under his breath.

"If that's mine, so help me God…"

"It's mine, Dr. Allen. Tricia?"

She turned toward the circulating nurse.

"I know you have thirty things to do right now, but could you see who that is?"

The young nurse nodded as Dr. Allen breezed past her and sidled back up to the operating table. "Any luck yet?"

Grayson shook her head. "I don't know if we're gonna get this reduction without opening it. Or at least putting a pin in to joystick this piece around."

She manipulated the leg around on the table, shooting several x-rays in the process. "See? It just doesn't want to reduce like it should. All I'm doing is pushing fat from one side to the other. The bone's hardly moving."

"Well, fuck. And on a day when we're swamped anyway. Goddamn it." Dr. Allen turned around. "Tricia! We're gonna need the major retractor tray and my instrument trays up here. We're gonna open."

"It'll take a few minutes to get those, Dr. Allen. Those trays are down in sterile storage."

"In the fucking basement?" he barked.

"Yes, sir."

"Shit. Whose goddamned brilliant idea was it to move our shit to the basement again? I'm gonna kill 'em."

Dr. Allen shook his head and walked back over to the x-rays displayed on the flat screen on the far wall. "Keep trying, Carter." He waved over his head.

Grayson rolled her eyes and grabbed the leg.

Oh yeah, sure, like I'm gonna come up with something

*brilliant flailing around by myself. We should've opened an hour
ago. Goddamn it.*

She was getting ready to suggest just cutting the damned
leg off, albeit sarcastically, when she saw Tricia waving to get
her attention across the room.

"Tricia, what's up?"

"Um, Dr. Carter, this page you got...it's from the head of
general surgery's office. You want me to call it back?"

"Does it say what he wants?"

"No, it just says to call the office ASAP."

"Well, I guess call 'em back and see what they want."

She shrugged.

What the heck does his office want this early in the week?

She feigned another attempt at lining the bone up properly
while listening to the conversation from across the room.

"Hi, this is Tricia, one of the nurses in the OR. Dr. Carter
got a page from this number. She's scrubbed in surgery; can I
take a message... Oh! I'm so sorry, sir, I didn't recognize your
voice...oh, um, let me see. Hold on one sec..."

She put the phone down on the counter.

"Dr. Carter?"

"Yeah?" *Stupid hundred-fifty-pound broken leg...reduce,
you stupid thing!*

"Dr. Sanders is on the phone. He said he wants to see you
in his office immediately."

Grayson paused and looked over at Dr. Allen, who already
had his eyebrows raised at her, and shrugged.

Shit.

"Um, that's usually not good. Did he say why?"

"No. He just said drop what you're doing and get to his office."

"Um, well…I can't just leave…crap…" She paused again, glancing over at her attending to gauge his reaction.

"Dr. Allen, what do you want me to do?"

He shook his head. "When you gotta go, you gotta go." He waved her off. "I'm not gonna argue with Sanders. We've gotta wait on trays anyway. Go see what he wants. Get back when you can."

She nodded and backed away from the surgical field, ripping off her gown and gloves.

"Thanks, Dr. Allen." She grabbed her pager and cell phone from the desk, hastily clipping them onto the top of her scrub pants.

"Hey, Carter?" Allen called after her.

"Yes, sir?"

"You might wanna change before you see the big man." He raised his chin, gesturing at her.

Grayson watched his eyes crinkle above his surgical mask. She knew he was smirking at her. She looked down at her scrubs. They were soaked in blood.

"Probably a good idea," she admitted.

She left the OR and headed straight for the locker rooms at a jog. Dr. Sanders was a nice man, as far as general surgeons went, but he did not like to be kept waiting. She pulled her phone out of its holster and looked at the screen. There were two missed calls and a text from Noah.

Just got called into Sanders' office ASAP. WTF is going on, Gray?

She suddenly had a bad feeling in the pit of her stomach.

10

IT WAS WELL past noon when Ryder and Nolan finally got a break and went to grab a bite to eat in the hospital cafeteria.

The facility itself was brand new, similar in style to the main lobby. Blue glass, modern countertops, the whole nine yards. And the place was swamped. It was all they could do to get two egg salad sandwiches and two bottles of water in under twenty minutes.

Not wanting to stay in the chaos of the cafeteria, they headed to the outdoor courtyard. There was only one other couple outside, a young woman and a thin, sickly-looking man with an IV pole attached to his right arm. A red bandanna was wrapped around his head. A little boy not more than two years old was playing in the grass in front of them.

Nolan jerked his chin in their direction as they sat down. "Sad, don't you think?"

Ryder glanced over and softly nodded.

"You think he'll even remember his dad?"

"It's not a done deal that he's dying, Blake."

"Gabe, look at the man."

He sighed. "Yeah."

"Well, you think the kid'll remember him?"

"I hope not."

Blake choked on his sandwich. "You don't want that poor kid to remember his father? You've said some heartless shit, Gabe, but fuck."

Ryder shook his head. "What's better, that boy remembering his father sick and dying, or strong and happy? That's how his mother will talk about him. I wouldn't want my son remembering me like that, gray and tied up to an IV pole."

Nolan didn't know what to say. Truth be told, if he got sick, he wouldn't want his girls remembering him dying in a hospital bed.

"Sorry," Ryder muttered. "You okay?"

"Yeah," Nolan nodded back. "I don't know why I pushed that."

"You're angry we're not getting anywhere. It's easier to pick a fight with me. And you miss your girls."

Blake cleared his throat, obviously uncomfortable. He changed the subject. "We're learning who she was, the Oakes girl. That's a start."

"I suppose."

Ryder leaned back in his chair and folded his hands behind his head.

Classic Ryder thinking posture. C'mon, man, give me something.

"We know she was well liked. She never had a formal complaint filed against her. All of the residents who have interacted with her liked her. Nurses and OR staff, too. She was on her way to becoming a very good asset to her department."

"And nothing crazy about that rough patch she hit, either," Blake chimed in. "Sounds like some of the senior surgery guys and a few of the rougher attendings got up in her face about minor crap and she took it hard. From what that Mason kid said, she perked right up after being partnered up with this Carter guy."

"It sounds like they were close," Ryder nodded.

"You think it got too close?"

Ryder shook his head. "Anything's possible, but I don't think so. Even if they were romantically involved, it doesn't sound like he was a particularly bad influence on her. And from Sanders' reaction, it sounds like the entire hospital would have known if they were sleeping together. But it's worth asking about."

"So, I'm supposed to be optimistic about this?"

"She has an isolated circle here. If nothing pans out in this group..."

"We start working a random crime angle?"

"It might come to that."

"Make your brain work overtime so it doesn't come to that, Gabe. I can't handle a wild goose chase this week."

"Next week okay for you?"

"Depends if the Broncos get their heads out of their asses and win a game."

"So, if they win, I don't have to work as hard?" Ryder smirked.

Nolan nodded.

"Remind me to put in a call to Elway."

"Manning's the quarterback now, idiot."

Blake tossed his empty water bottle across the table at his partner. It sailed wide to the right and bounced off the brick wall. He sighed and went running after it before the breeze took it out onto the grass. He dropped it in the recycling bin, then slapped his partner on the shoulder.

"C'mon, man. We're due back."

"How many more are there?"

"Seven or eight, I think.

"Great."

"Hey, you should be excited. You get to sink your teeth into that Carter guy next."

They walked back to the surgery office in silence, the mechanical din of the hospital carrying on in the background.

The hallways were much busier in the afternoon. White coats and green scrubs intermingled with jeans and cowboy hats. Occasionally, the crowd would part to allow a wheelchair or a stretcher through, then fold back in on itself just as quickly, like the parting of the Red Sea.

Nolan smiled to himself. They weren't particularly conspicuous. A good third of the people in this place were dressed in suits, just like they were. But his partner was drawing a lot of attention. Nurses and techs were walking by in pairs to lunch, and most of them were elbowing each other in the ribs as they passed.

There was a chattering gaggle of nursing students gathered near the coffee cart. They couldn't be bothered to notice the elderly couple waiting patiently for the creamer, but the second Gabriel walked by, they all went deathly silent. One or two of them probably pulled a muscle trying to get a better look at him.

Blake looked over at his partner.

Completely oblivious, just like always.

Sanders' secretary stood up and smiled when they walked through the door. If it was possible, she'd put on even more makeup since they'd gone to lunch.

There were several young people in white coats in the waiting room, each spread the polite two-to-three seats apart from one another, reading medical journals or checking their cell phones. They all looked a little nervous, but they were in their boss's office without an explanation. Nolan couldn't blame them.

The two men trudged back to their assigned conference room. It certainly wasn't as glamorous as Dr. Sanders' office, but it served its purpose well. A long, dark wooden table took up at least half of the floor space. There was a projector attached to the ceiling at one end of the room, and what he assumed was the projector screen rolled up against the ceiling at the other. Whiteboards adorned the other two walls, and from the looks of them, they were used often. The floor-to-ceiling windows behind the projector looked out over the main hospital entrance. Nolan took his jacket off and draped it over the chair he'd been plastered into the entire morning. He noticed that new coffee cups, water glasses, and several pitchers had been arranged in the middle of the table.

"Thought you boys could use a little pick-me-up this afternoon," Shelly said from the door.

"Thank you," Ryder turned and flashed a quick smile.

Nolan shook his head when he saw the woman blush.

"Are you two ready for the next one or do you need a few minutes?"

"I'm ready if you are, buddy," Nolan said.

Ryder had moved to stand by the window and was looking through some of the notes in his binder. He nodded. "Go ahead."

"All right, Shelly, let's have at it."

"Be right back."

The secretary disappeared down the hallway, shutting the door behind her.

"You having an epiphany back there or what?" Nolan nodded at the fumbling going on against the back wall.

"Huh? Oh, no, just…reorganizing."

"Whatever. Get over here and sit down like a civilized person. Can't have you scaring this guy the first five minutes he's in here. And pour me a cup of that coffee while you're at it."

Ryder smirked, dropped his binder on the table, and reached across for two cups and the carafe marked Regular. He poured some into his partner's cup, then went to pour his own. Nolan swiped the second cup.

"Uh, absolutely not. You're too perky today as it is." He motioned toward the middle of the table. "Decaf for you."

"You can't tell me what kind of coffee to drink, Blake."

"Sure I can. I have to be in an enclosed space with you for a good four more hours at least, and you're already acting like a caged hyena. If you get any antsier, I'm going to have to shoot you myself. Decaf." He pointed, for emphasis.

"Fine."

Ryder poured himself a cup and made his way back toward the window, scowling at his partner all the while. "If you're starting to pick out my coffee, then I'm changing your breakfast routine. No more bear claws. Steel-cut oatmeal and kale juice for you."

"I literally blacked out after 'no more bear claws'. What did you just say?"

Ryder was ready to sling a retort back at his partner when the door creaked open and Shelly shoved her head into view.

"Detectives, your next interview is here. This is Dr. Carter."

11

OUT OF HABIT, Nolan stood up from the table as the secretary stepped to the side and opened the door wider. He dropped his eyes to the table, frantically shuffling the papers around to find a clean sheet to write on.

The sound of Shelly's heels retreating down the hallway drew his attention back to the door. He cleared his throat and blindly extended his hand.

"I'm Detective Nolan, this is my partner Detective Ryder. Have a seat, Dr…"

He trailed off as he fully focused on the figure in the white coat standing by the door.

Wait, what the hell? He's a she? No, wait…well…what?

He shot a surprised look toward Ryder, whose own gaze was fixated on the new arrival. To someone who didn't know him, he looked calm and collected. Jaw set, eyes focused, one hand lazily placed in his front pocket. He didn't even have a wrinkle in his suit yet.

But something was wrong. Blake watched his partner's right hand clench into a fist so tight that the skin on his knuckles blanched. He was taking deeper and deeper breaths to calm himself down. He was completely on edge, clearly and quickly losing control.

Forget about Dr. Carter being a woman…

What the hell is wrong with my partner?

A soft cough from the young woman waiting by the door knocked Nolan out of his own head. Recognizing that the long, awkward pause was becoming longer and more awkward, Nolan cleared his own throat and tried again.

"Take a seat, Dr. Carter."

She nodded and made her way around the table, selecting a chair to Nolan's right. It put her directly in Ryder's line of sight.

Nolan watched her carefully. She was about five foot six, he guessed, subtracting a few inches for the heels she was wearing, with honey-brown hair and blue, almost green, eyes. She was dressed sharply in black slacks and a gray sweater, her white lab coat over them. Several pagers were clipped onto her belt and a pair of silver bandage scissors jutted out from her left pocket. She slipped out of her white coat and draped it over the back of her chair, sitting down and softly smiling at both of them.

"Thank you."

"Any idea why you're here?" Nolan asked, taking his own seat.

She shook her head.

"No clue at all?" Ryder snapped at her.

Grayson startled at his tone and sucked in a quick breath. Nolan glared over his shoulder.

"No, I'm sorry. I was scrubbed in when I got the page from Dr. Sanders telling me to get over here as soon as possible. I... I had a text from one of the other residents asking if I knew what was going on, and I said no. I got here as quickly as I could."

"Who's the resident?" he bit out.

Blake shot his partner another look over his shoulder.

Back the fuck off, Gabe.

Ryder blatantly ignored him.

Nolan watched as the young doctor struggled to contain the scowl threatening to spread across her face. Her guard had gone up the second his partner had opened his mouth. Her hands were wringing nervously in her lap. Her eyes were darting from one safe spot in the room to the other. She refused to look at either of them. She was angry, but she didn't want to show it.

"Noah Mason. From internal medicine."

Nolan shuffled through some of his notes. "Oh yeah, the British guy."

"Yeah, that's him." Grayson smiled brightly at the detective to her left.

He seemed nice. And harmless. Easy to talk to. His partner, on the other hand, made the hair on the back of her neck stand up.

She hazarded a quick glance in his direction. He was staring at her intently, resting back against the wall, a leather binder opened on his thigh.

Physically, he pushed all of her buttons. There was no denying it. He was tall and muscular. Even from her vantage point across the room, she could see the strength in his broad shoulders. His hair was dark brown, nearly black, which made his piercing blue eyes all the brighter. The immaculate suit was clearly custom.

But it had been his voice that had instantly brought her inner walls slamming up to their full height. For all the clean-cut elegance he presented, there was something else there... unrestrained power simmering beneath the surface that she couldn't see. And all of it was focused exclusively on her. She shivered.

He's dangerous.

"How do you know him?" Nolan continued.

"Noah and I started residency together. We've been friends for over four years."

"And he didn't tell you anything about his meeting with us? What we discussed with him?"

"No, he…he didn't answer my text," she replied warily, "but right now, I'm wishing he had. Am I in some kind of trouble?"

Her eyes darted between the two detectives. Nolan made an attempt to smile at her, to reassure her. His partner didn't move, his face hard and expressionless.

Wait, what the hell? Is he…? He is.

Ryder was scowling at her. She didn't miss the rhythmic clenching and unclenching of his right fist underneath the binder. Grayson could feel the intensity radiating off of him from across the room. She shrank back into her chair to get away from it.

Blake motioned toward the carafes. "Would you like something to drink?"

"I'd like to know what the hell is going on," she shot back.

Detective Ryder smirked at her from his perch near the window. Shoving himself off the wall, he approached the table while unbuttoning his suit jacket, and sat down across from her.

"Dr. Carter, you are one of the residents here at Saint Joseph Hospital, correct?"

"Yes," she replied, shifting in her chair to face him.

Up close, Detective Ryder made her even more nervous. There was something about him that had her on edge. It wasn't necessarily a bad edge. It just had her heart racing in her chest. Her cheeks were flushed. And she was suddenly very, very warm.

Is it getting hot in here? Why did I wear a sweater today?

His voice had changed. It was smooth and controlled. The bite from earlier was gone. And he still wouldn't stop staring at her. Grayson wrung her hands together nervously under the table.

Focus, focus.

It took everything she had to not reach up and twirl a piece of hair between her fingers, her usual nervous habit.

"Which department do you belong to?"

"Orthopedics."

Ryder's eyebrows shot up. "Really?"

He looked surprised. It wasn't the first time she'd seen the look in a man's eyes when he'd discovered her profession. This man's, however, was unique.

"Yes." She nodded, her eyes darting to the table as a small smile blossomed on her face.

Ryder watched the blush growing on her face.

"What does that mean?" Blake interjected.

Grayson brought her eyes back up. "I work on bones and joints, Detective Nolan."

"So, you do…what, exactly?" Nolan's forehead was full of deep wrinkles. He was clearly confused, and it was endearing. She smiled at him.

"Total joints, ACLs, sports, trauma, hand, spine…take your pick." She shrugged.

"Like, you personally do these things? You don't just watch?"

She nodded.

"But you're a girl."

"Nolan…" Ryder hissed violently under his breath.

"What? I assumed she was a guy, Ryder. So did you."

The young woman smiled and shook her head. "Don't worry about it. I get that a lot. I'm the only girl in my program. Everybody always thinks I'm a nurse or one of the other ortho guy's wives. Most of them do a double-take anyway because of my name; they automatically assume I'm a guy and then… surprise."

This isn't the first time I've had to explain myself.

"You're in your last year of training," Ryder stated sharply, taking control of the conversation again.

"Yes."

She took in the sound of his voice. It was deep and strained, a faint scratch at the edge of his words. The hair on the back of her neck stood up again.

Jesus, Gray, get a grip on yourself.

"Which means?"

"I'm a chief and currently running the ortho trauma service here. I'm in charge of taking care of all the inpatients, looking after my junior residents, operating, trauma-related conferences during the week…I guess the best way to describe it is like being a junior attending surgeon."

"How many other chiefs are there?"

"Three. One is at the children's hospital across town. One is on paternity leave this week but otherwise running the red team, and the last one is running the green team."

"And those are?"

"Oh, sorry. The red team is total joints and sports medicine. The green team covers spine and tumor."

Ryder nodded, scribbling notes in his binder, never taking his eyes off her. Grayson fidgeted in her chair, trying to work herself out from under the detective's stare. She gave up on trying to be subtle after several moments with a sigh and blatantly shifted her torso toward Detective Nolan. The flush on her chest instantly cooled and her breathing slowed.

What is wrong with me?

"So, my guess is you two didn't come here to ask about my day-to-day schedule as trauma chief. Can I know what's going on?"

Nolan looked to his partner for the okay to take over questioning the young woman, which he got with a slight nod.

"Dr. Carter, do you know a Lisa Oakes?"

"Lisa?" she parroted, wrinkling her forehead. "Of course I know her. She's been my unofficial little sister since right after she started residency."

"Tell me about that."

"She was having problems with some of the guys in the surgery program. She wasn't handling it well and threatened to quit. Sanders found out, and he matched her up with me in August."

"Why?" Ryder interjected.

"Why what? Why was she threatening to quit?" She looked at him, confused.

Didn't we just go over that? Does he want details or something?

"Why you," Ryder pressed.

"Oh. I, um…I didn't have the easiest introduction to residency either. It hasn't been a cakewalk here for five years, but I've managed. Dr. Sanders figured I could help her. You'd have to ask him on specifics."

"You had problems with the same people?"

"Yes. No. Well, not really," she stammered, rolling her eyes at herself.

Speak English, Gray.

"You have to understand, detectives. General surgeons aren't the nicest bunch of people in the hospital, and some of the more senior attendings are a bit, um…paternalistic. They're not happy when a girl shows up, especially a competent one. A few of the senior general surgery residents are carrying that same torch now. I had to deal with the attendings when I was an intern, and I've 'grown up' with those same problem residents. It's just something you get used to…eventually."

"Or it breaks you," Ryder added quietly.

"Sure," she nodded, narrowing her eyes slightly at the comment.

How the hell would he know that?

"Every few years, somebody quits. That's why this unofficial mentoring system started, to keep those numbers down. It's a black mark on a program to have a resident leave. And potential applicants start asking questions."

"She perked up after she met you?" Nolan asked.

"I guess you could say that. I think having someone to talk to helped her more than anything. She'd just moved to Denver and didn't know anybody here, so we took her in."

"We?"

"Noah and I. And my roommate. We go out to dinner or see a movie or run around downtown when we all have a day off. Anything to get our minds off of this place."

"Your roommate is also a resident?"

"Oh God, no." She stifled a laugh. "Barbara is a nutritionist and personal trainer."

Grayson's eyes darted back and forth again between the two men. She pulled her bottom lip in between her teeth when she caught Ryder's eyes on her.

Gabriel's breathing increased sharply when her teeth began working the pink flesh. He balled his right hand into a fist underneath the table until his hand went white, resisting the urge to reach across the table and stop her.

Keep it together, goddamn it. She doesn't know what she's doing.

"Look, detectives, no offense to either of you, but I'm getting tired of asking. What am I doing here? You could've gotten all of this from Dr. Sanders. And why bring up Lisa? Is she in trouble?"

Ryder sighed.

Damn it, Nolan. Don't make me tell her.

———

Grayson startled when she noticed the anxiety shoot over Detective Ryder's face. Her eyes darted over to Detective Nolan. He didn't look much better.

"Where were you Saturday night, Dr. Carter?"

"At home, watching a movie."

"Someone can confirm that?"

"Sure. Noah and Barbara can."

"And Sunday morning?"

"We all got up and went to brunch. Barbara had to get some new clothes for work, so we went shopping in Cherry Creek for the afternoon. We got home around dinnertime. I went to bed around ten, got here around three this morning."

"That's a usual time for you? Shit." Nolan balked.

Grayson chuckled softly under her breath at the outburst. "No, it isn't. I had the weekend off. It always means more work on Monday morning," she said with a shrug.

"When was the last time you saw Lisa?" Ryder interjected, his voice once again sharp and forced.

"Friday afternoon. I was leaving the hospital."

"Time?"

"Probably around six or so. I don't remember exactly."

"She seemed…"

"Fine. I mean, she was on call. Stressed out and busy, but nothing seemed off."

"You were aware of her plans for the weekend?"

"No, I assume she was working. Usually, we meet up if we share a day off, so I can check in with her. We didn't this weekend."

Gabriel dropped his eyes to scribble several notes in his binder. Nolan sighed heavily and leaned forward in his chair.

"Dr. Carter, I'm really sorry to tell you this," he said softly, "but Lisa Oakes was found dead early Sunday morning."

The conference room fell eerily quiet. The rhythmic tick-tick-tick of the clock on the wall was the only audible sound.

Grayson closed her eyes and took a deep, steadying breath. When she opened them again, she blinked wildly and promptly shoved herself back into her chair, startled. Detective Ryder had leaned forward, nearly halfway over the table, his chin resting in his hands. And he was glaring at her.

Grayson shook her head slightly and tried to reset.

Maybe I'm just reading that wrong. He can't seriously be glaring at me, can he?

She raised her eyes again and was met by the same deep blue, ice-cold eyes. The same subtle smirk on the edge of his lips. She leaned forward, matching his posture with hers.

"Say that again," she demanded, softly.

She was focused on the man across from her. Detective Nolan did not exist.

Say it.

"Lisa Oakes is dead," Ryder replied sharply, the annoyance clearly evident in his voice.

"Ryder..."

Grayson heard Nolan utter the warning under his breath. She didn't pay him any attention. Apparently, neither did Detective Ryder.

He's all over the place. Is he normally like this?

She continued to square off with him, daring him to make another snide remark. To her surprise, he didn't, instead breaking his concentration to glance over at his partner.

She took the opportunity to drop her eyes and suck in a shaky breath. It didn't take long for the overwhelming, crushing emotion to hit. She'd blocked it out for longer than she'd thought possible. She dropped her head into her hands. Her shoulders started shaking. She couldn't stop them.

Much to her chagrin, she did catch Detective Nolan giving his partner the "look-what-you've-done-now" look in her peripheral vision. She could almost hear him saying, "*Goddamn it, you animal, you've fucking scared her. Back off!*"

"How?" she asked, fighting back the first tears.

"We don't know yet," Ryder replied, his voice once again soft.

"Where...where was she..."

"At the Catholic seminary."

Her forehead wrinkled. "That doesn't make sense," she said, staring at the table in front of her and shaking her head. "Lisa isn't Catholic. I don't know if she even goes...went to church."

"She wasn't a practicing Christian?"

"She wears...wore a cross around her neck. Has someone called her parents?" Her voice had gone eerily monotone and flat.

Nolan wrestled control of the questioning. His partner wasn't the best at playing nice when delivering bad news, and from the rate of his leg tapping under the table, he was beyond the end of his rope.

"Yes, they're coming down to make arrangements."

"Somebody killed her?"

"We don't know that, either. From all we've heard, she was well liked. Nobody's come up with a grudge against her or an axe to grind. That true?"

"Yes."

"Was she romantically involved with anybody? Boyfriend? Casual fling?"

"Ha!" Grayson let out a shaky laugh, tipping her head back toward the ceiling. "No, in fact, that was one of her things. She couldn't find anybody around here she liked."

"Old boyfriend from college or medical school maybe?"

Grayson shook her head. "Nobody serious. At least that she told me about."

"No threats?"

"None that I know of."

A few silent tears started to run down her cheek. She felt one drop off of her face and onto the table. She wrinkled her nose in disgust at the sight of it on the varnished surface.

How embarrassing. Surgeons don't cry.

Grayson hastily tried to wipe her face with the back of her hand, but a flash of white in her peripheral vision made her pause. She looked up to see Detective Ryder standing beside her, holding out a handkerchief. A real one.

"Oh, it's all right," she mumbled. "I can just grab a tissue." She looked around the room absently.

Where's the stupid box?

"Just take it," he said softly, crouching down beside her chair to hand it over.

Grayson felt the tips of his fingers brush over hers as she grabbed the soft square of white fabric. She took in a sharp breath. She could've sworn he did, too, but when she looked up at his face, it was flat. Expressionless.

Talk about mercurial.

But he was still staring at her. So, she forced herself to stare back.

It wasn't hard to miss. She watched him struggle. Watched his eyes shift ever so slightly down toward the floor before he caught himself. Watched him swallow hard. It wasn't hard to miss because she was doing the same things. She startled when the detective shot to his feet and rounded the conference table.

Shelly took that moment to knock sharply at the door and poke her head in.

"I'm sorry, detectives. Dr. Allen just called over from the operating rooms. He's asking for Dr. Carter to come back over. Something about trying to fix a toothpick inside a whale?"

Grayson smiled and shook her head slightly. That was Dr. Allen's graceful way of describing operating on an exceptionally obese patient.

"That's fine. We're done with her," Ryder said brusquely, dismissing both women with a wave of his hand.

His tone earned him a warning in the form of violent throat-clearing from his partner, telling him to change his tone. Immediately. Ryder ignored him and headed back toward his perch by the windows.

Let it go, Gray.

Detective Nolan stood up from his chair, glaring at his idiot of a partner, and held out his card to her.

"If you think of anything, give us a call, Dr. Carter. We may have some more questions for you in a few days."

Grayson nodded as she stood and pulled on her white coat. She checked her pager out of habit and made her way toward the door.

She brushed her hair back behind her ear. She was shaking badly. Her arms were trembling, and her steps were unsteady. She barely got her hair to stay in place. Her twitching fingers just pulled it right back out again.

This has to be a bad dream.

It wasn't. She knew better. But the thought was nice all the same.

She was so lost inside of her own head that she didn't notice Detective Ryder standing in her way by the door. She hadn't noticed him move to patiently wait for her. She hadn't seen the embarrassed look flash across his face or notice the way he had his hands shoved in his pockets with his shoulders slumped over. She hadn't noticed him watch her circle around the conference table toward the door.

She plowed right into him, losing her balance and stumbling forward in her heels. She grimaced, anticipating a hard impact on the carpet. Instead, a strong arm wrapped around her waist as she pitched forward and pulled her upright...upright into a very warm, very strong torso. Instinctively, her hands flew up to steady herself. They rested on a set of broad shoulders encased in a rather fine black suit coat.

"Oh my God, I'm so sorry, I..." she stammered, losing her voice completely when she looked up.

I've been reduced to a blubbering mess. Speak English, Gray. Full sentences.

Detective Ryder looked down at her, a mix of curiosity and concern on his face. He didn't speak. Grayson became acutely aware of his arm wrapped firmly around her hip and the fact that he wasn't letting go. She tried stepping back, giving him the subtle cue to relax, but he held onto her. His bicep flexed against her back.

What the hell does he want?

For one brief moment, she let herself believe he wanted her. All of her. At that moment, she definitely wanted him. Then it dawned on her.

The handkerchief.

She still had it. She fumbled with it briefly and held it out to him, tearing her eyes away from his to stare at the floor.

"This is yours, detective," she whispered, her voice shaking.

He shook his head, took her fingers, and wrapped them back around the soft fabric.

"I said to keep it," he said gently. He leaned down next to her ear. "And I...I'm sorry."

Abruptly, Gabriel released her and backed away, grabbing his binder from the table.

Nolan watched him retreat, eyebrow raised, then turned back to the young doctor. She managed a small smile, then closed the door behind her without saying a word.

Blake sat back down in his chair and leaned back, hands behind his head, and gave his partner a minute to get his breathing under control. Then he went for it.

"All right, Gabe. What in the hell was that?"

12

ALL RIGHT—WHAT in the hell was that?

Grayson walked back to the women's locker room in a daze.

Lisa's dead. I just saw her on Friday. She looked fine. She smiled and wished me a good weekend. Said she'd see me on Monday. But she always smiled. Damn it, why didn't I think to call her?

She was so lost inside her own head she didn't hear someone at the end of the hall calling her name. It took Noah forcefully turning her around and shaking her by the shoulders to snap her out of it.

"Gray! Hello! Hey, focus, love. What's happened?"

She looked up at him, and from out of nowhere, the tears just started to fall.

"Noah," she choked out, "Lisa's dead."

"Aw, love," he shushed, wrapping her in a hug. "They told you."

She nodded into his chest. They stood together in the hallway for several minutes, Noah rocking back and forth with his arms around her. Grayson tried and failed to stop her tears.

"You need to take the day off."

She shook her head and pulled back. "I can't. Allen's calling for me in the OR."

"So, tell him what happened."

"He's not going to give a crap, Noah. You know that."

"Dr. Allen's a good man. He might surprise you."

"Ha ha." She laughed sarcastically. "You know I'm not the department's golden child. I'm not you."

Noah stiffened protectively. "Let me talk to him."

"Noah, don't…"

He shook his head. "No, you're shaking like crazy and shouldn't be operating. If I have to make it a patient safety thing, you bloody well know I will. What room is he in?"

"Six," she replied half-heartedly. "But he's actually right there…"

She pointed to a man in a white coat and scrubs walking down the hallway. Noah smiled down at her and took off to catch him. Reluctantly, Grayson followed behind him, slowly, her head down.

"Dr. Allen?" he called.

The man stopped mid-stride and turned, smiling widely when he saw the tall Brit sprinting toward him.

"Dr. Mason, what can I do for you, son?" he asked, extending his hand out in greeting.

Grayson managed a weary smile as she trudged down the hallway to catch up to them. Noah's British accent and good nature had won over the entire hospital staff rather quickly, including attendings from other departments. One couldn't help but like him.

"Could I speak to you a moment, sir?"

"Sure. My next patient isn't quite ready yet. What's on your mind?"

He saw Grayson come up behind Mason and clapped his hands together.

"Carter, glad they let you loose. What the hell did Sanders want? I had to finish fixing the whale by myself. You know Mrs. Ottman's up next."

Grayson opened her mouth to respond, but she never got a word out.

"Actually, sir, that's what I wanted to talk to you about," Noah interjected.

"Oh?"

"Dr. Sanders has been helping the Denver police."

"With what?"

"Do you know Lisa Oakes? One of the general surgery interns?"

"I think so. Redhead, right? Real spunky? People seem to like her." He shrugged.

"She was found dead yesterday."

"Aw, shit…" Allen's face dropped. He looked over Noah's shoulder at Grayson, immediately registering her puffy eyes and slumped shoulders. "You were close with her weren't you, Carter? Some mentorship thing?"

"Yes, sir. Kind of a big sister-little sister deal." She nodded.

"Then I'll tell you what. You help me get Mrs. Ottman's femur exposed and reduced, and I'll let you get out of here early."

"Really?" She eyed him suspiciously. *There's no way he's serious.*

"Of course," he replied. "You know I don't do this super-technical trauma crap anymore, but if you can get me there and get the articular shit done, I can be a monkey and put in screws through an outrigger. And we've got the good rep today, so he'll deal with me if shit goes south. Go change. I'll meet you in six."

"Thank you, Dr. Allen."

He nodded and walked off down the hallway.

Grayson stared at Noah with an open mouth. "How'd you do that?" she whispered so her voice wouldn't carry.

"I'm just that good, love." He smiled at her.

Grayson shook her head, wiping the tears from her eyes and inwardly scolding herself. "I don't understand why I'm so upset. I didn't know her that long."

"Yeah, but you liked her, and she depended on you. Don't worry, love, we'll get you through it. Do your case, sign out, and go home. I've already called Barbara."

"You did? Wait, why?"

"She's ordering pizza for dinner for us. Now go." He shooed her off toward the locker rooms.

Grayson turned in the general direction he was pointing, racking her brain for what Mrs. Ottman's femur x-rays looked like and exactly why they were going to be putting a plate on it.

"Hang on a tick, what's this?" Noah brought her right hand up to eye level and there, gripped in her hand, was the white handkerchief. "Since when do you carry one of these?"

"I don't. I mean, I didn't." She rubbed her fingers across her temple and shut her eyes tight. She could feel the beginning of a rip-roaring headache building behind her eyes.

"Ugh, never mind…"

Noah waited patiently and held her in place until she opened her eyes. When she did, he quirked his own eyebrows at her expectantly.

"It's Detective Ryder's."

The eyebrows went higher.

"That was my reaction, too." She smiled slightly.

"There's my girl." He nodded toward the white square. "We're going to have a chat about this later," he said, tugging lightly on the fabric.

"Get a move on it, Carter!" Allen's voice boomed down the hallway.

"Get going, hun," Noah echoed.

Grayson smiled a bit. All she had to do was get through half a case and go home.

God bless Noah Mason.

He could make things happen that she could only dream of. She made a mental note to pick up a six-pack of porter on the way home to say thank you.

13

TRUE TO HIS word, Dr. Allen let her break scrub and go home early. Grayson had been wary of how sincere the offer really was, but he'd all but shoved her out of the operating room an hour into the case.

She'd changed back into her street clothes, thrown on her coat, and headed solemnly to the parking deck. She half-expected Lisa to jump out from a dark corner and yell "Gotcha!" before she got out the main door.

It doesn't seem real.

It was still early by Denver rush hour standards. The streets were reasonably clear. She took City Park West to University Boulevard, then headed south toward Cherry Creek, making a quick detour into the local market.

She flew through the store, grabbing wine for herself and Barbara and a local porter for Noah. She let herself drift by the bakery and, on a whim, picked up a fresh fruit tart. If they were going to stuff themselves with pizza and alcohol, the least they could do was finish it off with a quasi-healthy dessert.

She got through the checkout line unscathed, except for her wallet, and threw her bags in the back of her 4Runner.

Grayson opened her windows, pulled out into the right lane so she could drive at a slower pace, and switched on the local country music station. Lisa had loved country music. She'd listened to it constantly, much to Noah's chagrin.

Grayson hadn't known the girl for very long, but damn it, she was brokenhearted over her death. Lisa was a sweetheart.

Naïve, but a sweetheart, and certainly didn't deserve to be murdered and dumped in a church. She shook her head violently at a red light, pieces of hair falling out of her loose ponytail to hang about her face.

Stop thinking about it. You're going to start bawling in the middle of the street.

Several minutes later, Grayson pulled off the main street and into a back alleyway, traveled four houses down, and maneuvered her SUV into the carport in the back of her Wash Park bungalow. Thank God Barbara knew how to parallel park and graciously parked on the street.

The back porch light was on, and the back door to the kitchen was unlocked. Barbara was already home. Grayson blindly pushed her way through the screen door, colliding head-on with her roommate, who was scuttling around glued to her cell phone.

"Shit, Babs!"

Grayson stumbled and sprawled out on the kitchen table, bags and all.

"Oh, damn it! I'm sorry! I didn't see you!" Barbara grabbed one of the grocery bags and hoisted it up onto the kitchen counter, talking into her phone simultaneously. "I've gotta go. No, I'm not doing any of that, they aren't my clients. If he's not working out, then fire him, Stephen. Cleaning up his mistakes is not my job. See you tomorrow."

Barbara Parker threw her phone onto the kitchen counter, opened her arms up and gave the universal *come here* gesture.

"C'mere, sweetie."

Grayson dropped the rest of her bags onto the kitchen table, tears already brimming in her eyes, and violently hugged her roommate.

"How the hell is this really happening?" she whispered into her shoulder.

Babs shook her head. "I don't know, hon. It doesn't make any sense."

"Why her?"

"Still don't know, hon," she replied, sarcastically rolling her eyes.

Grayson pulled away, wiping her eyes. "Sorry."

"Don't be. You're upset," she replied, taking the other grocery bags into the kitchen to unload them. "Go upstairs, put on some sweatpants, and come back down. Pizza should be here in a bit. Did you buy more wine?" she asked, pulling a bottle out of the bag and raising her eyebrows.

Grayson nodded.

"Good girl. Go change."

Grayson schlepped herself up the stairs and hung a left on the landing. She opened the door to her room and tossed her messenger bag on the floor. The room was thankfully only slightly a mess; a stray pair of shoes here, a pile of orthopedic journals there. But all in all, it was clean and coordinated. There was a chest of drawers on the nearest wall, a queen-sized bed in the center of the room, and a small desk in the corner. All in warm blues, oranges, crimson, and dark wood. Warm and soft.

The afternoon sun was still pouring in through her bedroom window. The tips of the snow-capped mountains were just visible in between the overgrown trees. Grayson closed her eyes and sighed, soaking in the rays of the remaining sunshine. She leaned back against the wall, lingering on the edge of her window seat until she heard a car door slam down on the street, followed by British-laced swearing.

Noah.

She scurried across to her chest of drawers and pulled out a pair of well-worn black yoga pants and a Broncos T-shirt. She skidded into the bathroom to change, hastily throwing her hair up and drying her eyes. She heard the front door open and shut, then the muffled sound of two voices talking on the landing.

Warm, fuzzy socks. Check. Hair in a messy bun. Check. Impending pizza and wine. Check.

"Hey, love," came a voice from her doorway.

Noah was leaning against the wall with his arms crossed, a soft smile his face.

"Pizza's getting cold."

"I bought wine," she said with a smile.

"And a porter for me, I see," he said, holding up a half-empty beer bottle. "C'mon downstairs. Barbara is starting to ask questions about the interviews."

"Yikes…" Grayson winced. Barbara Parker in an inquisitive mood was never a particularly pleasant thing.

She followed Noah down to the living room where Babs was already waiting, perched cross-legged on one side of the couch. Grayson took the other end. Noah took one of the side chairs.

Babs had never been one to beat around the bush, especially when the topic was important, but she at least had the good sense to wait until after everyone had a drink and a piece of pizza in front of them.

"So," she declared, "Lisa's dead."

The two young doctors looked across the coffee table at each other and nodded sadly.

"They found her dead yesterday at the Catholic seminary," Noah replied, biting into a slice.

"And the police decided bright and early Monday morning would be a great time to come ambush the hospital and interview everybody?"

They both nodded again.

"Sounds about right. Idiot cops," she muttered under her breath, scowling and slamming back the remainder of her first glass of wine.

"It wasn't bad," Grayson countered.

"Oh, please…"

"No, she's right," Noah agreed. "Well, the one detective was a bit of a wanker, but that Nolan chap was nice."

"Wait, which one is the other one?" Babs wrinkled her forehead while pouring herself a fresh glass.

"The one who gave our dear little Gray that handkerchief." Noah pointed toward Grayson's right hand.

She looked down, and her breath hitched when she realized she'd brought the little fabric square down with her. She looked at it like it was completely foreign, twisting it around in her fingers. But it wasn't. It was real. And the feel of it in her hand was already becoming familiar.

I don't even remember grabbing it.

"Wait, wait, what?"

Babs eyed her roommate from her perch on the couch. Grayson tried to tuck it behind her back, but it was too late. Her roommate was across the couch in a flash. She grabbed the fabric square and held it up to the light.

"Wow. This thing is a piece of art, Gray."

Grayson wrinkled her forehead skeptically. "What are you talking about?"

"It's an S. Godard. They've been in business since the 1700s. These are high end."

"And you know this because..."

"Because I know things," she muttered, then turned back to continue examining it. "I used to date this guy who was all into high-end guy accessories. Instead of electronics at Christmas, he got custom cufflinks and rare pocket squares. I picked up a few things."

Carter rolled her eyes. Of course, Babs had dated a guy like that.

"This has some initials on it...GMR."

"Ryder," Grayson mumbled under her breath, trying desperately to hide the blush on her face.

"Huh?" Barbara questioned, eyebrow raised.

"The detective. The one she's talking about. His last name is Ryder," Noah clarified.

"Oooooh," she cooed.

"Stop it," Grayson snapped, yanking the linen square out of her roommate's hand.

"So, you just swiped that?"

"What? No!" She paled.

"He just handed it out like a business card, then?"

Noah winked at Babs from across the couch.

"No. He didn't. I...I kind of lost it in the interview and started crying. He handed it to me."

"You know they make tissues, right?" Babs joked.

"Of course," she nodded, wringing the fabric in her hands. "He insisted I take it. I tried to give it back, and he just..."

She faded off. Babs and Noah looked from Grayson to each other, and back again. When she didn't look up from her lap after several long moments, Noah leaned across the coffee table, pizza balanced precariously in his lap.

"Hey, Earth to Gray! Come back!"

Noah snapped his fingers in her face. She shook her head sharply. "Sorry."

Babs softened.

"Are you okay, sweetie? Really?"

Barbara poured her roommate another glass of wine.

"Of course not. Lisa's dead. Nobody knows what happened to her. I've just been interrogated by two police detectives. One of them got seriously under my skin. And I'm hanging onto a high-end handkerchief like a security blanket. What about any of that makes it seem like I'm the slightest bit okay?" she quipped, throwing her hands up to her face and burying herself back in the couch cushions.

"Yeah, but was he cute?" Babs winked.

Grayson rolled her eyes behind her palms.

Blonde, 5'10", with a Barbie-esque figure, Barbara Parker was used to getting a lot of attention from the opposite sex. She blew most of it off. Grayson's light Italian skin, blue-green eyes, and honey-brown hair just couldn't keep up with Barbie's beauty.

"I didn't notice." *Oh please, please, Babs, drop this.*

"Oh, nonsense! I'm not even his type and I noticed, Gray. Barbara, he's gorgeous. Dark hair, blue eyes. There has to be something good to look at under that shirt. A little odd, though, I'll admit," Noah chattered, opening another beer.

"He wasn't odd."

"Um, what? Are you joking? All he did was pace in the back of the room during my interview. Everyone else I talked to said he was blunt and abrasive. Just nasty. You looked shaken up. I doubt Detective Nolan did that."

"Who's Nolan?" Babs questioned, clearly lost.

"Ryder's partner," Noah explained.

"Ah."

"He wasn't odd," Grayson repeated.

"So, letting you walk out of the room with an exceptionally expensive personalized accessory is something normal for this guy?"

"I don't know," she shook her head, looking down at the fabric in her hands again. "He told me to keep it."

And I want to.

She gripped it harder.

"So, then keep it. Or throw it out. Do what you want with it. Just hand me another piece of pizza," Babs replied.

Grayson passed over the pizza box and started opening another bottle of wine. Between the three of them, it was going to be a carbohydrate- and alcohol-fueled night.

They sat around the living room for hours and talked… about work, about Lisa, about what could have happened to her, and about the detectives.

Every now and again, Babs kept steering the conversation back to the interrogation. Every time she did, Grayson's grip tightened on a certain piece of white linen in her right hand.

14

THE REST OF the week passed by in a haze.

Noah watched Grayson bury herself in work. She was at the hospital by 3:30 in the morning, whether she needed to be or not, and she stayed long after the rest of her team had gone home. There was a new fierce concentration to her operating technique that made more than one attending do a double take. Her usual meek, laid-back demeanor was gone, replaced by cold precision. The abrupt personality change was a shock, but nobody complained. Her work was still excellent. What was there to complain about?

Noah had tried to catch her in between cases, to no avail. She was never free. She'd shot him a quick wave across the hallway when she'd dropped off a patient in the ICU, but that had been it for the entire week.

He knew she was avoiding thinking about Lisa.

And the funeral.

Lisa's parents were in town, arranging the service. At first, he'd thought it odd that they would hold it in Denver instead of back in Wyoming with family and close friends. Two days into the week, it started to make sense.

The entire hospital knew about Lisa's death, and most of the residents and staff wanted a chance to say their goodbyes. The Oakes family had instantly agreed to a service in town when they'd found out. Family and friends from Wyoming had been arriving for days. Everyone would get to say their good-byes without feeling rushed, including Grayson, who seemed to need it more than anybody. Noah knew that she didn't have many friends, just a few close people she trusted and loved, and somehow Lisa had become one of them. Very quickly.

Noah shrugged to himself.

Must've been something incredible about her that she could see before everybody else. Just like Babs. Just like me.

He rested his head in between his hands on the cold countertop and sighed. He jumped when his phone vibrated in his pocket.

Speak of the devil…

"Hello, Barbie-girl!" he singsonged into the phone.

"You know I hate it when you call me that, Mason," she shot back, annoyed.

"Of course I do. That's why I do it."

"Great."

"What's up?"

"Have you seen her today?"

"No, not at all." His smile faded, and he shook his head into the phone.

"Damn."

"Why?"

A long sigh filtered over through the speaker. "I honestly think she's surviving on coffee and fairy dust at this point. I know she's not sleeping. I caught a glimpse of her this morning—at three a.m., by the way—and she looked awful. Like eyes-sunken-in-pale-and-vacant-stare kind of awful."

"Really?" he asked worriedly. *Oh, that's really not good.*

"And I know she's not eating. Nothing's gone from the kitchen but half a sleeve of saltines, the coffee, and most of the creamer. That doesn't count as nutrition in my book."

"It does in mine, kitten…"

"Oh, shut up! I'm seriously worried, Noah. And I can't say anything to her because she's *never* here!"

"She doesn't want to be home, Barbara," he said calmly.

"Why not? It can't be good for her to be walking around with a bunch of white coats in a place where a dead girl worked."

"She can think here."

"She can think at home," Babs countered fiercely.

"No, she can't. Here she can focus on work. It's a distraction, I think. What's she going to think about at home when the surgeon part of her mind shuts off?"

There was a pause on the other end of the line, then another heavy sigh.

"A dead girl and the dead girl's upcoming funeral. Right, right. You're right."

Noah nodded, leaning back in his chair to let her talk.

"Well..." Babs sighed into the phone, "I get it. It wouldn't be my approach. I'd be at home with continuous pints of Ben and Jerry's ice cream and a romantic movie marathon. But that's not our Gray, is it?"

"No, it isn't."

"Damn her."

Noah smiled. "Yeah, I know. Damn her for being super-human."

"I think I need to start checking her closet for a cape and spandex outfit, honestly."

Noah chuckled. "So, what do you want to do?"

Another pause. "Do you think you'll have time to track her down later today?"

"Probably. I can get everything signed out in the unit in an hour or two. Why?"

"Just see if you can corner her into coming home. I'll cook something light, and we can force-feed her if necessary. She doesn't need to pass out from exhaustion tomorrow. Spin it that way if you have to."

"It might take me spending the night to keep her from bolting in the wee hours of the morning," he warned.

"I'll make up the couch."

"Okay." He smiled. "See you soon."

Noah returned his phone to the pocket of his white coat and headed toward the doctors' lounge in the ICU. He had a few consults to see and two critical patients to check on before he signed out to the night team.

Halfway down the hallway, he had an idea. He took out his phone, scrolled through his contact list, found the name he wanted, and hit dial. Three rings and a two-minute conversation later, he slid the phone back into his pocket.

He had what he wanted.

15

GRAYSON RIPPED THE green surgical mask off of her face, pushed her surgical glasses onto the top of her head, and breathed a sigh of relief. The seventh and final case, done. Not bad for one day. And they were an hour and a half ahead of schedule. She ripped down the bright blue surgical drapes, revealing the anesthesiologist at the head of the bed.

"William…William…Bill…wake up. Your surgery is all done. Everything went well. Your knee is fixed. Wake up. Open those eyes. Take a big deep breath for me…" The nurse anesthetist kept mumbling in the patient's ear.

The patient coughed and sputtered as his endotracheal tube was removed, and phlegm rocketed out of his mouth onto the front of his gown.

Grayson turned around, shielding her eyes.

Ick.

As much as she sometimes wondered if she had been crazy picking orthopedics as a subspecialty…long hours, physically demanding, pain-in-the-ass attendings…there was no way she could have ever gone into anesthesia. Dealing with the insides of peoples' mouths and the things that came out of them at the end of a case…

Yuck.

Grayson took two big steps backward and ripped off her surgical gown and gloves, throwing them in the nearest trash bag. Dr. Allen was standing over by the portable x-ray monitor, staring at the intra-operative fluoroscopy shots. She joined him.

"Whadda ya think, Carter?" he asked, glancing sideways at her.

"I think once we got the articular surface tamped up properly, things went a lot smoother."

"I agree," he replied. "I wouldn't have noticed the difference if you hadn't said something. And that filler was a good idea. How'd you know to do that?"

"I read about it." She shrugged. "Used it once or twice with Villamenta. His articular surface needed some additional support once we cranked on it."

Allen nodded. "Crappy bone. Maybe tell me next time when you haven't used something more than once or twice."

"Yes, sir," she said, wincing and dropping her head a bit.

Allen smiled at her. "You know what, never mind. You know what the hell you're doing. I would still have three cases left if you hadn't been my resident today. I can't believe I'm going to make it home for dinner. My wife might seriously make me buy you a car."

She laughed. "Tell her thank you, but I'm partial to my 4Runner."

"All right. Get out of here. You've got to be more wiped out than I am."

"Oh, thank you, but I have some things to do before…"

"Then go do them," he cut her off. "You've been burning it at both ends. Not that I mind. I mean, look at today. You fucking rocked it. But it's going to catch up to you. Go get your shit done and go home."

"Yes, sir," she promised, grabbing the side rail of Mr. Kasterson's hospital bed, steering him out the operating room door.

Grayson hastily slipped her pager and cell phone clip onto her scrubs and bolted ahead of the bed, hitting the steel plate on the wall to open the doors to recovery. They parted, and she immediately saw Noah leaning against the wall just inside the PACU threshold. His satchel was slung over one shoulder, and his coat was tucked securely under the other arm.

He didn't say anything to her and she didn't say anything to him as she helped anesthesia staff steer the old bed into recovery bay seven. She gave the recovery nurse a quick run-down on Mr. Kasterson before grabbing the chart and sitting down at a nearby table. She absently flipped the chart open and started filling out the same-day post-operative orders.

Noah slid into the chair directly across from her. "Avoiding me, love?"

Grayson looked up at him, eyes narrowed. "Of course not."

"So, we haven't seen each other this week because…"

"I've been busy." Her voice was flat.

"Right."

"What do you want, Mason?" she asked, concentrating on her orders.

She only used his last name when she was upset with him. She wasn't really upset now, just…tired. So very tired.

"I want you to get your stuff together, get in your car, and follow me home."

"I have things to do here."

"Bullshit."

Her eyes shot up. Noah hardly ever swore, especially at her. "Excuse me?" she balked.

"I said bullshit."

"You know nothing about my service," she spat.

"The hell I don't. I already called Adams. Your service is locked down. He's even on call, so you don't have to sign out to anybody. You couldn't have any less work to do."

"You've been checking in on my service?" she shot back.

"No, I just made one phone call."

"I have things to do," she repeated, shaking her head.

"No, you don't," he countered forcefully.

Noah reached across the table and grabbed the chart. He scanned the post-op orders, which were complete and immaculate, and signed his name at the bottom. He shut the front of the binder as he stood up, strode over to bay seven, and placed it on the table at the foot of the bed.

"That was your last piece of work for the entire day. You're done. Now, you're coming home if I have to drag you kicking and screaming from this hospital. You're not dropping over dead tomorrow if I have anything to say about it."

Noah scooped up his coat, slung his bag back over his shoulder, and pulled her backward, chair and all.

"Get up," he demanded.

Grayson looked up into his face and recognized that this was one of the rare times she wasn't going to be able to talk her way around Noah Mason. She sighed, shook her head, and slowly rose to her feet.

"Now go get your crap from your locker so we can go."

He pointed down the hallway toward the locker rooms.

Grayson set off in the direction he was pointing, and Noah fell into step silently behind her. She disappeared into the women's locker room for a few minutes and quickly re-emerged, her black North Face fleece jacket zipped up and a well-worn brown leather messenger bag slung cross-body over her left shoulder. She wound around through the halls of the hospital toward the main entrance with Noah still on her heels.

"You haven't been that pushy in a while," she said to the floor.

"You haven't given me a reason to be that pushy in a while, Gray."

"I haven't been that easy to deal with this week, have I?"

"No kidding."

"I'm sorry," she said as Noah held the door to the main lobby open for her.

She stepped out into the early night air. The sun had gone down, but there was still light hanging in the sky. The street lamps hadn't come on yet. There was hardly enough chill in the air to merit the heavy coat she was wearing, but when she'd come into work at three in the morning…

Noah playfully ran into her side to jostle her back into reality. "It's okay," he said gently.

"No, it's not."

"Sure it is. You've had a rough week."

"It doesn't excuse me treating you like crap."

"Who said you've been treating me like crap? You've been avoiding me and your roommate and burying yourself in work. You've made us all worry about you, that's all."

"Which isn't great."

"Buy me coffee sometime. And start getting some decent sleep. We'll call it even," he said, smiling at her.

They walked across the street and up to their respective cars. As luck would have it, Noah had parked his Civic directly across from her SUV. He grabbed her shoulders and turned her around to look at him in the middle of the ramp.

"Look, Grayson, Babs and I know you've been having a hard time with this. You and Lisa got close very quickly. I understand that keeping your mind busy at work keeps you from thinking about her. But running yourself down like this isn't doing you any good; you're going to kill yourself if you keep this up. You're going to have to think about her eventually. The longer you wait, the worse it's going to be. And you know that."

"I know," she nodded, avoiding looking at him.

"Buck up. You're human. Not Wonder Woman. Come home, have a good cry, and eat something."

"Okay."

"I'll follow you."

They separated, started their respective cars, and pulled out of the parking lot. True to his word, Noah stayed behind her the whole way home, and when she turned down the alleyway, he found a space to parallel park on the street.

She walked up her back steps and into the kitchen, just as Noah walked in the front door and Babs came down the stairs. Her roommate stopped on the stairway and stared at her for a second before looking at Noah.

"Holy crap, you actually got her to come home."

"Hi to you too, Barbara," she said sarcastically, dropping her bag onto the bench by the entryway and unzipping her coat.

The kitchen smelled wonderful, as it usually did whenever Babs Parker decided to actually follow the recipe. There was something in the oven, two somethings on the stove, and a chocolate something cooling under a kitchen towel on the counter.

"You having company over tonight?" Grayson joked.

"Well, supposedly I live with this genius doctor, but I haven't seen her in almost a week, so I thought I could bribe her with food," she replied, making a face.

"You can always bribe me with food," Noah said, also setting his things down.

"We both know that," she replied as she stirred something in one of the pots on the stove.

"What're you cooking? Can I help?" Grayson started in toward the kitchen.

"Absolutely not!" Babs turned around and shooed her away from the stove with a wooden spoon.

"Upstairs. Sweatpants. Slippers. I'll have it dished out when you get back down."

Grayson shrugged and did as she was told. Both of her friends were clearly in a mood. She came back down in gray sweatpants and a long-sleeved white shirt, hair pulled back into a ponytail.

Three plates of food were steaming on the kitchen table. Three glasses of red wine were waiting on the far countertop beside a plate of chocolate brownies. She smiled as she stepped up to the table. Of course, Babs had made comfort food. Tomato soup, grilled cheese, red wine, and brownies. For the first time in a few days, Grayson felt her stomach growl, and she realized how long it had been since she'd had any real food.

"Sit, sit!"

Her roommate shuffled back into the room, bringing the two of the three glasses of wine with her. Noah followed close behind her and grabbed the last glass for himself. Grayson did as she was told. When Barbara Parker was in mothering mode, it was best not to argue.

"You approve?" she asked as she sat down at the table.

"Of course," Grayson smiled. "Thank you for this," she added softly.

"Oh, honey, please..." Babs took a drink from her glass of wine and shook her head, "I'm just happy Mr. Suave over here was able to get you to come home and actually sit down to dinner."

"I'm sorry if I've been less than…um…gracious this week."

"Gray, nobody cares. At least I don't. I just want to be sure you're okay, and right now the first step in that is to get you to eat, so start eating."

Grayson smiled and started in on her grilled cheese. A bottle of wine and two brownies later, they put the dishes in the sink and headed into the living room. All three of them settled onto the couch with Grayson sandwiched in between her two friends. Babs curled her legs underneath her and turned toward her roommate.

"All right, now spill it. You've been running on coffee and no sleep this whole week."

"I know."

"It's all about Lisa?"

She nodded.

"What's gotten so far under your skin about this girl? I mean, don't get me wrong, she was sweet. We all enjoyed spending time with her, but you're acting like someone just told you your twin sister died. What is going on?"

"I don't really get it, either, to be honest," she replied, pulling the fleece blanket off of the back of the couch and wrapping it around her legs. "Lisa was assigned to me because she was having the same problems I had as an intern. There was some bonding in that, I guess. I didn't want to see her walk out on a great career because of the hospital pecking order. It became my responsibility to keep an eye on her, and I took it seriously."

She grabbed a tissue from the box on the coffee table and dabbed her eyes. Noah wrapped an arm around her shoulders.

"And then one day she just ends up dead. No reason. No warning signs. Nothing. At this point, I don't think anybody even knows *how* she died, let alone why. And I keep running things over and over in my head. I don't think she was acting any differently, but what if she was and I missed it? What if something was bothering her and she didn't feel like she could tell me? What if…I just…what if I could have done something to keep her from…"

Her voice was getting shakier by the second, and both Noah and Babs could see her mind clicking into overdrive.

Noah took over. "Hey, hey, enough. Stop it," he said, pulling her into a hug.

Babs leaned over and hugged her from the other side.

"The police are trying to figure out what the hell happened. You aren't helping anything by getting yourself worked up. If she'd had something going on that she was worried about, she would have come to you. She always did before."

Grayson nodded silently into his T-shirt, which was now damp.

"Lisa wouldn't want you sitting around like this." He pulled back from the hug and looked at her. "Answer me, yes or no?"

"Yes," she nodded, shakily.

"Okay. Remember Lisa as she would want to be remembered, a happy little redheaded firecracker."

Grayson took a few deep, shaky breaths and reached for another tissue. "You know, you can come up with a really good speech when you want to, Noah," she replied shakily.

"I only do it when it really matters, love. Now," he reached over to the coffee table, grabbing the unopened bottle of wine and corkscrew, "Why don't we toast to the memory of our little firecracker?"

Carter and Babs nodded, taking their glasses from Noah as he poured. Grayson raised hers, and the others followed.

"Ar dheis Dé go raibh sé."

Babs gave Noah a questioning look. He shot one back that said "just go with it", and they clinked glasses, sitting in silence for a moment.

"What did that mean?" she finally asked.

Grayson smiled. "Don't worry about it. She'll get it."

That was enough of an explanation for anybody.

Noah grabbed the remote and switched on the TV.

16

AT SUNRISE FRIDAY morning, Detective Blake Nolan stepped into the elevator, a coffee mug in one hand and a file folder in the other. He stifled a yawn as the old machine kick-started its ascent. Seven a.m. was his usual call-in time, but he was exhausted. He'd been pulling long hours all week, mostly trying to keep his partner in line.

He walked off the elevator, surprised to find Ryder's desk empty. He'd expected to find him pouring over the Lisa Oakes file, already on his second or third cup of coffee. Instead, it looked just as immaculate as it had when they'd left last night. Completely undisturbed.

Nolan set his coffee down on his own desk and shucked off his coat.

Strange.

"Nolan."

Captain McCallister was standing in the doorway to his office, motioning him over.

Shit. Now what?

Nolan shuffled into the office, alone and on guard. He hated going into the captain's office without Ryder around, especially when they weren't making much progress on a case. It sounded stupid, but apparently, if the Golden Boy couldn't catch a break, then it was okay. If *he* couldn't catch a break, well…

"So," the captain started, sitting on the edge of his desk. "Any movement on the Oakes case?"

"Not really." Nolan shook his head as he took his customary seat.

"Nothing from all those interviews?"

They had spent almost three days interviewing anyone and everyone who might have had regular contact with the young intern. They'd all said the same thing. She was a nice girl, always did her work well, and was getting more and more adjusted to residency, especially after she'd started hanging around with Dr. Carter.

Nobody had noticed a change for the worse in the weeks leading up to her death. The last documented person to see her alive was one of the nighttime security guards who had walked her out to her car on Saturday. She'd looked tired, but fine, and security footage proved as much.

Her neighbors in the apartment complex where she'd lived hadn't provided much else. They rarely saw her because of the hours she worked, but they all knew her as the happy redhead down the hall. No one had heard any fights, seen any male visitors, or witnessed anything strange in her behavior. The security cameras outside her building showed her getting into her car Saturday evening, dressed in jeans and a sweater, and heading north away from her building. No one had followed her, and she didn't look agitated on the tapes.

They were officially stuck.

"No, sir. Same thing we've been telling you all week. Everyone liked her. Nobody saw anything suspicious. Same thing on the security footage we have. Then she's in the wind."

"Damn."

"Yeah."

"And where's the wonder child?" he asked sarcastically.

"You mean Ryder?"

The captain nodded. "Who else would I mean?"

"No clue. I thought he would have beaten me here."

"He's doing okay?"

"As well as he usually does when we're not getting anywhere."

"So, borderline?"

Nolan reluctantly sighed, then nodded.

"All right. Figure out where he is. Hopefully, he's had an epiphany. I keep getting calls from the chief about this case."

"The seminary's putting pressure on us? I didn't figure that from a group of priests."

"No," McCallister said with a laugh. "Just the chief. He doesn't like an unsolved murder on holy ground. Thinks it's a bad omen."

"Hey, I don't either." Blake grinned, throwing up his hands. "Gotta be bad luck or something."

The captain opened his office door. "Just try to get me something I can run up the ladder to get him off my back."

"No promises, captain," he replied as he pushed himself out of the chair.

"Are you two attending the funeral tomorrow?"

Nolan paused, his mouth half open. They hadn't actually discussed it. "I don't know, captain. Probably. At least one of us will head over there."

"I'd prefer both of you. Figure it out."

Blake nodded and headed back toward his desk. He plopped down in his chair, took a big swig of what was left of his coffee, and sighed.

Where in the hell is my partner?

He looked up when he heard the elevator ding.

Speak of the devil...

In strode Ryder, immaculate as ever. Black suit, crimson tie, tailored overcoat.

Bastard. Nolan made a face as his partner sat down at his desk.

Gabriel raised his eyebrows. "What?"

"You late getting back from your modeling gig this morning?"

"Huh?"

Oh, dear Christ...

As usual, his partner was completely clueless. Nolan shook his head.

"This," Nolan motioned up and down. "Is there ever a day where you wake up and go, 'Hmmm. I think I'll put on a shirt with a few wrinkles in it today. I feel like slumming it'?"

"Not that I can think of. This bothers you?" Gabriel smiled.

"Occasionally, yes."

"Like today?"

"Like today."

"Fantastic, Blake. Glad we cleared that up."

"So, what was so important with the tie selection this morning that you were late?"

Gabriel looked at the clock on his desk.

"It's 7:15. Technically, I'm still early by department standards."

"Late for you."

"What's up your ass this morning?"

"How about a solo meeting with the captain and a lack of doughnuts?"

Ryder paused, his overcoat half-slung over the backside of his office chair. "Solo meeting?"

"While you were admiring yourself in a mirror somewhere, I got grilled about the Oakes case."

Ryder winced. "Sorry."

"I want an extra doughnut this week." Nolan feigned the beginnings of a tantrum.

"Fine," Ryder agreed, waving his hand in the air. "And for the record, I was down at the seminary."

"Oh?" His partner's eyebrows shot up. "Come up with something?"

He shook his head.

"Then why go?"

"It's been bothering me. I wanted to have another look around."

"Didn't they open the chapel back up?"

He nodded. "I wasn't there to take trace. I just wanted a look around. The Freedman kid let me in."

"But no epiphanies?"

"No."

"Well, unfortunately, that's what our captain wants. One of your glorious epiphanies."

"He's not getting one." Ryder scowled, shifting in his seat.

Nolan nodded and leaned back in his chair. "So, new topic. We going to the funeral tomorrow?"

"Lisa Oakes' funeral is on Saturday, Blake."

"Tomorrow is Saturday, Gabe."

Ryder stared for a moment, then blinked rapidly. "It's Friday," he stated, his voice flat.

"Brilliant, detective."

Nolan coughed and rolled his eyes.

"Shove it."

"You're not sleeping again, are you?"

Gabriel stayed quiet, so Blake sat back and laced his hands behind his head. That silence meant he was right. His partner wasn't sleeping.

"We should be there tomorrow."

"To stake it out?"

"Yes. And no."

"Let's start with yes."

"We need to be sure no one suspicious shows up at the church. And the Oakes family is going back to Wyoming after the service. We need to talk to them before they go."

"Let me handle the grieving family, Ryder. And the no?"

"We should pay our respects," he said, matter-of-factly.

"Can't argue with that. So, what adventures do we have today, partner?"

Ryder flipped his binder open. "We need to see the M.E. We still don't have a cause of death."

"You know it takes weeks for tox to come back, Gabe."

"It doesn't mean Carla doesn't have something for us now. And the family will ask tomorrow."

"You two on a first-name basis now?"

"I'm down there enough."

"Please don't start poking at the body today, Ryder. I haven't had enough coffee for that. Let the M.E. do it. With gloves on."

"No promises."

Ryder smiled as he stood up from his chair. Nolan followed.

"Can I at least get more coffee first?"

"Sure."

They stopped briefly in the break room, then headed to the elevator.

"So…" Blake drawled. "We have a date tomorrow afternoon then?"

"Sure."

"You want me to pick you up?" he mocked.

"Whatever floats your boat, Blake."

"I have to wear a suit, don't I?"

"You're supposed to wear a suit to work."

"I do."

"You're wearing a collared shirt and tie."

"My coat's in the car, I swear…"

"Right."

"…at least I think it's in the car…"

"Blake…" They stepped into the elevator car, and Ryder pushed the button for the morgue.

"Look, I'll look respectable, okay? I won't embarrass you."

"Didn't say you would."

The doors closed, and they were silent on the short ride down.

"Tomorrow's not going to be pleasant, is it?" Nolan asked as the doors opened.

Ryder shook his head. "I can't imagine a funeral being anyone's ideal way to spend an afternoon."

"Think the perp will show?"

Gabriel didn't answer as he walked into the hallway and opened the door to the M.E.'s office. He didn't say anything to his partner because, honestly, he didn't know what to tell him.

17

SATURDAY DAWNED COOL and dark. The weather had turned ugly overnight. The skies were covered in threatening gray clouds that were intermittently spitting rain, and the wind was whipping relentlessly through the trees.

Grayson stood in the warmth of her living room, looking out the window onto the street. If the weather was supposed to sum up her mood, she'd give Mother Nature an A+ on this one.

She could hear Barbara jostling around upstairs, putting the finishing touches on herself before it was time to leave. Babs was always running late, but today she had given herself a ridiculous amount of time to get ready to go...and was about to put every last second of it to good use.

Grayson smiled to herself, appreciating the fact that her roommate had woken up so early just to be sure she was on time for once. She tightened her grip on the cup of coffee she held in her hands and breathed deeply. Today was going to be awful.

Lisa's family had come down from Wyoming. Her mother, father, brother, and sister were all in town. Aunts and uncles had flown in from as far as New York City. By last count, half of Lisa's hometown had made the drive down, all for this service. It was going to be the only service for her. Her family was taking her body home and burying her on the family farm tomorrow.

She'd gone to see Lisa's parents last night. The thought of the visit had been torture enough, but to make things worse, they had been wonderful to her. She had expected tears, anger, grief...something painful. Instead, there were hugs. Her mother had gone on and on about how much Lisa talked about her. About how happy she was to finally meet the famed Dr. Carter in person. And then, Lisa's father had asked her to say something at the funeral service.

Shit.

What could she possibly have said, no? So at 10:30 last night, she'd sat down at her desk and tried to put something on paper. As of 2:15 this afternoon, she still had nothing.

The front door opened, and as expected, in walked Noah Mason. He was sharply dressed. Black suit, white shirt, skinny black tie, and a pink pocket square.

Grayson smiled.

Lisa's favorite color.

Noah quickly shut the door to keep the cold air out, then took time to give his friend a once-over. Grayson was dressed in a modest wrap dress—black, of course—with long sleeves and a V-neck, and three-inch leather heels. Her hair had been straightened, pulled off the right side of her face by a small jeweled comb, and her makeup had been softly done.

Barbara Parker has struck again.

"Well, don't you look lovely."

"Oh, ha ha," she replied sarcastically, rolling her eyes.

"No, I'm serious, lovie. Babs worked her magic."

"So, I need war paint to pull off being a girl, huh?"

"Rubbish. It just puts on the final touches for a special occasion, that's all. You know I think you're gorgeous in sweatpants." He smiled at her and pulled her into a hug. "How're you doing? You figure out what you're going to say yet?"

She shook her head.

"Don't worry. You'll think of something."

"And if I become a blubbering idiot up there?"

"Then you're blubbering from the heart and who cares?"

"I'll care, Noah."

"Nobody else will."

She smiled into his chest. "Just promise me you'll give me a signal if I'm making a complete fool of myself."

"I promise. I won't have to, but I promise anyway."

Babs took that moment to come racing down the stairs, stumbling in the attempt to put on her second stiletto.

"I'm sorry, I'm sorry, I'm sorry, I know I'm running late," she mumbled.

"You're fine," Grayson replied. "We have plenty of time. You look nice."

"Thanks," she said, adjusting her sweater and walking into the kitchen.

She'd dressed in black slacks, a cashmere cardigan, and fluffed her hair a la Farrah Fawcett. She came back with two cups of coffee, handing one to Noah.

"You don't look too shabby, Mason. What do you think of our girl?" she asked, taking a sip.

"Very nice job, I must say," he replied, taking the cup.

"You two know I'm standing right here, right?"

"We know, love," Noah said, hugging her sideways. "What time do we have to leave?"

"Probably in the next fifteen minutes if we're going to be on time."

"Who's driving?" Babs asked.

"I can," Grayson volunteered.

"Um, absolutely not. I'll drive," Noah stated.

Babs reached for both of their coffee cups, eyeing the storm. "Let's just get going before this weather gets any worse. You have umbrellas, right?"

"Of course. I'm British. Gray, you ready?" Noah asked softly, placing a hand on her shoulder.

Grayson shrugged. "As ready as I'll ever be, I guess."

Babs opened the coat closet and handed her roommate her long black wool coat, pulling her own khaki coat on in a flourish.

"Deep breath, Gray," Noah whispered in her ear.

She obeyed him. In fact, he noticed she kept repeating the mantra quietly under her breath, all the way to the church.

18

NOLAN PULLED UP outside of his partner's apartment building behind the wheel of one of the department's SUVs. Black exterior, black interior, tinted windows.

Perfect vehicle for a funeral, he mused.

The weather was crappy, to put it nicely, and it was projected to get worse throughout the day. He flipped on the windshield wipers as another spurt of rain hit the glass. Of course, he'd forgotten an umbrella. He'd also left the house without a tie. He'd managed the suit but forgotten the tie.

He saw his partner walk into the lobby of his building, and he honked the horn twice. Ryder came out immediately, and Blake inwardly groaned. This was seriously getting old. He even had leather gloves and a classic black umbrella hooked over his arm.

Gabriel opened the passenger door and slid gracefully into the seat. He immediately noticed Blake's face. "What?"

"Okay, I really have to ask. Do you have someone pick out your clothes or something?"

"No. Why?"

"You look like a fucking Ken doll."

"A what?" he asked, chuckling.

"Ken. Barbie's boyfriend. Always super-masculine and color-coordinated."

"Isn't he blond?" Ryder smirked.

"That's beside the point. I have two girls. I'm supposed to know who Ken is, and it's still a fucking miracle that I actually know. How the fuck do you know anything about Ken dolls?"

Ryder silently shrugged.

"Look at you…" He motioned up and down. "You have matching gloves."

"They're black, Nolan. And it's cold outside."

"They match."

"I'm dressed in black. I would hope so."

"Shut up, asshole."

"You have a problem with the way I'm dressed?"

"You look good."

"Again…wait, what?"

"Damn it, just hand over my tie."

"You mean *my* tie. The one you're borrowing?"

"Yes." He held out his hand impatiently.

Ryder dug into his coat pocket and produced a burgundy tie. "Here."

"Not black?"

"I didn't know which suit you were wearing."

"It makes a difference?"

"Yes." His partner nodded.

"You know I have more than one black suit?"

"Yes." More nodding.

"They don't all look the same?"

"No."

"Okay, stop. You're making my head hurt. Tell me we have time for coffee."

Ryder looked at his watch. "Of course."

"Fine. Let's go," Blake grumbled, turning the key in the ignition.

"Put your tie on."

"I'll do it later. I can tie a tie."

"I know that…"

"I'll tie it when I'm good and ready, ass. And I need coffee before that."

Blake flipped on his turn signal and pulled out into traffic. Usually, he'd be dodging bicyclists and families out with a multitude of strollers, wayward toddlers, and various retrievers. Today, there was barely anyone on the road. One of the only good things about bad weather.

"At least tell me you didn't go running this morning," he said as he turned left at the second light.

He glanced across the car at the man in the passenger seat, who just ran a hand through his hair and smiled. Blake shook his head. "Damn it, Ryder."

"I don't see why that should bother you."

"I could barely drag my butt out of bed this morning to eat waffles with my girls."

"So, you want me to eat a bunch of cake, sit on my couch, and get fat?"

"Would you, please? It'd make so many of us feel better about ourselves," he sniped sarcastically.

"Maybe next year, Blake," he replied. "Just get your coffee. We need to get to the church before people start showing up."

"You think there'll be a big turnout?"

He nodded. "She was a good kid. And half of her hometown drove down. I'm expecting standing room only."

"Great. And I wore uncomfortable shoes."

19

PARKING IN FRONT of the seminary, Noah shut off the car. It was raining constantly now, and the sky had turned a much darker shade of gray on the drive over.

The ride down had been quiet. Babs had attempted some small talk, but she'd ended up talking to herself. Grayson had been eerily silent in the backseat. Noah glanced back at her in the rearview mirror. Her eyes were glazed over. Her face was blank. She looked lost.

He hurt for her.

Noah cracked the driver's side door and popped his umbrella open, handing another to Babs across the console. He stepped out of the car and opened the backseat door, holding out his hand.

Grayson snapped out of her daze with a quick shake of her head, grabbed his hand, and stepped out. She looked around absently. Lisa's parents' truck was in the parking lot, alongside some other cars she recognized from the hospital parking deck. It was still early. The lot would be full by the time the ceremony started.

"C'mon, honey," Noah said, gently guiding her up the front stairs and into the building, his left hand pressed on her back. Barbara followed behind them.

The lights were on full blast in the chapel foyer, but the weather still threw a muted, gloomy glow around the room. Candles were flickering on the sideboards. Gentle organ music drifted out through the chapel doors. Dozens of flower arrangements lined the walls, all various shades of pink. The trio handed over their coats to a young man at the door and started milling around the arrangements.

"Miss Carter?" A portly, well-manicured Hispanic man in white robes crossed the room, his hand outstretched.

Grayson put on the best smile she could manage and turned toward him. "Yes?"

"I'm Father Dominic," he said, clasping her hand. "It's wonderful to meet you. The Oakes family has spoken very highly of you. I'm sorry to meet under such circumstances."

She nodded.

"I understand you've been asked to say a few words today?"

Another nod.

"Well, don't worry. Speak from your heart, and she will hear you. You will be speaking after Lisa's brother, Jake. Take all the time you need."

"Thank you."

The priest seemed to notice the hesitation and anxiety in her eyes but didn't press, instead turning to address the young woman's friends. "And you are?"

"Noah Mason," the young man said as he stepped forward, shaking the father's hand. "I work with Grayson. This is Barbara Parker."

"Wonderful to meet you both," he replied, grasping Babs' hand in greeting just as he'd done to Grayson. "If any of you would like a private moment with Lisa, now would be the time."

Noah and Babs nodded. Grayson stared at the floor and shook her head. She was in no hurry to talk to a corpse.

"C'mon, love. Let's go see her," Noah prodded.

Father Dominic motioned toward the large wooden doors that led into the chapel.

"Please take a seat in the second pew to the left. When you're ready, of course."

Babs grabbed her left hand and started guiding her toward the door. Grayson took three steps, then turned around to face the priest. "Father Dominic?"

"Yes?"

"One of your students found her, right?"

"Yes, that's true."

"Did he, um, give her...her last rites?"

"To a point, yes. As much as he was able," he agreed.

"Is he here?" she asked softly.

"He insisted. So did I. First pew on the right. Andrew Freedman."

"Thank you."

Grayson let her friends steer her into the chapel and down the aisle.

———

Father Dominic peered in after them for a quick moment. It was clear the young woman hadn't come to terms with Lisa's passing. If she couldn't find peace for herself, perhaps she would bring peace to Andy.

He crossed his fingers, just in case.

20

NOLAN AND RYDER arrived at the church early and parked the SUV under a tree across the street. It gave them an unobstructed view of the front door so they could monitor the arrival of the guests.

Lisa's parents had arrived first, followed closely by what were probably family friends. Mrs. Oakes already had tissues in her left hand and was being supported on either side by her husband and her son.

Nolan didn't blame her. He'd be a mess if he had to bury one of his daughters, and they were only a few years old. He couldn't imagine burying one after twenty-odd years' worth of memories.

Gabriel sat in the passenger seat, drumming his fingers on the dashboard and thumbing through his binder. He barely paid attention to the arrivals across the street until a dark Honda Civic parked several car lengths ahead of them. Ryder's fingers paused in midair. He sat up slightly in his seat.

Blake eyed the car.

What's got him excited all of a sudden? It's a goddamned Civic. My car looks like more of a threat than that thing.

Nolan watched the car with one eye and kept his partner in view with the other. A tall, leggy blonde stepped out of the passenger seat, quickly popping open a pink umbrella to shield herself from the ongoing rain. A man stepped out of the driver's door, his face hidden by an open umbrella, and held his hand out to someone in the backseat. Gabriel sat up further in the passenger seat. Nolan opened his mouth to say something, then shut it just as quickly.

Huh. That has him worked up?

Dr. Carter emerged from the backseat, holding onto a man Blake now recognized as one of the other interviewees, Dr. Mason. The trio headed into the seminary without any fanfare. A few more cars drove past them on the street and headed into the parking lot.

Nolan waited a few moments, then his curiosity got the best of him. "So, people are startin' to show."

"Mm-hmm."

"Aren't they a bit early?"

"Some of them might be speaking at the service."

"You have to be early for that?"

"To meet the priest," he replied. "Maybe spend a moment alone with the deceased. Haven't you ever been to a funeral?"

"I was six, and it was my grandpa, thanks for asking." Nolan scowled. "I remember not getting to have the cookie I wanted."

"How sweet," Gabriel replied sarcastically.

"Are we going to just sit here all day?"

"Itching to get a cookie?"

"No, I'm freezing my ass off in this car."

"Then I guess we should get you warmed up before your attitude gets any worse."

———

Gabriel pushed open the passenger door and opened his umbrella. He walked around to the driver's side, where his partner had his door half-cracked.

"If you think I'm getting under that thing with you, you better think again," Nolan griped, attempting to step down from the SUV without stepping directly into a puddle.

"You have a better idea?" came the humored reply.

"I'll run like a normal man," he replied, shutting the car door and pulling his coat collar up around his neck.

"Or you could be civil and walk fifty yards under an umbrella."

"When have you ever known me to be highbrow, Gabe?"

"You more than me, Blake."

Nolan shrugged, pulled his collar up higher around his neck, and then dashed off toward the church.

Ryder shook his head and followed, at a much more leisurely pace. He looked calm and collected, but he felt terrible. He hadn't slept well the entire week, and oddly, it wasn't because of the case. He was invested in it, of course, and frustrated that they didn't have any leads.

But that wasn't it. Not this time. He couldn't pinpoint the source. And his two-hour run in the rain this morning hadn't clarified a damned thing.

What in the hell is wrong with me?

21

THE STAINED GLASS windows lining both walls were serenely beautiful, despite the gloomy weather. Two massive bouquets of bright pink roses in white vases decorated the altar, and a large picture of Lisa sat on an easel on the right-hand side. Behind that, the walls were lit up with dozens of flickering candles. It was all very pretty, very pink, and very Lisa.

But Grayson wasn't paying attention to it. She was focused on the young man in the front row sitting with his head between his hands. She was three rows back from him when she turned and nodded at Noah. He pushed Babs into a pew. She continued on.

"Andrew Freedman?" she asked softly.

The young man looked up and nodded. Grayson winced. He looked as terrible as she felt. His eyes were bloodshot and sunken in, and he was quite pale.

"I'm Grayson, one of Lisa's friend. Can I sit down?"

He nodded and scooted over on the bench.

"You all did a beautiful job. Lisa would be very happy."

"I hope so," he said, his voice scratchy like he hadn't spoken in days. "I pulled together what I could."

"She would like this. Especially the flowers."

"I didn't do that. Her parents did."

"But you're the one who asked the fathers if she could have a service here, didn't you?"

He nodded.

"That was a wonderful thing to do. Otherwise, nobody here in town would have been able to say goodbye to her, you know?"

He stayed silent, his gaze focused on the coffin in front of them.

"Father Dominic told me that you were the one who found her on Sunday."

"Yes, I ... I was."

"He also said you gave her her last rites."

"That's n…not really true," he stammered. "I… I tried, but my Latin's not very good yet."

"That's a pretty brave thing to do for her."

The young man didn't say anything for a long moment, then he sighed. "It wasn't brave at all. I did it because I had to. She died all alone and scared, and there was probably nothing she could do to stop it. Someone just *left* her here, all alone. I didn't want her to be alone anymore. "

He hid it well, but he'd started to cry. Grayson reached into her pocket and withdrew a tissue she had been saving for herself.

"I still think that's pretty brave, Andrew."

He took it from her, his hand shaking. "She looks just like my damned sister," he muttered under his breath.

Grayson's eyebrows shot up.

Well, that explains it.

She turned and hugged the young man on instinct. He hugged her back and cried into her shoulder. It took a few minutes, but he eventually got ahold of himself. He wiped his eyes roughly and shoved the tissue into his pocket, embarrassed.

"Sorry," he murmured.

"Don't be," Grayson said, gently touching him on the shoulder. "Everyone is allowed to grieve, even if the reason isn't straightforward. I'm glad you stayed with her. And I know her family is, too."

Grayson caught her lower lip between her teeth and glanced hesitantly at the coffin. "If you'll excuse me, there's someone I need to say hello to."

———

Andrew watched the young woman walk up the few steps to the altar. It took a minute, but she eventually started softly talking to the young girl lying pale and still in the coffin. He couldn't hear what she was saying, so he watched her face instead. Her eyes were watering and, after another minute, tears slipped down her cheeks. But she was smiling. Half-heartedly maybe, but smiling. Almost as if she didn't want Lisa to see how upset she really was.

She reached out and plucked one of the pink roses out of its vase. She snapped off most of the stem, unfurled a few of the petals, and then the flower disappeared into the casket. She murmured what sounded like "sweet dreams, kiddo" before stepping down to join a young man and woman in the second pew. The young man offered her a tissue, but she waved him off, taking a white handkerchief out of her pocket and dabbing her eyes.

Andrew stood and made his way up to the altar. More and more people were steadily trickling into the chapel. It wouldn't do for him to be taking up a whole pew to himself, and he had a few odds and ends to check on at the back of the sanctuary before the service started.

As he crossed in front of the altar, he hazarded a glance into the coffin. She really did look like his sister: curly red hair, pale skin, just a hint of freckles. But what caught his attention was a pink rose that had been placed just above her left ear. It was the only piece of pink in the entire casket, and for some reason, it was perfect.

She should be buried with a pink flower in her hair.

He turned around to face the pews, hoping to be able to catch Grayson's attention and somehow relay how perfect it was.

What he saw instead was a vaguely familiar tall figure in a black suit and wool coat standing at the back of the church, watching her.

22

THE FUNERAL SERVICE started on time.

As predicted, the chapel was packed, standing room only. The seminary students had started bringing their desk chairs down from the second floor so people would have somewhere to sit down.

When Lisa's parents had mentioned that a few people from their hometown were driving down from Wyoming, Grayson had pictured twenty or so. It was more like a hundred and twenty. They were taking up the entire right-hand side of the chapel and spilling out into the aisles.

The members of the hospital staff that had been able to get away were all sitting on the left side, behind the pews that held Lisa's immediate family and the people who were slated to speak, including herself. There were even a few last-minute arrivals in the back, trying their best to respectfully hide their brightly-colored scrubs underneath black coats.

Grayson smiled to herself. It was like they were all stuck in some kind of twisted wedding: bride's family on the left, bride's other family on the right. She was able to pick a few people out in the crowd. Dr. Sanders was sitting with the general surgery residents a few rows back. *All* of the residents, in fact. He had shut down the department, save for the sole attending surgeon on call. Grayson hadn't expected that. She even recognized a few medical students toward the back of the room.

A line of white robes took up the very back of the chapel: the seminary students, standing in support of Andrew, who was seated next to Father Dominic at the altar.

Father Dominic started the service, welcoming everyone to the seminary and apologizing for the weather. Bible verses were interspersed in between hymns and speeches from family. Grayson didn't pay much attention to what was going on. She was still lost in her own head, frantically trying to think of what to say. She stood up when Noah tugged on her sleeve and sat down when Babs told her to. In between the ups and downs of the service, she kept her eyes focused on the floor.

Eventually, she felt a *tap-tap* on her shoulder and looked at Noah, who pointed toward the lectern. Father Dominic was gesturing her toward the altar. She took a deep breath and sighed.

Okay, here we go.

She shakily got to her feet, scooted out of the pew, and took her position behind the lectern as quickly as her legs would carry her. She had nothing to read from. No notes, no cue cards, nothing. She hadn't been able to put one single word onto paper.

Grayson looked out over the sea of expectant faces. She focused on Noah, who shot her his usual you've-got-this smile.

Deep breath.

"Hello, everyone. My name is Grayson Carter. Um," she stammered, "for those of you who don't know me, I'm one of the residents at St. Joe's here in Denver. Mr. and Mrs. Oakes asked me to say a few words about Lisa," she paused and looked over at the casket.

"I've been thinking a lot about what I should say and trying to put something down on paper has been…difficult. So, I'm just going to tell you a few stories about her instead."

She took a deep, steadying breath.

"Every year, when the new interns start, there's a big ceremony where each intern comes up on stage and receives his or her first new long white coat. The long white coat is very important. Ask any medical student. They have short white coats, we have long white coats. It means you're a 'real doctor.'" She winked at Noah.

There was snickering in the crowd from the interns.

"So, picture a nice summer day, everyone's dressed in a suit, very conservative, and here comes Lisa: hot pink dress, matching strappy sandals, and fire-red hair. She, um…stood out a bit. Her turn finally comes, they open up her coat, and it was absolutely gigantic. It looked like it had been made for someone three times her size. It was a circus tent. Of course, we didn't have any extras, and we were all horrified. Here's this momentous occasion, and it's totally ruined. The auditorium was dead silent. And what did Lisa do? She just shrugged, turned around, held her arms out, and said 'Well, what're you waiting for? I've been waiting for this for eight years! Put it on me!'"

Laughter trickled up the aisle from the interns. Dr. Sanders cracked a grin and nodded his approval. He'd been the one to put the coat on her shoulders that day. Grayson found herself smiling at the memory.

"The entire auditorium lost it. All the interns go to walk off the stage, and here's Lisa trying to schlep this huge coat in four-inch heels. Two of the other interns ended up carrying it behind her like it was a train on a wedding dress.

"But the best part was that she wore that white coat around the hospital for the first two weeks like it was the most normal thing in the world. Tiny resident, fire-red hair, high heels, massive white coat. That's how we all knew her."

Several rows of residents were wiping their eyes or doubled over laughing. The rest were smiling broadly. Dr. Sanders looked like he was ready to start howling.

"A few weeks later, I was formally introduced to Lisa. I knew nothing about her, except that she was *that intern* with the super-sized white coat. She was about to start a rotation on my orthopedic service, so I took her out for coffee to go over my expectations. Out of nowhere, these two little girls came tearing up the sidewalk pointing at her and screaming. They thought they'd found a real-life Disney princess, Merida. Nothing their poor dad did to get them moving worked. The one little girl asked Lisa to come to her birthday party in the park down the street. So, instead of coffee, I spent two hours watching her pretend to be this princess character. Sixteen little girls were dressed up in their princess costumes and following her around like she was a momma duck. She even had to shoot a bow and arrow...and she was a pretty good shot. Who knew?"

Guests on both sides of the aisle were nodding and smiling. Grayson continued.

"I grew to like Lisa a lot when she was on my service, and we became friends. She was a hard worker and always had a smile on her face. A few weeks after she rotated off my service, I bought her coffee at the same coffee shop, but this time we were talking about why she was thinking about quitting the program."

That raised a few eyebrows in the audience. Clearly, Lisa's hard time had been kept quiet, especially back in her hometown.

"Lisa hit a rough patch, and I was tasked with deciding whether or not she had what it takes to survive a five-year surgical residency program."

Grayson closed her eyes for a quick moment, then chuckled.

"What a ridiculous assignment that was. Of course, she did. She would get up and start work early because she knew that her senior resident had been up all night at home with a colicky baby. She stayed late to teach the medical students and sit with families while their loved ones passed away in the ICU. She brought romance novels to the ladies on the geriatric unit and told them their daily milk of magnesia mixed with orange juice was a screwdriver so they would drink it. She even bought one of our patient's little kids a cupcake, so he could give it to his dad...who happened to be celebrating his last birthday in the hospital with terminal cancer. I challenge anybody in this room to come up with a resident, past or present, who can top Lisa's generosity and resilience."

Grayson paused for a moment and looked around the room. No one said a word.

"Exactly. We all know there isn't one."

Her voice was starting to shake. She took a deep steadying breath and another long look back at the casket.

"Today is a day of mourning. A day to grieve for the loss of a colleague, a friend, a sister, a daughter. And we should mourn her, and grieve for her, and spend time wiping tears from our eyes as we say our goodbyes to her. But only for today. Lisa would not want us to live our lives remembering her with tears in our eyes or sorrow in our hearts. She lived to care for others, to put a smile on someone else's face, to ease someone else's suffering. She's the redheaded firecracker who ran around the hospital for two weeks in a giant white coat on principle and was a real-life Disney princess. We need to remember her as the incredible young woman she was and use the joy in those memories to care for each other the way that

Lisa would have. Be spontaneous. Eat a piece of chocolate cake for breakfast because you can. Wear hot pink. That's what she would want us to do, so that's what we should do."

Grayson looked up from the lectern. There wasn't a dry eye in the house. There was a lot of sniffling, hiding of eyes behind tissue, and head nodding. Lisa's mother was sobbing into her husband's shoulder, and her father was looking up at the lectern with moist eyes and a trembling smile.

Grayson smiled back at him. She was able to keep it together until she saw him mouth the words "thank you" as the first tears trickled down his weathered face. She closed her eyes and felt the first of her own tears let loose.

Father Dominic gently took her elbow and led her down the stairs. Noah had already jumped out of his seat. He met her at the bottom and gently started guiding her back toward the pew.

"Well, you did it, sweetheart. You brought the house down," he whispered.

She kept her head down and nodded.

"Lisa would've loved it."

That did it. Grayson stifled a sob, and suddenly the packed chapel felt too warm and too small. Her heart started racing. She needed to get outside, and quickly. She started moving down the side aisle, but Noah grabbed her arm.

"Hey, where are you going?" he whispered.

"I need a minute," she replied, shakily.

It was a miracle she got those four words out. A gentle tap on her other shoulder made her turn. Andy Freedman stood next to her, eyes red from crying. "The easiest way outside is this way."

He turned on his heels and circled around the back of the sanctuary. Grayson followed him without hesitating. He pushed open a side door to the chapel.

"I'll leave the door unlocked for you. Come back in whenever you'd like," he murmured and held the door open for her as she stepped out into the evening rain.

23

GRAYSON LAUNCHED HERSELF out into the thunderstorm. The wind had increased. The skies were a mass of swirling, dark gray clouds, and the rain was falling hard against the sidewalk. The awning over the door sheltered her from the majority of the storm, but a few stray raindrops pelted against her legs.

She took a moment to take in her surroundings. A stone walkway wound around the side of the chapel to the back quadrangle. Two metal benches looked out over the lawn, shielded by the stone archway. The roses that surrounded it were still in bloom, just barely clinging to the last warm days. She stood stock-still, taking slow, deep breaths, willing her heart rate to return to normal. In and out, in and out. The faint sound of singing filtered outside through the crack in the door.

They must be singing another hymn.

A gust of wind blew past, whipping her hair out of place and throwing the bottom of her dress off to one side. The raindrops sliced against her calf, and she winced.

I'm so cold.

A throat cleared in the shadow of the church wall. She startled at the sound, wrapping her arms even tighter around her waist.

Gabriel stepped out into what little ambient light there was, the collar of his long wool coat pulled up around his neck. His hair moved with the wind, back and forth. His deep blue eyes were steadily trained on her. Grayson felt her heart speed up.

"Detective Ryder?"

"Dr. Carter," he murmured, nodding in greeting.

"What are you doing out here?"

She was at a loss for anything else to say.

Why is he here? What is he doing outside? Breathe, Gray.

"I could ask you the same question," he replied sharply.

Immediately, Grayson's guard went up. The tone of his voice made the hair on the back of her neck stand straight on end. Short, sharp, and accusatory. Just like it had been the first time she'd met him at the hospital. Of all days, this was not the day to be a snarky bastard. At least, not with her.

"Then do it. Or leave me alone, detective," she snapped.

She turned her back to him and focused on the storm. It was clearly getting worse. A crack of lightning lit up the clouds to the east and was followed by a deep roar of thunder. And another. And then another. It was getting colder. Despite the long sleeves of her dress, she was beginning to feel the chill creep under her skin. Goosebumps formed underneath her stockings. She wrapped her arms tightly around her waist and rubbed her hands along her arms, trying to ward off the cold. It didn't work.

Grayson was just about to admit defeat and head back inside when she felt something warm drape around her shoulders. She looked up, shocked to find Detective Ryder standing in front of her, wrapping his long wool coat around her. He placed himself in between Grayson and the edge of the sidewalk, effectively shielding her from the violent wind.

"Here. You're freezing."

Grayson started to shrug the coat off on instinct, shaking her head and training her eyes on the cobblestones underneath her feet.

"No, I'm okay, I…"

A sharp tug against the coat forced her to take a shaky step forward. She threw her hands up and collided with fine, warm cotton. Grayson looked up at Gabriel's face, and she immediately lost all impulse to talk.

Ryder's jaw was set tight. His eyes were fixated on her, dark and intense like she'd never seen. The muscles in his neck strained against…something she couldn't see. Something inside of him. It was unsettling. It had her breath caught in her chest. Arguing about the coat was off the table.

I don't want him to stop looking at me like that…wait, what? Focus, Gray. You're at a funeral.

"You're cold," he said softly.

It was a statement, not a question. The harsh tone he'd had a moment earlier was gone, completely. His voice was soft and comforting. She nodded.

"Then put the coat on. Properly."

On command, she slipped her arms through the sleeves and overlapped the front edges of the fabric. The inside was lined with silk. It was still warm from the heat of his body and smelled of musk and sandalwood. The bottom hem would have brushed the floor if she hadn't been wearing heels.

"Won't you be cold?" she asked softly.

"I'll be fine," he shrugged.

"But…"

He waved her off and shook his head. "The storm is getting worse. You should be inside."

"And you're going to stay out here by yourself?" she scoffed.

He didn't respond.

"If it's all the same to you, detective, I'd like to stay here."

Something flashed across his eyes. It was dark and unguarded and incredibly intense. It disappeared just as quickly as it came on before she had a chance to identify it.

Gabriel moved back away from her. Grayson walked past him, under the archway, and took a seat on the nearest bench. He leaned against one of the stone pillars, his knee bent, and right foot kicked up to rest against it.

"What are you doing here?" she asked after several long minutes.

"I needed air. You?"

"I needed air," she parroted.

He smirked.

"What are you doing here, detective?" she asked again, staring nervously at the floor.

"I thought we just covered that."

"No, not outside. I mean here. At…at the seminary."

"I came to pay my respects. So did Detective Nolan."

"You didn't know Lisa," she said, eyes narrowed.

"No, I didn't, but I've been charged with finding the person who took her away from all of the people who cared about her. The least I can do is pay my respects."

"Thank you," she murmured after a moment.

Gabriel didn't miss the shine in her eyes.

Fuck. She's going to start crying again.

Ryder kicked off the pillar, sat down next to her on the bench and wrapped his right arm around her. Grayson let her head fall onto his shoulder. They stayed silent for several moments, watching the rise and flow of the storm clouds.

"So…" he began, "…hot pink and chocolate cake, huh?"

Grayson burst out laughing. For a brief moment, the grief left her eyes and she smiled. Gabriel smiled back at her.

"You heard that?"

"Of course. I heard all of it."

"Did I sound like a rambling idiot?"

The smile faded from his face. "Absolutely not. You spoke from your heart. You gave everyone something to aspire to: to bring joy to another person on behalf of someone who was taken away from this world too soon."

Grayson awkwardly craned her neck sideways and narrowed her eyes at him again. "Do you work for Hallmark?"

"No."

"Consider it for a second career."

"I'll keep that in mind, Dr. Carter."

"Grayson."

"Hm?"

"You can call me Grayson, detective."

What did she just say?

The sound of organ music began to softly filter out from inside the chapel. Someone had turned up the lights in the chapel. The service was over. Grayson heaved a long sigh.

"I should go back inside."

Gabriel glanced down at her, his eyes narrowing.

"But you don't want to?"

"No, I don't," she said, shaking her head against his shoulder.

"Why not?"

She stayed quiet.

"Because you've said your goodbyes," he stated knowingly.

She nodded, and he tightened his right arm around her. He felt rather than saw her close her eyes.

We can stay a while longer. She's not shaking from the cold anymore.

The thought had only just crossed his mind when lightning cracked directly overhead. The rumble of thunder was almost deafening.

"The storm is getting worse…" he murmured into her hair.

"I don't care," she whispered back.

The side door suddenly flung wide open, spilling a warm column of yellow light onto the sodden grass. Grayson and Ryder were just out of range, hidden underneath the arch.

Barbara's elongated shadow spilled out across the lawn.

"Gray? Gray!" she called out over the wind.

Grayson watched her roommate crane her neck to the right, to the left, and then, not seeing any signs of life, start out into the rain. She was five steps out the door before she saw Grayson's hand go up.

"I'll be back in in a minute, Barbara."

"Gray, the storm…" she started.

"Just…just give me a minute," came the response.

The tone of her voice was all she needed to send Barbara grumpily back into the warmth of the chapel. She didn't like using it, and it was rare that she ever had to, but it always meant back off. Immediately.

Grayson sighed and shut her eyes again. She just needed the world to put itself on pause. Just for a minute. Reluctantly, she stood up from the bench and begrudgingly started removing herself from the warmth of Detective Ryder's coat. Gabriel quickly shot to his feet beside her.

"I should get back inside, I…I guess…I…" she stammered. Her eyes darted from left to right across the stone floor.

"Keep it on," he said huskily, grabbing the lapels of his coat together to keep it on her.

"I'm not keeping your coat, detective."

"You'll keep it on until you get back inside, Grayson."

She narrowed her eyes at him.

"I'm not kidding. Keep. It. On."

The sudden power in his voice made her shudder. It wasn't a request. He tugged his coat roughly back onto her shoulders and pulled the collar up around her neck.

"Come on," he said, his voice softened again.

He guided her toward the side door, his palm gently pressed to the small of her back and stepped in front of her to open it. The sudden brightness and warmth of the chapel were overwhelming. Grayson sidestepped into his chest, burying her head against his shoulder to get away from it. His left hand settled automatically on her hip. Gabriel possessively flexed his fingers over the fabric of the coat.

"I...I can't..."

"Yes, you can. Find Mason. He'll get you out of there."

"And you...?"

"...will stay until you leave. Now go."

He moved his left hand and pressed it into the small of her back. She stepped forward and was instantly swallowed by the onslaught of hospital employees and Wyoming townspeople who wanted to talk to her about Lisa. She made her way through the crowd, respectfully but efficiently, until she collided with Noah.

"Whoa, sweetheart, I've been looking for you!" he exclaimed.

"Really?"

"Where did you run off to?"

"I just needed some air," she said, being evasive.

"Well, there are a few people who want to talk to you."

"Noah..."

"You need to talk to them, Gray. Then we can bolt. Ten minutes," he chided, gently steering her through the crowd.

"Okay."

Two minutes later, she was standing awkwardly in front of Mr. Ronald Oakes, his wife Marie, and their remaining children. Grayson felt sick to her stomach.

"Miss Carter!" the young girl exclaimed, launching herself at Grayson with her arms wide open.

She hugged her almost violently. If Grayson hadn't seen the young blonde with her own eyes before her assault, she would've been sure it was Lisa hugging her, instead of her younger sister.

"Sheila," came Mr. Oakes' scolding.

The young girl pulled back from the hug. "I'm sorry. I just really wanted to say thank you."

"For what?" Grayson eyed her quizzically.

"For what you said about Lisa," she replied, grinning from ear to ear. "I was so afraid everyone was only going to say sad things about my sister. But…she wasn't a sad person. She was always so happy. It's nice that someone could remember the happy parts of her, even in the middle of a funeral."

Mr. Oakes stepped up behind his daughter. "How about you take your mother to the car with Jake, honey?"

The young girl nodded, hugged Grayson one more time, and then trotted off on one side of her still-weeping mother.

Grayson turned her attention back to the older man standing in front of her. His face was wrinkled and weathered from a lifetime of working outside, but his eyes were kind and brimming with tears. She felt her own welling up. Before she could react, he had wrapped her up in a hug, not unlike his daughter's.

"I really can't thank you enough, young lady," he whispered shakily.

"For what?" she asked, honestly confused as he loosened his hold on her.

Mr. Oakes guided her toward one of the back pews, sat down, and then gestured to the still-full chapel.

"For all of this. We're still going home to bury our daughter. There's nothing that can change that. But this...this has brought some life back into my family. Do you have any idea what it was like for my wife to hear so many people from our town were going to make the drive down here for our little girl?"

Carter shook her head.

"I don't think Marie's even processed how many people from the hospital were really here. Just to say goodbye to our Lisa. She hadn't even been here more than a few months..."

"And she made an impact on most people she touched here. If we'd had some way to contact any of the patients she has taken care of..."

"We would have needed the football stadium?" Mr. Oakes grinned.

"Something like that." Grayson smiled back.

"And what my younger daughter said was true. It was very nice to hear something happy about her during her time here. We so rarely got to talk to her because of her schedule."

"I'm sorry."

"It wasn't your fault. It was part of the job."

She shook her head. "It shouldn't be."

"Well, at any rate, I am incredibly thankful that she had someone like you looking after her. She was happy. When we did talk, we inevitably talked about you. You're the reason she stuck it out down here."

Grayson focused on the floor. Mr. Oakes waited a moment, then stood. "I'd better be getting to the car. The love of my life is waiting," he said softly

"I won't keep you," she replied.

"Take care of yourself, Miss Carter."

"I will, sir."

"We'll be in touch with you."

"I would like that."

With a silent nod, Ronald Oakes left the chapel and climbed into his truck. His wife was crying on his son's shoulder in the backseat. The grief wasn't about to stop anytime soon. But his heart was lighter for coming to Denver.

Inside the church, Grayson took a deep breath. This was becoming too much. She felt Noah grab her shoulders. "Please tell me we can go now."

"Yeah, we can go now."

She breathed a sigh of relief and stood up, turning herself toward the back of the chapel. She caught Noah's arched eyebrow and smirking face out of the corner of her eye.

"What?" she asked.

He kept quiet, but also kept looking at her with his eyebrows raised.

"Noah, answer me! What? Why are you staring?" she sighed, very near the end of her rope.

He reached out and gently ran the edge of the wool collar between his two fingers. "Warm enough?" he smirked.

It was only then that she realized that she was still clutching Detective Ryder's coat around her shoulders. She reached up and pulled it tighter, shooting her eyes down to the floor and not saying a word.

"That's what I thought," Noah chuckled. "Let's go."

He put his arm protectively around her and walked her toward the door. They said goodbye to Father Dominic and Andy Freedman, then made their way to the car.

Babs was already in the passenger seat, having pulled the car around and cranked the heat up minutes ago. She whipped around in her seat when Grayson slid into the backseat.

"Are you okay?" she asked worriedly.

"Of course."

"You're sure?"

"Yes, Babs." She rolled her eyes.

"Gray..."

"Just drop it for now, hon," Noah interjected. "Let's just go home and crack a bottle of wine, shall we? We've all had a rough day."

Babs nodded and turned back into her seat. Noah pulled away from the church, the windshield wipers working frantically against the pouring rain.

24

BACK INSIDE THE church, Detective Nolan was milling around in the lobby, hands stuffed deep in his pockets. He'd sat through the entire funeral. It had actually been quite nice, and the turnout had been incredible. He'd kept his eyes out for anyone suspicious during the service and had come up with nothing. Everyone seemed to have a right and a reason to be at Lisa's funeral.

When Dr. Carter had finished giving her eulogy, he'd leaned over to say something snarky to his partner. He'd fallen over into a vacated wall.

How in the hell does he just disappear like that?

When the service was over, he'd moved from the chapel to his current perch in the lobby and waited. And waited. And gotten annoyed. And waited some more. And was just about ready to get in the car and leave his partner's sorry ass stranded at the seminary.

"You couldn't look any more bored if you tried, Blake."

Nolan spun around and came face-to-face with his partner. "You can tell that from the back of my head, smart guy?"

"No," he replied, shaking his head, "I've been making the rounds. You've had that look on your face for a good ten minutes now."

"How observant of you," he snapped. "Where have you been?"

"I just told you. Making the rounds."

"With or without your coat?"

"What?"

"Where's your coat, Ryder? That thing you wear when it's cold out. The black one you were wearing when we walked in here."

"Don't worry about it. We can go."

"Without your coat?" Blake smirked.

"What does the damned coat have to do with anything?" he hissed.

"It probably cost more than a month's salary, knowing you."

"Start walking toward the damned car, Blake."

Ryder grabbed his umbrella from the entryway and headed out into the raging storm, his partner on his heels. They threw themselves into the SUV, started it up, and set out toward downtown without a word.

Blake let his partner get comfortable in the passenger seat for a few minutes before he started in on him.

"So, did you find out anything useful on your little walkabout?"

"Nothing we didn't already know."

"Talk to anyone in particular?"

His partner fidgeted in the passenger seat. "No."

"Bullshit, Gabe."

"Excuse me?"

"C'mon, I know you well enough."

"I don't know what you're talking about."

"Fine, fine…" Blake trailed off with another grin on his face. "So, how's the young Dr. Carter holding up?" Nolan kept his eyes straight ahead on the road, but he could feel the venom seeping toward his side of the car.

"What?" Ryder ground out through his teeth.

"Dr. Carter. She seemed a little worked up after her eulogy. Just wondering if you bumped into her on your walkabout."

"Right."

"Well?"

"Well, what?"

"Did you see her?"

"Why is that any of your business?"

"Um, because she's someone we talked to as part of a murder investigation and I'm your partner and usually partners share this kind of thing when they go to a funeral for work-related reasons?"

There was a long pause.

"She's fine."

"Mmm-hmm."

"What?"

"You going to get your coat back?"

"What?"

"I saw her leave with it on, Ryder. I'm not stupid. You're zero for two getting stuff back from that girl."

"I don't give a damn about the coat, Nolan."

"That's a first. What about her?"

"Excuse me?"

"Carter. Giving a damn."

"She was upset, Blake. And alone. And freezing. What was I supposed to do?"

Blake smiled. "Just don't keep this habit up, Gabe, or you'll be showing up to work naked in no time."

25

THE SHRILL RING of his cell phone snapped Ryder out of a dead sleep. He rolled over and briefly glanced at the clock on his nightstand. 03:30 a.m.

Shit.

He'd only fallen asleep an hour ago, and that was with the help of a decently-sized glass of scotch. Or two. He grabbed his cell phone and looked at the display.

Nolan.

He rolled his eyes and answered. "Ryder."

"Morning, sunshine."

"Morning is several hours away, Blake. What do you want?"

"Don't tell me that you were actually sleeping this time."

"Surprise," he spat sarcastically.

"Sorry, man."

His partner genuinely sounded glum. Ryder mentally cursed himself and took the sting out of his voice. "What do you want?"

"Get out of bed. We've gotta go."

"Call dispatch back and tell them we're not on until eight."

"I would if it was dispatch that called. McCallister woke me up."

"What?" Ryder sat straight up in bed. McCallister never called them out of bed unless it was an emergency. Two weeks in a row was not a good sign.

"You're not going to believe this."

Gabriel groaned, flung himself back onto his bed and threw his free arm over his eyes.

"Another one?"

"Yup."

"Another young girl?"

"No."

"Another doctor?"

"Yup."

"In a church."

"Catholic church, to be specific."

"Lovely."

"Get your pretty self out of bed and dress warm. Looks like we're spending another Sunday with the padres."

Just before five a.m., the two detectives pulled up outside of Good Shepherd Catholic Church. Seventh Avenue was jammed solid with squad cars, their blue and white lights flashing across the rain-soaked trees. The coroner's van was pulled up onto the lawn, its back doors hanging wide open. The gurney was missing.

Ryder followed Nolan through the continuing rain and into the church without a word. The whole scene gave off an eerie feeling of déjà vu. Yellow crime tape was strung up everywhere. Pairs of uniformed officers were interviewing several people in the main lobby: an elderly man in a black robe and round wire-framed glasses, a somewhat younger man in a wrinkled tracksuit with awful bed-head, and a ragged-looking homeless man who had to be wearing at least three different winter coats.

Nolan looked back and gave his partner the "which-one-do-you-want" look, and Ryder nodded at the homeless man. Nolan smiled and headed toward the other two.

Ryder shucked off his coat and approached the uniformed officers interviewing the homeless man. He didn't recognize either of them. The petite blonde one was babbling on at a mile a minute; her balding bowling ball of a partner couldn't have looked more bored if he'd tried.

"Detective Ryder from Major Crimes," he stated flatly as he flashed his badge at them.

"Officers Jeffries and Tomlin. Nice to meet you, sir."

The young blonde extended her hand and shook Ryder's. Her cheeks flushed crimson when she got a good look at his face.

"Catch me up to speed."

She gave him a mega-watt smile and eagerly batted her eyes.

"This is Miles. Not his real name, but the one he goes by. He's one of the local homeless guys in the community. Frequent flyer, according to Father Rinaldi." She jutted her chin toward the older man in the wire glasses. "Seems to come in here every week or so to sleep it off, more often if the weather's bad. He came in to get out of the rain after his usual haunts closed last night. The shelters were all at max capacity because of the storms. He says he was almost asleep in the front pew before he noticed it."

Ryder glanced quickly over his left shoulder and down the aisle. A white sheet had been pulled over a body near the altar. Several of the medical examiner's staff were lurking close by.

"I'll take over here for a minute. You're booking him?"

"We're taking him to the ER after this to get him checked out. He may have a psych history, and since no one can corroborate his story..."

"…if he's acutely psychotic, they'll put him on a hold. Understood. Give me five minutes with him."

"Yes, sir."

Officer Jeffries nodded and walked over to join several of the other uniforms, her partner schlepping along loudly after her. Ryder absently wondered if the poor guy ever got a word in edgewise. He approached the disheveled man, sitting down on the chair next to him.

Miles was thin, pale, and smelled of cheap vodka. His beard was unkempt. Pieces of food and dirt were matted into the greasy hair. His clothes were covered in dirt, and he hadn't bathed in at least a week.

"Miles?"

The man looked at him with glassy eyes. "Who're you, fancy man?" he slurred.

"I'm Detective Ryder. I need to ask you some questions."

"I dun't answer qwushuns from fancy pants. Bring the gurl back here an' I'll talk. You got any shine?"

"Not a chance, Miles. You found the body?"

Miles made a face, then nodded.

"Did you touch it?"

He shook his head violently.

"You're sure?"

"Don't like blood."

"Do you know who it is?"

"Nope."

"You're certain?"

"Dun't know nobody like that."

"Where were you last night?"

"Merlin's Bar, then the motel where my buddy's got a room. Him n' his gurl got drunk an' started…you know…an' kicked me out. Went back to th' bar, then here. Just wanted to sleep."

"This buddy have a name?"

"Larry."

"And Larry's girl?"

"Toya."

"Last names?"

"Don't know 'em. Toya's a stripper. Big tits. I'm still fucked up, man."

"Yeah, I've got that. Can you think of anything else to tell me?"

"Nope." He yawned and settled down into his chair.

"Don't go anywhere, Miles."

There wasn't any chance of that. The homeless man was already snoring sitting straight up.

Blake caught his partner's eye and waved him over. Ryder gathered his binder, grabbed his coat, and made his way to the back of the chapel.

"Any stunning revelations from your bar buddy?"

"No. He'll be sleeping it off in the ER or in holding. He may have a psych history on top of it."

"You don't think he did it?"

"No, I don't. He's still too drunk to hold himself up straight. What did you find out?"

"Well, he was sober enough to start yelling at the top of his lungs. Father Rinaldi here found Miles standing on a pew and screaming and got a full-on view of our vic. He called 911, called the deacon Mr. Rosemont, and then got Miles outta there. Rosemont's the one in the tracksuit. They actually went outside and stood by the door until the uniforms arrived. They thought they'd screw up something by staying inside with the body."

"You believe them?"

"We'll need formal statements about it all, but they're both freaked out. I don't see either one of these guys doing whatever went on in here."

Nolan turned and pointed down the main aisle where the crime scene techs were packing up.

"You want a quick look? The coroner's people want to get the body out of here ASAP. So does Father Rinaldi. He's got mass in a few hours."

"The Father's going to be skipping services today, Blake," he replied sarcastically, starting down the aisle.

"Yeah, I know, I told him. But you know somebody's not going to be on the phone tree or checking the website, and we really don't need this ruining anyone else's Sunday morning."

They approached the altar, stepping on each side of the sheet. Ryder pulled it back.

"Holy fuck, Gabe…"

Ryder smirked. "We're in a church," he scolded.

"Under the circumstances, I think God will forgive that one," Blake muttered, his face turning a pale shade of green.

Underneath the sheet, a middle-aged man was naked and sprawled on his back. His face had been sliced from ear to ear. Repeatedly. There were bruises developing over his chest and on his wrists. He'd been restrained, forcibly. But Blake's comments had been referring to the injury a little further south. The victim's genitalia were gone. They weren't mutilated or mangled or mauled; they simply weren't there.

"Well, that's one I've never seen."

"I hope not, Ryder. Jesus."

Blake turned away from the body, focusing all his efforts on keeping the bile out of his throat.

"There's not enough blood here."

Nolan shot a look toward his partner. "I'm sorry, you want *more* blood here? For what, aesthetics?"

"No. I'm saying he wasn't killed here. For the amount of damage to the body, there should be blood running halfway down the aisle. This looks pretty clean. He was killed somewhere else and brought here."

"Like Lisa Oakes."

Ryder wrinkled his forehead and shook his head. "Not necessarily. Lisa was wrapped up and posed. There wasn't a mark on her. We still don't know how she died. I get the feeling that whoever killed her tried to take care of her afterward."

"You're assuming the person who killed her is the same person that put her in the chapel."

"That's true."

Ryder started pacing up and down the length of the sanctuary. His voice became more and more pressured. "But we don't have any evidence to suggest more than one killer in the Oakes case. This man was brutally tortured and mutilated, then dumped. He didn't die peacefully."

Nolan threw up his hands in defeat.

"All right, so these two murders aren't related?"

"They don't have much in common except being found in a church."

"On Sunday morning."

Ryder nodded, then frowned. "You told me on the phone that the vic was a doctor."

"Yeah."

"How do we know that? He's naked and mutilated. The homeless guy doesn't know him."

Nolan motioned toward the main doors of the church where Father Rinaldi and the deacon were still standing.

"Rinaldi knows him. Not only does this guy go to church here, but he's the priest's personal doc. Meet Dr. Alan Nelson, prominent Denver-area cardiologist," he said with a flourish. "He was treating Rinaldi for some kind of irregular heartbeat thing."

Ryder nodded. "Based on his age, probably atrial fibrillation. It's an abnormal heart rhythm characterized by..."

Nolan quickly raised a hand in front of his face. "So help me God, Ryder, if you start in on a lecture about heart rhythms before I've had my coffee, I will punch you."

"Sorry."

"Just promise me coffee."

"Of course. Where did Dr. Nelson practice?"

"He's a partner in one of the bigger groups here in town and sees patients at two different offices, according to Google. But it sounds like he spends a good amount of time seeing patients admitted in the hospital. You'll never guess which one."

"St. Joseph's."

Shit.

"Yup. Looks like we'll be spending another Monday with the white coats."

Ryder nodded, placed the sheet back over the body, and started gathering his belongings.

"Hey, did you notice this guy at the funeral yesterday?"

Gabriel paused briefly, still bent over the pew where he'd thrown his coat, then shook his head. "No, I didn't. But we should find out who has the guest book. He might have signed in and left before we noticed him."

Nolan threw his jacket on and followed his partner out to the lobby of the church. They spoke briefly to Father Rinaldi, who was still in shock, and asked him to come down to the department within the next few days with Mr. Rosemont to give their formal statements.

The storm was still raging as they jogged across the lawn to the SUV, and it didn't seem to have any intention of slowing up anytime soon.

"Well, where to?" Nolan asked as he put the keys in the ignition and started the car.

"Didn't you want coffee?"

"Dear God, yes."

"Then let's get coffee. You can drop me off at home after that. You need to get back to your girls."

"They're at their mother's," Blake said flatly.

"Oh."

"It's easier."

They drove off in silence. Nolan had an uneasy feeling in the pit of his stomach. Two bodies in a week did not bode well. His partner was right, the crimes weren't all that alike, but he was worried about the St. Joe's connection.

Looking at his partner's reflection in the passenger window, he could tell he wasn't the only one.

26

GRAYSON WAS BACK to her usual routine on Monday morning. Rounds, clinic, surgery, repeat. It had been a blessing to have the rest of the weekend free, courtesy of Dr. Sanders, to recuperate.

She'd been a wreck by the time Noah had finally pulled up outside of her house Saturday night after the funeral. He'd gently prodded her inside, sat her down on the sofa, and run into the kitchen to get the wine.

Babs had done her best to figure out how their little group of three had come home with an extra overcoat, but Noah had shooed her off of the couch and sent her out to get something for dinner. The Oakes family hadn't felt the need to host a reception after the service, and Grayson had been grateful. Frankly, most people had wanted to get home quickly because of the worsening storm.

Once Barbara had driven off to pick up Thai food from the hole-in-the-wall down the street, Noah had started in with the questions.

"All right, I got her out of the house for fifteen minutes. Spill it."

"What are you talking about?" she asked, holding her stemless wineglass in both hands.

"About your little meltdown back at the church. Are you okay?"

Grayson raised her eyebrows. That wasn't the line of questioning she had been anticipating, and Noah knew it. He was building up to it.

"Yes, I'm fine now."

"You weren't then?"

"Not really, no."

"Did you get what you needed outside in the middle of a violent storm?" he asked, a mischievous grin on his face.

Grayson looked at him warily. "Sure. I just needed some air." She stood and set her glass down. "I'm going to go change, Noah."

"I'll join you."

"Huh?"

"I brought a bag to stay over." He shrugged.

Grayson didn't say anything as she grabbed a coat from the rack by the door, climbed up the stairs, and went into her room. She found a pair of silk pajama pants and a long-sleeved black T-shirt then headed into the bathroom, leaving the door cracked. Noah stayed in her bedroom, rifling through his overnight bag for his sweatpants. She had her dress halfway over her head when he started talking.

"So, you gonna ever 'fess up how you ended up with that nice black coat? As gorgeous as it is, love, it isn't quite your size."

She paused for a split second, and considered answering him, but decided to keep her mouth shut. She washed her face, pulled her hair back, and grabbed her clothes from the side of the clawfoot tub. Noah was leaning against the side of her bed in sweatpants and a hoodie, smirking.

"Well?"

"Well, what?"

She slid past him and dropped her clothes in the hamper, then grabbed a spare hanger from the closet.

"Are you going to tell me what happened out there?"

"There's nothing to tell."

"Just a new coat as a souvenir." He rolled his eyes.

"A coat that is going to be dry-cleaned and returned, Noah," she said, clearly annoyed as she hung the garment up in her closet.

"Not kept?"

"Of course not. Why would I keep his coat?"

"Whose coat is it?"

"Detective Ryder's."

"So, it is his! Ooo, I knew it!" Noah clapped his hands giddily.

Grayson rolled her eyes at him and opened her bedroom door, hoping that going back downstairs would end her friend's line of questioning. No such luck.

"Was he out there waiting for you? What did he say?" he asked as he bounded down the stairs two at a time after her.

"Nothing important."

"What did who say?" came a voice from the kitchen.

Crap.

Crap.

Barbara was already home. On cue, she walked into the family room with three boxes of take-out balanced on one arm, her glass of wine in the other hand. Grayson quickly grabbed the two most precarious boxes from her.

"Detective Ryder! That's who she was talking to outside." Noah clapped enthusiastically.

Babs sat down on the sofa and wrinkled her nose. "Didn't you say he was the one that gave you the creeps, Gray? He just kept pacing around and doodling in a notebook or something?"

"I never said he was creepy," she replied, grabbing her wineglass from the coffee table.

"Well, that's the vibe I got," Babs replied, taking a drink from her own glass.

"He's also the one that's the stone-cold fox," Noah interjected, reaching across the table for his to-go box.

That got Babs to refocus and shoot a scowl toward her roommate. "You didn't mention that, Grayson."

"I didn't think it was really relevant to the conversation we were having at the time, Babs."

"But he's hot?"

She sighed heavily and rolled her eyes. "Do we need to be having this conversation? We just came home from a funeral, for God's sake."

"Since you came home with his coat on instead of your own, yes," Noah replied.

"Wait, what?" Babs nearly choked on her noodles.

"And it's a gorgeous coat, too. Not something I'd just up and give away."

Barbara fixed her gaze on her roommate. "Out with it. Like now. What's going on?"

"Nothing's going on!" Grayson protested. "I went outside without my coat, like a bumbling idiot, and he was nice enough to make sure I didn't freeze to death. It's going to the dry cleaner first thing Monday, and I'll figure out how to get it back to him at some point. Now, can we all refocus and calm down? All I really want to do tonight is eat dinner, get a little tipsy, and go to bed."

Babs put her fork down and scooted closer to her friend. "I'm sorry, honey. Don't be mad. Here..." she grabbed the bottle of wine from the side table and refilled Grayson's glass. "Get going. It tastes great with the pad thai."

"Thanks."

The three friends ate in silence until Babs' cell phone started ringing in the next room. She huffed and put her food down on the coffee table.

"Just don't think you've gotten away with anything, Gray," she murmured and then winked.

Grayson rolled her eyes again.

Noah laughed and reached over her for another spoonful of rice.

———

Grayson opened her eyes at the sound of snapping fingers. Adams and Thompson were both staring at her like she had a communicable disease.

"What?"

"Holy shit, I didn't think it was actually possible for you to sleep, Carter," Adams joked.

"Shut up, Adams," she replied, grinning. "Did I miss anything?"

"No, but we're ready to run the list."

"Okay," she said, grabbing her pen and focusing her eyes on the patient list in front of her. "Go for it."

Ten minutes later, they had divided the list and broken off from each other to get all of the patients seen for afternoon rounds. She flew through the ICU, then dropped down two floors to the cardiac unit to check on Mr. Ippolito. She slid her badge through the reader by the double doors, and they popped open with a soft click.

Even in the middle of the day, the cardiac wing was nearly silent. It was a sealed-off ward. Only certain people had full access; thankfully, that included subspecialty residents.

Grayson found room 406 and took a quick peek in through the glass door. George Ippolito was an unfortunate man. He'd had several days of chest pain before his admission, which he'd ignored, but he'd slipped in his garden pulling weeds and broken his hip yesterday. A routine EKG in the ER had shown a several-days-old heart attack and he'd been transferred up to the cardiac wing for possible stenting. Interventional cardiology had been consulted...only there weren't any notes from them in the chart.

Grayson frowned.

He's been here for over 24 hours and cardiology can't get their asses in here to see him? What the hell?

She double-checked the chart, just to be sure the consult hadn't been filed in the wrong spot. Nothing. She walked into the room to examine him anyway. Mr. Ippolito was sleepy but awake enough to wiggle his toes and give her a thumbs-up. His vital signs looked good, and he wasn't hooked up to any vasopressors, which was a good sign, but her last rotation on cardiology had been in medical school. Properly managing a heart attack was way outside of her job description.

Grayson snapped her gloves off and walked down the hallway in search of his nurse. From an orthopedic perspective, if he didn't get his hip fixed soon, his complication rate was going to shoot through the roof. She needed to talk to the cardiologist.

She found the nurse two doors down and gently knocked on the doorframe. "Excuse me?"

The nurse, an older woman with gray hair and scrubs covered in cats, looked up. "Can I help you, sweetie?"

"Um, I hope so. Are you taking care of the guy next door? Mr. Ippolito?"

The nurse sighed and motioned with one finger to give her a moment. Grayson nodded and waited around outside the patient's room. The nurse came out a few minutes later.

"I'm so sorry," she apologized. "Mrs. Moskowicz is a big sundowner, and if she wakes up now, she's going to give the nightshift nurses hell. Her delirium will just be out of control. If she stays asleep for another twenty minutes, we're golden."

"It's okay. Do you know what's going on with Mr. Ippolito's heart? Last I heard he had a STEMI but I don't see any cardiology notes anywhere."

The nurse eyed her warily. "And you are…?"

"Carter, one of the ortho chiefs. He's on our surgery schedule for today still, but I have no idea if he's cleared from a heart standpoint."

The nurse's face instantly softened. "Oh, honey, nobody told you?"

"No. Told me what?"

"Well, Dr. Nelson was on call all weekend, and nobody's been able to get ahold of him. Not his residents, not his partners, nobody. It's been chaos down here. One of the ICU doctors got ahold of Dr. Preston, his partner, and he's come in to cover the gaps. He's in the cath lab right now with another patient. Mr. Ippolito is on deck."

"So, probably no major hip surgery today then?" she replied sarcastically.

"I'd say probably not." The nurse smiled back.

"Thanks. We actually have a few of Dr. Nelson's patients on our list. Is Dr. Preston covering the whole hospital right now?"

The nurse nodded. "Until somebody says otherwise, that's what I hear."

"Okay. Um, if I leave my pager number on the chart, could you ask Dr. Preston to get in touch with me about surgery timing for George over there? We'd like to take him in the next few days if possible, but we don't want to kill him."

"Sure, sweetie, no problem. It'll be a few hours, though."

"I'm in no rush. The heart stuff comes first."

Grayson grabbed a sticky note from the nurse's station and put her pager number on the outside of Mr. Ippolito's chart.

Dr. Nelson was known for several things around the hospital but passing up taking a patient to the cath lab was not one of them. Procedures meant more money, especially to cardiologists.

She finished her rounds and made it back to the OR in time for her last case of the day. She was in the recovery room, dropping the patient off in the bay when she noticed several of the nurses were gathered around a computer monitor. She walked up behind them to grab a post-op order form.

"Excuse me, ladies. Could I grab one of those order sheets?"

"Oh, Dr. Carter, of course. Let me grab you one," Irene sniffled as she moved sideways.

Irene had worked in the surgical recovery unit of St. Joe's for longer than Grayson had been alive. She was the momma bear of the unit. You wanted Irene to like you. If you pissed her off, you were in for a long residency…or even worse, if you were an attending, you were in for a long and painful career. Thankfully, Grayson had turned up on Irene's nice list.

"What's going on?" Grayson asked, taking the offered paperwork.

"We just found out. The head of the hospital sent out an email."

"About what?"

"Dr. Nelson."

"Oh yeah, he was a no-show this weekend I heard. Dr. Preston's taken over all of his patients. That's not like him."

"Well, now we know why."

"What happened?"

"He's dead, dear."

"What?"

Carter's eyes went wide and she felt her blood run cold.

Another one?

Irene nodded. "That's what all us old birds are blubbering about. It says he was found dead early Sunday morning. Poor dear, we all liked him a lot. No wonder no one could get ahold of him." She shook her head. "I'm sorry, dear. Do you need something else?"

"No, no. I just dropped off one of Dr. Hoppe's patients."

"Oh, well, don't worry. We know what he likes. Go get yourself a coffee," she smiled.

Grayson nodded and left the PACU. She immediately pulled out her cell phone and hit speed-dial. It took two rings, then she heard the click of the other side of the line picking up.

"Hey, stranger."

"Hey. What're you doing right now?"

"Nothing."

"Meet me for coffee?"

"M'kay. See you in a minute, love."

27

AT 3:07 MONDAY afternoon, a black SUV pulled up outside of Saint Joseph Hospital and smoothly parallel parked across from the main entrance. Nolan squinted against the sunlight and rummaged around in his suit coat pocket for his sunglasses. He pulled out a pair of plastic kid-sized purple Ray-Bans.

Damn.

His youngest had decided to steal Daddy's glasses again and had hidden them somewhere in the house. He made a mental note to check the refrigerator when he got home. That was where she normally hid them.

He waited by the hood for his partner, who was taking his time getting out of the car. Ryder hadn't said much on the ride over. That wasn't a great omen for how this meeting was going to go. Blake looked up at the edifice of the hospital building and shook his head.

This is some sick kind of déjà vu.

Gabriel rounded the hood of the car and stood beside his partner, his binder clutched under his left arm.

"Weren't we just here?" Nolan groaned, tossing him a sideways glance.

"Always one for stating the obvious, Blake."

"It's Monday. Give me a break. Where are we going?"

"The private office block in the back of the hospital. That's where Nelson's cardiology group has an office."

"And we're meeting…?"

"The head of the group and two of the partners."

"Tell me we don't have to spend another two and a half days interviewing everybody."

"I doubt it."

"Good. I can't live on hospital food this week."

"I'll spring for dinner if we're stuck here late."

"The day's getting better all the time," Nolan replied. "Lead the way."

The two detectives made their way through the familiar lobby and took an elevator up several floors to a skybridge, which led to a separate building that contained the office block. There was a carpet change halfway across. Suddenly, instead of uncomfortable plastic chairs, there were tufted leather wingbacks every thirty or forty feet with side tables and fresh flowers.

The skybridge opened up to a massive five-story lobby which had a large marble waterfall installation at the far end. Looking up, an ornate crystal chandelier was suspended from the ceiling.

"Hot damn," Nolan let out a whistle. "They put some money into this place."

"It's overdone."

"Says the guy in Armani, or whatever the hell you're wearing today. All I can say is my doctor's office doesn't look like this."

"The office we want is on the eighth floor."

"Beauty before age."

The two detectives rode an all-glass elevator to the eighth floor. They were pinned against the back panel behind an arguing elderly couple.

The wife was talking a mile a minute, her high-pitched voice going on and on about something the husband had done last night. He was quietly standing next to her, holding her hand. She was waving her free hand all over the place, occasionally pointing a bony finger in his face. The elevator door dinged when they hit the sixth floor, and the old man tapped his wife on the behind to get her to move out of the door. She stormed off the elevator in front of him, and he followed after her, chuckling to himself.

"I can't tell who won that fight," Nolan grinned as the doors closed.

"They weren't fighting."

"Oh? That looked like a fight to me. Had a ton with my ex-wife just like that."

"She was yelling at him for ignoring a two-year cough. There's an oncologist listed on the sixth floor. He probably has lung cancer. She's scared, Blake."

"Oh." *Shit, I totally missed that.*

The elevator dinged again.

"Arguments in hospitals tend to be more complicated than they look."

Ryder stepped off the elevator, headed to the right, and stopped outside of a set of frosted glass doors with *Elite Denver Cardiology* stenciled across them in bold, jagged script. Nolan opened it and walked into the waiting room. There were still several patients waiting to be seen, spaced out reading *People* and *Popular Mechanics*. They walked up to the desk where a young blonde was incredibly busy chewing gum.

"Sign in and take a seat," she singsonged without looking up.

"Um, no offense, but we're not patients and we're not waiting to see anybody," Blake flashed his badge at her.

"Uh…um…" she stuttered. "Hold on…"

She disappeared behind a door, then reappeared with a petite older woman wearing bright red lipstick and a brown pantsuit.

"Detectives, please come around to the office door. I'll let you through." Her voice was raspy from a longstanding pack-a-day cigarette habit.

They walked around to the door that led to the main part of the office, and it clicked open. The woman in the red lipstick met them on the other side.

"Mindy, go back to the front desk. I've got them."

The young blonde took a long once-over of Ryder, licking her lips before almost skipping back to her desk.

"I'm Glenda, the office manager. The partners are waiting for you. Thank you for coming," she said as she led them toward the back part of the office.

"Not a problem, Glenda," Nolan smiled as she opened the door to a small conference room.

Three older gentlemen in expensive suits sat on one side of a polished wooden desk; two seats were waiting for the detectives opposite them.

"Okay, Ryder. These look like your kind of people." Nolan looked over his shoulder. "Turn on the charm, partner."

The detectives entered the conference room and Glenda shut the door behind them.

———

Hours later, Blake rested his head on the glass elevator's wall as it descended into the overdone lobby. Gabriel was leaning against the side panel, his binder stuffed under one arm.

"Well, that was almost useless," Nolan said with a sigh.

"Agreed."

"Apart from being the 'world's best cardiologist', did we learn anything about Dr. Nelson?"

"No." He shook his head.

The elevator dinged.

"Well, I dunno about you, but I need some coffee after that."

"The coffee cart is in the main hospital."

"Fine, fine."

Blake waved his left hand in the air and stalked off the elevator. Ryder followed close behind him.

28

THE TWO DETECTIVES wound through the maze of hospital hallways toward the western wing, where the oncology unit was housed. A well-kept secret of many hospitals was the major step-up in coffee quality of the cancer units, and St. Joseph's was no exception. The coffee cart (which was really a kiosk, but no one made the distinction) was an outpost of one of the local Denver coffee companies, so everything—from the seasonal blend to the puff pastries—was locally sourced. Business was helped significantly by the rather attractive college junior who manned the cappuccino machine on the weekends.

Today, however, Maria, the weekday 4'10" pink-haired grandma of six, was manning the cash register. She might have been a little slower than her hunky weekend counterpart, but she always knew who needed a real pick-me-up. Nolan had spotted the place during their first trip to St. Joseph's, and he'd been more drawn in by the pastries in the glass case than the prospect of good coffee. Food always came first.

The oncology lobby was calm and quiet. The entire outer wall was floor to ceiling glass panels pushed out into a crescent, facing west. The back walls were painted a soft, muted green. Worn-in leather couches and an eclectic mix of café tables were spaced out around the lobby and along the outer wall. A few patients were pushing IV poles across the carpet. A family with three rowdy children was checking in at the information desk, but overall, the place was serene. A few floors up was the infusion unit; windows from the private chemotherapy bays looked out over the lobby.

"C'mon, I'm buying."

Nolan jabbed his partner in the shoulder and got in line for the coffee cart. Ryder followed silently behind him. A few short minutes later, they were at the head of the line.

"Hi, boys." Maria smiled at them. "What can I get ya?"

"A large black coffee and that chocolate fancy thing in the glass case," Nolan replied, pointing.

"That's a double-chocolate cream puff with vanilla bean filling and caramel glaze, hon."

"Yeah, that thing." Nolan nodded enthusiastically.

"Okay. Anything else?" She looked expectantly at Ryder.

"Just a black coffee please, Maria," he replied, reading her nametag.

She nodded and turned her back to start on the coffee.

Nolan leaned over toward his partner. "Have you ever seen a grandmother with pink hair?" he whispered.

"I heard that," Maria said over her shoulder. She turned and brought their coffees up to the counter.

"It's breast cancer awareness month, and I'm here five days a week. I've let my granddaughters dye my hair like this for years. They love it. The patients appreciate the support," she explained, taking Nolan's credit card in exchange for the coffee cups.

"And it's cathartic for a survivor," Gabriel added.

Nolan shot him a questioning look, and Maria raised her eyebrows at him.

"How did you know?"

He nodded toward her left hand, which was slightly swollen compared to her right. "Mild lymphedema. It's not noticeable unless you're looking for it. You've had a resection."

She smiled. "You're right. Fifteen years clean, but I've got a swollen arm because of it. I got lucky."

"Congratulations, ma'am."

"Thank you, sonny. Here." She plucked a small macaroon out of the glass case. "I made these myself this morning. Hope you like coconut."

"I do."

She handed Nolan his receipt, winked at him, and moved on to the next customer.

"Now you get free cookies, too? I've had it with you, Gabe." Nolan pouted.

Gabriel chuckled and handed the macaroon over to his partner.

The detectives took one of the café tables by the windows. They sat in silence, Ryder perusing his notes and Nolan wolfing down his cream puff. Once he was done, Blake relaxed back and sipped on his damned good coffee.

I've gotta ask Maria what she puts in this stuff. It's a thousand times better than the sludge at the precinct.

Blake was halfway to his feet, intending to do exactly that when he spotted a familiar face walk into the lobby. He stopped, smiled, and sat back down. He cautiously glanced at his partner, who was absolutely clueless.

Why am I having so much fun with this?

He cleared his throat.

"Yes?" Ryder didn't look up from his notes, but his eyebrow arched up.

"So, you have any epiphanies over there?"

"No."

"Who else do we need to talk to today?"

"I'm not sure."

"I've got an idea."

Ryder looked up from his binder and grabbed his coffee cup, taking a long drink.

"We've talked to Nelson's partners, and obviously we'll talk to his family, but you know that's not enough. We need to find someone here who knew him from a different perspective. Someone who would know the dirt on him…"

"…and be willing to talk to us," Ryder finished. "You have someone in mind?"

"Well, I was gonna start with the hottie at the coffee cart."

"I doubt Maria knows much about Dr. Nelson's dark side if he had one." Ryder smirked sarcastically.

"I'm not talking about the coffee clerk, ass. Try again."

Ryder wrinkled his forehead at his partner and turned around in his seat.

Nolan sat back and grinned at him.

29

GRAYSON WALKED AS fast as she could from the PACU over to the oncology unit. Whenever either she or Noah were stressed out and needed coffee, this was where they would meet. Apart from having the best coffee in the hospital, it was the most relaxing spot in the whole building. She yanked her hair out of the elastic band and ran her fingers through it a few times.

Maria saw her coming. "Hi, honey. What'll it be?"

Grayson smiled. Maria always started talking like a bartender when she knew something was wrong, a holdover habit from her previous career.

"How about two medium coffees the usual way and two biscotti?"

The older woman smiled. "How about two biscotti and two macaroons?"

"You made your macaroons?" she asked, the excitement audible in her voice.

"I did. And I have two left."

"You know I would kill for those, Maria."

The elderly woman brought up the coffees, cream for Grayson and cream with four sugars for Noah, and the cookies.

"You okay?" Maria asked as she took the ten-dollar bill from her hand.

"I don't know yet. We'll see how the rest of the day goes."

"You come back tomorrow for another cookie if you don't feel better. I'm making chocolate chip tonight."

"Thanks, Maria. Love the hair." She winked.

Grayson dropped her change in the tip jar, like she always did, and carried the coffees and cookies over to one of the couches. She had just enough time to sit down and take a sip before Noah swooped in over the back of the couch.

"Hello, love," he said, reaching for his coffee.

"Hi."

"So, why the 9-1-1? You sounded really upset."

"Did you hear the news?"

Noah shook his head. "No, what? I've been buried in ventilator settings all morning."

"Dr. Nelson's dead."

"Wait, what now?" Noah nearly dropped his coffee cup onto the carpet.

"I'm serious. I just found out from the PACU nurses. Apparently, all of the surgical services got an email from the head of the hospital. It's being forwarded around."

"What happened?"

"I don't know." She shook her head and grasped her coffee with both hands. "The email was very vague. He didn't answer his pages starting Saturday night. They found him on Sunday."

"Yikes."

"Yeah."

"Why are you so worked up?"

"I don't know. It's a bit weird, don't you think? Two Mondays in a row and two people are dead."

"Lisa and Dr. Nelson have nothing in common. You know that."

"Yeah, but still. It just sent a chill down my spine. Now all they have to say is that they found him in a Catholic church, and I'll really lose it."

"Oh right, like that's happening."

Grayson shrugged. "How's your service?"

"Buggered after the weekend. What else is new? How's yours?"

"Still a mess. Everybody and their brother got drunk and crashed a car last night."

"That means you get to operate quite a bit, though."

"Eventually. Most of them are simmering down in the ICU today."

"Gotcha."

He paused, taking the opportunity to change the subject. "Have you given any more thought to Halloween?"

She rolled her eyes. "Really?"

"Yes, really. You're off this year for once, and you're coming out whether you like it or not. Have you thought about a costume?"

"Can't I just wear a pair of scrubs and my white coat?"

Noah made a face. "Absolutely not."

"Then I have no thoughts." She shrugged, taking a long drink from her coffee cup.

"Well, I can always dress you up like a hooker." He grinned at Grayson's horrified expression.

"Um, I think I'll start looking into costumes…"

Noah laughed into his coffee and shifted his position on the couch to reach for a biscotti. Almost immediately, he saw two familiar figures sitting at one of the café tables, and one of them, in particular, was staring straight at them.

"Don't look now, sweetheart, but I think we're about to have company."

Noah motioned toward the small table, and Grayson followed his pointed finger. In the short interim, one of the men had gotten to his feet and placed a leather binder under his arm.

Grayson startled. Her hands shot out to the edge of the couch cushions, her fingers gripping hard into the fabric. Her knuckles blanched white. Her breathing accelerated.

What the hell is he doing here?

30

RYDER KEPT HIS eyes focused on the young brunette at the coffee stand. She had her hair down and was chatting with the cashier. The natural waves in her hair nearly masked it, but he could pick up the wrinkle where her hair elastic had been holding it up for most of the day. Two cups of coffee, two biscotti, two macaroons.

She's meeting someone.

The hair on the back of his neck stood on end, and he clenched his fist under the table.

What the hell? What do I care if she's meeting someone?

He looked over at his partner, who had a shit-eating grin on his face. When he looked back to the counter, it was vacant. She'd already moved to one of the couches and been joined by someone in a white coat. He recognized the back of the man's head.

Mason.

They spoke for a few moments. She looked upset. Frightened, even. Mason shifted on the couch and got a good line of sight on him. The coy bastard actually grinned at him.

That's it.

He stood up, grabbed his binder off of the table, and headed directly for the couch. Startled, Nolan grabbed their coffees and stumbled after him. Gabriel weaved his way through the lobby and stopped directly in front of the young brunette, who had coincidentally jumped to her feet at the sight of him coming. They stood stock-still in front of one another, neither breaking eye contact. Ryder watched the blush creep up on her cheeks and run down the length of her neck.

Blake sidled up next to the couch, coffee cups balanced precariously in one hand.

"Dr. Mason," Nolan held out his free hand to the young doctor, who was still seated.

Noah took it readily, eager to break the thick silence hanging between Grayson and Detective Ryder. "Detectives. Surprised to see you so soon," he replied.

"Us, too," Nolan admitted, grinning.

Gabriel refused to break eye contact with the young woman in front of him. His left hand was still balled into a tight fist.

"Dr. Carter," Ryder cleared his throat.

"Det…Detective Ryder," she replied, her eyes suddenly glued to the floor.

"So, what can we do for you gentlemen?" Noah asked lazily, leaning back onto the couch.

Nolan and Ryder sat down in two chairs facing the couch. Nolan handed Ryder his coffee.

"We were hoping to ask you a few questions about a Dr. Nelson from cardiology," Nolan said, nonchalantly.

"I figured."

"So, you know he's dead?"

"She just brought me up to speed." Mason nodded, gesturing toward Grayson.

"And how did you find out, Dr. Carter?"

"An email was sent out to some of the staff. I happened to be around when the nurses upstairs got the news," she explained.

"Did you know him well?" Ryder asked, focusing on Grayson.

He was leaning his forearms on his thighs, his blue eyes dark and fixated on her.

"No." She shook her head. "My service consulted on some of his patients. He's consulted on some of ours. I don't know him well personally."

"You're certain?" he pressed.

"Yes," she said, emphatically. "You don't believe me?"

He didn't answer.

"We were hoping you could fill us in on his dark side, so to speak." Nolan took over.

"Who says he had one?" Mason asked suspiciously.

"Everyone has a dark side," Ryder replied forcefully. "Some show it more readily than others."

"And how would you know that, detective? Personal experience?" he snapped.

"Noah…" Grayson warned softly, laying a hand on his forearm.

"So, about Dr. Nelson then…" Blake prodded.

Noah continued to glare across the coffee table at Detective Ryder, who had an equally ferocious look on his face. His blue eyes were completely focused on the spot where Grayson's hand met Noah's skin. Nolan inched forward, ready to break up a fight if Gabriel decided to start one.

Grayson looked back and forth between her friend and the exceptionally angry detective, sighed, and then spoke.

"Dr. Nelson had a reputation."

"What kind of reputation?" Nolan pressed, sipping his coffee.

"Well…ummm…let me put it this way. When I started as a resident, there was a list that was passed around. A list of attendings to be aware of."

"Gray…" Mason hissed.

"What? They're going to find out eventually."

"Keep going, Dr. Carter," Nolan prodded.

Grayson took a long sip from her coffee cup. "Look, there are two ways to get through residency as a girl. You can work yourself to the bone and prove yourself, just like everybody else, or you put your legs up and sleep your way through. It happens everywhere. When I started here, if you were a female internal medicine resident, making nice with Dr. Nelson was a way to do the latter. He wasn't subtle about it, either." She shuddered.

"He approached you, didn't he?" Ryder spat through his teeth.

Grayson dropped her eyes to the floor and blushed. Nolan nodded in understanding. Ryder softened his gaze.

She's embarrassed.

"Only once. He thought I was one of his."

"One of his?"

"A medicine resident; someone he had power over. Not a surgeon. I made it clear he was barking up the wrong tree. I never had a problem after that."

"How did you 'make it clear'?"

Grayson shifted uncomfortably in her seat. Her eyes never left the floor.

After a few long, silent moments, Noah cleared his throat and answered for her. "Something that took rows of stitches and a turtleneck to hide. Can we move on?"

"Did you report him?"

She chuckled. The sound was soft and hollow. "Are you kidding? A first-year resident reporting an untouchable attending like Nelson? There's a sure way to get yourself fired," she replied, sipping her coffee.

Ryder growled under his breath.

"Anything else?" Nolan asked.

"Since my intern year, he's changed focus. He's chasing nurses now. The last resident he got involved with got upset when he got bored and dumped her. She called his wife, and that created a few waves."

"Those waves didn't end in divorce papers?"

"No. From what I understand, Mrs. Nelson is a pill-popping drunk, and his children are spoiled brats lining up for their inheritance. I don't agree with how he handled himself, but I can understand why he tried finding some kind of happiness outside of his own home."

Nolan shifted in his seat. "Anything you can think of, Dr. Mason?"

"Not anything more than she's told you. Nelson was a pig—probably king of them around here—but most doctors have their vices if they hang around long enough. I don't know of any residents having problems with him for quite some time."

Nolan glanced in between Dr. Mason, who was glaring at his partner, to Ryder, who hadn't taken his eyes off of Dr. Carter. He was staring at her like she was an animal, prey to be stalked. The hunger in his eyes was obvious.

Noah cleared his throat. "We should be getting back to the ward. Anything else, detectives?" he asked.

"Any names come to the top of your head for nurses he was involved with?" Nolan asked.

Noah shook his head.

"Try Becky, a nurse on the sixth floor," Grayson replied softly. "If she wasn't still seeing him, she'd know who he moved on to next."

Nolan nodded, then stood. "Thanks for the help. We'll let you two get back. Let's go, Gabe." He lightly punched Ryder in the shoulder as he passed behind him.

Ryder stood up and turned to follow. He was less than ten yards from the couch when he stopped in his tracks. Someone was following him.

"Detective?" Her shy voice came over his left shoulder.

He turned around to find Grayson standing meekly behind him, eyes still glued to the floor.

"Can I help you, Dr. Carter?"

"I, um…I have your coat. I'm sorry I left with it on Saturday."

"It's all right. You needed it," he countered. "I didn't expect to get it back."

"I'm going to have it dry-cleaned. I just haven't had time to drop it off yet…"

"Don't bother with it." He waved his hand dismissively.

"I can't give it back to you dirty," she protested.

"Unless you dropped it in mud, it's not dirty."

"I wore it," she protested again.

"It's not dirty," he repeated.

"I need to get it back to you…"

He stepped closer to her, as close as he possibly could without touching her.

———

Grayson felt her heart-rate shoot up when his shoes came into her field of view. Suddenly she felt very, very warm. The room started to spin, and she frantically tried to find something to focus on besides sage green carpet. In her panic, she raised her gaze up and found herself locked into a pair of dark blue eyes.

Gabriel gently grabbed her chin to keep her from looking away. "I'd rather you keep it. I'll figure something out," he said quietly. "Besides, it looks good on you." He smiled slightly before turning away from her and quickly following Nolan out of the lobby.

Grayson stood still for a moment, willing her heart to slow itself down, before turning back to the couch.

Noah was sprawled out on the cushions with his chin resting on his upturned palms. "Well, well," he teased, eyebrows raised.

"Stop smiling," she warned. "Now, give me one of those macaroons. We've gotta go back to work."

31

DETECTIVE NOLAN WALKED off of the elevator into Major Crimes bright and early Thursday morning, travel mug of coffee in hand, expecting his partner to be at his desk. It was empty, but the desk lamp was on and several books were opened haphazardly across the surface. He was in the building; he just wasn't at his desk.

The older detective plopped himself into his desk chair and fired up his laptop. Today was not shaping up to be a good day. They had another meeting scheduled with the captain, and just like last week, they didn't have much to go on.

After running into the two young doctors at the hospital, they'd followed up on the lead about the nurse, which had panned out. Then they had tracked down the good Dr. Nelson's widow, which had been a less-than-pleasant experience. Even with all of the information they had on him, they weren't any closer to figuring out who killed the man.

And there was still Lisa Oakes' case to think about. Evidence was still being processed, the M.E. had toxicology pending, but it was looking less and less like they were going to get anywhere. That poor girl wouldn't get justice and this womanizing, egotistical cardiologist was taking time away from her case.

Nolan caught a shadow out of the corner of his eye and turned quickly enough to catch his partner heading toward the break room.

More coffee, most likely. Not a good sign this early in the day.

Blake shook his head. Ryder never slept. He grabbed his near-empty travel mug and headed in the same direction. Muttered swearing filtered under the break room door. Blake cautiously pushed it open and there was his partner, trying to force the centuries-old coffeepot into submission.

"You could just try hitting it with a hammer," he said smoothly.

Ryder jumped and nearly dropped the glass pot. "Shit. What the hell, Nolan?"

There were bags under his eyes, and he looked paler than he had yesterday afternoon.

"Sorry." Blake sauntered up behind his partner, grabbed the coffeepot out of his hand, and placed it correctly underneath the machine. "If you break this thing, even more people in this department are going to hate your ass."

"Thanks for the warning."

Nolan leaned back against the Formica counter. "So, since you're clearly not getting any sleep, any epiphanies since yesterday?"

"How do you know I'm not sleeping?"

"You're already on your second coffee and it's not past 6:15, Gabe. There's nobody else in the department. You're clearly not sleeping."

"Whatever, Blake."

All right, asshole. I can be a hard-ass, too.

"All right, so thrill me. What has you so uptight that you can't sleep?"

"This case."

"Which one? The Oakes girl or Mr. Casanova heart doc?"

"Either. Both."

"That's clear, thanks."

"I just…" He started to pour himself a cup of coffee from the now-finished brewing pot. "There's something about the way that each one of them died. Something about the crime scenes. I can't put my finger on it. Something's not right."

"I'll say. We have a sweet young girl who doesn't have a scratch on her and a womanizing cardiologist who's lost his most prized possession. Two totally different crimes, though."

"Both found in churches."

"You were mocking me for bringing that up earlier."

"I was not. And I'm not saying they're related. Not yet."

"We don't even know how Lisa died, Ryder."

"Thanks for reminding me," he grumbled. He grabbed his coffee and left the break room, heading back toward the interrogation rooms.

Nolan silently followed him to the far end of the hallway. Whenever Ryder got something under his skin during a case, he took over the back interview room and lived among the evidence files until something clicked. Blake affectionately called it the Bat Cave. As disorganized and frankly psychotic as it sometimes looked, the ritual had worked every single time. But if he was resorting to it this early…that definitely meant something was wrong.

Fuck. This day just keeps getting better and better.

And sure enough, when Nolan opened the door to the interview room, he walked into chaos. He tried, unsuccessfully, to shake the queasiness from his stomach. One whole wall was covered with crime scene photographs from the seminary. Witness statements and pages ripped out of Gabe's binder were tagged to their accompanying photographs. Another wall was dedicated to the Nelson case.

"Setting up the cave a bit early, aren't we?" he mused.

Ryder looked up from the photos he had strewn out on the table in front of him. He hadn't heard Nolan follow him. He just nodded and returned his focus to the table.

"And the cave isn't speaking to you yet?"

Gabriel shook his head.

"Fine."

We've been partners long enough for me to know how this works.

Nolan took a seat on one of the incredibly uncomfortable metal chairs and kicked his feet up. "If the cave's not talking to you, then you talk to me. You put all this shit up, called me into work early in the middle of the week, and then get grumpy over coffee. What's going on?"

Ryder scowled. "Look at these two pictures. What do you see?"

Nolan pawed the two photographs that were shoved at him. One was of Lisa Oakes, the other was of Dr. Nelson. They were both taken on the examination table at the medical examiner's office. Naked bodies on metal slabs. Nolan scanned the pictures over and over; nothing jumped out at him, except the obvious missing anatomy on Nelson and the slash marks across his face.

"What am I missing?" he asked, pushing the pictures back at his partner.

"Look on the abdomen."

"There's nothing there."

Ryder pointed to Lisa's picture.

"It's a mole or something. Whoop-de-doo, Ryder."

"Nelson has one, too. In the same spot."

"Who cares? It's a coincidence. It's not like she has the number one drawn on her and he has the number two on his."

Ryder swore under his breath. Nolan kept talking.

"I probably have a mole around there somewhere, Ryder, and I'm not lying on an autopsy table. You want me to check?"

Nolan made a move to pull his shirttails out from his waistband. Ryder held his hand up.

"Keep your fucking shirt on, Blake. And they're not moles."

"Fine. Whatever other skin tag or growth or whatever you want to call it, I don't care. I think you're making something out of nothing. But I'll humor you since I'm your partner and that's my job. You think it means something. So, what is it?"

Ryder dropped his eyes to the photographs and remained silent.

"I…I don't know."

"That's what I thought. Just let it go. Focus on something else."

"Then what ideas do you have?"

Blake shrugged. "You know I haven't any clue. Speaking of which, what are we going to tell McCallister? Last time didn't go so well. Now we've got a prominent murdered doctor on top of it."

"We tell him what information we do have." Ryder shrugged. "That's the best we can do."

"You going to tell him about your dot theory?"

"I'll save it for next week," Ryder replied sarcastically.

"Great. I'll have time to practice my I-don't-know-what-the-hell-he's-talking-about face."

"Thanks for the support."

"Tell you what. If vic number three has a dot anywhere close, I'll consider it."

"You think there will be a number three?"

Nolan did a double-take. "Don't you?" he asked, not bothering to hide the shock in his voice.

"I hope not."

"That wasn't the question."

Ryder put his head in his hands. "If Lisa Oakes was a random murder and Dr. Nelson's death is coincidental, then I'm wrong and there won't be a third."

"And if there's a number three?"

"Then we'll have to try to make the connection between all three of them. Start working the cases as a serial spree."

"Why is that such a problem to do now if you already think they're connected?"

"Because I can't make *her* fit with *him*. I can come up with good reasons for why someone would leave Lisa Oakes in a church the way she was left. And I can come up with some very good reasons Nelson was left like he was. But the profile for Oakes is completely different from the one for Nelson. It's like two separate people are at work here."

"So maybe it *is* two separate people."

"Hence the crimes wouldn't be related."

"No, two people working together."

Ryder paused to consider the thought, then shook his head. "It's not impossible, but it makes even less sense. Both crimes were deeply personal. There's guilt in the Oakes case; rage and disgust in Nelson's."

"So, if it is one person, he's a total whack job."

"That's the technical term, yes."

"Fantastic."

"Yeah."

Nolan shook his head and looked at the photographs again.

Ten-thirty came around sooner than they expected. Neither Nolan nor Ryder noticed the time tick away. Their captain's curt knock on the doorjamb came as a violent surprise. Blake was halfway through a swig of coffee and nearly choked as he stood up.

"Shit! Captain, I'm sorry..." he hacked through coffee-coated lungs.

"Jesus, Nolan, sit down and cough that crap out of your lungs." The captain laughed as he patted his detective on the back. "No use trying to kill yourself with coffee for being a few minutes late to a meeting." McCallister looked toward the younger detective sitting across the table. "I figured you two were working on something."

"Trying to, captain." Gabriel stood.

"Oh, sit the hell down, Ryder. I'm not your prom date. Fill me in."

Over the next half hour, the two detectives relayed all they had to their captain, who leaned back in one of the uncomfortable metal chairs and didn't say a word. Ryder didn't say anything about connecting the two cases, and Nolan didn't see a need to fill in that particular gap just yet.

When they stopped, McCallister stood up and examined the haphazardly-decorated walls for a few minutes before sighing.

"So, we have nothing," he said solemnly. "On either case."

"Well, I'd say we have stuff, captain, just none of it's shining a spotlight on a potential suspect," Nolan replied.

"For either case," Ryder added.

"You're certain the wife didn't have a hand in her husband's death? She had motive."

Ryder shook his head. "With all due respect to Mrs. Nelson,

sir, she doesn't have the capacity to follow a network TV crime show, let alone hire someone to track down her husband and kill him. She's never sober enough."

"One of the kids?"

"They all have a lock on their inheritance money based on age restrictions," Ryder said flatly. "They get enough of an allowance every month to keep them more than happy. They were only served by their father being alive. The longer he worked, the more money he made, the more money they'd have when he died."

"Lovely."

"Yeah, that's what we thought when we interviewed the brood from hell," Nolan agreed.

"And the nurse angle?"

"We talked to one who worked on the sixth floor. She'd been a longtime hookup of the doctor's. Only ended it with him a few weeks ago when she decided she didn't like feeling like a hole in a mattress after a twelve-hour shift. He'd apparently gone after a new hire in the cardiology wing after she gave him the boot, but the old nursing guard there put a stop to that. So, he'd moved on to a day-shift scrub tech. And she was gaga over him. No one looks good for it."

"And all of their alibis for the night Nelson was murdered checked out," Ryder added. "They're all clean."

"Okay. Well, if that's all you've got, I trust you. Keep at it. Something's bound to come up sooner or later."

Captain McCallister stood and walked out of the interview room.

Nolan just shook his head. "Bring on victim number three I guess, then?"

Ryder chuckled. "I suppose so."

"Well, keep your damned phone on Sunday. Chances are you'll be buying me coffee before church."

32

SUNDAY MORNING DAWNED clear and cool. A burst of overnight rain had washed the streets clean. The wind was calm. The roads were deserted. A perfect morning to run.

His mind had been running wild since two a.m., waking him out of a dead sleep in anticipation of another callout from Nolan that didn't come. By a quarter to six, he'd had enough, and he'd hit the pavement to try to focus. Crime scene photos and witness statements ticked through his mind one at a time as his sneakers connected with concrete, at the same damnable rhythm.

Think horses, not zebras.

It was unlikely that there was anything but coincidence connecting the Oakes and Nelson cases. Minor skin markings and conspiracy theories were less than nothing to go on. Still, he wasn't sleeping. That meant he was missing something.

Something's not right.

He turned southeast down the Cherry Creek Trail and picked up his pace. The creek was running high after all the recent rain, and the sound of the water running over smooth river rocks echoed peacefully off of the gulley walls. A misty fog hung low over the flowing water. There was only one other runner in sight, on the other side of the creek and running in the other direction.

Perfect.

With any luck, he'd get five or six miles in before the rest of the city woke up and clogged the trail with power-walkers and strollers. Gabriel put his head down and forced himself to move faster, his hamstrings protesting against the new pace.

Ten minutes later, sweat was pouring off his face and down his back, soaking his T-shirt. He was just about to slow up when he felt his phone vibrate in his pocket. He pulled himself off the trail, leaned up against a large tree, and answered.

"Ryder," he panted, wiping the sweat out of his eyes.

"Please tell me I'm interrupting you getting laid," came the chuckling voice on the other end of the line.

"Fuck off, Nolan. What do you want?"

"Soooo…you're grouchy. You're not getting laid, are you?"

"Blake…"

"You're out being all healthy and whatnot, huh?"

"Sure."

"Where are you?"

"On the trail."

"How far are you from your apartment?"

"About thirty minutes or so. Why?"

"Get your butt off the trail and figure out what cross-streets you're at."

"What the hell for?"

"Because I'm coming to pick you up, that's why. I'm not waiting outside your damned building for another half-hour."

"Why are you outside my building?"

"Remember when I said you'd be buying me coffee…"

Gabriel leaned his head back against the trunk of the tree and closed his eyes. His stomach dropped to the floor.

"Fuck."

"Yeah. Vic number three just popped in Littleton. Their squad leader called me."

"Directly?"

Ryder pushed off the tree and climbed up the embankment to the main street.

"His kids go to school with my kids. We do the preschool soccer-dad thing together in the summer."

Gabriel took inventory of his surroundings while nodding into the phone.

"I'm up by the country club off of Speer and First."

"Ugh. Of course you are, you pretentious bastard. Just stay there."

"I'm in running gear."

"I didn't figure you'd be in a tux," came the sarcastic reply.

"I need to shower and change."

"Nope. I'm not waiting for you to come all the way back here and get pretty."

"Blake..."

"Seriously, no. We're going now. How many times do I have to tell you that you don't have to dress up for a crime scene?"

"Fine."

"Finish your pouting by the time I get there."

The phone went dead.

"Pain in the ass," Ryder mumbled as he leaned against a streetlight and started to stretch.

At least he'd remembered to put some cash in the pocket of his running shorts this morning. Nolan would never forgive him if he didn't pony up for coffee.

33

IT TOOK NOLAN almost twenty-five minutes to drive down to the suburbs and find Our Lady of Mount Carmel Catholic Church. A rather large crowd of people was already gathered on the opposite side of the street when they arrived.

He inwardly groaned. For some reason, people were drawn toward the flashing blue lights of cop cars like swamp bugs to a bug zapper, and it always made parking a pain in the ass. Thankfully, this church had its own parking lot around back, and Littleton PD had been proactive enough to block it off early.

A pudgy officer in uniform saw the badge Blake flashed through his window and clumsily moved the barricade. There was no sign of the medical examiner's meat wagon yet, but there was no doubt they'd be down shortly. Ryder had called the captain, after he'd made good on his promise to spring for coffee, and then the M.E.'s office to get their on-call team in gear.

Nolan shut off the engine, grabbed his coffee cup from the console, and hoisted himself out of the car. The church certainly wasn't the most elaborate thing he'd ever seen, but it was substantial in size. Weathered brick, stained glass windows, a large cross towering over the front door…a typical church.

Nolan heard the passenger door shut and smirked as Ryder tried to get a handle on his sweat-drenched hair in the rearview mirror. He'd debated about snapping a picture for later blackmail purposes but had thought better of it. "You look fine, princess."

"Shut up." Gabriel scowled. "Let's get this over with before Pelton's team gets here."

"Don't want your girlfriend to see you without your suit on?" he countered, chuckling at his own joke.

Nolan kicked himself away from the car and made for the side door of the church with Ryder on his heels. Two uniformed officers held up the crime scene tape when Nolan flashed his badge. They wound around through a dark hallway and emerged at the front vestibule.

Nolan managed a quick glance into the church itself and whistled. "Wow. Wouldn't think of this from the outside of the place, huh?" He pointed.

The inside of the church was vast, with high domed ceilings painted in blue and spotted with white sunbursts and stars. A beautiful white marble altar, complete with white spires soaring high into the air to the ceiling, took center stage. The only blemish on the scene was the white sheet half-pulled up over a mass at the base of the altar steps. A crime scene photographer was precariously balancing on a set of pews, trying to get a decent aerial shot.

A loud call from the street ripped their attention from the body.

"Oy! Nolan! Give me a second. I'll be right there!"

A rather round, ginger-haired man with a handlebar mustache and wearing a Denver Broncos sweatshirt slapped a uniformed officer on the back, then waddled up the front steps. He held out his hand to Nolan, who took it and pulled him in to clap him on the back several times.

"Blake, how the hell are ya?" he boomed.

"Been better rested, Dan. You?" he replied, gasping for air.

"Well, I was okay until this landed in my lap this morning. Thanks for coming down." He looked Ryder up and down. "This your partner?"

"Yup. Dan Greene, meet Gabe Ryder."

"Sir," Ryder nodded.

Greene looked the younger man up and down again with an eyebrow cocked. A wide grin spread underneath his mustache. "I never knew you to be the better dressed one at a crime scene, Blake."

"I'm usually not, trust me." Blake grinned at his partner, who was scowling back at him over the rim of his coffee cup.

"So, what's the story here?"

"Eh, let me show ya. Come on."

The three men ducked under a strip of crime scene tape and started down the main aisle.

"I got the call after five this morning. A couple of my night patrol guys were finishing their shift and noticed the front door was open. They stopped to check on things. Almost left without coming in. They figured the priest had come in early and just left the door open. But then Johnson decided he saw a bear in the aisle."

"A bear. Seriously?" Nolan laughed sarcastically.

"He's new," Greene rolled his eyes. "Grew up in LA. Anything bigger than a Chihuahua is a man-eating monster to this kid. Anyway, they came in to see what this hulking thing in the aisle was, and now here we all are."

"How'd you know to call me?"

"I listen to the department gossip. And this," he said, grabbing an evidence bag with a man's wallet in it.

He pressed the wallet toward the side of the bag and handed it over.

Nolan read the front of the driver's license. "Marcus Porter. Littleton address. Okay. So?"

"Here." Greene threw another bag over, which Nolan missed catching when it sailed wide. Ryder picked it up off of the floor.

"Saint Joseph's ID. Department of Gastroenterology," he read.

"Yeah, that's it," Greene nodded. "A quick Google search said that he's one of their department's fellows, whatever the hell that means. Works out of the same hospital as your other two vics. I figured this would come to you one way or the other. Best to get you involved early."

"And get it off your desk," Ryder finished.

"Exactly, m'boy." The older man grinned. "Now, I've got to go say something to all the people outside who won't be coming to church here today. My patrol guys are headed downtown to give their statements. If you need anything, Blake, call me."

The two men shook hands. As Greene headed back outside, Nolan turned toward the body. Ryder already had the sheet pulled back. Looking at their victim up close, Blake didn't particularly blame the poor rookie for thinking there had been a bear in the church. The dead guy had to be a good four hundred pounds.

At least.

Dr. Marcus Porter was a bloated, balding, blue, awful sight to behold on a Sunday morning. Nolan gave his partner a few minutes to pace and circle the body before he opened his mouth.

"Well?"

"Well, what?"

"What do you think? They connected?"

"It's hard to say no. All three victims are physicians from the same hospital." Ryder shrugged.

"Anything jumping out at you about this guy?"

"Not really. No major signs of trauma."

"Like Lisa," Blake nodded.

"But he was dumped here, like Nelson."

"You don't think he was killed here?"

"Why would he have been?"

"Well, I dunno about you, super-stud, but I couldn't carry this guy anywhere. Lisa, sure. Nelson, yeah, if I had to. This guy? I'd need a forklift."

Ryder looked around the church haphazardly, then back at the body. "Uh, good point."

He stared at the floor for a minute, then narrowed his eyes slightly and dropped to the floor. He grabbed a pair of gloves out of the CSU kit resting on the pew behind him and leaned in toward Porter's face.

"All right, all right, stop," Nolan said hastily.

Ryder stopped mid-lean. "What?"

"Before you get too close, what the hell are you doing?"

"Trying to figure out what he last had to eat."

"Probably whatever crossed his path. McDonald's. Cold Stone. Small children."

Ryder opened the victim's mouth and sniffed.

Nolan shot backward several feet down the aisle and grimaced. "Okay, stop immediately or I'm gonna be sick." He turned his head away.

"Oh, please..."

"Seriously. I am never going to get used to you doing that kind of shit."

"Then don't watch."

"You're smelling a dead guy, Ryder."

"I'm aware of that," he countered.

Nolan glared at his partner, then sat down on the edge of a pew. "Well?"

"Italian."

"I'm never eating a meatball again."

Ryder smirked. "Probably for the best."

"Shut up."

"Now what?"

"Are you done sniffing corpses?"

"For now," Ryder nodded, peeling off the gloves and standing up from the floor.

"Then let's start by making you look more respectable. We can search this guy's house after lunch."

"I thought you weren't eating."

"*Meatballs*," Blake said forcibly. "I'm not eating meatballs. There are other food groups."

The two detectives stepped back out into the morning sun through the side door and headed toward the car.

"Meatballs are a food group?"

"Just like beer. And nachos. Get in the damned car."

34

THE WEEK, NOT to mention the weekend, had passed by in a blur. Two of Denver's rival drug gangs had decided to get into an all-out war Wednesday night, which sent the hospital into lockdown. Police officers were patrolling the halls in pairs with loaded guns. No hospital employees were allowed to walk to or from their cars without an armed escort. It was setting everyone on edge.

To add to the chaos, a bus loaded down with tourists had overturned on black ice coming into town from the ski resorts. Six people were dead. The survivors had been spread out over all of the area hospitals, but St. Joe's had accepted thirteen of the worst. Add on the usual smattering of hip fractures, broken ankles, and drunk redneck accidents, and the orthopedic trauma service had exploded.

Grayson looked over the three-page rounding list in front of her and sighed. The names, medical record numbers, and diagnoses were all starting to blur together. This was going to be her life in less than two years. Taking on a trauma fellow-ship would put her right smack-dab in the middle of this chaos for the rest of her career. Thankfully, she would be looking at it as an attending, which at the moment seemed infinitely easier. They never had to start rounding at four a.m. on a Sunday. She signed in to one of the computers and pulled up her patient list.

"Okay…" she said quietly to herself, clicking through lab results. "Let's see who's causing problems this morning."

Several hours later, she met up with Ethan Adams, her junior resident on call. They finished rounding together and then headed to the cafeteria for a well-deserved breakfast. Thankfully, the doctors' lounge in the cafeteria let residents and attendings eat in peace, away from the chaos of the main dining room.

Grayson glanced over at her list as she munched on a bagel and cream cheese. Adams plopped down in a chair beside her with a tray full of sausage, scrambled eggs, and hash browns.

"Got enough food there?" she teased.

"Hey, breakfast of champions, man," he replied, shoveling the first forkful into his mouth.

"Thank God you were on this weekend, Adams. No offense to Thompson, but he would've just been in the way."

"Ha! Yeah. The kid tries, but he's so shy. The patients bulldoze over him, for Christ's sake."

"Anybody on your end causing problems this morning?"

He pulled his list out of his pocket mid-bite.

"Umm...Jones and Marsters needed blood this morning, but you knew that already. Mrs. Adams, no relation, is still refusing to get out of bed and work with therapy. I told her she's leaving today whether she likes it or not and put in an aggressive PT order. I'm keeping my fingers crossed. And our one guy over in oncology isn't doing so hot. I think they're gonna make him palliative today or tomorrow."

"He looks that bad?"

"Yeah, just tired and depressed and pale. I don't know how to explain it. Just...bad."

"Gotcha."

"Either way, we're done with him, surgery-wise, so we can just keep checking his chart while he's here. Everybody else was fine. Should be four coming off my side of the list today. Anybody from your side I should know about for call today?"

"Yeah. Six, fifteen, and twenty in the SICU are all getting blood, so check their repeat hemoglobin levels. Six is that bad four-limb bus victim, so he may end up needing quite a bit. Talk to general surgery if you give more than four units. He may need a TEG, and they manage that stuff. Mr. Alroy is also refusing to get out of bed, and he and I had a similar conversation this morning. Get him out of here. Whatever it takes. Four of the bus-crash people are going back to the OR today with gen surg; we're only involved with the one. Bilateral femoral nails at eight a.m."

"So, it's going to be an uber-simple day?"

"Oh, of course," she said sarcastically.

"What up, ortho bitches!" came a high-pitched screech from the lounge door.

A rail-thin resident in plaster-covered scrubs stood in the doorway holding a tray of food and a large cup of coffee. He proceeded to bow in greeting.

"Francis, good morning," Grayson replied, mocking his formality and motioning for him to take a seat next to her. "Where's your junior?"

"Finishing up paperwork in the ED," he said, setting his tray down. "I figured you'd want to run this call list before your case."

"Do I wanna know?" She groaned.

"It wasn't awful, but you have two add-ons today. The rest are for tomorrow."

"Okay, hit me."

She readied her pen.

"534, Mendez, 82 years old, displaced femoral neck. Hemi today. Medicine is looking into new onset arrhythmia. The night hospitalist said he should clear, but you know how that goes."

"M'kay."

"806, Hamilton, geriatric fall with an ankle, a distal radius, and a proximal humerus. Two of the three are operative. I'll let you guess which."

"Ankle and radius."

"Yeah."

"I'm going to put two more hips and a tibial plateau on your list after breakfast. They're all going Monday or Tuesday. Everything's done for them. There's one more guy, new consult over on oncology."

"To the trauma service? Are we becoming the oncology service now, too?" Grayson shook her head.

"I know. I tried to turf it, but he's a family friend of somebody who knows somebody who knows our department chair. They requested an ortho trauma doc. They don't like our onc guy."

"For what?"

"Pathologic fracture of the femur. Through a met."

"So, a totally appropriate ortho trauma case…" She rolled her eyes.

"I know. Didn't you guys just have one of these?"

"Yeah. We did a hemi on that guy's hip, but apparently, he's going palliative."

"That's nothing you guys did."

"He's still gonna die, Francis."

"I hear that," the young man said as took a sip of his coffee.

Timothy Francis was a good guy. Father of two, he was one of the most inappropriate residents in their entire orthopedics program. He told the dirtiest jokes and had the foulest mouth in the entire department, but he worked hard and did a reasonable job. Some people didn't like him, but she had always gotten along with him. They were at least friendly at work. He was in his fourth year and looking into hand surgery fellowships. Their tallest resident in a decade was going to spend his career sitting behind a microscope repairing tiny nerves and sewing together chopped-off fingers. Oh, the irony.

"Anything else?"

"Nope. Everything else went to other services. I don't think you need any more people on your trauma list." He threw his head back and drained the last of his coffee. "Okay, Nguyen's making me nervous. He should've been here by now. Gonna go track down his ass. Have fun."

"Bye, Francis."

He sauntered out of the dining room, mumbling to himself about inefficient interns.

"So, how do you wanna play it this morning?" Adams asked in between bites.

"I'll take the bilateral femurs. That hemi will probably go in another room, as long as it clears, and should be quick. Why don't you try to get all the floor stuff handled during that time? Then you can come up for the combo. You and Dr. Allen can blow through the ankle while I handle the wrist. You can even do the hemi if you get done with the floor fast enough."

"Sounds like a plan to me."

"I've gotta get upstairs. Call if you need anything, okay? I'll plan on seeing you for the third case unless another bus rolls over."

Grayson stood up and headed straight for the OR.

35

THANKFULLY, THE MORNING cases went well. Dr. Allen sat in the back of the room and played solitaire on his phone while she took care of the femurs, then held retractors for her while she did the hemi.

"I'm going to miss you when you go off service, Carter," he said as they were closing the incision on the second case.

"Huh?"

"Really. You make being on trauma call bearable. You come in and operate. I get to sit back and fuck around. And you bail me out of shit I haven't done for years. You think any of your co-chiefs can pull that off?"

"They're good residents, sir."

"Yeah, I know. But I scrub in if any of them are rodding a femur."

"Thanks, Dr. Allen," she said as the scrub tech handed her another stitch.

"Eh. Just tellin' it like it is. You're gonna do the next one?"

"Yeah. And Adams is coming, too, I think. As long as he's not swamped downstairs."

"Divide and conquer?"

"It'll get you out of the hospital faster."

"That's all I needed to hear. Which do you want?"

"I thought I could do the wrist while you two handle the ankle."

"Have you seen the films yet? I didn't bother."

She nodded.

"Weber B bimal equivalent. Should just need a lag screw and neutralization plate. Syndesmosis looked questionable on the stress view, so it may need a few screws, too."

"And the wrist?"

"Four-part intra articular. Not a ton of comminution on the plain films, but the patient's old, so I bet it'll looks worse when I get in there."

"Still think you can plate it?"

"Sure. The fragments are big enough. She doesn't need an ex-fix."

"Sounds like a plan."

Grayson smiled behind her mask as she took the skin stapler from the scrub tech. Dr. Allen had been a very pleasant surprise this time around on trauma. He let her operate, gave her great feedback, and was actually nice to her. That was in stark contrast to the rest of the department.

Now, all she had to do was figure out what he was putting in his coffee in the morning and spike the ortho department's coffeepot with it.

By the time five o'clock rolled around, she was exhausted. Two more gang shootings had come through the ER. Of course, both teenagers had had open fractures and bullets floating around in loops of bowel. That had meant more time spent in the OR and fights with general surgery about who took care of what and in what order.

I'm exhausted.

Grayson opened the door to her call room and sat down on the edge of the bed. The little room, with its peeling paint, ancient mattress draped in threadbare sheets, small desk, and lonely bedside lamp, had been her home-away-from-home for almost five years. She'd spent more nights sleeping here than in her own bed at home.

She stretched her neck from side to side and sighed. Her feet hurt. Her back hurt. Everything hurt. She grabbed a bottle of Aleve from the bedside table, took a swig of water, and knocked back two pills. She took off her shoes and brought her right leg up on the bed, rubbing the instep of her foot.

At some point, I should really go with Babs to get a pedicure again.

She felt a vibration at her hip, and she instinctively reached for her pager, bringing the obnoxious black box up to eye level. But the screen wasn't lit up, and the vibration at her hip continued.

Shit.

She shoved her pager back into its holster and unclipped her phone from the waistband of her scrubs. She answered it without looking at the screen.

"Carter."

"Hello, lovie."

Her anxiety instantly dropped off, and she smiled. "Hi, Noah."

"How's the service from hell?"

"Busy. I just got out of the OR."

"Yikes. That's awful. I thought you were supposed to have an easy go of it today."

"Two add-ons from last night and another two emergent from the ER. Great experience. Just exhausting."

"Understandable."

"What's going on? You're calling a hospital-trapped resident on a weekend when you're not on call."

"I wanted to see how you were handling things."

"Ummm…fine, I guess…" she replied, confusion evident in her voice. "Why wouldn't I be?"

"Have you watched the news today? Hasn't anybody told you?"

"Told me what?"

"Marcus Porter died."

She paused and wrinkled her forehead.

"Who?"

"Marcus Porter. The big GI fellow. The slob."

"Oh my God, seriously? Oh crap, hang on!" She swore as her phone slipped from its perch on her shoulder.

She scrambled to pick it back up and shifted on the bed.

"Sorry, I dropped the damned phone." She sucked in a long breath. "I didn't know him well, but that's horrible. What happened?"

"I don't know. Police found him this morning not too far from his house in Littleton."

"He didn't have a great reputation, but still…"

"They found him inside a church, Gray."

Grayson didn't reply. She felt her heart rate skyrocket and shut her eyes against the suddenly-spinning walls of the call room.

Oh no. Another one?

"Gray…?"

"That's three people in two weeks," she whispered, eyes still closed.

"I know. Weird, right?"

"Are they saying if they're connected?"

"No, but all kinds of rumors are flying around. You know Nelson was found in his own church, right?"

"I heard," she replied, nodding like he could actually see her.

"I can't think of anything Lisa had in common with those two."

"Me either."

"Well, just be careful, love. Something's up. Keep walking out with somebody at night, okay?"

"You know I hate doing that. And that rule about the armed escort is only in effect because of the gang activity right now. It doesn't have anything to do with the three doctors who have died recently."

"I don't care. I'm not there to do it, so just do it for me, okay? Don't try to duck the guards again."

"What do you mean *again*?" She tried to feign ignorance.

"I know you got caught trying to leave by yourself yesterday," he huffed through the phone line.

"Oh, all right—" she rolled her eyes, "—but I think you're being overprotective."

"I don't."

Despite his words, she could hear the smile in his voice on the other end of the line.

"Okay, Mr. Protective, I need to nap before the next wave of chaos. I'm hanging up now."

"All right. Remember, car escort."

"Yeah, yeah, I know. I'll see you tomorrow, Noah." Grayson lay back onto her bed and shut her eyes.

What in the hell is going on around here?

She didn't notice herself drifting off to sleep.

The strident screech of her pager pulled her violently out of a deep sleep. The ceiling lights were still on full blast and blindingly bright. She slammed her eyes shut. The blaring noise from the pager persisted. She searched the bedside table for the damned box. Once she found it, she hit the button to silence the alert and focused her blurry vision on the alarm clock by the bed.

Forty minutes.

She'd been asleep for forty minutes. She moaned, then looked at her pager.

9-1-1. ER ADAMS.

Grayson grabbed the phone off the side table, dialed the ER's extension, and waited while the secretary transferred her over. She heard her junior pick up, breathing heavily into the receiver.

"Carter? Carter, you there?" he called out, clearly panicked.

"Hey, buddy, what's going on?" She was fighting to keep the fatigue out of her voice.

"Um, can…can you come down to the ER?"

"Sure. You okay?" Grayson leaned over the side of the bed and felt around on the floor for her shoes.

"They just brought in some guy by chopper. Highway, high speed, I don't have any other details. But his legs are like…off. Like *off* off. He's bleeding everywhere. It's on the walls. And his one hand is blue and…and…I am so out of my league here."

She threw her hair up into a ponytail and wrapped it up in her scrub cap.

"Go grab tourniquets from our crash cart. Page Dr. Allen to the ER. I'll be right there."

"Okay. See you in a minute. Bye."

She was already halfway down the hallway.

36

TRYING TO GET any information about their third victim had been more painful than pulling teeth, as far as Blake was concerned. The guy wasn't well-liked by his own department at St. Joseph's, let alone the rest of the hospital. His department chair was just biding his time until he could give Porter his credentials and get him the hell out. The sooner he was gone, the better.

Porter had a reputation for being gruff, sloppy, and personally going against every principle of gastrointestinal health. He smoked like a chimney, drank like a fish, and more than once he'd been suspected of coming to work high on something. Nothing had ever been proven, so he'd kept his job with a running tally of warnings and reprimands.

He lived alone in a rental house in Littleton. His neighbors knew about as much about him as they knew about quantum physics. His car was still in his driveway, locked and untouched. The house was in order; well, at least it didn't look like someone had ransacked the place. It definitely wasn't clean.

Ryder had been sequestering himself more and more in the back interview room. The walls were progressively becoming covered with crime scene photos and reports from the M.E.'s office as they were sent up. The Oakes girl's toxicology reports were still pending, something about re-running the tests. The official cause of death for Dr. Nelson was exsanguination.

Big surprise.

No one had recovered the missing parts, and the good doctor had been buried without them late last week. Ryder's

228 | A. R. Nicole

going theory was that whoever murdered him had kept them as some kind of trophy. Disgusting, but if they happened to find them hanging out in someone's freezer, they'd have an open-and-shut case.

Speaking of my partner...

Nolan made a quick detour into the break room and grabbed two cups of "fresh" coffee before leisurely walking back to the closed interview room. He knocked and, without waiting for an answer, pushed the door open with his foot.

"Hey, man," he said by way of greeting. "Looks like you could use this."

Gabriel looked like hell. He had bags under his eyes, and his hair was a mess. By the looks of it, today had already been particularly rough.

"Thanks," he replied, taking the mug and pushing the two empty ones further away on the desk.

"So," Blake said, sitting down, "is the good Dr. Porter telling you anything today?"

"No, not really. Pelton's as stumped with him as she was with Oakes."

"Carla's running out of ideas? That's never good. She's sharp."

"I went down there this morning."

"To look at the body again?"

He nodded.

"Of course you did." Nolan rolled his eyes sarcastically. "Did you get in on the autopsy, too?"

"No," he chuckled. "She had both of her assistants today. Didn't need the help."

"She'll need 'em with a guy that size. I got the rest of his records from his medical school in New York. Not the most stellar student, but no big red flags. He was in the middle of the pack. Got written up a few times for being late and lazy. No surprise there. Had six parking tickets from his time in Manhattan, but I can't fault the guy for that. It's freaking Manhattan."

Ryder nodded. "I talked to the directors at the church again. A few parishioners remembered seeing him in the neighborhood off and on, but nobody knew his name or knew what he did for a living, much less where he worked. He was the neighborhood ghost."

"Fuckin' huge ghost. His family didn't have very nice things to say about him."

"Oh, really?"

"Yeah. Finally got them to answer the phone today. Dad was waking up with a hangover and Mom was screaming at someone named Jim at the other end of the house. Sounds like he left home after high school and hasn't been back to Jersey since then. Not even for his brother's wedding last year. They don't have anything to do with him. It sounds like the hatred was mutual."

"So, another dead end." Ryder sighed.

"You said if we got a third body, we could connect the first two. All found in Catholic churches, all from St. Joe's…"

"…and nothing else besides that, Blake. I'm stuck."

"Well, yeah…but it's a place to start."

"We're going on three weeks here. I shouldn't just be finding a fucking starting place."

"Maybe this psycho's just picking people at random in the hospital parking lot."

"There's something else there, Blake. There has to be." Gabriel shoved his hands through his hair and rested his elbows on the table. His heavy sigh echoed off the walls.

"Ryder, are you talking in fucking circles again?" A smooth voice crept in from the doorway.

Both detectives twisted in their chairs. A 6'2" plainclothes detective with early salt-and-pepper hair was leaning against the door jam, watching them. His arms were folded across his chest, and he had a wicked grin on his face.

Nolan glanced back at his partner, who suddenly had an equally wide grin on his face. Clearly, these two knew each other. Nolan bristled.

"Shit." Ryder stood up, shook the man's hand, and clapped him on the back. "Harrison, what the hell are you doing here?"

"Sightseeing in Major Crimes."

"Bullshit."

Ryder turned toward his partner. "Blake Nolan, meet Logan Harrison. He was my partner in narcotics."

Nolan instantly relaxed.

Detective Logan Harrison had one of the best and most colorful reputations in the entire department. He was a good cop and got the job done, sometimes with questionable tactics, but then again, he worked in narcotics. They were a different breed altogether, as far as Nolan was concerned. He was only in his late thirties, but he was already tipped to be the next captain if he didn't ruffle too many feathers. He was part of the reason Ryder had caught the attention of the brass so early in his career, and the word was Harrison had helped him get his place at Major Crimes.

Nolan stood up and shook the man's outstretched hand. "I've heard a lot about you."

"Eh, only about half of the good stuff's true, but thanks."

Logan smiled back, then swept his arm around the room in one dramatic gesture. "Jesus, Ryder, what are you doing in here? Putting up wallpaper?"

"Not really."

"You used to do this shit in narcotics, too."

"And it worked then."

"How about now?"

"I'll get back to you on that," he said, sitting down as the smile faded from his face.

"Why don't you just walk me through what you have so far?"

Gabriel raised an eyebrow at him. "Why would I do that?"

"Because it's rude to leave one of the three musketeers out of the loop," Harrison replied as he pulled another chair up to the table.

"All right, you've lost me," Blake interjected.

Harrison grinned at him. "As of today, I'm officially on loan from narcotics with the express purpose of helping with this investigation," he singsonged, then rolled his eyes.

"They don't trust us?" Blake scowled.

"Nah. Sounds like the opposite," Harrison said, shaking his head. "The story I got from my captain is you've got three bodies, all from a hospital that treats both the scum of the earth and the richest of the rich, and they're connected. If it's something seedy, I have connections to that world. And it never hurts to have another badge on a case to placate the mayor's office and the chief of detectives."

"They are chomping at the bit for something to tell the press," Nolan conceded.

"Champing," Gabriel corrected.

"So, they're buying time by adding me into the mix. I'm here to help, not get in your way."

"We know that," Ryder replied, glancing nervously at Nolan. "Don't we?"

Blake smiled and waved him off. Harrison wasn't a threat.

"Okay. So, stop trying to read that file and get me up to speed with all of this. You only have two hours before lunch."

Nolan sat back down in his chair as Ryder started talking. He wasn't entirely happy with Harrison being brought into the mix without warning, but he had to admit, his partner had perked up a bit. If he was what it took to get this shit off their desk and get a psychopath behind bars, then so be it.

Plus, he'd already mentioned lunch.

37

BY THE END of the week, Grayson was at her wit's end with her service and the whole damned hospital. The trauma service had been overrun with patients. Five residents wouldn't have been enough to properly take care of everyone, and they were trying to hold it together with three. Everything would just get settled down, and the floor would come out from underneath her feet an hour later. They were so busy that attendings had had to operate without resident coverage for the first time in over a year. The ones who'd drawn the short straws weren't happy about it, but extra hands were needed to fix pelvic fractures and pull traction on femurs. A fibula fracture was a one-man show. It was complete chaos.

The other hospital services weren't faring much better. General surgery was inundated. The intensive care unit was completely full. Noah had been pulling sixteen-hour shifts all week just to stay afloat. Elective surgeries had been canceled because there weren't any post-operative beds. The hospital had gone on divert twice. Top it all off with a phone call from her department chair telling her that she was going to be giving surgical Grand Rounds next Friday, and she was completely spent.

Grayson pulled her cell phone off of her hip and hit speed dial.

"Dr. Mason speaking."

"Wow. You're formal today," she teased.

"Oh, Gray! Sorry, love, I've been fielding hospital calls from my cell. You okay?"

She nodded into the receiver.

"What're you up to tonight?"

"You mean now?"

"Technically yes, since it's dark out."

"I'm going to finish signing out, then get the hell out of here. Why?"

"Feel like a greasy cheeseburger and a beer? I desperately need a drink."

He chuckled into the receiver. "I think this entire hospital needs a round of tequila shots, hun."

"So that's a yes?"

"Yeah, that's a yes. When will you be done?"

"I'm tucking in my last patient now, and then I'm done."

"I'll meet you in the lobby in twenty."

"Make it fifteen, or I'm bolting without you."

"Okay, okay. Fifteen. Tops."

"Bye."

Grayson clipped her phone back onto her scrubs and focused on the computer screen in front of her. All that stood between her and freedom was a post-op order set and a change of clothes.

Fifteen minutes later, she walked into the main lobby to find Noah leaning up against the back of one of the modern sofas, checking his phone. She snuck up behind him and looped her right arm through his left.

"Ready to go?" she asked, smiling.

"Dear God, yes. Let's go before they lock the doors."

They quickly crossed the street to the parking deck.

"It's going to be awful to try to park down there," Grayson moaned.

"Just leave your car here. I'll drive. You're not working tomorrow, right?"

She shook her head.

"So, worst case, Barbara or I bring you to get it tomorrow or Sunday. No big deal."

His car chirped as he unlocked the doors with his key fob.

"Someday you're going to have to teach me how to parallel park," she said as she slid into the passenger seat.

"In *your* car."

"Yeah, yeah, in my car."

Noah smiled at her out of the corner of his eye and started the engine. "Okay, honey, let's go eat cheeseburgers and make bad decisions."

The Duck and Coach was a hole-in-the-wall British-style pub that had sprung up north of Saint Joseph Hospital about a decade before Grayson had started her residency training. For the first year, the place struggled to bring in business. The owners had been considering closing up shop and cutting their losses before one overly-tired obstetrics resident realized that the initials for the place resembled a well-used surgical abbreviation from his department.

Overnight, the D&C—as it was now affectionately known—transformed into the go-to after-work hangout for the entire residency staff. It still kept its English pub-like decor but altered its menu to include cheeseburgers along with the fish and chips. There was always local beer on tap, a few select sports games on the televisions by the bar, and the staff always knew how to liven up a Friday night.

The place never got rowdy or obnoxious. Grayson couldn't remember ever seeing a bar fight, but that was likely due to the staff. Mitch and Kyle were the regular bartenders. There was easily 500 pounds of pure muscle between them, and they didn't tolerate anyone getting out of line.

Every year, there was an intern or two who tried to flex their muscles and get nasty. The last thing anyone wanted to see after a few drinks was Mitch or Kyle halfway over the bar and headed in their direction. Of course, they were both giant teddy bears once you got to know them. Mitch had a little boy and another on the way. Kyle was gay. Grayson had wanted to set Noah up with him for ages, and he kept putting her off.

One of these days...

Noah maneuvered his car into an impossibly small parking space, and they both headed directly for the front door. It was lively and warm inside, just like usual.

Mitch waved at them from behind the bar and pointed toward a booth in the back. Grayson narrowed her eyes at him, but Noah pushed her through the crowd toward it before she could say anything. She slid into one side and he took the opposite, sliding his coat off.

"I called ahead and asked him to save us a spot," he said without prompting.

"And you managed to sweet-talk him into doing that how exactly?" she asked.

"Never mind."

"Noah..."

"I'll tell you later," he grinned.

She rolled her eyes. He'd never tell her.

Carly, one of the waitresses, appeared at the side of their table. "What'll it be tonight, you two?" she asked sweetly, placing two cocktail napkins on the table.

"Blue Moon for me. Fat Tire seasonal for her. And keep 'em coming."

"Sure. You getting dinner tonight?" she twittered.

"Fish and chips for me. Gray?"

"Cheeseburger, medium. My usual."

"Give me a minute on the drinks. And the kitchen's behind, so give me a few extra minutes on the food."

"We're not going anywhere."

Carly smiled at Noah as she sauntered off. Most of the waitresses had schoolgirl crushes on him, even though they knew they were barking up the wrong tree.

"Well, how in the hell was your week?" Noah asked, plopping his head in between his hands.

For some reason, the move struck Grayson as incredibly hilarious, and she started laughing. Noah raised an eyebrow at her but didn't say anything. He just waited until her laughing fit faded away before opening his mouth again.

"I don't think things could've been much worse, honestly. You?"

"About the same."

"People need to quit being idiots."

"Yeah, but that keeps us both in business. I'd run naked across the field at a Broncos game if I could get just one of my patients to take their goddamned insulin on a regular basis."

"I'd become a compliant diabetic just to see that happen."

"I know." He grinned. "The gossip mill isn't helping, either."

"Tell me about it. If I hear one more conspiracy theory, I'm going to slap someone. What's your favorite so far?"

"It's a tie between a jealous wife on a rampage and underground poker debts gone bad."

"Neither of those make sense."

"You asked for my favorites, not the most plausible," he shrugged.

"True."

Carly placed their beers on the table, and Grayson took a long drink.

"What's yours?" Noah asked when she'd placed her glass back down.

"Love triangle gone bad. Supposedly, Lisa was sleeping with both of them. Porter found out, went ballistic, killed her, then Nelson, and then committed suicide."

Noah was silent for a minute. "That's actually not bad."

"Except that Porter was disgusting."

"So was Nelson, in his way."

"The more I hear about the both of them, the more I feel like getting sick."

"You've got some winners over in surgery too, you know."

"Oh, I know. But I've had almost five years to get used to them."

"Ha!"

The two friends drank in comfortable silence and watched the orderly chaos of the bar unfold around them. There was a group of family medicine interns at the end of the bar, clearly already a couple of shots in, digging into a plate of nachos. The obstetrics chiefs were at the other end, fascinated by something on an iPad they had positioned in the middle of their group.

The general surgery guys were taking up the majority of the long end of the bar with a few of the orthopedic residents speckled in between, all glued to ESPN, and cheering or booing at appropriate intervals. Mitch was talking intently to one of them. Most of the booths were taken.

The door was intermittently opening and closing as people came and left. The rush of cold air that came through each time was actually pleasant. Carly walked up to the table a few moments later with their food and two new beers on a large wooden tray.

"So, what're your plans for this weekend?" Noah's voice drifted across the table as they dug into their dinners.

"Now that the week from hell is over?"

He nodded.

"I haven't a clue. Babs has been going on and on about some benefit that she has in a couple of weeks. I think she wants to go shopping for a new dress."

"Just a dress?"

"When is it ever just a dress with Barbara?" she asked, sarcastically rolling her eyes.

"This is true." He nodded in agreement. "Big fancy thing?"

"I don't know. She makes it seem like it must be. Babs has some great dresses. If it's anything less than black tie, she already has something she can wear."

"Maybe she just wants a new dress."

"That's a distinct possibility."

"So, you're doomed to a weekend at the mall?"

"I wouldn't say doomed. She's fun to shop with. Besides, it's fun to dream about wearing some of that stuff. Makes me remember there's more to a wardrobe than scrubs and sweatpants."

"Someday, I'm going to make a ton of money and throw a big party just so I can see you all fancied up. You'd be a stunner."

Grayson blushed. Maybe it was just the alcohol catching up to her. "I wouldn't say no to a nice party," she said shyly. "And you need to stop exaggerating."

"Gray…"

"Don't, Noah." She shook her head at him and went back to eating her cheeseburger.

Noah went back to his fish and chips, a mild scowl on his face. He'd never been able to understand why her self-esteem seemed to take a nose dive every time the conversation got away from medicine. She could talk the talk and hang in there with the best of them in the hospital but once she walked outside of those walls, she was a different person.

He glanced up from his food. Grayson didn't have the Barbie-doll-come-to-life looks like Babs did, but she was pretty in her own right. Even eating a cheeseburger in a dive bar after a sixteen-hour shift, her hair pulled back in a messy bun, she looked good. Not to mention she was a great person. If he'd been straight, he would've put a ring on her finger a long time ago. But since life had had other plans, he'd settled for making her his best friend, and that seemed to be working out extremely well for both of them.

He snapped himself out of his head when a fry hit him square in the face.

"Hey, you gonna stare off into space or eat your dinner?" she asked, grinning at him from across the table.

"Sorry..." He shook his head to clear it. "I'm more tired than I thought I was."

"Let's just finish eating and go. I could do with an early night."

Twenty minutes later, the check was paid, and the two doctors were heading out the door into the chilly October night.

38

NOAH DROPPED HER off at her front door, blew a quick kiss to her out the passenger window, and headed off into the night.

Grayson waved back at him, heading inside after he'd turned the corner. She shucked out of her coat, kicked her shoes off, and walked into the living room. Barbara was bent over the coffee table painting her toenails.

"Hi, Babs," she said as she plopped onto the couch.

"You sound exhausted," she replied.

"I am exhausted. It's been the week from hell." She yawned. "How're you?"

"Oh, not too bad. Work was busy from my standards, but nothing like yours. I'm not even going to try to complain." She dipped the nailbrush into the color several times, then moved on to the next toe. "So, do you have to work tomorrow?" she asked, clearly building up to something.

"No. This is one of my weekends off. Oh, which reminds me, I need you to take me to get my car tomorrow."

"I wondered why you came in the front door."

"I didn't want to try parking at the D&C."

"Makes sense. We'll go tomorrow early."

"M'kay."

"By early I mean before noon, not five a.m."

Grayson rolled her eyes. "I figured that."

"Good. Just checking." Barbara finished painting the last toe and sat back a bit to look at the handiwork.

"Looks good."

Barbara wrinkled her nose. "I prefer the professionals do it, but I didn't have time." She twisted the cap back onto the nail polish. "Do you have a bunch of things you have to do this weekend?"

"No," Grayson shook her head. "I have to make a PowerPoint presentation for Grand Rounds, but that should only take a couple of hours."

"Is that that horrific lecture thing where someone has to stand at the front of the room and get yelled at for two hours straight?"

Grayson cringed. "Yeah, that's the one."

"When did you get assigned to that mess?"

"Today. Imagine my excitement," Grayson said sarcastically.

"Well, would you be interested in a little shopping trip? I need to find a dress for that benefit."

"What is this you're going to again? Noah was asking."

"It's for work. A whole bunch of ridiculously wealthy people get together in a room and raise money to help one charity or another once a year. My office works with the charity that won this year. I just have to show up with a smile on my face, according to my boss."

"And be your usual charming self."

"Well, obviously." She winked. "Please, Gray, come with me. You always pick out the best things."

"You do fine on your own."

"Yeah, but you do better and you do it faster. The quicker I find a dress, the sooner I can move on to shoes!" she squealed. "I'll throw in dinner if we're out too late."

"All right. I'll come with you." *Can't say no to dinner.*

"Great!" She jumped up and started hobbling toward the

kitchen on her heels, her pink-tipped toes pointed toward the ceiling. "Do you want some tea?"

"Sure, if you're making."

"What do you want?"

"Whatever you're having."

Babs came hobbling back several minutes later, teacups in hand. "So, what're you going to do your presentation on?"

"I have a few ideas," she said, softly blowing over the top of the steaming tea to cool it off. "The last few have been ridiculously boring. I need to come up with something just interesting enough to keep people awake, but not too interesting that they actually start asking me questions."

"Everybody comes to this?"

"All of the departments with residents, yeah. Next week is the all-department one. Which makes it even more fantastic." She rolled her eyes.

"Give 'em hell. You usually do."

"Can we change topics? I'd rather not focus on work until tomorrow morning."

"Okay, fine." Barbara smirked behind her teacup. "Run into Detective Hot 'n Handsome lately?"

Carter nearly spat her tea across the room. "Ex…excuse me?" she stuttered.

"You know who I'm talking about."

"Yes, I do," she hissed, the annoyance clear. "Why are you so focused on him? He's just one of the detectives assigned to Lisa's murder, that's all."

"And the other two that have happened since then."

"I really only care about the one, Babs."

"Well, me too, but you still haven't answered my question."

Grayson rolled her eyes again.

"C'mon…" Babs elbowed her in the ribs, grinning from ear to ear.

"Fine. Yes. I saw him last week," she replied tersely.

"Ooooh!"

Grayson scowled over the edge of her teacup. "I was having coffee with Noah, Babs. He and his partner happened to be in the oncology lobby at the same time."

"And…"

"And what? He asked me a few questions about that cardiologist that died, Dr. Nelson. His partner asked a few, too, if it matters. And then they left," she answered, annoyed.

"And…"

"And what?" she asked, throwing her hands up in the air. "What is it with you? You're acting like the guy is showing up at the hospital with roses and spouting sonnets. He's investigating a crime, for heaven's sake. Whatever Shakespearean romance you've concocted inside that head of yours is ludicrous."

"That's not what I heard."

Grayson narrowed her eyes. "That's not what you heard from who?"

Babs took a long sip of her tea. "Never mind," she smiled into her cup.

"Barbara Parker, you tell me right now or I'm not going shopping with you tomorrow."

"Then I'm not taking you to get your car."

"I'll walk."

The young blonde faked a frown and sad puppy-dog eyes. Her roommate continued to glare at her from across the couch. "Oh, you never let me have any fun."

"Fine, have your few hours of fun," Grayson replied. "I'm pretty sure I already know anyway. I'm exhausted. I'm going to bed."

"Okay. Night-night. I'll see you tomorrow morning."

As Grayson stumbled up the stairs in her exhausted stupor, she had a slight smile on her face. At least her roommate didn't know that a certain black coat was still hung up in her closet.

She'd have a freaking field day.

39

THREE HOURS AND a bacon burger later, Blake was back at his desk, watching Ryder and Harrison interact. The older man had been nice enough to call time on the catch-me-up session around noon and take them both out to a hole-in-the-wall sports bar for lunch. Nolan had to admit, the more he was around Logan, the more he liked the guy. And Ryder seemed to be in a better mood.

"Well, Ryder, you couldn't pick something easy for me to help you with, like a drug cartel, could you?" Logan joked.

"Sorry. I'll remember that for next time." Gabriel smirked.

"So, what now? It sounds like you've hit a wall."

"Yeah, kind of," Nolan chimed in when he saw his partner's face drop. "We're supposed to catch up with the M.E. later on today to see if she's come up with anything. You've gotta admit, the pickings are slim."

"You're sure they're connected?"

"Three docs dead from the same hospital like this? Yeah. After all that, you don't?"

"Nah, didn't say that," he joked. "Just checking."

The phone on Ryder's desk rang, and he picked it up.

Harrison turned his back on his former partner and leaned over toward Blake. "Tell me the truth. Is he sleeping?"

Nolan's eyebrows shot up in surprise, but he quickly recovered and shook his head. "I don't think so."

"I figured."

"How'd you know?"

"He didn't sleep much when we had a bad case in narcotics, either. I worried about him then. Still do," he confessed.

Blake opened his mouth to reply, but a loud cough from the opposite desk stopped him. Ryder was glaring at them.

"If you two are quite finished gossiping…"

"You've solved the case!" Logan joked, throwing his arms up in the air in mock celebration.

"No, asshole. That was Pelton. She wants us downstairs. Now."

"She's found something?" Blake asked as he stood.

"She just said to come down. I didn't push it," Ryder replied, gathering up his binder.

"Good call, knowing you."

"Shut up, Blake."

"Get your ass up, Ryder. The closest thing you have to a girlfriend is calling," he teased. He was rewarded with a pen being tossed at his head.

"Wait…you're screwing the M.E.?" Harrison wrinkled his forehead. "Isn't she married?"

"Don't listen to a goddamned word he says, Logan," Gabriel replied as he headed toward the elevators.

Harrison looked over at Blake, silently asking the question again.

"No, it was a joke. He spends too much time here to be seeing someone. But recently…"

"What?" Logan's eyebrows raised up, a fine addition to the smirk developing on his face.

"Hey! I'm not holding this goddamned thing all day!" Ryder called out from the other end of the hall.

Blake waved him off. "Remind me to tell you later, man."

40

DR. CARLA PELTON was stewing at her desk when the three detectives walked into her office. Normally, she loved her job, despite the long hours and the pesky detectives she fended off on a daily basis. It was becoming harder and harder to romanticize things when she'd been shoulder-deep in a three hundred-plus-pound corpse for the third time in as many days.

She brushed her platinum blonde hair out of her face and rounded her desk in a huff. The extra twenty pounds she still needed to lose after baby number two jiggled underneath her scrubs as she walked.

"Detectives," she said, coolly eyeing up Harrison in her peripheral vision.

"Carla, meet Logan Harrison, on loan from narcotics," Blake replied.

Logan flashed his trademark smile and stuck his hand out. She took it.

"We've met before, long time ago. Firm grip," he remarked.

"You, too," she quipped.

Carla pushed past them and headed around the corner, back toward her exam room. Ryder and Nolan followed, with Harrison not far behind. She shed her white lab coat and grabbed a pair of latex gloves from a box by the door.

Ryder set his binder down on a side table and grabbed a pair for himself. Nolan and Harrison kept their hands shoved in their pockets.

"I see you take after Nolan, Detective Harrison," she said with a grin.

Ryder smirked as he snapped on his gloves and approached the body on the table.

Nolan blushed. Harrison just gave all of them a confused look.

She rolled her eyes at all three of them. "Never mind. Look, you wanted an update on this chaos you've sent down here, so here it is. Lisa Oakes. I have a cause of death for you," she said, picking up the first of several manila files from a metal table.

"Oh?" Blake raised his eyebrows. "What took so long?"

"Send-out blood levels for tox. Twice. And don't complain. These were rushed." She flipped open the file, then tossed it down on the table in front of them. "Turns out, she overdosed."

"On what?" Ryder asked.

"A cocktail of fentanyl, versed, and dilaudid. All quick-acting, all exceptionally strong, especially the fentanyl. Quick on, quick off. They're hard to detect in the blood after a certain period of time but thankfully, pharmacology gives us a wonderful property called a drug's half-life. Working back in time, I can tell you roughly how much she had in her system at the time she died."

"And?"

"The dilaudid alone would have put her at risk, but the fentanyl and versed pushed her over the edge. The sedative effects would have knocked her out within a few minutes, and the respiratory depression that followed wouldn't have resolved without a whopping dose of narcan and some time on a ventilator."

"So, she got knocked out with drugs, then stopped breathing?" Logan scowled.

Carla nodded.

"Would she have been in pain?" Ryder asked.

"No. I don't think there's any way she would have known what was going on. She would have drifted off to sleep very quickly. People used to overdose on morphine to commit suicide if they had access to the drug. Some states in this country have authorized euthanasia to one degree or another, and cocktails very similar to this are used to do it. All in all, not the worst way to go, if I'm picking between the three vics you've sent me."

"So, it was a suicide? She took her drugs herself?" Blake asked.

"No, I highly doubt it." She took a few photos out of the file and spread them out on the table. "When I got the results back, I went over my pictures again. I found this." She pointed to a small black dot along the young girl's right clavicle. "It was hidden so well, I almost missed it. It's a needle mark."

"Why in the hell does she have a needle mark in her shoulder?" Harrison asked, picking up the photo to get a closer look.

"It's a good spot," she replied. "Just below your clavicle is your subclavian vein. It's a beeline to the heart. It's used for IV access in critically ill patients all the time in the hospital. It's big, high-volume flow, and relatively easy to hit if you know what you're doing. It would have made her react to the medications that much quicker. One big shot and bam—lights out."

"So, whoever did this to her is a doc?" Harrison asked, handing the photo back to her.

Carla tossed her hair and shrugged. "That's for you to find out, detective. But if you're asking me if only physicians could hit this vein, the answer is no. Anyone with even a basic knowledge of anatomy can do it. Hell, there's a good cohort of chronic drug abusers who know how to hit it."

"Excuse me?" Nolan balked.

"They blow out their peripheral veins, so they only have two options: shoot up in the subclavian or the jugular." She shrugged.

"Lovely," he replied, shaking his head. "You don't think she could've done this to herself?"

"Most likely not. She was right-handed, so it would have been easier to go for her left side. But it's a shitty angle and she would've had to do it in front of a mirror; turning your neck to watch what you're doing changes the anatomy. I'd say somebody did this to her."

"Anything else?" Ryder asked.

"No. Besides that one puncture mark, she's clean. I'll look over everything again to be sure. She's not a chronic user. That's it."

"Anything new with Nelson, the cardiologist?"

She opened a second file. "His blood alcohol level was a little elevated, but I found white wine in his stomach along with what was left of his dinner, so no surprise there...." Her voice trailed off as she scanned her notes. "Well, well, this is interesting. I guess I was right."

"Huh?" Nolan wrinkled his forehead.

"It seems our dear doctor had a little visitor."

Ryder took the file, nearly ripping it right out of Pelton's hands. She scowled at him but didn't move to take it back.

"Syphilis?" he read aloud.

"I doubt he knew he had it. I saw a few abnormalities on routine x-rays. It had spread to his spine. Dr. Nelson was not going to be practicing medicine much longer at the rate he was going. With cirrhosis of the liver on top of it...yikes."

"Do we need to notify anyone?"

"I'll take care of all that, but yes," she replied.

"Anything else on him?"

"Not unless you brought his missing parts with you."

"Nope," Blake chuckled. "They're still missing."

"Then no."

Ryder leaned back against one of the empty gurneys resting in the corner. "What about our victim from this week? Porter."

"Ugh," she groaned. "You guys owe me for this one. I'm serious. I haven't had one this bad in a while."

Ryder smirked. "We aim to please at Major Crimes, Dr. Pelton."

"Can it, Ryder," she hissed. "You've had me shoulder-deep in this body for days."

"Will you two lovebirds stop bickering and get on with it already?" Blake snapped.

"Calm down, detective," she soothed. "Look, I haven't had time to get toxicology or tissue samples back, but here's what I do have. The report from the scene said he was blue and coming out of rigor in the church, but that doesn't make sense. Body temp puts his time of death only a few hours before you showed up. "

"So, he shouldn't have been in rigor yet, let alone coming out of it," Ryder stated.

"Right. I got a feeling something was off, so I came in on Sunday to do the prelim exam myself. He was extremely floppy. So, I did the jumpstart test."

"Which is?" Harrison asked, eyebrow raised.

"I shocked him."

"Huh?" Nolan squinted in confusion.

"I shocked him," she repeated, stone-faced.

"Still not understanding, doc," Logan said.

"I took my defibrillator out of my car, charged it, and shocked him. Nothing happened."

"Well duh, he was dead. What did you expect him to do, wake up and start singing?" Logan asked sarcastically.

"No. I expected his muscle fibers, which would have been starved of oxygen but still viable, to jump at the electric impulse. Nothing. Not one muscle fired. So, I got suspicious."

"Of?" Ryder questioned.

"Botulism."

Blake and Logan looked at each other and shrugged. Ryder was grinning.

"Well, clearly Wonder Boy over there understands what's going on. As usual. Wanna fill in the rest of us, Carla?" Blake grumbled.

"Not until I confirm that I'm right. I'll let you know in a few days. Now shoo…out of my room. I have work to do."

The detectives made a hasty exit and piled into the elevator without another word.

"You wanna fill us in there, Gabe?" Logan mumbled after the doors closed.

"It's a toxin secreted by clostridium bacteria. If ingested, it can cause a flaccid paralysis. Your arms and legs don't work, but more importantly, neither does your diaphragm. You can't breathe. Even with the best of medical care, you can stay on a ventilator for weeks to months."

"And if you don't get treatment?"

"You die. It doesn't take much. Botulinum toxin is one of the most potent toxins known to man. Coincidentally, it's the main ingredient in Botox."

"Botox," Harrison chuckled. "That crap women are putting in their faces to hide wrinkles?"

"One and the same. Except it doesn't hide wrinkles. It just prevents you from being able to move the muscles in your forehead that cause wrinkles in the first place."

"Thank God I'm not a woman."

"Amen to that," Nolan seconded.

"So, what now?" Logan asked as they exited the elevator and headed back toward the desks.

Nolan plopped into his chair and Logan leaned up against the side of his desk. Ryder paused beside him, blankly staring at the desk surface.

"Why don't you two take off?" he said suddenly, grabbing a few books from his desk and putting them into his messenger bag.

"And you'll be…?" Harrison asked.

"I have some reading to do," he said vaguely.

"Ryder…"

"I'll see you both tomorrow." He abruptly walked away, passed up the elevator, and headed for the stairs. Both Nolan and Logan stared after him.

"Well, that's a classic Ryder mood swing. Haven't seen one of those in a while," Logan chuckled.

"Oh good, so it's not just me?" Nolan replied.

"No, it's not just you. When he gets something in his head…"

"Yeah, I know. Just get out of the way."

Harrison looked at his watch. "Look, I've gotta run by the narc unit and check in on a few things. Unofficially, of course." He grinned.

"I thought you were on loan to us."

"I am. But that's left my partner with all the heavy lifting and I feel for the guy. Worked it out with my captain so I can work through this weekend to get him caught up before I officially become all highbrow with you guys."

"Makes sense."

"I'll be in touch. If he doesn't get himself out of the house by Sunday, promise me you'll kick his ass."

"Sure thing."

"See ya!" Logan waved over his head as he walked toward the elevator.

Nolan smiled and started rummaging around in one of the drawers for his car keys.

41

BRIGHT AND EARLY Saturday morning, Grayson padded down the stairs with her laptop tucked underneath her right arm and put a pot of coffee on in the kitchen. She was dreading having to put the Grand Rounds presentation together, but it was only going to be worse if she did it at the last minute. She knew she could put most of it together off the top of her head; it was just going to be mind-numbing and tedious.

The coffeepot beeped in no time, and she poured herself a cup, heavy on the cream.

"All right," she whispered to the computer screen, "let's make up something at least marginally entertaining."

True to her word, Babs was up early. At least, early for her. She took Grayson up to the hospital to pick up her car well before noon. It was still safe and sound in the parking lot. They dropped it off back at the house, then drove down into Cherry Creek for their day of shopping. Well, technically, it was Barbara's day of shopping and Grayson's day of following her around the mall.

The first two boutiques they visited were a complete waste of time, so they switched gears and went into Saks Fifth Avenue, hoping for a larger selection.

"Ugh, this is ridiculous. I'm never going to find anything that doesn't make me look fifty years old!" Babs whined, weaving her way through racks full of embellished evening wear.

"You do realize that there's no possible way, short of a mask and very good stage makeup, to make you look fifty, right?" Grayson trailed behind her.

"Look at this!" Babs yanked a dress off the rack and held it up.

"What?"

"It has shoulder pads!"

"Aren't those in right now or something?" Grayson chuckled under her breath.

"Gray, shoulder pads haven't been in since the eighties, and even then, there were limits." Barbara rolled her eyes.

"Have I suggested you wear shoulder pads?"

"No. But they're everywhere!"

"Well, maybe it's because you dragged me into the sixty-and-older section of the store," Grayson replied. "Stop panicking and turn around."

"Oh, thank God!" Babs squealed, lunging at a slinky black Calvin Klein gown.

Grayson just smiled and shook her head. "Here, give me your coffee before you spill it on something."

Babs handed over her iced latte, never taking her eyes off the rack in front of her. "What do you think of this?" she asked, holding up a neon-pink, one-shoulder gown with rhinestones around the neckline.

"Eh. A little loud for a benefit, don't you think, Barbie?"

"Oh, shut up," Babs frowned, putting it back on the rack.

"If you like the cut, try the red one behind it," Grayson replied, moving around her friend toward another rack.

"Oooooh," she cooed, pulling the suggested garment off the rack in the proper size. "I like this one. And this one..." she said, handing over another red dress. "And I like this one even more," Babs nodded, taking it and holding it up against her.

"I thought you might."

They spent forty minutes scavenging the department before Barbara finally relented and headed back to the fitting rooms. Grayson sat down in a tall wingback chair by the 270-degree full-length mirrors while her roommate went back to change.

Barbara came out in a bright blue dress and stepped up to the mirror. "What do you think?" she asked, looking hopefully at Grayson's reflection in the mirror. "You don't like it," she moaned when she saw Grayson's facial expression in the glass.

"No, I don't."

"What's wrong with it?

"It just looks cheap."

"Really? It does?" Babs spun around in a circle, trying to get a better look at herself.

Grayson nodded. "Yeah…I don't know. It just looks like a prom dress you could pick up at a thrift store. The fabric doesn't fall right, and the strap needs to be taken in."

"All right, all right. Next." She hurried back into the dressing room and changed into the black Calvin Klein dress.

"Well?" she asked, admiring herself.

"Better. You'll need to do something to accessorize it, though, or you're going to look like a blonde Morticia Addams."

"Accessories are so not a problem. You know me."

"I do." Grayson smiled. "We'll keep that one in mind. Next."

Several moments later, Barbara was back out in the second red dress. "What about this one?"

"Now that I like. It's got color to it, and the fit is incredible."

Babs spent a few minutes admiring herself in front of the mirror, turning one way and then the other, while Grayson checked her phone. "So, when am I going to get you in something like this?" she asked, admiring the slit up the back.

Grayson's eyes shot up. "In that? Um, don't take this the wrong way, but never."

"Why not?"

"Apart from the fact it's wrong for my skin tone and three sizes too small?"

"Yeah."

"I have absolutely nowhere to wear it, Babs."

"You'd look hot."

"I don't do hot, Babs. That's your department," she said as she looked back down at her phone and took a drink of her coffee.

"Oh, that's total crap."

"Barbara..."

"What? I'm just saying..."

"Whatever you're thinking, don't. Go put another dress on," she snapped.

"Fine," she scowled, turning away from the mirror and stalking down the hall.

Babs pulled off the red dress inside the changing room, threw it onto the floor, and reached for one with a large floral print.

She's so damned stubborn!

Barbara knew Grayson would follow her around the mall all day and wouldn't take a second to look at something for herself. Her roommate wore the equivalent of shapeless green pajamas to work in a department with fifteen raunchy guys and had a slight dent in her hair from putting it up in the same ponytail every day. Before Lisa's funeral, she couldn't remember the last time she'd seen her in a dress. It made her furious.

"Are you going to grace me with your presence at some point?" came her roommate's voice from outside the door.

Shit.

She was half naked, staring off into space. "I'm coming," she called back.

She was halfway up to the mirror when Grayson burst out laughing.

"What?" Barbara wrinkled her nose.

"Ummm, hon, you've got the dress on backward. It's a high neck-low back, not a recreation of JLo's Grammy look," she giggled.

"Oh, shit!"

"Just take it off," Grayson cackled, holding her ribcage. "You look like walking wallpaper in that thing anyway. Next!"

They stopped for a late lunch, then headed back out into the mall. They hadn't had much luck.

Grayson inwardly groaned at the prospect of spending her entire Saturday trailing behind her roommate, but it was better than moping around the house. They flew through a few more boutiques and another department store before Barbara insisted on a second coffee. They were standing in line when it suddenly dawned on Grayson that the blonde had some 'fessing up to do.

"So, you've had your Saturday of shopping."

"We're not done yet, Gray. I don't even have a dress, let alone shoes."

"I know that. Stop worrying. We'll find something. I'm talking about what you said last night."

Babs scrunched her nose up in mock confusion. "Hmmm?"

"It's time. Spill it."

"I don't know what you're talking about."

"Spill or I'm leaving."

"You wouldn't."

"Try me," she countered.

Babs opened her mouth to say something, then shut it. Grayson smiled. It was very hard to silence the sarcastic side of Barbara Parker.

"Just let me order first."

"Fine."

They waited around for almost ten minutes before the fancy latte was complete. Barbara grabbed the paper cup from the pickup counter and took off toward Nordstrom without a word.

Grayson followed quickly behind her. "Barbara...now."

"All right, Miss Bossy-pants. What do you want to know?"

"I want to know A, what's going on inside that head of yours so I can tell you you're insane, and B, who's reinforcing this madness so I can kill them."

"Easy answer first," she replied with a grin. "Noah." Barbara scampered into Nordstrom, cackling like a hyena, leaving Grayson scowling in the entrance to the store.

What the hell? What nonsense is Noah feeding her now?

She shook herself out of it and walked toward the escalators. Babs was in the center of the department, holding out a sky-blue ball gown and examining the slit in the skirt.

"Welcome back," she chuckled.

"Shut up," Grayson seethed. "What nonsense has he been telling you now?"

"About you?"

"Yes, about me," she rolled her eyes, exasperated.

"Oh, not much," Barbara singsonged. "Just that you have a very attractive secret admirer."

"Oooo, yay, Justin Bieber..." Grayson moaned sarcastically.

"No, and stop being so sarcastic. Bieber is a creep."

"Babs..."

The tall blonde leaned down close to her friend's right ear and whispered, "It's that detective." She grinned like a Cheshire cat and nearly skipped over to the next wall filled with dresses.

"What?"

"That's what he told me," she confessed, shrugging. "And honestly, from the story he told me, I agree. What do you think of this one?" She held up a dark gray dress and stood up on her toes to mimic wearing heels.

"It's fine," Grayson waved her hand in dismissal. "And you agree with what, specifically?"

"That he likes you!"

"Based on what? You've never met the man."

Oh, this conversation is ridiculous!

"No, but I did interrupt a little something-something at that church and a little British birdie told me about that coffee run-in at the hospital."

"*I* told you about that," Grayson hissed, ducking her head.

"...over a week later." Barbara stuck out her tongue at her roommate, who was looking aimlessly through a rack of Vera Wang. "He called me that day and told me all about it. Apparently, Detective Hot Stuff was staring at you from across the room the whole time you two were there. Like, *intensely.*"

"Probably trying to figure out if I'm a serial killer or something." *He was staring at me?*

"Huh? No, you know what, never mind. That's another put-down on yourself. I've had enough of that shit today."

Barbara put the dresses she had been carrying down over a nearby chair and grabbed Grayson by the shoulders.

"Listen up. I'm sick and tired of you acting like you're a second-class human. You're smart, gorgeous, and a to-die-for catch. Stop rolling your eyes at me!" she snapped, catching Grayson mid-eye-roll. "Now, get your butt in gear and find me something fabulous."

Babs nodded emphatically to solidify her point, and then picked up her dresses again. As her roommate stalked off toward the dressing rooms, Grayson stood rooted to the ground, shaking her head.

Both of my best friends have gone completely insane. Great.

She began wandering around the racks of ridiculously expensive eveningwear, lost inside her own head. They had to be crazy, the both of them. But the thought of him staring at her from across the room, just at her...

Why am I breathing so fast?

She pulled her phone out of her purse, picked out Noah's number and typed a quick text message.

I'm going to track you down and murder you was probably not the best thing to say to him, considering recent events, but her choice of words conveyed the same meaning.

42

SUNDAY MORNING, GRAYSON piled herself back into Barbara's car, and the pair headed back to Cherry Creek.

The sun was shining. The air was cool and crisp. She would have given anything to just lie in bed with the window open and read a book. Instead, Babs had knocked on her bedroom door before nine a.m., all dressed up in her new gown, babbling about accessories and shoes and completely insistent on going back for a second round.

"So, explain to me again exactly what it is we're looking for?"

"In short?"

"Yes, please."

"Sky-high heels and bling." Babs grinned from behind the wheel.

"Lovely."

"Oh, you'll love it. Hush."

"No more life lessons today, right?" Grayson looked over at her roommate hesitantly, referring to the confrontation in Nordstrom yesterday afternoon.

"Eh, I haven't decided yet." Babs looked back at her and grinned. "You let Noah have it last night, didn't you?"

"I should have let you both have it." Grayson scowled.

"You're so cranky this morning," she countered.

"I'm sorry."

"Don't be. I should've gotten you drunk before I said all that stuff."

"A glass of wine would've helped."

Babs pulled the car over and parallel parked on a side street in North Cherry Creek, the trendy neighborhood and outside shopping district just north of the mall itself.

Grayson looked around, confused. "What're we doing out here?"

"I can't handle another day stuck inside the mall. Ick," Babs said, wrinkling her nose as she climbed out of the car. "Besides, you know, I've gotta find something unique to go with that dress."

In the end, she had gone with a pale pink strapless dress with a vampy purple lace overlay. It was gorgeous, but still a tad bit understated for her.

Grayson sighed, got out of the passenger side, and squinted her eyes against the sun.

"C'mon." Babs grabbed her by the arm and started dragging her toward the nearest corner. "I'll get you a coffee, sweetie."

———

Three hours later, Grayson was biding her time in yet another eclectic boutique, absentmindedly looking at the racks of clothing. Classic white and black pieces were chicly paired with camel and gunmetal gray accents. If she could have had a wardrobe built from one store, this would've been it. Of course, the fact that a T-shirt cost well over a hundred dollars meant that was a tad unrealistic, but still…a girl could dream.

Babs was at the other side of the store, dripping in jewelry and staring into a mirror, a saleswoman babbling away on either side of her. Grayson smiled at the sight. It really was like dressing a live Barbie doll.

She ambled around the store, ending up at a jewelry case pressed against the back wall. In the upper right-hand corner, a pair of earrings sparkled back at her. There was no way she could possibly afford them, but they were beautiful. Square emerald-green studs were turned forty-five degrees on edge and attached to substantial teardrops of the same color. They were classic, elegant, and exceptionally decadent. Way out of her league.

"Something I can help you with, dear?" Out of nowhere, an elderly saleswoman had materialized beside her.

"Oh, no, I was just…" She glanced back at the case.

"The green ones on the right?" the saleswoman asked, sticking a key into the lock.

"Really, that's not necessary," she tried again.

"Oh, don't worry, honey. It's always okay to look," the woman smiled sweetly and unhooked the first earring from its stand. "Here, try them on."

Grayson took the earring from her hand and put it on, followed by the second. In the interim, the saleswoman found an antique-looking hand mirror.

"Here. Take a look."

She smiled shyly and accepted the mirror, pushing some of her hair behind her right ear. Much to her own chagrin, she smiled at her reflection.

They actually look…

"Holy shit, Gray! Look at you!" Babs squealed, coming up behind her in the mirror.

Grayson immediately put the mirror facedown on the counter.

"Oh no you don't!" Babs said, steering her roommate toward a full-length mirror. "Those look awesome. You have to buy them."

"I can't afford these," she whispered, hastily reaching up to take them off. She handed the set back to the saleswoman. "Thank you," she murmured quietly. Her face was flaming red.

"Anytime, sweetie." The elderly woman smiled back.

"Besides, we're looking for you," Grayson said, changing topics and plastering a fake smile on her face for her roommate. "Now, show me what you found to go with your dress."

Barbara glared as Grayson steered her back toward the front of the store.

Another twenty minutes later and they were out on the street, having finally secured the perfect jewelry to accent the equally perfect dress. Barbara had her arm linked in her roommate's and was grinning ear to ear.

"Thanks for coming, Gray."

"No problem."

"You think I got the right stuff?"

"Of course. You'll look great."

"Thanks. Now, let's go find somewhere yummy for lunch. I'm starving."

43

NOLAN SLAMMED HIS cell phone onto the console of his Subaru and swore under his breath. Three calls straight to voicemail and no answer yesterday. Another two today.

Damn that jackass. His phone had better be at the bottom of a fucking lake or he'd better be dead.

Those were the only two explanations he was going to accept today. It was 11:30 on a Sunday, the first time in three weeks they hadn't been forced to go to a murder scene before dawn, and the day was already ruined.

He'd just been through the visit from hell with his ex-wife, who was now on boyfriend number four. The fact that the bitch was trying to take away some of his visitation weekends wasn't helping his mood. Add on a phone call from a pissed-off chief of detectives, and he was just about ready to say the hell with everybody.

He pulled up to the front of Ryder's building and tossed his keys to the concierge.

"I won't be long, Jack," he mumbled.

The elderly man caught the keys swiftly, placed them on his front counter, and nodded.

Nolan liked the old timer. Jack liked football. He knew his bourbon. He always wanted to see the most recent pictures of his two girls. Blake had chatted with him a few times over the years when he'd been waiting for his partner to come down.

Nolan stepped into the elevator and aggressively hit the number for his partner's floor. "He'd better be dead," he mumbled repeatedly under his breath.

The doors opened onto a stark white hallway.

It's too fucking clean here.

He marched down the hall to the last door on the right and started banging away.

"Ryder? Ryder! Open the goddamned door! I mean it."

It took a full minute, but eventually, he heard the deadbolt slide, and the door cracked open. Nolan shoved himself into the apartment.

"Blake, what the…" a sleep-heavy voice began.

"Don't fucking start, Ryder. I've been calling you for two days. What the fuck have you been doing?"

When he didn't get an immediate response, Blake took a minute to take stock of his partner's apartment.

The usually spotless living room had textbooks, papers, and beer bottles strewn all over the place. There was an empty pizza box on the counter in the kitchen and an open bottle of very good scotch next to it. He frowned, noting how much was missing from the bottle, then turned back around to take a better look at his partner. Ryder was in a pair of sweatpants, no shirt, hair a mess and bags under his eyes. From the looks of things, he'd been asleep on the couch.

"You know what? Never mind. Why didn't you pick up your phone?"

His partner looked down at the floor sheepishly. "I probably didn't remember to charge it."

Nolan smirked and shook his head. "You're an idiot."

"Thanks for the reminder. Why are you here?"

"I was worried about you, you ass."

Ryder's eyebrows rose. "Why?"

"Because that's what I do." He rolled his eyes. "Frequently. It's what I do when you're moody and don't pick up the phone." He sat down on the gray sofa and picked up a textbook.

"*Modern Interpretations of Body Disfigurement: The Signature of a Serial Killer,*" he quoted from the first page. "This seems like some light bedtime reading."

"For me, yes." Ryder shrugged and leaned back against the bar. "What's wrong with you?" he asked.

"Nothing."

"You saw Miranda today, didn't you?"

"Didn't we have an agreement that you wouldn't fucking profile me when I'm angry?" Nolan snapped.

"Yes. Are you angry?"

"You can't tell?"

"Sorry." Gabriel lifted his palm to his forehead, his telltale trying to massage away the hangover throbbing behind his eyes.

"Did you get anywhere with all this?" Nolan asked, softening his voice and looking around the room.

Ryder dropped his eyes to the floor. "No." He looked up. "Did you come here to tell me there's another body?"

"No," Blake smiled. "I came to make good on a promise to your old partner."

"What?" Ryder eyed his partner warily.

"Never mind. Just go get dressed. We're going to lunch."

"I'm not..."

"I don't care if you're not hungry. You're going to get dressed, clean up this mess, and then come out to lunch. I'm hungry and pissed off and not eating alone. You're coming with me."

Ryder reluctantly headed back toward his bedroom and turned on the shower. He felt like hell, but he wasn't about to piss off his partner anymore. His partner's ex, Miranda, was a sociopathic piece of work. There was no need for him to personally add to his partner's Sunday misery.

Thirty minutes later, he emerged dressed in a black T-shirt and jeans.

"Put a coat on. It's cold outside." Nolan motioned toward the coat rack.

"Thanks, Mom," Ryder replied, instead grabbing a black cashmere sweater from the back of a barstool.

He tucked his keys in his pocket, grabbed his halfway-charged phone from the counter, and followed his partner out the door.

44

BLAKE WAVED TO Jack as he pulled away from Spire and maneuvered his car onto Speer Boulevard. The breeze through the open window felt good and so did the warm sunshine. Days with this kind of weather were numbered. Pretty soon, parkas and scarves would become mandatory, even in the city. He was determined to enjoy the good weather while he could.

"Where are you dragging me off to?" Ryder asked, staring out his own partially-open window.

"Guess."

"Blake, I'm really not in the mood."

"You're never in the mood."

"We could've just walked around the corner from my apartment to get lunch."

"We do that when *you* choose where we eat, and I usually end up eating something I can't pronounce. Today we're going somewhere I want to go."

"Fantastic."

"Oh, shut up and be happy. You're getting lunch and we're not stuck at a damned crime scene."

Blake waited for another snarky remark from the passenger seat. When he didn't get one, he flashed a sideways glance at Ryder. The smile started fading from his face. "Please don't tell me you'd rather be at a crime scene, Ryder."

Gabriel looked like he wanted to say something but changed his mind and kept staring silently out the passenger window.

Nolan shook his head. "Dear God, you've got to be kidding me."

"I'm not saying I want another victim. It just bothers me."

"That we don't have another one?"

"Yes," he confessed. "Last week, I was so sure that they were all connected. We had a third victim. Third Sunday. It made sense. It was supposed to come together. But I...I still can't connect them. If...if we don't get a fourth body, then where are we?"

"Back to three half-connected crimes with no leads," Blake groaned.

"Exactly."

"Well, shit. Way to ruin my Sunday, partner."

"In my defense, it didn't seem to be going all that well when you burst into my apartment."

"Shut up." Nolan steadily maneuvered through traffic and the intermittent swarms of pedestrians. It was busier than he'd expected for a Sunday. Everybody had decided to get out and enjoy the weather.

He made two passes around the main block before giving up and heading north a few streets to park in a residential district. The overgrown trees leaned over the street under the weight of their branches, bright reds, and oranges intermixed with yellows and small patches of brown. The multimillion-dollar townhouses were nearly hidden behind them. With the breeze, leaves were continuously falling down to the pavement. Blake hit his key fob, and the car doors locked.

"Well, if we have to walk, at least it's a nice day," he mused as he started down the sidewalk.

Ryder nodded silently and fell into step beside him.

So much for small talk.

"You wanna tell me about the shit you had strewn around your apartment?" he asked, switching topics to get his partner out of his shell.

"No, I…well…you don't want to know about some of that stuff…"

"I'm your partner, Gabe. If you need a sounding board, go ahead. I'm usually not much help, but it can't hurt."

"You don't want to talk about your morning with your ex?"

"I'd rather forget all about it, asshole," he scowled, then softened. "Nice attempt at an evasive maneuver, buddy, but it's not gonna work."

Ryder swore under his breath as they rounded the corner.

"All right. I went digging into some old cold cases. Ones where the bodies kept piling up before anybody connected them. Nothing specifically fits our victims, but each case ultimately had one small thread that connected all the victims. Line of work, hair color, birth date. Something."

"Our vics all share place and line of work."

"Place, yes. Line of work, kind of."

"You've lost me. They're all doctors."

"Lisa Oakes was a resident, a doctor in training. Porter was a fellow. More advanced, but still technically in training. Nelson was an attending with ten years of practice under his belt. Lisa was a general surgeon. Porter was a gastroenterologist. Nelson was a cardiologist. Oakes was a DO; the others were MDs."

"What's the difference?"

"Two different schools of thought," he replied as they crossed onto 3rd Street. "MDs are 'traditional' doctors. DOs are physicians who tend to have a more holistic approach to things. They were originally trained to be general practitioners and family docs. That's changed. There are DO neurosurgeons now."

"Learn something new every day from you, don't I?"

"I try to broaden your horizons, Blake."

"Continue broadening. So being a doctor might not be the connection. Then what is?"

"They all practice at the same hospital. It's the only exposure they all have in common."

"So, we're looking for somebody at the hospital?"

"Or somehow associated with it. A patient, maybe, or hospital employee."

"Please don't tell me we have to start pulling common patients," Blake groaned.

"It might be the only avenue we have left to pursue."

"Seriously. Sunday just keeps getting better and better," Nolan groused as he opened the door to their destination and followed his partner inside.

The Cherry Cricket was a popular neighborhood hangout in the North Cherry Creek shopping district. Part dive bar, part burger joint, it was always packed full and lively. If you lived, worked, or shopped in the neighborhood with any frequency, you'd had a meal or two at the Cricket. Today was no exception. There were already a few parties waiting to be seated.

Damn, Nolan thought to himself as he walked up to the hostess.

"Can I help you?" the pretty brunette asked.

"Yeah, uh, what's the wait time for a table for two?"

"Ummm…" she looked down at her seating chart. "If you want inside, it'll be about a half hour."

"And outside?" *Probably double that.*

"Outside…I can seat you right now, actually." She smiled.

"We'll take it."

He motioned to his partner, who begrudgingly followed him outside to a square metal table near the end of the patio. It was a patio in name only; it was just a concrete extension of the restaurant that bordered up on the main street. There were Christmas lights wrapped around the guard railing that separated the diners from the pedestrians. An overhanging green awning provided some shade.

The hostess set their menus down, gave Gabriel a once-over, and disappeared back into the restaurant. He sat down in a huff, while Nolan just smiled.

"What?" he snapped.

"Do you ever even notice when a cute girl checks you out?"

"She's a child, Blake. She can't be over twenty."

"Still, though. You're a detective and completely oblivious."

Ryder rolled his eyes at his partner and opened the menu. After a few minutes, a kid with scruffy blond hair who looked younger than the hostess introduced himself as Tim, their waiter. Blake ordered a beer; Ryder hesitated momentarily before following suit. The kid scampered away toward the bar.

"We're not on call, buddy. It's okay to have a beer with lunch."

"Yeah, I just…" he trailed off.

"You keep thinking we're going to get called in."

He nodded.

"Look, it's noon. Everybody's already been to church. Some places have had a second service by now. If there'd been a body to deal with, we would've gotten a call by now. Maybe the guy took the week off. Who knows? Just let it go."

Ryder nodded and refocused on his menu. Tim returned with their drinks, and they ordered. Within minutes, their food was steaming in red plastic baskets in front of them.

"I gotta hand it to this place," Nolan said when he looked at the size of his meal, "they know how to put out a good burger."

His partner nodded in silent agreement, and they both dug into their food. Ryder was hungrier than he'd thought, and the burger was surprisingly quite good. The two partners ate in companionable silence, stopping every now and again to lean back, drink some beer, and watch the pedestrians go by.

During one such pause, Nolan did a double-take. At first, he'd just noticed the leggy blonde walking toward them on the same side of the street, talking animatedly to her shopping companion. She had several bags draped over one arm, all from expensive boutiques nearby.

Too rich for my blood, but it never hurts to look.

He was prepared to just sit back and appreciate the view, but then the brunette on her left looked up from the sidewalk and took off her sunglasses.

Nolan smiled and nonchalantly took another swig of his beer.

Aw, hell, now this could get interesting.

45

BABS STRODE GRACEFULLY up 3rd Street, shopping bags slung onto her right arm, the other linked with Grayson's. The weather was gorgeous. She'd found her shoes and all of the accessories to go with her dress, not to mention a few extras. All in all, a damn good morning. Now she had to find a good spot for lunch to repay her roommate for putting up with her.

She knew Grayson's time, especially weekend time, was precious, and she'd monopolized her last thirty-plus hours without a second thought. Kind of a bitchy move, even for Barbara Parker, and she was determined to start making up for it with lunch. And maybe dinner and a good movie at home later.

They'd passed several good restaurants already. Sushi. Italian. Mexican. There was no shortage of great food around, but Grayson was being less than helpful picking a restaurant. If anything, she seemed a little down.

"So, you made a choice for lunch yet?" Babs asked, trying to get some kind of reaction out of her roommate.

"What? Oh, no…not really. You really don't need to waste money taking me to lunch," Grayson replied absently.

"Why wouldn't I?"

"You've just spent quite a bit on this charity thing. And I can afford to pay for my own lunch."

"Call it penance, honey," she replied gently.

"Babs, I really don't care."

"Gray…"

The young doctor stopped, took off her sunglasses, and ran a hand through her hair. "Look, I'm just not hungry. I'd rather go home."

"Fine. Then I'm getting ridiculously expensive takeout tonight for dinner."

"Can I somehow stop you?"

"Absolutely not."

"Fine. I give up."

Babs hoisted her bags up a bit higher on her forearm, having every intention of heading straight for her car. A brief glance at the Cricket's patio stopped her from walking forward.

Two men were eating lunch at a table in the back corner. One had his back to her, but the other one was blatantly staring at them. And smiling. He was reasonably good-looking, probably mid-thirties, with a Broncos baseball cap on his head. Not her type, but still pretty easy to look at.

Wait, he's not staring at me.

He was staring at Grayson.

"Hey, you've got an admirer," she murmured quietly, elbowing her roommate in the ribs.

Grayson narrowed her eyes and shot Babs a look. Her roommate tossed her head subtly in the direction of the restaurant patio. She followed the line of sight. It took a moment to place him with the baseball cap, but realization quickly dawned.

"He's totally checking you out," Babs whispered encouragingly.

"No, he's not." She rolled her eyes.

"Yes, he is!"

"Babs, that's Detective Nolan," she scolded.

It took a moment for Barbara to register the name. "Oh! That's why he looks like he knows you. Who's that he's with?"

Grayson switched her focus from Nolan to the back of the head of his lunch buddy and instantly blushed.

Babs immediately caught on. "Ooooohhhhhh…"

"Enough," Grayson hissed, trying to get her suddenly out-of-control heart rate back below two hundred beats per minute. She was starting to feel claustrophobic in her sweater.

"C'mon. Let's go say hi," Babs said, starting toward the patio.

"What? No! Absolutely not!" Grayson stuttered, pulling back on her roommate's arm and forcing her to turn around.

I can't. Please, Babs, don't push this. Let's just go home.

Barbara Parker wasn't having any of it.

"He's recognized you. I haven't met either of them. We have to walk that way anyway to get to the car. What's a two-minute hello?"

Grayson didn't have a response. Babs rolled her eyes. She watched her roommate's face turn a darker shade of crimson, and the blush was heading south down her neck.

"Honestly. You're the worst introvert I know," Barbara griped. She linked her arm in Grayson's so she couldn't try to escape, which was a very real possibility, and started toward the patio.

Grayson stared straight down at the concrete, her face flaming. Barbara saw the smirk on Nolan's face; she returned it, and knowingly, he nodded.

"Hey, Ryder…" Nolan said as he watched the young blonde half-drag her companion toward the patio. "Heads up."

Gabriel had just enough time to look up and register the

smirk on his partner's face before two shadows came over their table.

His partner stood up, his hand out. "Dr. Carter. What a pleasant surprise," he said, shaking her hand.

"Detective Nolan." She slightly nodded back in greeting, removing her hand as quickly as she could. "This is my roommate, Barbara Parker. Babs, this is Detective Nolan."

"Charmed," Nolan winked, warmly shaking the blonde's already outstretched hand.

The sudden screech of metal on concrete drew everyone's eyes to the other side of the table. Ryder had awkwardly sprung to his feet.

"Oh, and um, this…this is Detective Ryder," Grayson said softly. "Detective, Babs Parker."

Ryder shook Barbara's hand, completely on autopilot. His eyes never even glanced in her direction. His attention was completely focused on Grayson.

A few moments of awkward silence ensued, with Nolan scrambling to come up with a way to break it. "Uh, what brings you two down to the district today?" he asked politely.

"Shopping," Barbara replied, holding up her bags. "I've been dragging her all over trying to find something for a benefit I have in a few weeks. You two?"

Carter stared at her roommate, mouth half open. She knew these people and couldn't get a word out without sounding like an awkward idiot. Babs had met them thirty seconds ago and was already chattering away like she'd known them for years.

Queen of the social butterflies.

"Lunch," Nolan replied. "A well-deserved one."

"Well, I'm jealous. A lunchtime patio table at the Cricket is a hot commodity."

Blake immediately took the hint. "Would you like to join us? We have two extra chairs here."

"Oh, no, we wouldn't want to intrude..." Grayson started to protest, backing away from the railing.

"You're not intruding," a low voice replied.

Grayson felt a low, slow shiver make its way down her spine. She was stupidly staring at the concrete, and she could feel his eyes on her.

Look up, look up, look up, idiot...

She forced her eyes up from the pavement. Gabriel was as close to her as was physically possible without jumping the guard railing around the patio.

Wait a minute, is he breathing harder? It looks like he's in pain.

"Gray, I'm hungry, and we have absolutely nothing at home. If you're not hungry, don't eat. But we can't pass up the Cricket's patio. Please?" Barbara whined.

She sighed. "All right."

"M'kay, around the corner and in the door you go!" Babs said, pushing her roommate back toward the main door.

Satisfied, Nolan sat down at the table and looked across the metal surface into the glaring eyes of his partner.

"What?" he chuckled, the humor clearly evident in his voice.

"What. Do. You. Think. You. Are. Doing?" Ryder ground out through gritted teeth.

"Asking them if they want to have lunch," he replied nonchalantly. "What's the problem?"

"Nothing," Ryder said as he sat down, pinching the bridge of his nose.

"Oh, cool off. Have another beer." He motioned for two more from Tim, who nodded from across the patio.

Back at the main entrance, Babs maneuvered Grayson through the door and up toward the hostess station. There were a few parties crowded around waiting to be seated, and there wasn't any way around them. She stopped and turned toward her friend.

"So, that's Detective Ryder, huh?" She raised her eyebrows and whistled in appreciation.

"Stop it, Barbara," Grayson replied, wrapping her arms protectively around her waist.

"What?"

"I can see what's going on inside that mind of yours, especially after what Noah's said to you. Just drop it."

"Well, if you don't go after him, I'm going to. He's one hot hunk of man, Gray. Damn."

The crowd opened up slightly, and Barbara pushed through, heading straight for the door that led to the patio. Grayson stayed rooted to the floor.

Well, what the hell did I think would happen when she met him? More importantly, why do I care?

Anyone who met Barbara Parker fell for her. Looks, charm, an outgoing personality; she had it all. Half of the patrons at the restaurant had already craned their necks around to watch her saunter out the patio door in her so-called fat jeans and a Rockies T-shirt. And here she was, plain Jane in a wrap dress and flats, utterly inferior. Grayson shook her head clear.

It's not like this is news. Why do I have such an issue with this? And why won't my goddamned heart rate go back to normal?

Grayson put the best smile on her face she could manage and made her way out to the patio. Babs waved her over, already comfortable in the seat next to Detective Nolan. She reluctantly slid into the only chair left and kept her eyes focused on the tabletop.

Barbara's smile dropped off her face when she saw how dejected and shut down her roommate looked.

"So, how were you two lucky enough to get a table on the patio at the Cricket on a Sunday?"

"We lucked into it." Nolan shrugged, waving their waiter over to the table. "There was a wait inside but open tables out here. Go figure."

"The NFL games," she replied. Barbara pointed to the TVs above the bar. "No TV out on the patio. Just inside." She smiled.

"Good point."

Tim sidled up next to the table beside Babs. "Can I get you ladies something to drink?"

"Um, I'll take your seasonal wheat beer," Babs said, quickly glancing over the menu, then at Nolan's half-eaten burger, "... and one of whatever he had to eat," she replied, handing the menu across the table.

Grayson took it but didn't open it. "I don't think..." she began quietly.

Babs cut her off. "She'll take a Fat Tire and a goddamned side of fries," she said tersely, yanking the menu from her friend's hands and handing it over to the stunned waiter.

Tim looked briefly at the young brunette, who nodded sheepishly, then took off to get the drinks as quickly as possible.

Grayson didn't look up from the table, her face flushing.

How humiliating.

Nolan tried to get the flow of conversation back on track. "I see you had success shopping," he said, nodding toward the shopping bags that Barbara had deposited by her feet.

"Oh, yeah, I found the dress yesterday, thank goodness, but today I had to come back for the rest."

"The rest?"

"Jewelry, shoes, shawl. You know, everything a girl needs to attend a charity gala."

"I'll take your word for it." Nolan chuckled into his beer.

"Gray's been an incredible help. She literally picked out the whole thing," Barbara gushed. "Of course, the one thing she tried on for herself looked incredible, but she walked out of the store without it."

Gabriel glanced to his left, expecting a response, but Grayson had her eyes focused on her lap. Her hands were nervously wringing back and forth under the table.

"What was it?" Blake asked, looking at the young brunette.

It took her a minute to realize Nolan had asked her the question, not Barbara.

"Oh, um...nothing."

"What was it?" Ryder's voice softly rumbled across the table.

Grayson shifted slightly toward him, thrown off by his interest in something so inconsequential. She startled in her seat when she looked up and registered how intently focused he was on her.

"Um, just a...a pair of earrings. That's all," she said shyly, unconsciously pulling some of her hair behind her right ear.

"They were gorgeous," Babs interjected. "They were these beautiful emerald-drop earrings. And she just left them there. Unbelievable," she said, shaking her head. "At least I found my shoes at the same place," she said, kicking a particular bag by her feet.

Tim returned to the table with their drinks. Grayson gratefully drank from hers to steady her nerves.

"Just a few minutes on the food, folks," he said before disappearing.

"Well, is there anything remaining on the list?"

"Not a thing," Babs replied, taking a drink of her beer. "You two have plans for the rest of the day?"

"Taking an easy day, for once," Nolan replied.

Grayson looked up from her glass. "You didn't have to, um…" she trailed off, unsure if she could even actually ask such a question.

"…go to a crime scene this morning?" Ryder finished.

She nodded.

"No, we didn't. Oddly enough," he smiled reassuringly.

"You thought you would have to?" she said, raising her eyebrows.

"I'd anticipated it, yes." He nodded.

"Oh," she replied flatly, taking another drink from her beer. "Can I ask if you have any leads yet?"

"You can," he said, taking a drink of his own, "but I'm afraid we don't have any."

"Hence your wanting another body," she replied.

Ryder looked at her with hesitation but found no malice or horror on her face. Just understanding. He nodded quickly, the relief spreading across his face.

Grayson bit her bottom lip.

Nolan and Babs looked at each other. *Did we miss something here?*

Tim arrived with the food. Babs dug into her burger with gusto. Grayson intermittently picked at her fries. Nolan and Ryder attempted to finish their now-lukewarm lunches. The crowds on the street meandered by, providing passing entertainment from time to time.

Ryder took a bite of a stone-cold french fry and wrinkled his nose, dropping the remaining piece back down into the basket. Something gently slid into the side of his forearm, which was propped on the table. Grayson's basket of fries, still warm, was pushed up against him.

She nodded at it. "They're still warm," she said softly.

"They're yours," he countered.

"I'm not going to eat them all." She smiled, then looked away into the passing crowd. A faint smile crossed his face as he reached for one. They finished the basket between them.

Nolan and Barbara tried to continue small talk across the table. Neither failed to notice the side glances Gabriel and Grayson were giving each other. Any attempt at conversation between them failed before it ever started.

Suddenly, Grayson jumped in her seat and placed her hand on her right thigh. She pulled her phone out of a hidden pocket in her dress and wrinkled her forehead as she looked at the screen.

Ryder was instantly on edge as she answered the call.

"Carter. Adams, what's up? You've got what?" She put a finger into her other ear, trying to drown out the noise of the passing foot traffic. "Hang on, I can't hear a thing you're saying," she said as she stood up and headed back into the restaurant.

Gabriel looked after her until she disappeared inside the building, then turned back to the table. His partner and Barbara Parker were both staring at him, grinning.

"What?"

"You're such an idiot, Ryder," Blake said, shaking his head.

"Excuse me?"

"Nothing," he replied as his own phone began to ring.

He slid his finger across the screen and answered. Babs just continued to stare.

"Hello? Yeah, speaking. What?" Nolan's face fell. "You've got to be shitting me. Okay, okay, yeah. We'll be there. Okay, thanks," he said, ending the call. "You're not going to believe this…"

46

GRAYSON HAD HER phone clamped to her right ear and a finger plugged into her left as she made her way back to the inside lobby of the restaurant. She squirreled herself away in a corner near the door and tried again.

"Okay, now I can hear you. What's up?"

"Hey, I'm so sorry to bother you on a Sunday. I know it's your day off…" her junior resident began apologetically.

"You're fine. Don't worry. Tell me what's going on."

"I've got a guy here in the ER. He's thirty-six, uninsured, doesn't speak a word of English, and has a blown-apart tibia. Fell off some scaffolding. Has some stuff in his belly, too, according to trauma, so they're gonna take him to the OR shortly here. Kramer's on, and he said he'd take care of the ex-fix today, but he doesn't want to do anything definitive. Told me to turf it to the house clinic. I guess I wanted to see if you wanted it."

The house orthopedic clinic was responsible for taking care of any uninsured or minimally insured patients who came through the hospital. It was staffed by the chief residents, and while it was a great learning experience, it was sometimes the most dreaded part of the workweek.

"You have a name for me?"

"Yeah, Ramirez. Alejandro J. Ramirez. Films are all in the system."

"Okay. Put him on the trauma list, and I'll see him tomorrow. Tell Dr. Kramer I'll assume care."

"Awesome. You're a lifesaver."

"Why's that?"

"I've talked to the other chiefs and the other attendings who were on this weekend. They all took one look and said hell no. It's a pretty bad fracture."

"They just don't want the challenge," she scoffed halfheartedly. "Don't worry about it. I'll do it. If we can swing it, you and I can do the case together later this week."

"Sweet!"

"Okay, go get back to work. Let me know if anything major happens to him tonight from the trauma standpoint. And don't forget to check his hips and his heels if he fell from a significant height."

"Will do. Thanks."

Grayson ended the call and made a note in her phone with the name. She'd look up the x-rays later from home. She turned around, still completely focused on the small screen, and collided head-on with another person. She stumbled backward, stunned, tripping over her own two feet. Two strong hands reached out to steady her, one on each shoulder. She muttered an apology and glanced up.

Gabriel had hold of her, concern written plainly on his face. He held her at arm's length and looked her over, inch by inch.

I'm going to get hurt if I don't start paying attention...wait, why is he looking at me like that?

"Are you all right?" he asked.

"Oh, um...yes. Thanks," she muttered, grabbing her left elbow with her right hand and rubbing her arm up and down. "Sorry about that."

"Don't be," he replied.

"Are you headed back outside?" she asked lamely.

He nodded. "But not to the patio. Nolan and I just got called out." He held up his partner's keys. "He's having me get the car."

"Oh." She sighed. *Am I disappointed?*

"My partner and Barbara are still at the table." He gestured back toward the door. "If you'd rather take a walk, I can drop you off back here to meet her."

"I'd like a walk."

"Good," he replied as he moved to open the door for her. His shoulders visibly relaxed.

Does he look relieved?

She shook her head at herself and headed out into the sunshine.

Stop trying to imagine things that aren't there, stupid girl. You're letting Noah and Barbara's nonsense get to you.

Ryder motioned for her to go ahead of him into the crowd. Their path took them directly past the patio, where two sets of raised eyebrows awaited them. Grayson tried her best to avoid looking at Barbara. Ryder waved off his partner and nonchalantly dropped his credit card on the table before striding past the restaurant altogether.

The crowd was thick with families out shopping, nannies out with young children, and gaggles of high school girls talking about homecoming. Grayson felt herself starting to panic, afraid she had lost him in the crowd, but a warm hand came to rest tentatively around her waist. Gabriel started steering her through the traffic, and without hesitating, she let him. They rounded a corner, broke through the crowd, and headed north onto a quiet residential street.

"So, you got called to a new case?" she asked, trying to break the silence.

She was admittedly awful at small talk. Chit-chat was not her forté.

He shook his head. "New body. Same case."

"Oh."

"Why did she call you Gray?" Gabriel asked, looking down at her, his arm still wrapped around her waist. He could feel the heat of her skin through the thin fabric of her dress. It was soft and broken in, worn often.

"What?"

"Barbara. Your roommate. She called you Gray."

"It's short for Grayson, I guess," she replied.

"Do you like it?"

"I suppose. It's a nickname, or as close to one as I have. Noah, um…Dr. Mason, was the first person to call me that. It kind of stuck."

"What do you prefer to be called?"

"I, um…I don't really have a preference. Why?"

Why does that matter?

"It's not important. Why didn't you buy the earrings?"

Grayson stopped dead in her tracks. Gabriel turned around to face her.

"What does that have to do with anything?"

"I'm curious."

"Why?"

Her eyes shot down to the concrete.

"I just am," he shrugged.

She couldn't help herself. She couldn't hide it. Before she could tell her body no, her face went red and her arms reflexively wrapped themselves around her waist. Her shoulders hunched. She swallowed hard. Her shame spread full-force across her body. Just as quickly, she tried to recover. The small smile that she'd seen ghosting across the detective's lips vanished.

Shit. He noticed.

Before he could say anything, she started babbling.

"I, um…I can't afford them," she said, staring at the pavement. "And besides, I don't need them."

She pushed past him and started walking. Ryder fell into step beside her.

"But you liked them," he stated simply.

"Yes, I liked them," she admitted softly.

I really, really liked them.

"Babs was right. They were beautiful." That jogged her memory. "Oh, by the way, I still have your coat. It's cleaned and everything."

"I told you it wasn't dirty."

"I had it cleaned anyway."

He nodded but didn't say anything. Grayson looked at him quizzically.

"Where do you want me to…um…" *Drop it off? Send it?*

Ryder waved her off mid-sentence. "Don't worry about the coat."

"You have to be joking."

"No, I'm not."

"So, you have a habit of leaving expensive custom-cut clothing with people you barely know?" she asked.

"How did you know it was custom cut?"

She just smiled at him and shrugged.

"Don't worry about the coat," he repeated, pressing a button on the key fob.

A Subaru parallel parked on the other side of the street chirped twice.

"You drive a Subaru?" she asked, surprised.

"My partner does," he replied, looking back at her as they crossed the street. "Why?"

"You don't seem like a Subaru kind of guy."

"Well, what kind of guy do I seem like, Dr. Carter?" he asked, leaning across the center console and opening the passenger door for her.

She took a moment to think.

"I'd guess somewhere between an Audi R8 and a Mercedes SL65 AMG," she replied, slipping gracefully into the passenger seat.

Working with fifteen testosterone-fueled guys who adore their toys more than their wives has its advantages.

His head twitched and his eyes briefly narrowed as he situated himself in the driver's seat. Grayson didn't notice.

He shut the car door but didn't put the key into the ignition. "I need you to do something for me," he said softly.

Grayson shook her head quickly.

What's with him and changing topics? Oh, and by the way, there's probably nothing you could ask that I wouldn't do when you use that voice...wait, what? Where did that come from?

"Okay..." she replied, her hesitation obvious.

He turned in his seat to look at her.

"I need you to promise me you'll be careful. At work. At home. I don't care."

Her eyes widened.

"Is there something going on..." she started, only to be cut off by his waving hand.

"No, no, there's not. I don't have any reason for asking this.

But please, promise me you'll look out for yourself. Whatever is going on is connected to that hospital, and I don't want you getting hurt."

"Okay."

"Promise me, Grayson," he demanded.

It was the first time she had heard him say her name. His voice was low and strained. She really wanted to hear it again.

"I promise, detective," she replied.

For some reason, she felt the need to touch him, to reassure him. She rested a tentative hand on his tensed forearm.

He startled for the briefest moment, reacting to her soft touch through his cashmere sweater, then relaxed. "Gabriel," he said as he started the car.

"What?"

"I'd prefer it if you called me Gabriel."

He pulled out into the street and kept his eyes firmly fixed on the road. Her hand didn't leave his arm until they pulled up outside the restaurant, and he never made a move to remove it.

Ryder easily maneuvered into an open spot in front of the Cricket and shut off the engine. Grayson reached to open her door but he stopped her, shaking his head as he got out and rounded the hood. She shot him a questioning look through the front windshield, then realized what he was doing. She waited patiently, then popped the broken door so he could swing it open.

She stepped out, noticing that Detective Nolan and Barbara were already heading toward the car. She only had a second, and maybe it was the beer talking, but she certainly felt braver than she had an hour ago. She leaned in a bit as she stepped onto the sidewalk, placing her left hand on his bicep.

She felt him tense again, the muscle straining under her fingers. When she looked up at him, she found him staring right at her.

"I like that," she whispered.

"What?"

"Being able to call you Gabriel," she said, coolly walking past him to stand beside her roommate.

Ryder didn't move for a moment, breathing heavily, then spun around on his heels and lobbed Nolan's keys at him. Blake caught them and grinned.

"Well, ladies, we must be off. Enjoy your afternoon."

He walked around to the driver's seat and got in just as his partner was settling into the passenger seat. He pulled away from the curb when traffic allowed. The two young women stood on the curb until the car disappeared around the next corner.

"What in the hell was that?" Babs immediately spun Grayson around to look at her.

"What was what?"

"You run off to take a work call and come back twenty minutes later with Hot and Handsome as your personal chauffeur."

"He had to get the car. I wanted to go for a walk," she replied.

"Bullshit, Gray."

She rolled her eyes at her roommate's temper tantrum. "Just let me go in and pay our tab," Grayson said, starting toward the door.

"Don't bother. Didn't you notice him drop his credit card? He paid for everything."

Grayson did a double take and looked back at her roommate.

"Go in and ask if you don't believe me," Babs replied.

"No, I believe you."

"Then will you tell me what the hell that was?"

"I'd prefer to just go home," she replied.

Babs just rolled her eyes and started walking down the street, making a mental note to call Noah when they got home.

———————

Down the street, Blake Nolan had waited what he considered to be a reasonable amount of time. It was time to lay into his partner.

"So, wanna tell me what that was?" he asked, handing over the credit card.

His partner shook his head and silently shoved it back into his wallet.

"You wanna tell me how or why that girl has gotten under your skin?"

He shook his head again.

"Do you have any idea how or why she's gotten under your skin?"

He paused. "No."

Blake smirked. He turned onto a side street, preparing to make his way out of the shopping district.

"Turn right here."

Blake shot his passenger a look.

"What?"

"Just do it."

"What for?"

"I have something to do."

Nolan sighed. "All right. You have ten goddamned minutes, Gabe."

"I won't need that long."

47

NOLAN TURNED THE car north, toward City Park, and put his cell phone up to his ear. The line clicked through on the fourth ring.

"McCallister."

"Captain, it's Nolan."

"Why are you calling me? Isn't this your day off?"

"Technically, yes, but we just got a call from a patrol team up at St. Ignatius. That big church on the western side of City Park."

The line was eerily quiet. Nolan could almost see his captain shaking his head and rubbing the bridge of his nose.

"Don't tell me…"

"Yeah, you've got it."

"It's Sunday afternoon. How in the hell…? Don't these fuckers get noticed in the morning?"

"Dunno, captain. I'll let you know when we figure that out. We're headed up there now."

"Do you need backup?"

"No, I doubt it."

"Harrison is still on loan to his home department today, correct?"

"From what he told me."

"Just update him before you pack it in tonight. Anything earth-shattering, call me. Otherwise, I'll catch up tomorrow."

"Okay, captain," he replied, ending the call.

Traffic wasn't too heavy. The park quickly loomed into view after they passed onto York Street. A few more streets north and Nolan turned into the parking lot of the church. It was an impressive gothic structure, red brick trimmed in ivory colored stone. A set of uniformed officers were standing by a side door with a middle-aged man dressed in jeans and a paint-splattered collared button-down shirt.

"That must be one of the priests," Blake motioned with his head as he pulled into a spot. "The patrolman I talked to said a priest found the body. I didn't know they wore jeans."

Ryder nodded, then turned in his seat. "How did they know to call you?"

"They called the find into dispatch. I guess our case has been flagged, so anything similar gets filtered straight to us. Courtesy of the chief of detectives."

"Lovely. I'm glad they have your cell number and not mine."

"Thanks, jackass," he replied, rolling his eyes. "Look, play nice with these guys. They look like newbies. I don't think they have three years on the force between them."

"Why wouldn't I?"

"You're agitated." He motioned to his partner's clenched fists. "And you have a short fuse when you're worked up."

"Fine. You do most of the talking."

They climbed out of the Subaru and made their way toward the awaiting officers. Nolan held out his hand.

"Detective Nolan. I think I talked to one of you on the phone."

"That'd be me, sir," said the blond. "Sorry to ruin your day off."

"Not your fault."

"This is my partner, Finn. And this is Father Bennett. He found the body."

The middle-aged man held out his hand and weakly smiled. He was obviously shaken up.

"Good to meet you, Father. This is my partner, Detective Ryder. You want to tell us what happened today? Starting with why there's nobody here on a Sunday?"

The man smiled slightly. "I explained that to the officers when I called. Our church has been undergoing a few renovations over the summer. We got behind schedule, and we're in a race to get things finished before winter shows up. We asked our parishioners to give us this week, including the weekend, to catch up. With the nice weather, we were able to hold mass outdoors at a different location today. I came here after noon to start on some of the inside chores, and…" he trailed off.

"And?"

"Why don't we just show you, sir," the blond officer said, pushing open the side door.

The detectives nodded and followed the uniformed officers and Father Bennett into the church. Most of the pews and decorative pieces were covered in construction plastic, but even so, the vaulted ceilings and white altar were impressive.

Blake whistled up toward the ceiling. "Must be something to spend Sundays in this place."

Father Bennett smiled. "Our congregation is blessed to worship God in a place like this, detective. Hence the passion to keep it in good repair."

The officers climbed up several steps and moved behind the altar itself. A low wooden wall separated the altar from the back wall. Father Bennett pushed on a portion to open it and stepped inside. Nolan followed, then Ryder.

Sprawled out in the middle of the floor, arms and legs spread wide, was the body of a young man. He was thin, with slightly-too-long sandy brown hair, and well dressed. Very well dressed.

For once, someone's outdone my partner, Nolan thought to himself.

The victim had an expensive-looking class ring on his right ring finger and a gold watch on his left wrist. There were several hundred-dollar bills scattered around on the floor.

Ryder knelt down next to the body. "Nobody's touched him?" he asked.

"No, sir."

"Gloves?"

"Here."

Finn handed over a pair. Ryder snapped them on, opened one of the victim's eyes, and immediately loosened the tie around his neck.

"I don't think it's causing him any discomfort, Gabe," Nolan scoffed.

His partner glared up at him and unbuttoned the top two buttons on the collared shirt, pulling the collar open to show dark purple ligature marks around the neck.

"Not now, but it looks like it might have been used to kill him."

Nolan frowned. "Oh, yikes."

"No signs of blunt force trauma to the head. Nothing under the nails. No signs that he fought back."

"You told dispatch you had an ID on this guy?" Nolan asked, glancing over at the patrol officers.

"Yes, sir. He had his wallet on him," the blond replied, handing over a sealed evidence bag.

"Elliot James III. Denver address," Blake said, handing it back.

"Is he affiliated with St. Joseph's?" Ryder asked.

"Hang on, let me check," Nolan replied, pulling out his phone. "Google says..." he paused momentarily, "yup. Here he is. Resident at St. Joe's. Internal medicine. Second year."

He flashed his phone screen toward his partner.

"Well, call Pelton," Ryder grumbled.

"Oh, hell no. I'm not pissing her off on a weekend. And I already had to call the captain. You're calling her."

"Fine." Gabriel pulled off his gloves and grabbed his phone out of his pocket. He quickly dialed and walked off, holding it to his ear.

"We're going to need to get your formal statement at the department, Father Bennett," Nolan said.

"Um, well, I...I hate to be rude, detective, but is there any way it could wait until tomorrow? All of this is going to put us even further behind, and it would be such a help..."

Nolan cut him off mid-sentence. "Go do what you need to do. Obviously, this is a crime scene, so you can't touch anything, but phone calls and coordinating are fine. Here's my card. Just come on by the department tomorrow."

"Thank you."

"No problem. Two questions, though."

"Of course."

"Did you know this kid? You know, before finding him this morning."

"No." The priest shook his head. "I've never seen him before, and he's not one of our parishioners. I'd have to double-check, but my guess is no immediate family of his attends church here, either. The name isn't familiar."

"Were all the doors locked?"

"To the church?"

"Yeah."

"Yes, of course. With all of the equipment in here, not to mention the wood and nails and everything else. All of the doors were locked last night before I left. That was around ten o'clock or so."

"Thanks."

His partner materialized at his side. "She's not happy."

"I figured. The good father is coming down for a statement tomorrow."

"Okay."

"I think the uniforms can handle things before the meat wagon gets here."

Ryder nodded in agreement as Blake motioned them over.

"We're leaving you two in charge. The crime lab and medical examiner should be here shortly."

"Yes, sir."

The two detectives turned on their heels and headed out the side door to the car. The weather was still beautiful. There were birds chirping in the yellowing trees. No one would have ever suspected a gruesome crime scene lurked only fifty feet away.

"Well, crap, I thought we were gonna get away with it today, buddy. You called it. Too good to be true."

Blake stretched his arms over his head and yawned. He was trying to lighten the mood, but one look at his partner's wrinkled forehead told him there was something wrong.

"What?"

"Something's off. Every other body was found early in the morning. Before mass. Not this one. Why?"

"You heard Bennett. He didn't get here until noon."

"But why break the pattern now?"

"Maybe he didn't mean to." Blake shrugged and kept moving toward the car.

"Wait, what?"

Ryder reached out and roughly grabbed his partner's arm.

"What, what?"

"Repeat what you just said."

"Um, 'maybe he didn't mean to'?"

"Meaning what?"

"Jesus, I don't know," Blake hissed, wrestling his arm out of his partner's viselike grip. "Maybe whoever dumped our vic here didn't realize there wasn't going to be a normal mass today. Bennett said the church has only been shut down for the week. It's not like there was a notice posted on the door or anything."

"Right…"

Ahhhh, fuck me. There he goes.

Nolan rolled his eyes. That tone meant his partner was already lost in his own little world. He steered him toward the car and started the engine.

"If you're going to get lost in your head, I'm taking you home. I need a nap."

"I have a couch."

"You're offering me your couch?"

"If you want it," he countered.

"I don't really, but it's more comfortable than mine," Nolan replied, smiling and pulling out into traffic.

48

ON WEDNESDAY NIGHT, Gabriel sat on his couch, the same one Nolan had occupied for the better part of Sunday afternoon. He was poring over the notes he had scattered across the coffee table, the floor, and tacked to the mantel above the fireplace. They were four bodies in, and he was getting fucking nowhere. Early morning back-to-back meetings with the captain and the chief of detectives detailing their lack of progress despite the bodies stacked up in the morgue hadn't helped his mounting frustration.

Nolan and Harrison had made a trip back to the hospital to talk to the head of the internal medicine department, who'd had nothing but a glowing review of Dr. James and his year-plus tenure at the program. He was smart and driven, good with patients…whatever. Nothing useful.

Dr. James' parents were on safari somewhere in Africa, and no one had been able to reach them. The butler had suggested they might have better luck when Mr. and Mrs. James reached Paris next week. Harrison's face had been priceless when he'd heard that.

The M.E.'s office had added a few small pieces to the puzzle. Carla had confirmed botulism as the cause of death for victim number three, Dr. Porter. Their newest victim had been strangled to death with his own necktie. The indentations on his neck had matched impressions taken from the tie itself, and his hyoid bone was shattered.

Speaking of which…

Gabriel grabbed two crime scene photographs off the floor. A class ring, gold Rolex, probably three thousand dollars in designer clothes, and a money clip with a thousand in cash and active credit cards were all found with the body. Several thousand more were scattered around the body. His expensive Yves Saint Laurent tie had been retied into a perfect Windsor knot.

That's clearly sending a message.

The crime was about the kill and the staging, not robbery. That realization had Ryder on edge. It would have been so easy to lift the watch or the cash, make it look like an assault gone bad. But the killer had made a point not to do that. There was now no doubt that each scene had been purposefully stylized. If that didn't scream serial killer, nothing else did.

Gabriel shook his head clear and eyed the glass tumbler on the side table. It was empty. He scowled, shoved himself to his feet, and went into the kitchen for the bottle. It was more than half empty, which darkened his mood even further. He stumbled back into the living room, poured himself another full glass, and picked up another photograph from the floor.

Carla had come through on one other big thing today: the marks on the abdomen. He'd asked her to look for them. All four victims had one. She'd had to dig around in Porter's fat folds before she'd finally found his, but it was there. The number of similarities between the cases was too obvious to ignore.

He was jolted out of his drunken stream of consciousness by someone knocking at his front door. Persistently.

"Goddamn it," he muttered. He recognized the knock. "What do you want?" he hissed.

"Is that any way to say hi to me?" Harrison asked as he strolled through the door.

"By all means, come on in," Ryder said sarcastically, closing the door behind him. "And yes, it is."

"What are you rambling on about now?" his former partner replied, shucking off his suit coat and throwing it over the back of one of the bar stools.

"Usually you want something when you show up unannounced. So, cut the crap and get to it. What do you want?"

"How much of this have you had?" Harrison asked, picking up the glass of scotch from the side table and eyeing the near-empty bottle on the counter.

"None of your fucking business."

Logan raised his eyebrows and, without a word, walked into the kitchen. He reappeared a moment later with a clean glass.

"Well, then, you won't mind me helping you kill this bottle," he said, grabbing it from the side table.

"There are three more in the cabinet," Ryder countered.

"Of course there are three more ridiculously expensive bottles of scotch in your apartment," he said, eyeing the disheveled living room. "Can I sit down somewhere or am I going to cause a disturbance in the force?"

Ryder pointed toward the set of high-end leather recliners near the fireplace. Harrison grabbed his glass and the nearly empty bottle. He slumped down into a chair and took a long drink from his glass.

"I should come here to drink more often. This is good stuff," he admitted.

"What do you want, Logan?" Gabriel asked, slumping into the other chair.

"Why the rush? Am I keeping you from something important?" he asked, motioning toward the papers scattered on the floor.

"Yes. Well, no, I…"

"Make up your mind."

"No. It's fine. I'll get back to it after you leave."

"Or you could sleep like a normal person. You're going to have a hell of a hangover tomorrow."

"Screw off."

Harrison just smiled into his glass.

"For the last time, Logan, what are you doing here?"

"I wanted to talk to you."

"About?"

"The James kid."

"What about him?"

"I think he might have a bad side."

"You told me the department chair gave him a glowing review."

"He did. But look at the kid. He's a resident, making less than a nurse, and he's running around with a Rolex and a few thousand cash in his back pocket. Drinking really expensive scotch on a regular basis, according to friends. C'mon, man, I didn't know this shit existed before I met you," he said, raising his own half-empty glass.

"His parents seem to have the means to support his lifestyle. You think he's a drug dealer or something?" Ryder wrinkled his forehead.

"Not necessarily, but that's a good idea. He'd have access to some strong stuff working at the hospital."

"Maybe he's just flaunting an inheritance. His parents are going from a safari straight to Paris. His dad's a partner in a high-flying law firm back in New York City. It isn't a crime to show off, Logan."

"True, but you can piss people off doing it, Gabe. And having family money doesn't mean he didn't get himself into a debt so deep Daddy's pockets can't cover it. Gambling, the track, girls, whatever. C'mon, think like a narco cop for once."

Ryder took a drink of scotch, turning the idea over in his head. There wasn't anything to suggest James had been involved in drugs, dealing or otherwise, but a careful investigator would be sure to tick it off his list, one way or another.

Especially considering how Lisa Oakes died.

And if James had been throwing money around like an idiot, he could have caught the eye of any number of people who would kill for it. But whoever had ultimately taken his life didn't seem interested in the money.

And we're back to that again…It just doesn't make sense.

"The money was left on him."

"Hmm?"

"The cash, the Rolex…."

"So, whoever killed him didn't give a shit about robbing him. Like I said, maybe he pissed off somebody just by flaunting it. Murder sends a much stronger message than an ass-kicking or robbery." Harrison sipped at his rapidly dwindling drink. "Oh, we found his car outside the last bar he visited. Stupid thing was in a private garage. High-end BMW convertible, of course, untouched."

"Of course."

The two former partners sat in amicable silence for a while. Eventually, Harrison cracked open another bottle of scotch, and Ryder put on an old Sinatra vinyl.

"Still a decent taste in music, I see, Gabe."

"Learned from the best, didn't I?" he replied, as he sat back down.

"Yeah, you did. Don't forget it."

"You're doing okay in narcotics, I hear."

"As good as I was before you left."

"They're pegging you for captain over there."

"Don't listen to all that bullshit. I don't."

"Whatever, Logan."

"Look, I didn't come over here for you to analyze me and my career."

"So, answer the question I asked you an hour ago. What are you doing here? Really. You didn't come to talk about the case. That shit could've waited until morning."

Harrison smirked into his glass.

You're not getting by me that easy, Logan. I can still read you.

"Blake and I had a little chat on the way back from the hospital this week."

"About me."

It was a statement, not a question. It also wasn't a surprise to Logan.

"Of course about you. What else would we talk about?"

"Sports? Girls? Getting laid? Ex-wives?"

"Asshole."

"What atrocity have I committed now?" Ryder spat. "Something bad enough to get me put on desk duty?"

Somebody else is coming after my badge. Goddamn it. I knew getting stuck on this damned case was going to get me into trouble again.

"What? What the hell are you...no, idiot." Harrison's initial surprise quickly faded and the smirk settled back onto his face. "I wanna know about the girl."

What. The. Fuck?

"What are you talking about?" Ryder replied, as smoothly as possible. Inside, he was boiling.

"Don't bullshit me, buddy. I got the whole story."

"Then you don't need any details from me, do you?"

"There are details, huh?" he queried, eyebrow raised.

"Oh, for the love of God, Logan." Ryder made a move to stand.

Logan motioned for him to keep his seat. "Look, I've known you for over seven years. In that time, you've had one-night stands. Period."

"Nothing's changed," Gabriel replied coolly, swirling the scotch around in the bottom of the heavy crystal glass.

"Something's changed."

"Leave it," he growled.

"Prove me wrong," Harrison challenged, turning in his chair. "I think that James kid is dirty, but we can't prove it. Blake said she gave you good information about Nelson. Let's go talk to her. We get a better profile, and you can prove to me that this is all bullshit."

"Why the fuck do you care?"

"I just do. Humor me."

"Fine."

"Good."

Logan looked at the small clock at the end of the mantel.

"Shit, it's after midnight," he said, standing up and draining his glass.

Ryder followed him to the door.

"Get some sleep, man. We've got work in the morning."

"Yeah, sure. After I'm done here."

Logan turned in the doorway and shook his head.

"Why don't we go to the hospital on Friday? Give you a day to get over your hangover."

"I'll be fine tomorrow."

"Let me rephrase. We are going to the hospital on Friday so you have a day to get over your hangover."

"Whatever. Good night, Logan."

"G'night, Ryder."

49

THURSDAY NIGHT WAS shaping up to be one hell of a night on call.

After a full day in the operating room, Grayson had had all of five minutes to breathe before Adams was calling her with consults from the ER. Everyone had decided to get in their last ATV ride or motocross race before winter set in, and they had all decided to do so after a fifth of Jack Daniels. Every single patient, save for one sweet elderly woman with a broken wrist, had been rip-roaring drunk and had needed emergency surgery.

At 10:30, she wearily followed her junior up to the ICU to see another STAT consult. Grayson leaned back against the wall of the elevator, rubbing the palms of her hands over her tired eyes.

"Okay, so tell me about this one again," she said, followed by a yawn.

"Sure," Adams said, taking a look at his notes. "Mr. Griega, sixty-year-old guy, diabetic, came in today just feeling crappy, according to the ER note. They did their usual bullshit workup and found a high white count. He spiked a fever downstairs, so medicine said they'd admit him. That was around eleven this morning. By the time they actually got him up to his room around five, he was hypotensive and delirious. ICU got called. They tubed and lined him, brought him up to the unit, and called us."

"Who's the attending?"

"Uh…no clue. Sorry."

"What did the resident tell you when he called?"

"He doesn't know what to think. The chest x-ray looked fine. Urine looked fine. There's no source for this guy's sepsis. So, since he didn't have any ideas…"

"…they asked us to take a look," Grayson finished.

"Yup. I hate these consults. They're a goddamned waste of time."

"Most of the time." She nodded in agreement. "But every now and again we catch something they miss and save somebody. You'll get jaded. We all do. Think of it like a game. See if you, the dumb ortho monkey with a hammer, can figure it out before they do."

The elevator dinged. Grayson trailed behind her junior resident to the room. She snuck a quick peek through the side window. Mr. Griega was hooked up to a ventilator, on pressors, and there was no family to be seen.

"Why don't you go in and have a look?" she suggested, grabbing the chart out of the chart box. "Come back and tell me what you think. I'll do a little digging in the chart and look at his labs."

"Okay," Adams said, reaching for a pair of gloves from a box on the wall.

Grayson sat down at the nurses' station and flipped open the chart. She was reading through the ICU admission note when she heard someone walk up next to her.

"Honey, I hope you're seeing Mr. Griega."

She looked up to see Linda, one of her favorite ICU nurses, standing next to the table.

Linda was in her forties. She was an imposing 6'1", two hundred thirty pounds, and had a mess of fire-red curls all over her head. She was also one of the smartest nurses in the unit. Grayson had seen her get right up in an attending's face and tell him he was being an inconsiderate asshole if she needed to, so she had no problem putting residents in their place. They had bonded while Grayson had been on her ICU rotation as an intern, and Linda had looked out for the orthopedic consults in the unit ever since.

"Yeah. What's his deal?"

The nurse shook her head and leaned her elbows on the countertop. "Honey, I don't know. Nobody knows. He's acting sick and looking sick, but there's no source."

"Yeah, I see that. Is there anything you found on him that isn't in his H&P paperwork here?"

"Ummm, let me see…" she said, grabbing the chart. "No, well…the only thing I noticed was this bruise down by his foot. It had a few little blisters on it. I don't think they took x-rays or anything."

"Really?" Grayson's head shot up.

"Yeah."

"Can…can you show me?"

"Sure, honey."

Grayson followed the nurse into the room; Adams was just finishing checking over the patient's arms. He looked up sheepishly.

"Oh, sorry, I'm going slowly."

"It's fine." She waved off his concern. "Linda said she saw a bruise on his foot. Let's take a look."

Adams pulled the sheet and blankets off of Mr. Griega's feet. The left foot looked completely normal. The right foot was covered with a purple bruise and markedly swollen, with black, weeping blisters.

"Holy crap," Linda whispered.

"I take it his foot didn't look like this when you looked at it?" Grayson asked, rapidly putting gloves on.

"No, not at all. It couldn't have been more than a quarter-sized bruise when I saw it."

Carter gently pressed on the top of the foot.

"Rice Krispies," she muttered.

"What? He has cereal in his foot?" Adams wrinkled his brow.

"Yup."

Adams and Linda looked at her with blank stares.

"Here, feel on top of the skin. Press gently. Feel that?"

They both pressed down on the top of Mr. Griega's foot and nodded instantly.

"That's air underneath the skin."

"That's bad," Adams said.

"Yeah, that's really bad," Grayson echoed.

"So, what happens now?" Linda asked.

"Does he have any family?" she asked, hastily snapping off her gloves and washing her hands in a nearby sink.

The nurse sadly shook her head.

"Power of attorney?"

"None that we know of or have paperwork on."

"Okay. Doesn't matter anyway. Who's his ICU doc tonight? The day shift guys have gone home by now."

"Cain."

"Okay, STAT page him to the bedside, please."

Linda nodded and immediately left the room.

"Adams, I need you to do the same for Dr. Allen since he's on call for us. Page him up to the room. Then call the OR and tell them we're bringing down an emergent case."

"What's going on?" he asked.

"He's got necrotizing fasciitis. Flesh-eating bacteria. We have to cut him open or he's going to be dead in an hour or two. Get going," she said calmly.

"You've got it."

"This is all we have pending, right? No other consults?"

"Right."

"Then tell the OR it'll be you, me, and Allen scrubbing in. We'll need the hands."

"Awesome." He nodded, then picked up the phone receiver.

Carter looked back at Mr. Griega and saw that the 'bruise' was almost at his ankle.

Shit.

They needed to move fast. She walked back out to where Linda was standing, absorbed in her phone call. She grabbed the chart off of the counter and flipped it open, starting on an emergent progress note.

"You're taking him now?" Linda asked, popping up beside her.

"As quickly as we can." Grayson nodded.

"I'm getting two of the other girls. We'll get him all disconnected from the wall and mobile. Respiratory is on their way with a portable vent. I paged anesthesia, too. When you say roll, we'll go."

"You rock, you know that?"

"I know, honey," she agreed, winking before walking off down the hall.

Grayson went back to writing her note. Her cell phone went off thirty seconds later. She yanked it out of its holster.

"Dr. Allen?"

"Carter," he answered, clearly still half asleep. "Why is Adams paging me to the ICU?"

"We've got a problem up here."

"Oh yeah?"

"Sixty-year-old diabetic on pressors with nec fasc. It's literally crawling up his leg in front of me."

Grayson heard Dr. Allen sit up on the other end of the phone line. She could hear the distinct rustling of sheets and clattering of a pager over the receiver.

"Shit. Family?"

"None. That's why I paged. You and the ICU doc have to double-sign the consent so we can take him to surgery."

"See you in two minutes."

She hung up her phone. Adams appeared at her side. The OR would be ready in ten minutes. She handed him the H&P paperwork to finish while she started on the consent. Adams disappeared around the corner to find a computer.

A moment later, Grayson felt someone close in on her. She assumed it was either Linda or Dr. Allen. She looked up and instead found herself face to face with Dr. Douglas Cain.

"Dr. Carter," he said, nodding slightly by way of greeting.

"Dr. Cain," she replied.

"Nurse Collins said that you needed to see me urgently about Mr. Griega."

"Yes. We're taking him to surgery in a few minutes, and I need your signature on the consent. He has no family to sign for him."

"Surgery?" he asked smoothly. "What on earth for?"

"His necrotizing fasciitis."

"He doesn't have any signs of that. He's admitted to my service for septicemia, presumably from a bloodstream infection. That is not a surgical issue."

"No, but the infection tracking up his leg is," she fired back.

Is he for real?

Cain was looking at her like she was speaking in Japanese.

"Here, look," she said, hooking the chart underneath her arm and walking into Mr. Griega's room. His leg was still on display. Dr. Cain followed, standing directly behind her by the bedside. Way too close for comfort. Grayson fought down the hair standing on end at the back of her neck.

"That was quarter-sized when Linda did her intake. It was over his whole foot when we got here. It's gone above his ankle since I've been here, maybe fifteen minutes." She turned to face him. "That needs to go to the OR. Now."

"You're sure?"

"Yes."

It's a good thing I'm exhausted; otherwise, I'd slap this guy. What ICU doc doesn't know what necrotizing fasciitis is?

Thankfully, Dr. Allen chose that exact moment to come flying through the door, his hair askew and scrub top on inside out. Dr. Cain pulled back, and Grayson took the opportunity to sidestep around him.

"This our guy?" Allen asked.

"Yeah. Linda's his nurse. Quarter-sized when she got him from the floor. By the time I saw it, it was over most of his dorsal foot. Since we've been here it's gone over his ankle."

I sound like a damned broken record. Can we just get this guy downstairs before he dies right in front of us?

"Rice Crunchies below the skin?" Allen quirked an eyebrow.

"Krispies," she corrected, "and yes."

"Well, okay then. Cain, let's get this consent signed so I can save a life," he barked as Grayson handed over the chart.

Dr. Allen turned on his heels, walking swiftly out of the room. Grayson turned around, intent on marking out the level of the mottled skin on Mr. Griega's leg, but instead ran right into Dr. Cain. His hands shot out, grasping her arms to keep her still. He was standing stock-still, and ruthlessly glaring at her. His fingertips dug violently into her shoulders.

What the...

"Cain! Time's important here; let's go!" Allen hollered from the hallway.

Dr. Cain nodded and backed out of the room. Adams came in once he was gone.

"Man, what is his deal?"

"I have no idea. He's just...special?" Grayson chuckled, trying for nonchalant.

It wasn't the first time a hospital employee had been a bit odd after midnight, and certainly wouldn't be the last. She rubbed the bruised skin around her shoulders.

"That's a nice way of saying he's psycho."

"You know ICU docs are all a bit off."

"Yeah, but he's way, way off."

Grayson glanced out the window at the two attendings hovering around the nurses' station.

Douglas Cain was certainly one of the odder ducks at St. Joseph's. He was in his early thirties as far as anybody knew. He was tall, over 6'3", with sandy blond hair that was always a little bit askew, green eyes, and a runner's build, certainly easy on the eyes.

He'd been recruited right out of his fellowship in California and had quickly made a name for himself at St. Joseph's as a brilliant intensivist. When his partners were out of ideas, they went to him for advice. Cain also had a reputation for being socially awkward. He was always invading the staff's personal space and was definitely not able to "read the room", so to speak. He'd had more than one sucker punch thrown at him by an irritated family member or spouse.

That didn't seem to ward off any of the interest in him. There were always nurses, residents, and medical students looking after him with goo-goo eyes. He never seemed to pay any of them any attention. Grayson had seriously considered if he was secretly gay, but Noah had readily shot that theory down. He paid even less attention to interest from the same sex than he did from the opposite one.

"Hey, honey, snap out of it. We're moving him."

Linda's voice jolted Grayson back to the present.

"You need some sleep, honey," she chided.

"I'll sleep after Grand Rounds tomorrow."

"Oh, you're giving it, right?"

She nodded.

"Well, I'll be there. I can't wait to see you whip those boys!"

"Don't get your hopes up. If we're in there with this guy all night, I might not be able to stand."

"I'll bring you a chair."

"Deal."

Carter took hold of one of the side rails of the bed as they rolled Mr. Griega down the hallway toward the elevators. Dr. Allen fell into step beside her while Adams grabbed the opposite side rail.

"Good call, Carter. He'll lose his leg, but you probably saved his life."

She turned her head to look back at him and say thanks, but all she saw was Dr. Cain standing in the middle of the hallway, staring after them. She shivered and forced her eyes forward.

"Oh, by the way, never put me down as the consultant for another one of Cain's patients again. I know he's the best and all that, but…he's weird."

"That's what I said," Adams chimed in.

"I'll do my best," Grayson said as they maneuvered the bed into the elevator and hit the button for the OR.

Thankfully, the rest of the night had been calm. After Mr. Griega's surgery, Grayson had had a few hours of fitful sleep before her alarm went off.

Preparing for Grand Rounds in the minuscule bathroom attached to the chief's call room was not exactly ideal, but it would have to do. It was a relic of the fifties with teal blue tile (or what had once been teal blue tile) and faux marble countertops. The vanity mirror above the sink was missing a hinge and the overhead light flickered on and off occasionally. It probably would have made a great set for a horror movie.

Grayson managed to get her hair under control and use her minimal makeup skills to apply some mascara before getting dressed and heading out to rounds.

"Good morning, boys," she said, grabbing a rounding list from the desk.

"Morning, Dr…whoa there," Thompson said, turning around.

"What?" Adams said, glancing at the tubby intern, then turning to look at whatever he was staring at.

He did a complete double-take when he saw his senior resident standing in the doorway.

"Holy crap, Carter. You look like a girl."

"Umm…thanks, I guess?"

"No, like, I mean, I don't think I've ever seen you dressed up. Not too shabby, coming right off of call."

She rolled her eyes. "Get back to vitals, Adams."

He shrugged and turned around in his chair, hitting Thompson on the back of the head to get him to do the same.

Grayson glanced down at herself. It certainly wasn't anything special. Black pencil skirt, dark green silk blouse, and black leather heels. She shrugged and got to work.

Men are idiots.

50

HARRISON HAD BEEN right, the bastard. Thursday had been rough.

Nolan had hovered around him like a mother hen all day, trying to force one hangover cure concoction or another down his throat. He'd even called it an early day and gone home, attempting to stop the power drill boring a hole into the front of his skull with a dark, silent room. It had only marginally helped.

Why in the hell did I think downing a bottle of scotch would be a good idea?

He bent forward in his desk chair and rubbed his right temple. There was still a very faint throbbing behind his eye this morning.

Fucking two-day hangover...

Logan smirked from his temporary desk across the room. He'd called to arrange a meeting with the young doctor on Thursday afternoon after Ryder had gone home. When the secretary had started rambling on about something called Grand Rounds, he hadn't been able to resist. They now had an open invitation to attend.

He stood up and crossed the bullpen, slapping Ryder on the back of the head. "C'mon. We've gotta go now, or we're gonna be late."

"You had to make this a morning meeting, didn't you?" he scowled, rubbing the back of his skull to dull the stinging skin.

"Hey, don't be mad at me because you're still licking your wounds from Wednesday. Get up."

Gabriel nodded and stood, wordlessly making his way to the elevator. Blake leaned over and whispered to Logan when they hit the parking deck. "Does he have any idea?"

Harrison chuckled. "Hell no."

"Well, at least this should be interesting."

Logan led the way through the hospital lobby and wound around the side hallway toward the main lecture hall.

At the moment, Nolan was more interested in where he could get breakfast than where they were actually headed. Ryder, on the other hand, was eyeing his former partner suspiciously. Logan was in too good of a mood for the early hour. When he started chuckling to himself, Ryder decided he'd had enough of being kept in the dark.

"You want to let us in on the joke, Harrison?"

"Nah, I'm good. C'mon, let's get coffee. We've got a few minutes," he replied, strolling over to the coffee cart that had been pulled up outside the lecture hall.

Nolan eagerly followed behind him, already scouting out the donuts over his shoulder in line. Ryder scowled at them both. Minutes later, coffee in hand, the three detectives made their way through a small entryway and ended up in the foyer of a rather large auditorium.

"We're meeting her here?" Nolan asked, playing along with the ruse in between bites of a rather large bear claw.

Harrison nodded.

"Why here?" Ryder asked.

"Where the hell else would she be?" Logan replied, waving toward a sign on the wall.

Nolan walked over to it and read aloud.

"'*Acute Management of Traumatic Pelvic Ring Injuries in Hemodynamically Unstable Patients.* A lecture by Dr. Grayson Carter, Chief Resident, Department of Orthopedic Surgery.'"

Ryder shot his former partner a look over the rim of his coffee cup.

Harrison just shrugged. "Surprise, buddy," he said. "If she doesn't show up, I think people are gonna be pissed. C'mon, let's go get a seat."

The three detectives entered the lecture hall and took seats in the back row. Harrison leaned in toward his former partner, who was silently bent forward, forearms resting on his legs, clearly trying to rein in his impulse to start pacing.

"According to the little secretary I talked to yesterday, this is a pretty big deal. The whole hospital's invited. Bigwigs, attendings from all departments. All the residents show. This got dropped on her last minute. Thought you might want to see her under pressure."

"Why in the hell would that be necessary?" Ryder ground out through gritted teeth.

"Why not?" He smiled back.

"You're an asshole, Logan."

"What? Why?"

"Did it ever occur to you that seeing three cops in the back row might be a bit of an issue for her?"

"I don't see you getting up to leave and wait in the hall, bud."

"Will the two of you stop bitching at each other like you're a married couple?" Blake interjected. "If you weren't so busy running your mouths, you could've seen *that* walk in. Fucking pay attention."

Nolan pointed toward the front stage. Ryder and Harrison followed his line of sight. Ryder visibly stiffened.

Logan grinned.

Well now, Blake wasn't kidding. This is gonna get interesting.

51

GRAYSON WALKED INTO the lecture hall and nervously glanced at the front two rows of seats. The rows of honor. Several attendings from her department were already seated and chatting amongst themselves. What looked like internal medicine and subspecialty attendings, most of whom she didn't immediately recognize, were scattered around behind them. Residents from all departments were starting to crowd into the seats on the side wings according to the usual unspoken seating chart. Surgeons, stage right; non-surgeons, stage left. General surgery and internal medicine in the front rows, specialists in the back.

The pattern had been in place for decades.

Nobody messed with the pattern.

Dr. Carrol, one of the general surgery attendings, plopped unceremoniously into a seat a few to the left of Dr. Allen. Grayson winced. Dr. Carrol was known for causing chaos at Grand Rounds, and he loved doing it. He had a knack for making residents squirm under pressure. It made his day if somebody cried. And since her presentation happened to feature one of his patients…this was going to make for a fun morning.

Fuck.

She walked up to the lectern and handed her jump drive over to the A/V guy who was setting up the computer and the projector. Two other residents scampered down the stairs, obviously intending to do the same. Her presentation might've been posted as the main attraction, but tumor board and morbidity and mortality conference were scheduled to follow after her.

What a cheery way to start the morning.

She paced up and down across the stage for a few moments. Someone tapped her on the shoulder and she nearly jumped out of her own skin. She spun around and found Noah smiling at her, a cup of coffee in each hand.

"Morning, love," he said, handing her the cup in his left hand.

"Oh, I could kiss you right now," she said, taking a long drink. "Although, I'm not sure caffeine is going to help with my nerves."

"I got you half regular, half decaf."

"Always thinking, Dr. Mason."

She tipped the cup to him in thanks.

"Indeed. Did you see who's in the audience?"

"Carrol." She made a face.

"Yup. Still excited about the case you chose?"

"Not really, no. But there's no time to change it now." She shrugged.

"You'll be fine. You always are. Just don't let him rattle you. He'll probably just be trying to look down your shirt anyway."

"Noah!" she admonished, hitting him on the shoulder.

"What? If you don't want them looking, wear pants and a turtleneck next time," he chuckled. "I'd better go take a seat with my flock. Knock 'em dead, Gray."

She smiled and stepped across the stage to the lectern. The hall was nearly full, and the din of small talk and medical chatter was beginning to become overwhelming. The A/V guy came up, clipped a microphone to the collar of her white coat and slid the battery pack into her pocket. She hit the little microphone twice to be sure it was working appropriately. He held out a small device to her.

"This is the remote for the computer. This button advances your slides, this one goes backward. I'll be back in the booth. If you have any audio or videos that need to be played, just give me a cue and I'll handle that. I can access the jump drive from back there and bring up the internet if you need it. This black button runs your laser pointer. Just point and hold. If it runs out, there's a backup in the top drawer."

"Thanks." She smiled nervously.

Okay, here goes nothing.

She stepped up behind the lectern and cleared her throat.

"Good morning, everyone. Thank you for getting up early. We have three presentations to get through this morning, so let's get things started. For those of you in the audience who don't know me, I'm Grayson Carter, one of the orthopedic surgery chiefs, and I will be giving the first talk."

She clicked a button, and her presentation popped up onto the large projection screen behind her.

Dear God, I hope nobody can see me shaking. Deep breath…

"Today, we're going to discuss the acute management of pelvic ring injuries, specifically in unstable patients. I know, this seems geared more toward the right side of the room…" she smiled, and a rumble of laughter softly echoed around the hall, as it was well known that surgery chiefs usually gave surgery-oriented presentations, "…but we see enough trauma in this hospital that I think every service needs to be aware of these patients. There's a large spectrum of injury here, and everyone from general surgery to urology to neurosurgery to psych can be involved. Even those of you going into general internal medicine. You'll have patients who have pelvic ring injuries. It's important to understand exactly what that means and what problems they might have, both short-term and long-term."

She clicked to the next slide.

"Now, I learn best by working through a patient case, so that's what we'll do. Ortho interns, stay on your toes. These questions will be coming to you. PGY-2s and 3s, help 'em out. We are going to gloss over a little bit of the ATLS protocol stuff, just to save on time."

She clicked to the next slide.

"Meet T. B., twenty-four years old, just brought in by helicopter from up in the mountains somewhere. She was the passenger in a car that was hit head-on when a semi-truck crossed the midline. Unknown rate of speed. The driver's dead and the back-seat passenger is critical, headed across town to another hospital. You're already waiting down in the bay with general surgery when they roll her in. Okay guys, what do you do?"

"ABCs?" came a meek, squeaky voice from the audience.

"Correct. So, Airway…"

Click. New slide.

"She was intubated in the field by the paramedics. Breathing…she has breath sounds on the right, questionable on the left. Respiratory is hooking her up to a ventilator. Trachea appears basically midline. Now, circulation…"

Another *click.*

"There are your vital signs. The first set is from the field. The second set is in the bay. What do you see?"

"Tachycardia. Borderline hypotension. Looks like at least stage three shock," another voice called out.

"You don't know that." The imposing, lumbering voice of Dr. Carrol boomed back and forth between the auditorium walls.

Oh, here we go already.

Grayson chose to ignore him completely. "Anything you'd like to do for her now?"

One of the general surgery residents piped up. "What has she had in the helicopter on the ride down?"

"Good question. She's had two liters of saline, some morphine for pain control, and the drugs they gave her to intubate her."

"I'd give her blood, start with two units and go from there."

"Anything else with the blood?"

"I'd start ordering up platelets and FFP."

"I agree. And for the younger guys in the crowd, what blood are you ordering specifically?"

"She's a childbearing age female with no type and screen available, so O negative trauma blood."

Grayson smiled and nodded. *So far, so good.*

"Very good. Let's skip ahead then a bit." She clicked a few times. "Now, we got a chest x-ray which showed this. One of my ortho guys, what's this?"

"A pneumothorax," came the chorused, albeit mumbled reply from several interns.

"Good. This happens to be a rather large one, so even we should be able to spot it, right? Obviously, general surgery took care of that with a chest tube. We also got this AP pelvis in the trauma bay. My guys? Somebody read that x-ray for us, please."

Adams cleared his throat and sat forward in his chair.

"AP pelvis showing a widened pubic symphysis and gapping at the posterior right SI joint. I'd be worried about…"

"You can't say that SI joint is wide," came Carrol's voice again, cutting the younger man off mid-sentence.

Adams sank back into his chair. It was well known that, as a resident, you did not argue with any attending at Grand Rounds. Especially if you were sitting in the audience.

Grayson waited a beat, chewing her bottom lip. *How early on do I want to piss him off?*

"I actually agree with my resident, Dr. Carrol. While it's true that judging how wide the posterior gap is can be challenging on a trauma bay x-ray, it would be exceptionally rare to have such a wide gap in the front without any posterior injury. In fact, it is much more common to overlook a posterior injury on plain films than to call one. But with this mechanism, a hemodynamically unstable patient, and this x-ray, you're really tasked with proving there's no injury in the back."

Carter swung her gaze back up toward the resident-populated rows.

"For the residents, assume there's a posterior ring injury in a patient like this until proven otherwise."

"That's a crock of shit," Carrol spat.

Dr. Allen shot a nasty look over at Dr. Carrol, the 'fuck off' clearly evident on his face. Several other faculty members cleared their throats, uncomfortable with the early confrontation from the behemoth attending.

Grayson didn't acknowledge any of them. "So, what do you want to do now?" she asked, still looking up toward the residents.

"Put a binder on her."

"Correct. So, let's talk about pelvic binders…"

Grayson went on for another forty minutes, leading the audience through the case step by step. To everyone's amusement, she called Noah and a few of her junior residents

334 | A. R. Nicole

up to the stage to demonstrate how to stabilize a pelvic ring injury with a sheet, then a prefabricated pelvic binder.

Mason got a round of applause when he was finished and hammed it up with a bow before sauntering back into the crowd. Dr. Carrol grumbled intermittently throughout the presentation, but in general, it went off without much fanfare.

Halfway through, Nolan sat forward in his seat and hazarded a quick look at his partner. Ryder was leaning back in his chair, head cocked to one side, intently staring at the young brunette behind the lectern. Every time Carrol challenged her, his right-hand balled up into a fist.

Blake caught Harrison's eye during one episode, and the older detective just smirked and nodded. He'd seen it, too.

At the end of the hour, Grayson returned to her original spot behind the lectern and clicked on her last slide.

"So, that's a very brief crash course in pelvic ring injuries. We could spend hours on this, but hopefully, this overview was helpful. Thanks for staying awake. I'll take any questions you may have." She smiled and nodded at the audience.

A good deal of applause erupted from the wings of the lecture hall. One hand shot up into the air.

"Carter?"

"Yes, Dr. Allen?"

"What happened to your patient? How'd she do?"

Crap. I thought I'd gotten out of explaining that.

Grayson attempted to put a smile on her face, despite mentally running through a Rolodex of choice four-letter words.

"Well, she was initially managed quite well. She was placed in a pelvic sheet and, after several rounds of blood products, her vital signs stabilized. The decision was made to take her to the CT scanner."

"Was that the correct decision?" came another voice, one of the medicine attendings sitting a few rows back.

"I think you will find some people who say yes, some who say no. Certainly, she was unstable with an obvious pelvic ring injury. The argument could be made for taking her to the operating room acutely, or at least performing a FAST exam under ultrasound."

"Ultrasound doesn't show you where the injury is," Carrol spat icily.

Grayson dropped her eyes to look directly at him. He was foaming at the mouth and red in the face. "That's true, Dr. Carrol, but any fluid on the FAST above a certain threshold should be taken for exploration. At least, that's my understanding of the current trauma guidelines."

The other general surgery attendings in the audience nodded in silent agreement. She turned her attention back to a safer target, Dr. Allen.

"Anyway, the CT scan showed multiple intra-abdominal injuries, and she was taken to the OR. Intra-operatively, the binder was removed and orthopedics was not notified. We had offered to place a pelvic ex-fix or cut through the sheet if needed, and that was deemed unnecessary by the general surgery attending."

"That's fuckin' bullshit!" Carrol bellowed, raising his booming voice above the wave of hushed conversation that was bubbling around the auditorium.

Many of the residents sunk back into the safety of their chairs. Grayson closed her eyes, took a deep breath, and squared her shoulders in Dr. Carrol's direction.

Today is not the day to screw with me, buddy. Especially about this case.

"The conversation is well documented, Dr. Carrol. From both sides. I'll throw up copies of the chart if you would like. They're at the end of this presentation."

Carrol's eyes widened slightly.

Grayson kept talking.

"The patient required work on her kidneys, liver, bladder, uterus, and diaphragm. Her abdomen was left open due to compartment syndrome. Once the binder came off, she progressively became more and more unstable. Her pelvis was not packed. She did not go to interventional radiology for embolization. She went directly to the unit where she continued to require blood pressure support and blood products. Around midnight, she started having an irregular heart rate."

Carrol was visibly fuming. His teeth were bared and his eyes were narrowed directly at her.

"A recheck of her lab work showed she was in DIC, and a retrospective review of her chart showed that the attending surgeon had ordered only packed red cells for her postoperatively, canceling the FFP and platelets put in by the residents. She started bleeding uncontrollably around one a.m., according to the nursing documentation. She coded seven and a half minutes after that."

"How dare you stand there and fucking accuse me of doing the wrong thing," Carrol bellowed again, standing to his feet and pointing a fat, shaking finger at the stage.

Grayson's face remained cool and calm. Inside, she was screaming.

Don't get angry, don't get angry. Stay calm. Breathe…

"I am not accusing you of anything, Dr. Carrol. I am stating the facts of this patient's case. The intensivists worked on her for a half hour. She died."

"Tom, sit down," Dr. Sanders hissed from the neighboring chair.

"No! This little shit is up here trying to make a fool out of me!"

"You're doing a fine job of that yourself, Carrol," Dr. Allen chuckled.

"Shut your goddamned mouth, Allen."

"Tom, sit down," Dr. Sanders repeated, standing to his feet.

"You got in my way that whole night," Carrol spat, pointing his chubby finger back up toward the lectern. "All you did was bitch. Couldn't just shut up and do what I told you to. Why couldn't you just keep your fucking mouth shut and do your job?"

Grayson's face went blank, and she dropped her eyes down to the floor. When she looked back up, Dr. Carrol took a step back. The backs of his thighs collided awkwardly with the chair. Noah's eyebrows shot up and a hand came up over his mouth. Nolan even shivered in his seat.

Her posture had changed. It was aggressive. Predatory, even. Her eyes were dark and fierce and trained on only one person in the room. When she spoke, her voice was low and calm and still, the kind of voice that sends a chill down your spine that can't be shaken off. It was very clear to everyone in the room that Dr. Carter had had enough.

"My job is, and has always been, to take care of my patients. If that means standing in the way of an attending who is grossly violating the standard of care, then so be it. And may I respectfully remind you, Dr. Carrol, that I did not answer to you then. I definitely do not answer to you now. My department followed the standard of care, and I stand by both my clinical judgment and my conduct that night. Do you?"

The room fell completely silent. Everyone held their breath, waiting for the hammer to fall. The clock on the wall ticked the seconds by...one, two, three, four, five...and a low growl erupted into a battle cry.

"Why, you little cunt!"

Carrol launched himself forward toward Grayson, scrambling to get over the row of chairs blocking his path. He didn't get far. Dr. Sanders and Dr. Allen, who had personally jumped over two OBGYN attendings, hooked their arms around his to keep him in place.

"Get your hands off me, damn it!" he boomed.

"All of you, ten-minute break in the lobby. Now!" Dr. Sanders hollered as he struggled to contain the larger man's left arm.

Immediately, the attendees jumped to their feet and began hastily filing out the upper doors to the auditorium. Several security guards came in from the bottom doors and took over securing Carrol.

From their position in the back of the hall, the three detectives were helpless. Ryder had jumped up at Carrol's epithet and had been halfway over the backs of the chairs in front of them before Nolan and Harrison had grabbed hold of him.

"Quit it," Logan hissed in his ear as he struggled. "We're not here for you to be a fucking knight in shining armor, remember? They've got her." He motioned with his head.

"She's fine, Gabe," Nolan echoed, putting his free hand on his partner's shoulder.

Ryder looked down at the stage. Noah had stepped in between Carrol and Grayson with his arms held out, keeping them separated as the security guards took hold of the large attending. He was motioning her toward the side door.

Carrol kept lobbing obscenities at her as she backed away. When she was safely through the doorway, Noah dropped his arms and followed her, all to the tune of more threats.

The three detectives exited into the lobby and maneuvered around the small pockets of white coats that were huddled together and mumbling in hushed voices. Most of them, especially the residents, were praising Grayson for standing her ground. From the sounds of it, Carrol had had this coming for years, and it seemed to be common knowledge that the case had gone to court.

"This way," Logan motioned, and they followed him down a back stairway to the lower level of the auditorium.

52

WHEN CARROL LAUNCHED himself at her, everything slowed down. It was like something out of a movie. She saw Sanders and Allen jump up to restrain him. Noah appeared directly in front of her, out of thin air, snapping his fingers frantically in her face and motioning toward the side door.

"Gray. Gray! Move, damn it! Now!" he yelled.

One of the other residents rushed up from the side of the stage and grabbed her arm, hauling her off the stage and into the small conference room attached to the side wing of the auditorium. She shook her head clear once she was safely out of view and walked over to the small sidebar. Coffee had been set up for the conference presenters.

Grayson started pouring herself a cup on autopilot. Noah slid up beside her and took the carafe out of her hand. She shot him a quick glance. He shrugged and nodded at her hands. She was shaking. Badly.

"I'm not having you burn yourself after that performance."

She didn't argue. Grayson stretched her fingers out straight, too straight, then brought them into a tight grip.

In, out; in, out; in, out. The shaking didn't stop, but it became easier to hide.

"You okay?" he asked, angling his face down to look at her as he reached for the creamer.

"I'm fine."

I'm definitely not fine.

"You put on quite a show up there, love."

She shook her head.

"I shouldn't have lost it like that."

"Lost it? Are you kidding me?" he scoffed. "That was absolutely epic! Do you know how long everyone has been waiting to see someone put that arsehole in his place?"

"I shouldn't have done that," she said, accepting the offered foam cup of decaf and moving toward the window.

She feigned a sudden interest in the weather, but in all honesty, all she wanted was to stand in the sun. She felt very, very cold, and would have given anything for her ratty black North Face fleece.

Noah followed her.

"Look, he spent almost an hour belittling and undermining you. You smiled and hung in there until he decided to be a little shite and get in your face about his mistakes. *His* mistakes, Gray. And then he got up to attack you. I think this is going to fall in your favor."

"Not with my track record. I'm not perfect like you. They could take my job for that."

"Oh, please, like anybody would ever talk about firing you." Noah rolled his eyes. "Everybody knows Carrol got sued over that case anyway."

As luck would have it, his eye roll ended on the side doorway. Three plainclothes detectives were occupying it.

"Um, Gray?"

"What now?" she sighed, the fatigue now obvious in her voice.

"I think you have company," he said, motioning toward the door.

She followed his finger with her eyes.

"Oh, shit." *Did I just say that out loud? I really need to stop swearing.*

She gave Noah a pitiful look.

"Off you go," he smirked, pushing her forward from the small of her back and grabbing her coffee cup from her hands.

She half-stumbled forward, glaring back at him, and then proceeded as steadily as she could. She recognized Ryder and Nolan, but there was a third man with them that she hadn't seen before.

"Detectives," she said, nodding by way of greeting.

"Good morning, Dr. Carter," Blake replied. "This is Detective Logan Harrison. He's come on board to help us with the investigation."

"Nice to meet you, detective," she said, extending her hand.

"Quite a way to start the morning, doc," Logan replied, taking it.

"Oh, you saw that, huh?" She chuckled awkwardly. The laughter didn't reach her eyes. Only Ryder noticed. "Trust me. That little outburst was not planned."

She sighed and looked toward the door to the lecture hall. People were already starting to file back in.

"Most of the time, Grand Rounds is a time for attendings to take a nap or play Sudoku. But I'm assuming you didn't come for the lecture."

"No, we didn't. Is there someplace we could talk privately?"

She looked around the room. "This is about as private as it gets on a Friday morning, I'm afraid. And I have to get back to conference."

"Don't worry. I'll stall," Noah said, walking up behind her and pecking her on the cheek. "Morning, detectives."

Ryder scowled and balled his fist.

"Dr. Mason," Nolan nodded in greeting, "meet Detective Harrison."

The two shook hands.

"Take your time, love. You're not going to miss anything in tumor board," he said.

Noah quickly hustled the few remaining residents out of the staging room and into the lecture hall, leaving the door open a crack. Grayson watched him leave, then turned her attention back to the three men in front of her.

"Well?" she asked.

"Why don't we take a seat?"

Logan motioned toward a bare circular banquet table pushed off to one side of the room. She nodded and followed them over to it, picking a seat for herself in the sun.

Ryder remained quiet but kept his eyes peripherally trained on Grayson. She was calming down, but she was still shaking. She kept flexing and extending her fingers, rubbing them together, trying to hide the tremor. She was more rattled than she let on.

Gabriel's own fingers gripped tightly into a fist underneath the table.

"What do you know about Elliot James?" Blake asked casually, leaning his chair back against the wall.

"From internal medicine?"

He nodded.

"Personally or professionally?"

Logan saw Gabriel's eyes shoot up from his binder, but he kept his mouth shut.

"Both. Start with professionally."

"He's a good resident, as far as I know. Seems to know his stuff for a second year. His department certainly likes him. He's not a problem resident."

"And personally?" Harrison asked.

"He's, um, got an attitude."

"An attitude?"

"Yeah."

"What does that mean exactly?"

"It's just who he is." She shrugged.

"Explain that to me," Blake interrupted, smiling warmly at her.

"He's from a pretty wealthy family. Dad runs a law firm in New York or Boston or somewhere on the east coast. He's used to having money and flaunting it. I think he still gets a monthly allowance, even though he's pulling in a paycheck. And he knows he's easy on the eyes."

"Excuse me?" Ryder interjected.

Harrison smirked and folded his arms in front of his chest. Grayson just smiled.

"You should've seen the first day he came to the hospital. It was like Justin Bieber was here. That's actually a good way to think of him. Pretty boy with too much money and he knows it."

She looked at Nolan. "Why so curious about him?"

When it took a moment for someone to answer her, she sighed and put her head in her hands.

"He's dead, isn't he?"

"Yes, he is," Logan replied.

"When?"

Her voice was suddenly flat, almost robotic.

"Sunday. That call at lunch…" Blake trailed off.

"Oh. Is it connected to the others?"

"We think so."

"How was he…?"

"Strangled."

"Probably wearing a two-thousand-dollar suit and a gold Rolex," she mused, sarcasm heavy in her voice.

"What was that?" Harrison asked, sitting forward in his chair.

"That was his go-to. He'd show up to the hospital in that if he thought it would get him laid before morning rounds. As far as I know, it usually worked."

Logan laughed and kicked back in his chair. He liked this girl already. Blake continued on.

"Did you ever have a negative interaction with him?"

"You mean did he ever hit on me?" she countered, eyebrows raised.

Logan cleared his throat and smiled. Ryder was clearly close to losing it, and he was loving watching every minute of it. It would be a miracle if he kept his seat for another sixty seconds.

"Sure."

"Yes, he did. When he first got here. It took the threat of me surgically removing some very important anatomy to get him to back off, but I never had problems with him after that."

A loud snap echoed from across the table. Three sets of surprised eyes turned to the source.

Ryder sat rigid and still in his chair, his fountain pen broken clean in half in his clenched fists. Ink was starting to leech out around his fingers and pool on the table. He didn't seem to notice. He kept his eyes fixated on the startled brunette across the table.

Before anyone could say a word, the door to the lecture hall opened slightly and Noah poked his head in around the corner.

"Sorry, blokes, but this meeting's over. Gray, they want you back in here. One of your bone tumors is up next, and the medicine attendings have questions. Weathers isn't here, and neither is Dr. Farley."

Grayson groaned and shook her head.

"Of course, our ortho-oncologist and his fellow are both no-shows for tumor board. Great." She stood, nodding apologetically at the detectives before slipping out the door. She quietly took a seat next to Noah.

"What did they want?" Noah whispered.

"James. From your department. He's dead," she whispered back.

"Shit. I thought he was on vacation or something."

"They found him Sunday."

"That's four, Gray."

She nodded.

"Hot and Handsome say anything to you?"

She shook her head. "You and Babs both need to stop."

"When you figure him out, let me know."

She smiled at him and tried to focus on tumor board.

Yeah, that's happening sometime soon.

53

THANKFULLY, THE REST of the morning went smoothly. By noon, Grayson was free from the hospital.

Dr. Sanders had called her into his office right after the conference had ended and assured her that no censure was planned for her actions. He'd actually winked at her.

Grayson was only partially relieved. Sure, Dr. Sanders could let her keep her job, but it didn't mean that Dr. Carrol wouldn't make her remaining time in residency a living hell.

She kept her windows rolled down as she drove home, letting the wind whip through her hair. It felt ridiculously good to be out in the fresh air.

She let her mind drift to Elliot James. He was a prick, sure, but she couldn't think of anybody who'd want him dead. He'd crossed the line a few times, but a good slap to the face usually brought him under control.

Grayson shook her head. *What in the hell is going on?*

She pulled up behind the house, shut the car off, and walked into a quiet kitchen. A note was sitting on the kitchen table, waiting for her.

Gray-
Had to run out for a few things. Get some sleep. We're going out tonight. Hope you got a costume!
-Babs

Grayson rolled her eyes. She wasn't getting out of Halloween this year, apparently. Her roommate and best friend both had it in for her. She climbed the stairs to her room, dropped onto her bed, and was dead asleep within minutes.

———

At seven o'clock on the dot, there was a soft knock at her bedroom door. Grayson rolled over in bed and threw a pillow over her head. Maybe if she hid deep enough under the covers, they wouldn't find her. She felt the side of the bed sink down and she sighed, relinquishing her death grip on the sides of the pillow.

"Rise and shine, love."

"How did you get in my room?" she groaned.

"You forgot to lock the door. Come downstairs. I brought dinner," he replied, grinning.

She sleepily looked Mason up and down.

Sweatpants and an old T-shirt. There might still be hope.

"So, no costume? Halloween's canceled?" she asked hopefully, sitting up and wiping the sleep from her eyes.

"Absolutely not. Didn't want to get anything on the outfit. Now come downstairs," he scoffed, pulling her off the side of her bed and down the stairs.

Five minutes later, she was sitting cross-legged at the kitchen table, eating Chinese and listening to Noah describe Carrol's outburst to her roommate.

"I wish I would've been there to see that jerk's face," Babs grinned, slurping down some noodles.

"It wasn't as big of a deal as Noah's making it out to be," she replied.

"Nonsense," he said. "It was glorious. The whole hospital's talking about it."

Grayson blushed, stuffing another piece of sesame chicken in her mouth.

"Well, what about that detective?" Babs asked.

"Which one?" she replied, evasively.

"Ryder," she pressed. "He gives me the creeps, Gray."

"You were falling all over yourself on Sunday," she snapped.

"Yeah, but remember, when you left to take that call? He couldn't keep his seat. I...I dunno. I can't explain it. Something's just off. Noah, back me up here."

"He's not your average bloke, but I don't find him creepy."

"Thanks for the backup, Mason," she hissed.

"Enough. Both of you. You've both tried to make something out of nothing. Enough is enough. Just quit it," Grayson sighed.

"All right, all right," Babs relented. "So, are you going to tell me what your costume is?"

"No."

"But you have one?"

"Yes."

"That's not scrubs and a white coat?" Noah specified.

"Of course. You both threatened me with dressing like a streetwalker, remember?"

"Isn't that half of the point of Halloween for women?" Noah chuckled.

"Pig."

Babs threw an eggroll at him. He caught it and made a face back at her.

"All right, I'm going to take a shower," Grayson sighed, standing up and putting her plate in the sink. "Um, Barbara, could I ask for your help in the makeup department?"

"Sure," she shrugged, watching her roommate walk up the stairs.

She made sure Grayson was out of earshot before turning back to Noah.

"Is she okay?"

"Carrol rattled her. Those cops showing up didn't help things."

"She needs a night out. A good one."

"We'll show her one. Don't worry."

"She's gonna kick and fight the whole way."

Noah chuckled. "She usually does. She'll enjoy herself."

When Grayson called her up thirty minutes later, Barbara dutifully followed instructions, applying dark, smoky-gray eyeshadow and pale lipstick, before she was unceremoniously shoved out the bathroom door. She'd shrugged and spent the next hour transforming herself into a sexy version of Glinda the Good Witch, complete with sparkly fairy wings and pink tulle skirt. She clicked her way down the stairs in her four-inch pink heels just before ten.

"You look pretty good there, Mason," she said with a smile.

"You don't look so bad yourself, Glinda," he replied, eyeing her dramatically over the rims of his aviators.

Noah was dressed in a fighter pilot costume, jumpsuit and all.

"Very *Top Gun* of you. Where are we going tonight?" she asked, securing her crown in her hair with a few extra bobby pins.

"I figured we could use a bit of a step-up from the usual downtown skin-fest. I have a few ideas."

"That sounds amazing. What is she doing up there?" Babs huffed, looking up the stairs impatiently. "Gray! Are you ready yet?" she called up.

A door lock clicked open, and the tell-tale click of stiletto heels on wooden floors drifted down the stairs. Noah walked to the bottom of the steps and tapped his fingers rhythmically on the banister.

"All righty, hon, let's see it," he chuckled, thoroughly expecting scrubs or jeans and a T-shirt.

Instead, he raised his eyebrows and motioned for Babs.

"Hey Glinda, come take a look at this."

54

HARRISON SPENT THE rest of Friday in the office, attempting to organize his former partner into something resembling a human being.

Ryder was all over the place, spinning his wheels. He was looking over the same files again and again, and the longer he did it, the more agitated he'd become. It was exhausting trying to keep up.

At least Nolan had finally been able to contact their latest victim's parents, who were graciously skipping the Paris leg of their vacation to come back to bury their son. Since it was going to be a few days before they could get out of Africa, that gave Pelton more than enough time to finish the autopsy.

By 8:30, Logan had had enough. He burst into the cluttered interview room without warning, grabbed his former partner's suit coat in one hand, and hauled said former partner to his feet with the other. Gabriel was too stunned to get a word in until they were out the door and halfway down the hallway.

"What the hell, Logan?" he hissed, wrenching himself out of the hold.

Nolan looked up from his desk at the commotion coming down the hallway and laughed. Logan stopped and leaned against an empty desk, his arms folded across his chest.

"You see this place? It's after eight o'clock on a Friday night, and we're still here. No more." He pointed in sequence. "You're driving me nuts. He's sulking because he doesn't get to take his girls out trick-or-treating. And quite frankly, I want a damned drink. Get your crap. We're going out."

Logan tossed Ryder his coat and turned on his heels toward the elevator.

"Can we keep him after this is all over?" Nolan cackled, pushing himself up from his desk chair and reaching for his jacket.

"So you have someone else who can handle me?" Ryder quipped, sliding his binder underneath his right arm.

"Maybe."

They rode down in the elevator in near silence, Logan tapping his fingers against the handrail. Gabriel's mind was clearly still working, his eyes narrowed and focused on the floor. No one said a word. They piled into Harrison's SUV, Blake in the passenger seat and Ryder in the back.

"So, where are we going at eight at night on Halloween?" Blake asked, throwing on his seat belt.

"I know a place," Logan replied, turning over the engine.

"You realize most places require costumes tonight, right?" Ryder smirked.

"Yes, smart ass. You're dressed up like a police detective. Any questions?"

Ryder threw his hands up in the air in mock defeat. "None whatsoever."

Mick's Tavern was a high-end pub with live music and an extensive cocktail menu located just off Larimer Square. The place catered to a higher caliber clientele than the nearby college bars and had a healthy group of regulars.

Tonight, it had been transformed into a swanky Halloween venue. The lights were low, the bar was saturated with black candles, and the staff was all dressed in coordinating zombie costumes. It was still relatively early, by nightclub standards, but it was already quite busy.

"This place went all out." Nolan whistled.

The hostess eyed the trio as they walked in the door and quickly held up her hands, mumbling about the night's required dress code. One flash of the badge on Harrison's hip and his trademark smile was all it took to calm her down. They were quickly shown to a table in the back. One of the zombies lankily sidled up to the table wearing a black apron.

"What'll it be, guys?" he asked.

"Is the kitchen still open?" Blake asked.

"Yeah, but it's a short menu tonight with the holiday."

He handed over a piece of black paper with white print. Blake perused it quickly, then handed it across the table to Logan.

"The burger. And whatever New Belgium you've got on tap."

"Shocker," Ryder mumbled.

"I'll have the same. But make it a porter," Logan said.

"Sure. And for you?" the waiter asked, looking at Ryder.

"Just a scotch. Neat."

"He means a burger and a scotch, neat," Logan corrected, shaking his head.

Ryder shot him a glare across the table, which earned him one for himself in return.

"Oh, get the fuck over yourself, Gabriel."

Their drinks came first, then dinner, which was thankfully quite good. The three men spent the hour after their plates had been cleared laughing and drinking, easing into a comfortable camaraderie with the help of the alcohol.

After ten, the place really picked up. The costumes proved to be a source of continual amusement. Nolan had a running list of best-dressed, worst-dressed, sluttiest, and most inventive. Their waiter kept the drinks coming, which helped considerably.

They had just started in on a new round when Logan looked up from his glass and kicked Nolan under the table. Hard.

Blake sputtered into his beer glass, foam flopping over the edges onto the table. He shot Logan a *what-the-hell* look, then craned his neck around in the general direction of the front door. It took him a moment to make the connection, but when he did, he grinned from ear to ear. Logan nodded and chuckled under his breath.

"You two lovebirds want to fill me in here?" Ryder asked, swirling his scotch around in his glass. His back was—like Nolan's—facing the door.

"Well, theoretically, what would do it for you, Gabe? A fighter pilot, a pink fairy, or..." Blake half-turned around in his chair again. "Shit, I can't tell."

"What?"

Nolan was still turned around, looking at the crowd at the front door, talking over his shoulder. "Shit...it's some kind of black thing."

"What the fuck are you talking about, idiot?"

Blake spun back around and took a long drink out of his glass. "I asked you a question. Fairy, pilot, or black thing?"

Ryder narrowed his eyes and glared at Logan, who was shooting him a smirk from across the table.

"Did you fucking drug him, Logan?" he asked, taking a drink from his own glass. "He's not making sense."

"He asked you a question, Gabe. Answer it."

"You two have both lost it."

"Turn around, idiot," Logan chuckled, shaking his head.

Ryder took a swig of scotch, rolled his eyes, and swung his body around, expecting his target to be another gaggle of inappropriately dressed college girls. He spotted the group in question easily enough.

The fighter pilot removed his sunglasses, and Gabriel immediately recognized Noah Mason. The pink fairy to his left, which he suspected was actually an attempt at sexing up Glinda from the Wizard of Oz, was Barbara Parker. They stepped down beyond the hostess station, and Mason looked back toward the door, beckoning a third person forward.

Oh, wow.

When she walked underneath the light, Gabriel's breath caught, and he struggled to keep his seat. He could feel Blake and Logan watching him. Any other day, their questioning eyes would have been unnerving. Right now, he couldn't give a damn.

"The raven," he mumbled.

"What was that?" Harrison said.

"You heard me, asshole," he mumbled, turning back around in his chair.

Grayson was dressed in a long-sleeved black dress that dropped to the floor. The neckline, lower sleeves, shoulders, and skirt were full of black feathers that glittered in the low candlelight.

How the hell are black feathers reflecting light?

Her hair was slicked back into a ponytail that tapered at the nape of her neck, and two plumes of feathers were attached to either side of her head near her ears. Her blue eyes shone brightly, even in the dim light, enhanced by the black kohl around them.

"That's a raven, huh?" Harrison asked from across the table. "Pretty bird."

"Yes, she is," Gabriel mumbled. He hunched his shoulders over his nearly-drained glass.

Logan leaned forward and hit him on the back of the head.

55

GRAYSON HESITANTLY FOLLOWED Noah and Babs into the bar. Mick's was a respectable place, and truthfully, she'd been thrilled at the choice. She hadn't felt up to spending the evening with drunk eighteen-year-olds who were dressed in little more than their underwear. The place was incredibly busy. She had to elbow for a position next to Noah at the bar.

"First one's on me, ladies." He grinned.

A bartender tossed a few cocktail napkins on the bar in front of them. "What'll it be, guys?"

"Cosmopolitan," Babs said.

"Gin and tonic." Noah nodded.

"And you?"

"Um, vodka and sparkling cranberry, please."

"Comin' up."

"Start a tab for us." Noah handed over his credit card and wrapped his arms around the girls' shoulders.

"You ladies do a bloke proud," he admitted.

"Thanks." Babs winked.

She grabbed her drink the moment it hit the bar and walked off to say hello to some friends from work she had spotted across the room.

"You too, love." Noah smiled, handing Grayson her drink.

He grabbed her free hand and spun her around once for effect.

"How'd you pull that off?"

"The costume? Oh, I just put it together. I had most of it at home, except for the feathers," she smiled meekly, pulling at one of her sleeves.

"Very well done. You've already got more than one admirer."

"I'm dressed up like a bird, Noah, and I'm fully covered. Nothing special."

Grayson took a sip of her cocktail. *Whoa, this is strong.*

"Doesn't mean they're not looking," he countered.

"I'm showing the least amount of skin in the whole bar, Noah. Guys included. If that isn't a back-off message on Halloween, I don't know what is."

The pair sat at the bar and chatted amicably, watching Babs flutter from one group of people to the next. After a while, Noah excused himself to say hello to some of the internal medicine residents who'd shown up.

Grayson sat for a few moments by herself, quietly soaking up her surroundings. She was about to signal the bartender for another round when someone slid onto the barstool her friend had just vacated. She turned slightly, intending to tell whoever it was that the seat was already spoken for. Instead, she ended up staring gape-mouthed at a rather handsome, incredibly agitated Detective Ryder.

Grayson jumped back slightly in her seat, startled at the sight of him. He was still dressed in his black suit and white shirt from earlier in the day, but the collar was open and his tie was gone. His hair was askew, his five-o'clock shadow had more than fully arrived, and she could smell the faint hint of scotch. He had just enough bad boy about him in the candle-light to make him exceptionally dangerous. She bit her lower lip and held her breath.

Oh, dear God, he looks good…Shit, mind out of the gutter, Gray.

"Grayson," he nodded.

"Gabriel," she breathed when she'd recovered herself.

She felt the blush rising from her chest. Thankfully, it was hidden under black fabric. They sat face to face, staring at each other. Grayson nervously wrung her hands in her lap. She ducked her eyes down to the floor when she couldn't take his gaze any longer.

Gabriel continued to stare at her, silently, unable to think of a single thing to say.

"What can I get you, bud?" the bartender asked, appearing out of nowhere and addressing Ryder.

"Scotch, neat," he replied, nodding to the particular bottle behind the bar he was interested in. "And whatever she wants."

"Another of the same, please," she said quietly, handing over her empty glass.

She looked him over carefully, her eyes narrowed.

"And what exactly are you supposed to be?" she asked.

Gabriel lifted the side of his jacket and pointed toward the badge clipped on his hip.

"A police detective."

"I'm assuming the gun is real, too?"

Gabriel nodded.

"That's cheating," she argued.

He winked at her as their drinks arrived. Grayson nervously wrapped both her hands around her glass.

"I suppose it is, compared to yours," he admitted. "It looks incredible, by the way."

She laughed into her glass.

"What?"

"You're lying, but thanks."

His face dropped into a dark scowl. "Why would I lie to you?"

"You probably don't even know what I'm supposed to be."

"A raven, of course."

She looked up from the bar, shocked that he'd guessed correctly. He smiled back at her and leaned heavily against the marble.

"Lucky guess."

"Maybe." He shrugged.

"What are you doing here?"

"I'm being held against my will," he replied, pointing over his shoulder toward a table in the back corner of the bar.

Grayson looked back over his shoulder to see Detectives Harrison and Nolan laughing like hyenas at one another. Blake was falling halfway out of his chair.

"They look well occupied," she said. "Now would be a good time to make a run for it."

Gabriel looked back at them, then trained his eyes on Grayson. He held his hand out to her underneath the bar.

"You coming?"

She hastily looked sideways, from one edge of the bar to the other. No one was looking at them. Barbara and Noah were nowhere to be found. She smiled meekly, then nodded. He grabbed her hand and stood up, pulling her with him.

Gabriel quickly wove his way around to the other side of the bar. Tables had been cleared away to make room for a dance floor. He kept their hands linked tightly together as he steered her along the outskirts. Grayson's heart was pounding in her chest.

Where is he taking me? Wait, could this be dangerous? Oh, who the hell cares...

Gabriel found a dark corner against the back wall and pulled her next to him. Grayson tried to turn to face him, but a rough hand pinned her back against his chest. The touch of his hand through the fabric of her dress sent electricity through her skin. She stopped trying to talk.

They stood in silence for several minutes, watching the crowd ebb and flow with the music. At some point, a round of drinks magically appeared, but she was too overwhelmed to notice how. Gabriel placed hers into a shaking set of hands. Grayson fought to keep her head from lolling back against his shoulder. She was warm. And protected. When she felt her resolve was desperately holding on by its last thread, she spoke.

"I thought your escape would include a getaway car," she teased, leaning in closer to be heard over the music.

"Next time," he replied, leaning down and whispering in her ear.

His hot breath on her neck sent a shiver down her spine.

Oh, do that again.

She looked sideways at him and, trembling, raised her glass to her lips. Gabriel leaned back against the wall, holding his glass of scotch in one hand and keeping contact with Grayson with the other. He watched her closely.

She was nervous. The feathers on her dress were shaking just enough to be noticeable in the low light. She kept flicking her eyes back over her shoulder to look at him. She never kept them up for long, but when she did...

...those eyes...

For her part, Grayson was trying to focus on her breathing and keep from making a complete fool of herself. He was looking at her. He was *still* looking at her. He hadn't *stopped* looking at her.

She gripped tightly onto her cocktail glass with both hands, wishing that the damned thing would magically refill itself. It didn't, and she set it aside. The alcohol was suddenly not doing a thing to help her nerves. Instead, she felt every quickening beat of her heart, every gasped breath.

I have to be blushing from my toes to my nose. Not a great look, Gray, even in the candlelight.

An overly rambunctious group dressed as characters from Super Mario Brothers pushed by, more than eager to get to the bar. They slammed directly into her, knocking the wind from her lungs and spinning her sideways.

Grayson stumbled and swore under her breath, bracing herself for a fall to the floor. Instead, she felt two strong arms wrap around her. They held her suspended in midair. She felt warm fingers splay protectively over her hip and in between her shoulder blades as she dipped toward the floor.

"Careful."

"Thanks. I…I mean, sorry," she mumbled.

She straightened herself up, and his arms went with her. Gabriel didn't make an attempt to let her go, and she didn't attempt to move away. He was looking down at her with that fire in his eyes like she was the only other person in the bar. It was painful. And he wouldn't let her look away. She took in a shaky breath and held it.

"Monster Mash" faded away, and something decidedly sultrier came over the speaker system. The DJ's voice filtered in over the introductory bars.

"For those of you who have a little witch in your life, why don't you lead her onto the floor? It's 'Witchcraft,' by ol' Blue Eyes himself."

Frank Sinatra started singing about fingers in his hair and a sly come-hither stare. Couples partnered off on the floor, giving the singles a chance to hit the bar and give their feet a break.

Grayson hardly registered the music change, but she most definitely felt Gabriel shift on his feet. She tried to step back, break away, to give him room. Instead, the fingers across her back pushed her forward. The ones at her hip dug in harder. He brought her closer. Her right hand flew to his shoulder, her left to his bicep. It was the only place for them. She felt the muscles harden under her touch.

My God, he's so warm.

The heat of his chest was radiating through his shirt. Grayson stood stock still, immobile, and completely overpowered. By the feel of him. By the smell of him. For what seemed like days. She kept her eyes rooted to the white shirt in front of her. She didn't dare look up again.

"You like to dance." His deep, smooth voice drifted down to her ear.

"Hmm? Oh, um, no. I…I don't dance," she replied, shaking her head.

"You're swaying rather well to Sinatra."

Grayson startled in his arms, realizing she had subconsciously started moving in time with the music. And in time with him. She froze.

"Don't stop," he whispered, sending another long shiver down her spine.

"I…I don't know how…"

"Yes, you do."

"I…I can't…"

"Yes, you can," he said, starting to move again.

He kept her by the wall but pulled her in tightly, taking her right hand and wrapping it in his. "You know exactly what you're doing."

Grayson lolled her head back a bit, closing her eyes. *He can dance. Of course, he can.*

Sinatra faded away and Nina Simone followed, singing soulfully about putting a spell on a man. Grayson lost herself in the music. It was easy to block out everything but the feel of his lead and the dark tones of the song. He whispered something under his breath, and it snapped her back into reality. She looked up, directly into his eyes.

"What was that?" she asked lazily.

"What in the hell are you doing to me, Grayson?" he whispered, resting his forehead gently against hers.

"I could ask you the same question, Gabriel."

Where did that come from?

What did she just say?

"Minx."

"Raven," she corrected.

Nina drifted off and was replaced by the usual techno-pop club set.

Grayson sharply jolted back into reality, holding on to Gabriel for dear life against the sudden surge toward the dance floor. She heard him chuckle softly. She bristled, thinking he was laughing at her. Ryder felt her tense and leaned down, whispering in her ear.

"Easy, Raven. I've got you."

He eased her back against the wall, then pointed to the other side of the bar.

"My captors are looking for me," he said softly.

She followed his finger to see Harrison and Nolan walking slowly through the crowd, scanning from side to side, clearly looking for someone.

"Oh. Right. I…um…I should probably find Noah."

He nodded, his eyes darting to the floor for the briefest moment.

Am I imagining things or does he look disappointed?

Gabriel grasped her hand without warning and spun her around, his eyes watching the feathers on her skirt twirl and twist in the candlelight. He relaxed his hold, only enough to turn her fingers in his.

"Goodnight, detective," she managed to squeak out.

His eyes narrowed with disapproval. Grayson cocked her head slightly to one side, not grasping the sudden change.

"We're back to that, are we?"

Oh.

"Goodnight, Gabriel," she said quietly.

"Happy Halloween, Raven," he replied, gently kissing the top of her hand.

And then he was gone into the crowd.

Grayson closed her eyes and wrapped her left hand around the top of her right. It was still warm where he'd touched her. She searched the crowd for him. She caught him standing by the front door, hands shoved into his overcoat pockets, his eyes on her and only her. He drank her in like a man starving, then turned and followed Harrison and Nolan into the night.

She did her best to steady her breathing, quickly gave up, and walked back around to the bar. Noah and Babs were both sitting down, not far from their original spot.

"Gray! My God, where have you been? Sit down!" Babs squealed. Clearly, she'd had a few.

Grayson sat in the offered seat. The bartender immediately set a drink down in front of her.

"Oh, I'm sorry, I didn't order this."

The zombie leaned over the bar so he could be heard. "I know. The guy you were with, the one dressed like a cop? He did. Before he left."

"Oh. Okay, I…um…thanks."

The man winked at her, then went back to serving other customers. She took a timid first sip, then a much longer second. Simple and sweet and refreshing.

"Yum." *This is perfect.*

"What is that?" Babs pointed.

"I have no idea," she giggled.

"Devil's punch. Tequila, limoncello, sour mix, and orange," the bartender said in passing.

"Special-ordered?" Noah asked with a wink.

Grayson didn't answer.

"All right you two," Babs said, slamming an empty shot glass down on the bar. "Time to get out on the dance floor. I'm tired of shaking my ass by myself!"

She grabbed Noah's hand, who shrugged and grabbed Grayson's. She followed them out onto the floor and spent the next two and a half hours dancing around before they headed home, sore and exhausted and utterly spent.

56

THE SHRILL SOUND of a cell phone sliced through the alcohol-clouded haze of deep sleep. Logan reached around blindly on the bedside table, knocking the damned thing under the bed by accident. He cursed and attempted to reach underneath the mattress. He failed and, still cursing, flopped out of bed and got down on his hands and knees. By the time he found it, he had two more missed calls and as many voicemails. He didn't bother to listen to them. He just hit redial.

"Where the hell have you been?" came the voice over the line.

"Nice to hear from you too, Blake," he mumbled, yawning into the phone.

"Logan, we've got a callout."

"Oh, goody. Another dead body in a church?"

"Yeah, but there's something else."

"What?"

"It's who the body is. We already have an ID."

"You gonna tell me or do I have to start guessing?" Logan asked sarcastically, pushing off his knees and heading toward the bathroom.

"Just be out at your door in twenty minutes. I'll tell you on the way to get Ryder."

Logan paused with the toilet seat half up.

"We're not going to meet him there?"

"No. He doesn't know yet."

"You gonna call him?"

"I don't think that would be a good idea."

"Why not?"

"Just be outside, Logan."

The line went dead.

Logan stared at his cell for a minute and then put it down on the countertop. Something wasn't right. Whatever had Blake agitated enough to call *him* first instead of his partner couldn't be good. They hadn't worked together long, but Blake Nolan had pretty good instincts.

Logan hoped for once they were wrong.

The pair rode up the elevator to Gabriel's apartment in silence. Blake looked like he'd gotten ready in a hurry. Logan looked only marginally better. Ryder would be sure to pick up on it. Well that, and the fact that they were both a bit on edge. Nolan had given Logan what details he'd had on the ride over. He'd been right to keep his partner in the dark about this one.

At least for now.

Harrison took the lead when they got to the apartment door. He knocked repeatedly, and when he didn't get an answer, he fished a key out of his jacket pocket. Blake raised an eyebrow. In all their years together at Major Crimes, he'd hardly been inside his partner's apartment. He definitely didn't have a key.

"In case of emergencies," Logan shrugged, sensing Nolan's unease. "Usually that means too much scotch and a bad mood."

He entered the apartment without hesitating, aiming down a hallway that curved off to the right of the kitchen and dining room. Blake followed silently behind him. Three doors down, he hung a quick left and pushed into what Nolan quickly discovered was the master bedroom. There was nobody there.

The bed was neatly made, and there wasn't a thing out of place. Same for the bathroom, guest room, office, kitchen…the whole place was immaculate.

Gabriel wasn't in the apartment.

"God damn it," Harrison muttered under his breath, pulling out his phone.

He put it up to his ear and walked into the main living room, leaning up against the floor to ceiling windows that looked out over downtown Denver and the distant mountains to the west. The sky was still dark, without a hint of the sunrise that was still hours away.

Blake plopped down unceremoniously on the couch.

Ryder probably has a great view once the sun comes up. Lucky bastard.

"Ryder? Yeah, it's me. Where the fuck are you?"

There was a short pause and a long sigh.

"It's five in the goddamned morning. Exercise at a normal hour."

Another pause.

"Just get your ass back to your apartment. For the record, it wouldn't kill you to put up a family picture or two in here."

"No kidding," Blake griped.

Logan smiled into the receiver. "Yes, I'm at your apartment, ass. Run. Quickly." He ended the call.

"He's out being healthy again, isn't he?" Nolan groaned.

"Makes me want to slap him sometimes," Harrison replied, nodding.

"Oh well, he's getting rid of enough free radicals for all of us."

"How do you want to handle this? You want me to…"

"I'll tell him," Blake shrugged, aiming for nonchalant. "He's gonna find out soon anyway."

Logan shot him a "whatever-floats-your-boat" look and turned back to look out the window.

Fifteen minutes later, Ryder burst through the front door, drenched in sweat. He was out of breath and exceptionally irritated. He yanked the earbuds out of his ears and wound them around his phone, tossing the whole thing onto the nearest chair. He slammed his front door shut. The paintings hung on the walls rattled softly in protest.

"One of you want to tell me why the hell you're in my apartment at five in the goddamned morning?" he roared.

Harrison looked over at Nolan, who was just standing up from the couch.

"We've been called out."

"Another one?" he asked, wiping the sweat from his face.

Nolan nodded.

"Do we know who?"

He nodded again. Ryder frowned at his partner. Something was wrong.

"You could've told me that over the phone, Blake."

"I didn't want to. There's more, Ryder."

"What is it?" he asked warily

"The vic was identified by a hospital ID badge."

"We were expecting another hospital employee. No surprise there," Ryder said, peeling off his hoodie.

"Yeah, but we know this one already. Really well," Logan muttered.

Ryder's blood went cold. *No...*

He threw the sweatshirt over one of the bar stools and slammed his right fist down against the granite bar top. Nolan held up his hands in mock surrender and warily approached the counter.

"It's not Dr. Carter," he said.

Relief flooded Ryder's face, then disappeared just as quickly as his partner continued to speak.

"It's Dr. Carrol."

The apartment went deadly quiet. Nobody moved. Nobody dared to.

Ryder pushed past his partner, disappearing into his bedroom. He returned five minutes later, dressed in black and seething. He stalked out the door without a word to either of them. They scrambled to catch up with him at the elevator. Harrison dove into Ryder's front pants pocket the moment they were side by side.

"What the fuck, Logan?" he hissed.

The older man held up a set of car keys, jingling them in front of Ryder's face.

"You're not driving."

"You don't fucking tell me what to do." He made a wild grab for the set, which failed.

"I do now. Stop being a prick."

Logan shoved the keys into his own pocket and kept his hand inside for good measure.

Ryder muttered under his breath the entire ride down to the lobby but didn't make another grab for them.

The drive to Blessed Sacrament Catholic Church was silent and tense. Blake looked back at his partner in the rearview mirror from time to time. Gabriel was staring intently into his binder, which Logan had grabbed off the counter as they'd scrambled out the door. His right hand rhythmically clenched and unclenched into a fist at his side.

Not a good sign.

A few streets away from the church, Harrison suggested they stop off for coffee. Nolan was only too happy to forego the drive-through and go into the shop to get their order personally. Once he was inside, Logan swung his left leg onto the middle console and looked into the backseat of the SUV.

"You wanna tell me what's going on in that head of yours?" he asked.

"No." Ryder kept his head down, his eyes dark and sharply focused.

"You're not helping anybody here, Gabe. Tell me what's going on."

"Shut up."

"Something has you uptight. I know it's not great that this doc ended up dead, but..."

"Goddamn it, Logan, shut the fuck up!" Ryder shouted, his eyes blazing. His right fist slammed against the side door, leaving a dent below the window.

Blake picked that particular moment to open the driver's door and slide in, coffee and donuts in hand. He looked back and forth from Harrison, who was scowling, to his partner, who was foaming at the mouth.

"Okay, so, what did I miss?"

"Just drive the goddamned car, Blake," Ryder hissed, grabbing his coffee.

"You're welcome. Jeez," he replied, quickly turning the SUV over and maneuvered out into traffic.

They pulled up outside the church at little before dawn. The front door was open, and warm light filtered down the front steps.

Ryder stormed into the chapel. He pushed the uniformed officers that met him at the door aside and stalked up the center aisle, Nolan and Harrison hot on his heels. They mumbled apologies on his behalf.

Gabriel threw his binder down on a polished pew and ripped the top sheet away from the body.

Dr. Carrol was gray. His eyes were glazed over and chalky white. He was dressed, without any obvious signs of a struggle, and there were ligature marks around his wrists. A small drop of blood at the corner of his mouth drew Ryder's attention. The young detective snapped on a pair of gloves.

"Hey, Gabe, why don't you wait for…"

"Fuck off, Blake," he spat.

He violently forced the dead man's lips and teeth apart, then let them slam closed just as quickly. Ryder stood, ripped the gloves off, and threw them against the nearest wall. He grabbed his binder and stalked off toward the front doors of the church without a word.

"Ryder! Where the hell are you going?" Blake hollered after him.

"Don't bother," Harrison said, shaking his head and laying a hand on the younger detective's shoulder. "He's got the scent of something. At this point, just follow along and apologize for him."

57

GRAYSON WOKE UP to the sound of pots and pans banging around in the downstairs kitchen. She looked out her bedroom window to see inky-black sky still draped over the mountaintops. Her clock read just a little after six o'clock. The clamoring of more pans and a string of epithets had her instantly sitting up in bed.

What on earth…?

She swung her legs off the side of the bed and slid her feet into a pair of well-worn shearling-lined slippers. She threaded her arms through the sleeves of her gray robe and wrapped it around herself to ward off the morning chill, tying the sash into a bow on her right hip. She quietly opened her door and snuck down the stairs. The house was dark, but the kitchen lights were on full blast. She tiptoed forward, peeking around the corner, and smiled.

Barbara was balancing the refrigerator door open with one hand, trying to gather milk and eggs in the other. Every pot and skillet that they owned between them was scattered out on the countertop. Dirty measuring cups and spoons poked out over what little space was left. The coffeepot was bubbling in the far corner, and the oven was just about pre-heated from the looks of the temperature gauge.

Grayson slid silently into one of the kitchen chairs and watched Babs try to get a handle on breakfast. She noticed that her roommate had her headphones on and was singing along to something vaguely pop-ish under her breath.

No wonder she didn't hear me come in.

Suddenly, Babs spun toward the front countertop, looking for the cookbook she had set there. Instead of the recipe she needed, she found her smirking roommate.

"Shit, Gray!" she shrieked, pulling off her headphones.

Grayson smiled and threw her head back, laughing.

"Serves you right for making such a ruckus this early on a Sunday, Babs," she replied cheekily.

"Oh no, I woke you, didn't I?" She frowned.

"Don't worry about it," she waved absently. "This is sleeping in for me. What are you doing?"

"I wanted to make us a nice brunch, and knowing my cooking skills, I figured I'd need about four solid hours to pull it off."

"What's the occasion?"

"Umm, Sunday? Do I need a reason?"

"No," Grayson shook her head, "I suppose you don't. Do you want some help?"

Babs looked around the halfway-destroyed kitchen. "Well, it couldn't hurt," she said sheepishly.

Grayson shook her head slightly, then moved around behind her roommate to pour two cups of coffee.

"Oooooh, wait!" Babs squealed. She scampered to the refrigerator and grabbed a carton of orange juice and a bottle of champagne from the side of the door. "I thought we could have mimosas today!"

"Coffee first, sweetie," Grayson replied. "Mimosas with the actual food."

They were midway through stacks of cinnamon pancakes, bacon, and teacups of mimosas when there was a knock at the front door. Babs looked up from her plate, her fork halfway to her mouth.

"Expecting somebody, Gray?"

"No one I know of," she replied, starting to stand.

"Oh, sit down. I'll get it. This is my fifth pancake. I could use the exercise," she muttered, heading off toward the living room in her wrinkled sleep tank and shorts combination.

Grayson settled back into her chair, bringing her legs up to rest underneath her, and took a sip from her teacup.

Mimosas were definitely a nice touch.

She heard the muffled voices of at least one man mixed with Barbara's, followed by the sound of footsteps headed toward the kitchen. She looked up just in time to see Detectives Nolan, Harrison, and Ryder step into the doorway. They looked like they had been up for hours, and it was barely past seven a.m. Harrison and Nolan both offered her a weak smile, which she quickly returned.

When she looked at Gabriel, all she saw was fury. It nearly knocked her off of her chair. It was radiating off of him in waves. Unconsciously, she wrapped her arms around her waist. She'd taken her robe off to help Barbara cook. Now she desperately wanted it back. It was out of reach, across the room.

"You've got company, Gray," Babs said hesitantly, walking around the three men and taking up a spot behind her.

Grayson noticed that she didn't sit back down. Barbara Parker was clearly gearing up for a fight.

What the hell?

"I see that. Good morning, detectives. Can I get you some coffee?" she asked politely.

"No," Ryder spat menacingly.

"No, *thank you*," Nolan parroted, emphasizing the latter portion of the refusal. "Dr. Carter, I'm sorry we're here so early on a Sunday..."

"I figure you have a reason for it," she replied. "What can I do for you?"

"Could we sit down?" Harrison asked.

"Oh, sure," she motioned to the table. "Let me just clear these dishes..."

She grabbed her plate and Barbara's and moved them to the back counter. She found her coffee cup and brought it back to the table with her.

Probably better to drink coffee around the cops.

Harrison and Nolan had sat down by the time she turned back to the table.

Ryder was standing on the threshold between the living room and the kitchen, clearly struggling to keep himself under control. His fingers were rapidly clawing and extending at his sides, and he was forcing his breath out through clenched teeth. He looked like an animal ready to strike. Grayson swallowed hard. She could feel herself starting to shake.

"Look," she started as she took her own seat, "I'm sorry if this is direct, but why don't we just get it to it?"

"We need to know where you were last night," Blake said softly.

She narrowed her eyes and wrinkled her forehead in confusion.

"Where I was last night?" she parroted back. "Why?"

"Answer the question," Ryder hissed.

Babs glared at him. She rested a protective hand on her roommate's shoulder.

"I, I…I was here. I mean, for most of the night. We…we had dinner, sat around for a while. I went out for a run around eight, came back before nine. I went to bed around eleven," she stammered.

Grayson looked wildly back and forth between the detectives sitting at her table, then over her shoulder at Barbara for reassurance. Her roommate could only manage a small smile, but she nodded in agreement.

"Do you usually run at night?" Harrison asked.

"Oh, God no, I hardly run," she replied. "But I was antsy last night and just couldn't sit still. So, I took a lap around the neighborhood. It's more of a jog, really."

"No one went with you?"

"No."

"Can anyone verify your route?"

"Why the hell do you care about where she went running?" Babs interjected.

"Please answer the question, Dr. Carter," Harrison directed, blatantly ignoring the blonde.

"Um, I…I don't think so."

"We'll need the clothes you wore last night," Harrison stated flatly.

"Um, okay, but what for?"

"And the shoes you wore," Nolan added.

"Okay, enough!" Barbara pushed off from the counter where she'd been leaning. "Tell us what the hell you're doing here. Now. This is starting to sound like she needs to call a lawyer."

Grayson turned in her chair and shook her head softly at her roommate. "Babs, I don't have anything…"

"Be quiet, Grayson," she said quickly, fully concentrating her venom at the detectives sitting at the table. "Well?"

———

Harrison concentrated on the young doctor, who was wrinkling her forehead at them.

Great. Now she's getting suspicious of us. Why the hell did we let Ryder drag us here?

He didn't say a word. Ryder remained rooted to the wall by the entryway, his fists rhythmically clenching and staring straight ahead. Nolan cleared his throat.

"Dr. Thomas Carrol was found dead this morning."

All three detectives looked at Grayson, eager to gauge her reaction. All they saw was shock and surprise.

"Dr. Carrol? But I…I just saw him Friday."

"Yes, we know," Harrison said. "We were all there for that little display. Seen the good doctor since then?"

"What? No. Of course not. I haven't been to the hospital all weekend. I haven't been on call." Grayson's voice was becoming more and more high pitched.

"I didn't ask if you saw him in the hospital. I asked if you've seen him. At all."

"No, I just told you…" Grayson started, shaking her head slowly.

———

She stopped mid-sentence. The blood drained from her face. She looked up sharply at Nolan, then trained her eyes on Harrison.

They can't think…

She swung her head up to look at Ryder, and what blood she had left went ice-cold. She could see the venom in his eyes, the disgust and the malice, and it was all directed at her. She started breathing faster, shallower; a blush rushed into her face. Her heartbeat was screaming in her ears. It was hard to hear anything else. The kitchen was suddenly too small, too bright, and very, very warm.

"You...you can't possibly think I..." She stood up shakily from her chair and moved to the counter, leaning onto it for support. She forced herself to suck in a deep breath. "You think I killed him," she whispered.

It wasn't a question.

"What?" Babs shrieked. "You can't be serious!"

The kitchen went silent. Grayson leaned her head into her hands on the counter. Barbara's eyes threw daggers at the detectives from across the breakfast table.

"Why not?"

A raspy voice from the kitchen threshold broke the silence. Grayson raised her head toward the source. Ryder was inching toward her, his hands in his pockets, anger dripping in his voice. She looked at his eyes. They weren't blue anymore. They were black.

"We were all there. We watched him argue with you. Berate you in front of your colleagues. The other residents. Humiliate you. The man came after you. He tried to physically assault you. And it wasn't the first time, was it?"

Nolan gave Logan a worried look, and it was immediately returned. The older man pushed back quietly from the kitchen table. Blake did the same.

Ryder inched closer to her.

"You're right. I don't think you killed Dr. Carrol," he said.

Grayson's eyes momentarily relaxed.

Another inch closer.

"I think you had someone do your dirty work for you."

Her legs felt like they were going to give out. They offered no support. Her shallow breathing was making it very difficult to keep the room in focus. Grayson somehow managed to maintain eye contact with him.

His eyes were still dark. His pupils were dilated, an evolutionarily learned response to an increase in the sympathetic nervous system. He saw something he wanted. He was coming in for the kill. For her.

"Dr. Carrol used his words against you, so you had his tongue cut out. Elliot James threw around his money. Got whatever girl he wanted. You disapproved, you said so yourself. You had him killed with his most prized possessions. Dr. Porter was a pig. That one was easy enough. Kill him with something you could hide in his food. Dr. Nelson was screwing anything and everything he could, so you took away his most prized possession..."

Grayson stared at the floor, her fingers gripping the granite countertop, desperately trying not to pass out. He was close to her now. Well within striking distance. She could feel the heat radiating off of him. That same heat had been pleasant at Mike's, warm and protective and safe.

It wasn't now.

"Who did you use? Who did you coerce into doing your little dirty work for you, huh?"

His breath brushed against her ear. She didn't answer him. The kitchen went still. No one moved.

"And of course," he lowered his voice, "there was Lisa..."

The thundering sound of her heartbeat instantly cleared

from her ears. Grayson snapped her eyes up from the floor. He was smirking at her like he knew he had her caught.

Bastard.

Before she could think twice, Grayson launched forward, grabbed Gabriel by his shirt collar, and slapped him across his face.

Hard.

The sound of her palm connecting with his cheek echoed off the stainless steel. Grayson didn't stop. She kept moving forward. The momentum was overwhelming. She joined her right hand with her left on his chest and shoved him into the living room.

Ryder stumbled backward through the threshold, his heels catching on the edge of the coffee table. He sprawled out on the floor, completely caught off guard by the outburst.

Grayson started to advance on him, but Barbara grabbed her by the shoulders. She instantly backed off. She refused to fight against her roommate.

Logan and Blake rushed around either side of the pair and hauled Ryder to his feet. Gabriel could feel them tense up as he regained his balance and brushed the dust off of his trousers. He wrinkled his forehead, momentarily confused, but the look on Logan's face spoke volumes.

They're trying to keep me away from her. They think I'm going to attack.... wait...what?

He stilled and shook the fog out of his head. He blinked rapidly and looked at Harrison, who was shaking his head and then to Nolan, who wouldn't look at him at all. Gabriel gritted his teeth and raised his eyes.

Obviously furious, Barbara Parker had her hands on her roommate's shoulders, but he didn't give a damn about the blonde. His eyes found Grayson, and his stomach dropped through the floor.

She was pale. He could see the faint rippling of her pajama pants as she shook. Her fists were opening and shutting rhythmically at her sides, much like his had just been. But her face...

There was no smile, no hint of the laughter or mischief he'd seen there a day and a half ago. Her lips were tight. Her eyes were narrowed and aimed directly at him. She advanced on him. One step. He stepped back. When she spoke, her voice was soft, low, and lethal. His gut turned over. He fought the urge to vomit.

"You. All three of you," she said, never taking her eyes off of Ryder, "will get out of my house. Now. Do not think for one moment that you have my permission to set foot here again."

Gabriel's mind was clear for the first time in hours. Suddenly, Dr. Carrol was the last thing on his mind.

What in the hell did I just do? I just accused her of...oh, Jesus fucking hell no...

He took one step forward back into the living room.

"Grayson..."

———

"Don't you fucking dare," she spat.

She turned back into the kitchen, opened the door to the back porch, and slammed it behind her. In turn, Barbara pushed past the three of them and opened the front door.

"Get the hell out of here. All of you. And if you ever come back, I swear to God, there will be more waiting for you than a slap across the face." She glared at Ryder and pointed a finger in his face. "I should've let her beat the living shit out of you, you asshole."

Harrison shoved Ryder out the door and down the stairs to the SUV before she had time to say anything else. Nolan skittered out the door after them.

Babs closed and locked the front door, then sprinted to the back porch. Grayson was curled up under a blanket on one of the rocking Adirondack chairs. Babs squatted down in front of her. She could see the streams of silent tears running down her roommate's face.

"Oh, Gray…" She didn't know where to begin.

"I guess I ruined breakfast, huh?" the brunette hollowly chuckled.

"Fuck breakfast, Gray. Who cares about the damned breakfast? In fact…"

She stood up, walked back into the kitchen, and returned with the bottle of champagne and their teacups.

"We've eaten. Now we need to drink. Heavily."

Grayson wiped her eyes, little good it did her since the tears kept coming. She accepted the cup that Babs poured for her.

"The nerve of those bastards…I just can't believe they… he…argh!" Babs fumed, pouring a cup for herself and collapsing into the other chair. She took a long drink, then smiled. "I'll tell you what though if there was ever a slap to be heard 'round the world, that was it. Damn, I'll bet that hurt."

They sat outside for a while, not saying a word and slowly sipping on mimosas that were becoming mostly champagne. When she couldn't stand it any longer, Babs broke the silence.

"Gray, let me clean up down here and do all the house

chores today. You do whatever you want. Better yet, go upstairs and take a long bath. There's a whole second bottle of champagne in the fridge. Take it with you."

"The alcohol might just make things worse."

"Might make things better, too. Ooo, or even better, go plop yourself on the couch. I'll call British James Bond and have him bring over an excessive amount of fattening food and even more alcohol. We'll be ridiculous and watch cartoons and think of something wonderful to do with ourselves next weekend."

"Babs, I don't think I'm up for anything…"

"Right now, of course not. But I won't see my beautiful girl moping around the house. The weather will be cold and crappy, so we'll plan something fun indoors. Okay? Please? It will keep me from physically assaulting someone today."

After a moment of thought, Grayson weakly smiled over the edge of her teacup. "Okay."

"Okay then. Now," Babs pulled her roommate to her feet and pushed her into the kitchen, "upstairs with you. A nice warm bath, a refill on champagne, and new PJs. I'm calling in reinforcements."

Grayson started toward the living room, then turned.

"Did you say British James Bond?"

"Yeah."

"You know James Bond is British, right? Not just Noah, but the actual James Bond."

"Is he? Oh, whatever. All I know is, Daniel Craig is fine in a tux."

Grayson shook her head and headed upstairs as instructed. She peeled herself out of her pajamas and started the shower. She let the bathroom steam up, watching her reflection disappear in the mirror over the sink. She stepped into the warm spray, adjusting the temperature a bit, and looked around blankly. Her shampoo, conditioner, body wash, loofah…everything was in its place. Her body was itching to start in on the routine it knew by heart. But she just stood there, letting the spray hit her in the back and dampen her hair.

She closed her eyes and immediately saw his face. Only she saw it as it had been on Friday night, warm and mischievous, a hint of a smile on his lips.

Grayson sank to the floor, her knees curled up to her chest and shivered. She stayed there, sobbing, long after the water got cold.

———

Glossary of Medical Terms
(listed alphabetically)

16s: A measurement of IV gauge or size

ABCs: From the ATLS protocol, abbreviation for Airway, Breathing, and Circulation, the first steps in the algorithm

ACL: Abbreviation for Anterior Cruciate Ligament

Amiodarone: An antiarrhythmic cardiac medication

Antecubs: A description of an IV placed in the elbow crease, or antecubital fossa

AP Pelvis: A front-to-back x-ray view of the pelvis

APC-III Pelvis: A severe injury to the pelvic ring resulting in instability

Art line: Arterial line

Articular: As in articular reduction, at the level of the joint

ASIS: Abbreviation for Anterior Superior Iliac Spine, a bony landmark of the pelvis

ATLS protocol: Abbreviation for Advanced Trauma Life Support protocol; the algorithm followed for acute management of life-threatening trauma injuries

Benzodiazepines: A class of medication used for its sedating effect

Bilateral: Both sides, left and right

Borderline hypotension: Blood pressure that is nearly too low

Bounding pulses: Easily palpable, strong pulses

Catheter: A flexible tube inserted to drain fluid, often in the bladder

Chronically: Opposite of acute; for a long period of time

Cirrhosis: A chronic liver disease marked by degeneration of the cells and inflammation, usually caused by alcohol use or hepatitis

CK: Creatine kinase, a muscle protein released during rhabdomyolysis, that contributes to kidney failure

Clavicle: The collarbone

Comminuted fracture: A break in the bone that is in multiple pieces

Compartment syndrome: An increase to intra-compartment pressures within muscular compartments which causes cessation of blood flow and muscle death

DIC: Abbreviation for Diffuse Intravascular Coagulation, a life-threatening change in the ability of the body to stop bleeding

Dilaudid: A strong narcotic pain medication

Displaced: Not properly aligned, as in fracture ends that no longer align with one another

Distal radius: The end portion of one of the forearm bones at the level of the wrist

Divert: To change course

Dressings: Surgical bandages

Dysphagia: Trouble swallowing

ED: Abbreviation for Emergency Department

Electrolytes: Ions, often measured in the blood

Embolization: The process of obstructing a blood vessel with a mass, whether naturally or artificially

Epi: Short for epinephrine

Etomidate: A short acting anesthetic used for induction

Ex-fix/external fixator: A combination of pins and bars outside of the skin that temporarily stabilizes a fractured extremity until definitive fixation can be performed

Exsanguination: A severe and rapid loss of blood

Fasciotomy: Operative release of the fascia tissue surrounding the muscle compartments of an extremity, performed to release pressure within the compartment and prevent tissue death

FAST exam: Acronym for an ultrasound examination looking at four particular intra-abdominal recesses for blood

Femoral nails: A metal rod that is placed inside the femur for fracture reduction and fixation

Femoral neck: A particular anatomic portion of the proximal femur; part of the hip joint complex

Fentanyl: A strong narcotic pain medication

FFP: Abbreviation for Fresh Frozen Plasma, a blood bank component used during trauma resuscitation

Four part intraarticular proximal humerus fracture: A fracture involving with shoulder joint with four separate fracture fragments

GCS 5: Glasgow coma scale score of 5, a sign of significant injury and neurologic impairment in a trauma patient

GI: Abbreviation for Gastrointestinal; pertaining to the gastrointestinal tract

H&P: Abbreviation for History and Physical paperwork, the initial paperwork performed for an admission to the hospital

Hemi: Short for hemiarthroplasty, a partial joint replacement, a common treatment for the hip following fracture of the femoral neck

Hemodynamically unstable: The combination of an abnormal blood pressure, heart rate, oxygenation, and respiratory rate indicating physiologic instability

Hemoglobin: A protein responsible for transporting oxygen in the blood

Hyoid bone: A bone in the anterior neck, often fractured when a person has been strangled

Hypertensive: High blood pressure

Hypotensive: A descriptor indicating low blood pressure

ICU: Abbreviation for Intensive Care Unit

IV PPI's: Abbreviation for Intravenous Proton Pump Inhibitors, medications used to prevent gastric ulcers

Intensivist: A subspecialty physician who works exclusively in the ICU

Interventional radiology: A subspecialty of radiology which specializes in invasive procedures, including embolization

Intra-abdominal injury: An injury to the organs and structures on the inside of the abdomen

Intra-operative fluoroscopy: Use of mobile x-ray during a surgical procedure, common in orthopaedic surgery

Ivy-League gunner: A tongue-in-cheek description of an ambitious, type A college student intent on a particular career goal

Lag screw/neutralization plate: A type of construct used to fix fractures utilizing a particular screw and plate combination

McBurney's point: A location on the right lower abdomen, pain at which may be related to appendicitis

ME: Abbreviation for Medical Examiner; a subspecialty trained pathologist dedicated to the examination of a deceased person in order to determine cause of death

Mercury Cyanide: An extremely toxic salt composed of mercury and hydrocyanic acid

Midline: In the middle; central

M&M: Abbreviation for Morbidity and Mortality Conference; a medical conference examining the patient cases involving death or suboptimal outcome

MVC: Abbreviation for Motor Vehicle Crash

Narcan: A medication used to reverse an overdose of narcotics

Nasogastric tube: A tube inserted through the nose, down the esophagus, and into the stomach, used to introduce or remove fluid from the stomach

Nephrology: A subspecialty dedicated to the kidneys

Neurology: A subspecialty dedicated to the brain

New-onset arrhythmia: Newly diagnosed abnormal heart rhythm

PACU: Acronym for Post-Anesthesia Care Unit; the location where patients are transferred after surgery to recover prior to returning to their assigned hospital room

Palliative: Relieving pain without directing addressing the root cause of the problem, as in palliative care consult for a terminally ill patient

Palliative care fellow: A doctor who is undertaking additional training in the care of the terminally ill and actively dying patient

Pathologic fracture: A break in the bone secondary to abnormally weak bone, commonly due to cancer and metastatic disease

Pelvic binder: A device used to decrease intra-pelvic volume following fracture of the pelvic ring

Pelvic ex-fix: An external fixator applied to the pelvis; see ex-fix

Pelvic packing: A technique used to help decrease bleeding secondary to pelvic fractures which involves placing sterile towels along the pelvic rim inside the body

PGY2's/3's: Abbreviation for Post-Graduate Year; a particular year in residency training

Plate it: To place a plate and screw construct to stabilize a fracture

Platelets: Small, a-nuclear cells involved with blood clotting

Pneumo: See pneumothorax

Pneumothorax: A condition where air becomes trapped outside of the lung but inside the ribcage, causing collapse of the lung

Poly-extremity: Involving multiple limbs

Pressors: See vasopressors

Proximal humerus: The most cephalad portion of the upper arm bone, part of the shoulder complex

PT: Abbreviation for Physical Therapy

Pull traction: Use manual force to pull longitudinal traction on an extremity in order to lengthen and reduce a fracture or dislocation

Renal failure: Damage to the kidneys resulting in a lack of cell function and buildup of toxins in the bloodstream; kidney failure

Rhabdomyolysis: A serious syndrome resulting from muscle cell death and release of damaging proteins into the bloodstream, which can possibly lead to kidney failure

Rodding (as in a femur): Placement of a femoral nail

Sat's: Short for Saturation; intending to describe the level of oxygen in the blood

Sepsis: A state characterized by abnormal vital signs in the setting of infection

Septicemia: See sepsis

Stage-3 shock: A descriptor of vital signs and clinical findings describing a severe level of hemodynamic instability

STEMI: Acronym for ST-Elevation Myocardial Infarction, a type of heart attack

Stitch: Surgical suture

Stress steroids: A particular dosing protocol of intravenous steroid medication

Subclavian vein: A large vein underneath the collarbone that returns blood to the heart

Subspecialty: A particularly specific area of medicine, e.g. cardiology, neurosurgery, orthopaedic surgery

Succinylcholine: A synthetic compound used in anesthesia to induce paralysis for intubation

Syndesmosis: A ligamentous complex at the level of the ankle joint

Syphilis: An infectious disorder caused by a spirochete bacteria

T-waves: A marker on an EKG, or electrocardiogram, which can be normal or abnormal depending on its morphology

Tachycardia: An abnormally fast heart rate

TEG: Acronym for Thromboelastogram; an intricate method for analyzing blood clotting mechanisms in the bloodstream

Tibia: The shin bone, the larger of the two lower leg bones

Tibial plateau: The proximal portion of the tibia; part of the knee joint

Tubed and lined: A descriptor indicating that a patient has been intubated and has had central and peripheral IV access established

Turf it: Patient transfer to another service

Type-1 diabetic: Also called juvenile diabetes; an inability to produce insulin or a defect in the body's ability to use insulin to regulate blood sugar levels

V-fib: Abbreviation for Ventricular Fibrillation; a very dangerous heart rhythm

Vasopressors: Medications given to maintain appropriate blood pressure

VDRF: Abbreviation for Ventilator Dependent Respiratory Failure; a condition in which a patient has been unable to wean off of a mechanical ventilator machine because he/she cannot breathe well enough to maintain enough oxygen in the bloodstream on his/her own

Ventilator: A mechanical breathing machine

Versed: A strong benzodiazepine used for sedation

Weber B Bimal equivalent: A type of ankle fracture often requiring operative repair

Wide mediastinum: A description of the area in the chest containing the heart, bronchus, esophagus, and great vessels; a widened mediastinum can indicate severe injury

Widened pubic symphysis and gapping of the right posterior SI joint: A description of an particular injury pattern to the pelvic ring, including injury to the front and the back of the pelvic ring, indicating instability

Trademark Notice

THE INFERNO TRILOGY
BOOK TWO

TORMENT

A. R. NICOLE

Available Spring of 2019

1

THE SOUND OF leather gloves hitting hundred-pound heavy bags was usually therapeutic. Whenever the running and the scotch didn't take the edge off the job, he'd turn his mind off here. The physical release was always painful, but it was welcome. He knew he would hurt like hell in the morning. It didn't matter. His knuckles were bleeding, his arms were begging for a break, and he didn't stop. He couldn't stop.

It's not working.

He hadn't been able to calm down since the morning. Nolan had driven him home in silence and dumped him at the front door without a second glance. He'd spent hours endlessly pacing around his apartment, playing the scene over and over in his head. Each time it ended with her icy expression and her roommate's parting words.

"I should've let her beat the living shit out of you, you asshole."

After three hours of wearing a track in the carpet, he'd gone for a run. Two hours later, frustrated and cursing, he'd thrown his bag into his car and headed to the gym. His usual sparring partner wasn't around, so he'd picked a bag in the back corner and gone at it. Hard.

Ryder wiped the sweat off of his face. Every goddamned time his eyes shut...

Fuck.

He hit the bag harder.

The gym was busy, so it took a few minutes to find him. He was kicking the crap out of a heavy bag, and from the looks of it, he'd been at it for a while. Harrison stood back and watched him swing wildly, picking up his pace until he missed the bag altogether and lurched forward into the wall. The older detective chuckled under his breath and sauntered over toward the sweating, swearing heap in the corner.

"You know, the whole point is to actually hit the bag, Gabe."

Ryder looked up, surprised to find his former partner looming over him. He wearily pushed to his feet.

"What…what're you doing here, Logan?" he asked, steadying the bag and getting ready for another set.

"Why does anybody come to the gym?" he replied.

"Not for the reasons I do."

"Clearly. The run didn't do it for you today?" He nodded, moving to stand behind the bag and hold it still.

Ryder didn't argue or tell him to move. He just started hitting the bag.

"So," Logan said, in between hits, "you wanna talk about it?"

"About what?"

"You know what. The scene you made this morning."

Ryder put his head down and focused on the black bag in front of him. That earned him a slap to the side of the head. He ripped his eyes up and glared. "Hey! What the fuck?"

Harrison smirked. "Eyes up, dummy. You know you don't box like that. Did I teach you nothing?"

"Don't fucking hit me in the head again," he spat.

"Don't let yourself get hit."

"If you came here to try to piss me off, it's working."

"Great. Maybe you'll get pissed enough to tell me what the hell happened today."

Ryder was mid-swing. He stopped midair. Logan noticed his facial expression change. His eyes closed, then tore open just as fast. Logan's forehead wrinkled. Gabriel looked like he was going to be sick.

What the hell is up with him?

"Look, finish whatever you're doing here and meet me on the mat. You could use some agility work," Logan said, grabbing his gym bag and heading off toward the locker rooms.

He emerged several minutes later and found Ryder still going hard on the same bag. Logan stepped behind him and grabbed his right arm as he brought it back, locking it in place.

"Enough. I said get to the mat. Now."

Ryder glared at him but nodded, grabbed his towel, and followed him to the center of the gym. A large area had been cleared out to let fighters train in the open. Logan grabbed two small sparring pads, one for each hand, and put them on. Ryder slipped his hands out of his boxing gloves and rewrapped his hands up to the wrists. It didn't take long.

"C'mon, rookie. Start easy. Transition when you're ready." Logan grinned, holding out his hands.

Ryder started in, alternating jabs. Harrison moved backward, slowly, in a circle, forcing the younger man to move his feet to keep the pads within striking distance. After a few minutes, he started moving the pads themselves, forcing Ryder to concentrate even harder. Logan kept the pace slow. He wanted something more out of this session besides sore wrists and a pissed-off buddy.

"You didn't answer me."

Hit. Hit.

"About what?"

Hit. Slide to the right. *Hit.*

"About what the hell happened today."

Hit. Hit. Alternate. *Hit.*

"I don't want to talk about it."

Hit. Hit.

"Did your mind just short circuit?"

Hit. Alternate. *Hit. Hit.*

"I said…"

"Or have you decided bullying young girls is your thing now?"

Hit. Hit. Hit. Ryder picked up the pace.

"Shut the fuck up."

Hit.

"No. I'm curious," Harrison said, advancing forward, sarcasm dripping off his lips. "Just how did you think that would go?"

Hit. Hit.

"Drop it, Logan."

Hit. Hit. Alternate. *Hit.*

"She didn't deserve that attack, Gabe, and you fucking know it."

Ryder stopped in his tracks. Harrison powered forward, shoving him back with the pads. Ryder regained his footing quickly and squared up. He wasn't about to be dropped on his ass twice in one day.

"Did you think it would be fun? Bullying her into a half-assed confession?"

Hit. Hit. Hit. Faster.

"No."

Hit.

"Did you ever think to yourself 'hey, I'm acting like a complete nut job'?"

Harrison took a swipe at Ryder's head with the pad, which he dodged.

Hit. Hit.

"If you'd have told us what the hell you were thinking, I wouldn't have let you fucking near her."

Hit. Pause. *Hit.*

"Did you even give a damn about what you were doing to her? Did you see her face, Ryder?"

Hit. Hit. Alternate. *Hit. Hit.*

Gabriel picked up his pace again, and Logan compensated accordingly, still advancing. "Shut up."

"No. Fucking answer me."

Ryder's eyes blazed. Harrison just smirked and lowered his voice.

"So, you did it to, what, get your rocks off watching her cry? Was that fun for you, Gabe? She's prettier than your usual playthings."

Gabriel froze, glaring at his former partner. He tightened his fists. Logan wriggled his hands free from the pads. Ryder growled and lunged forward, his right fist intended for Harrison's face. At the last second, Logan dodged and threw him to the floor, the pads unceremoniously tossed to the side. He grabbed Ryder's right arm and wrenched it behind his back, then put a knee to the back of his neck. Gabriel struggled until he felt the pressure against his spine, then went limp to signal defeat. Logan had made his point. He didn't need a broken neck on top of it.

When he was sure the fight was out of him, Logan released his hold and let him roll onto his back. Gabriel sat up, draped his arms over his bent knees, and hung his head between them.

"Tell me this," Logan said, sitting down beside him, "and don't bullshit me. Do you honestly believe she's responsible? That she's pulling strings to have these people killed?"

Ryder shook his head.

"Then why the fuck did you accuse her like that?" he asked, sighing. "Gabe, you didn't just politely ask if she had anything to do with this shit. You hung her out to rot. Jesus."

Ryder mumbled under his breath. The older man smiled and nodded.

"That's what I thought. C'mon. You've beaten yourself up enough for one day."

Logan hauled Ryder to his feet. They walked back to the locker room in silence, showered, changed, and headed outside. The afternoon sun was up and, despite the low reading on the thermometer, it still felt warm outside. Ryder threw his gym bag in his car, and Harrison did the same. The younger detective opened his driver side door, his biceps screaming in protest.

"Nope."

Logan shoved the door closed before Ryder had a chance to even consider sitting down. He walked off down the sidewalk without looking back. Ryder followed, head down. He knew better than to argue.

They ended up at a coffee shop two blocks down from the gym. They both knew it well. Logan grabbed a table by the window while Ryder paid for the coffee. He gave his former partner a minute to compose himself.

"So, explain something to me."

"I thought we were done talking," came the exhausted reply.

"We're done fighting, dumbass, not talking."

Ryder sighed and closed his eyes, then instantly opened them again.

Every time.

Logan was smirking at him when he looked up. "All right. Where were we? Oh yeah, the part where you start talking."

"What do you want me to say?"

"I want you to tell me what the hell snapped in you this morning. Nolan was right about you taking the news about Carrol badly, but holy shit."

"I, I…" he stuttered, staring into his coffee, "I don't know. You saw how he treated her on Friday. What he called her. Then he turns up dead with his tongue cut out on Sunday morning? It fit."

"And so clearly she murdered him," Logan said sarcastically.

"She's connected to all of them, Logan, not just Carrol. She has ties to all of them."

"And since when does that mean she's a criminal master-mind? Not to mention it seems like she's really protective of your first vic, that Oakes girl. You've got a nasty bruise on your face to prove it. Why would she kill her?"

"I don't have an answer for that. She's the one that doesn't fit."

"Carter?"

"Oakes. I can't make her murder fit with the others. The other victims had something wrong with them. Some kind of vice. For all we can tell, Lisa Oakes was a good person. But she kicked this whole thing off."

"And again, how does this mean young Dr. Carter's to blame?"

Ryder dropped his head into his hands and sighed.

"Do you have a better idea, Logan?"

"You just said you don't believe she did this."

"I don't."

"But you're going after her anyway. That makes perfect fucking sense."

"She fits. I just need time…"

"No, she doesn't, Gabe. And you know it."

They sat in silence for a few minutes. Logan was just about to open his mouth when Ryder's face cleared.

"She's the link."

He waited, and when his partner didn't elaborate, he pushed.

"Yeah, you've said that…"

"I accused her because I didn't see any other options. Any…any other way this made sense."

"But you do now?"

"Maybe."

Harrison leaned back in his chair enough to take the front two legs off of the floor. "All right. I'll humor you. Start talking."

2

GRAYSON SPENT THE better part of her Sunday trying to keep control of herself. She attempted to smile at regular intervals and participate in small talk, but it was no use. She felt awful, and it showed. By noon, she'd completely given up the masquerade. She was miserable.

Noah had shown up at the house after he'd finished rounding at the hospital, and he'd spent the day trying to keep her spirits up. He had even brought groceries to cook a proper dinner. She never came right out and told him what had happened, but she had the feeling Babs had given him a play-by-play. He fussed over her more than usual, and both he and Barbara tried to keep the conversation as far away from the hospital and cops as possible.

Grayson waited until early evening, when Babs had gone upstairs to take a shower, to say anything. She was sitting on the couch with Noah when the time hit.

"You two can stop walking on eggshells around me, you know," she said softly.

Noah smiled at her and turned the TV volume down. "We're driving you nuts, aren't we, lovie?"

She nodded. "Kind of."

Noah flinched. "I'm sorry."

"Don't be. I appreciate it, I do. But it's getting a bit, um, unnecessary. We all know what happened this morning. Not talking about it isn't going to make it disappear."

Noah rested his arm on the back of the couch. "I heard you kicked his butt."

Grayson smiled shyly and diverted her eyes to the floor. "I wouldn't say that. He just wasn't expecting me to do anything like that. It caught him off guard."

"Neither was Babs. She told me she nearly peed her pants when you slapped him."

"It wasn't my finest hour, Noah." She shook her head. "I shouldn't have done that."

I actually HIT him. I attacked another person. Good God, what's wrong with me?

"It still would've been great to see," he said, his smile fading. "Do you think they're serious? About coming after you for all this?"

She hugged her knees to her chest. "I don't know, Noah. I know I didn't do any of this, but what does that prove?"

"If those idiots believe that, they need to reassign the case."

"I did a bit of digging right after Lisa's funeral." She shrugged. "Those detectives are some of the best in the department. Ryder included."

"What is his problem?"

"Who?"

Noah scooted closer on the couch. "You know who, Gray. Ryder. One minute, I think he's making eyes at you, and the next he barges into your house and talks to you like you're the scum of the planet."

"I told you that you were blowing things out of proportion," she scolded.

"I'm usually so good at picking up on that kind of thing," he moaned.

"I'll forgive you this once," she said grinning.

She didn't dare mention that since Halloween, she'd started to think the same thing, just for a quick, fleeting moment.

Noah sighed and nodded. "Thanks. Are you going to be okay?"

"We'll see. Probably. I just need a few days to get my head around the fact that I'm being accused of murder."

"Shouldn't they have arrested you or something?"

"How should I know? All of my police knowledge comes from watching *Law and Order* reruns."

Noah smiled at her, then opened up his arms. She gladly settled into his side and threw a blanket over her legs. They flipped channels until they found a movie they could both agree on and watched in amicable silence until Babs came back downstairs. Her hair was wet, thrown back in her hair towel and twisted in that way that only women seem to know how to do.

"I swear, you two are going to give me diabetes," she said, rolling her eyes and sitting down on the side chair.

"What?"

"This…" she motioned with her hand moving in between the two of them, "This…sickeningly sweet display. Ugh. It's like biting into a sugar cube," she said, feigning annoyance.

"We'll keep that in mind," Grayson replied.

"So, J.B., what're we planning for our girl?" Babs asked, looking at Noah.

He wrinkled his forehead at her, confused.

"She's calling you James Bond right now, J.B. for short," Grayson explained.

"Original," he returned sarcastically.

"Don't be too harsh. She was strongly influenced by mimosas," Grayson chided.

"Well?" Babs pressed.

"It's a surprise."

"You really don't have to do anything," Grayson started in protest.

"Nope. Stop right there. You've had a shitty few days. Maybe the week gets better; maybe it doesn't. But I wanna take you out for a fun night. A real grown-up night out. No costumes. Babs is coming, too. Just deal with it." He smiled.

"You know I don't like big surprises," she moaned. "I don't have time to…"

"Stop being so difficult. We'll take care of everything. You just have to show your pretty face," Noah said with a wink.

Barbara nodded enthusiastically from her chair. Grayson leaned back on the couch and sighed. She was going out next Friday whether she liked it or not.

Continue on with Grayson and Gabriel in Book Two and Three of *The Inferno Trilogy*. Torment—Spring 2019 and Ascent—Summer 2019

Accused of orchestrating the murders of five of her colleagues, Dr. Grayson Carter attempts to continue life as usual, working harder and longer than ever in an attempt to block out the horrors slowly consuming her daily life. But the reality of her situation continues to deteriorate, inch by inch, day by day. Hidden in the shadows, a threat looms that she never could have imagined…that no one can protect her from.

———

Detective Gabriel Ryder, the best and brightest of Major Crimes, is floundering. A serial killer is on the loose, preying on the physicians at Saint Joseph Hospital. He has no leads, no motive, and no suspects. He knows he's running on borrowed time, but just how little…no one could have guessed. Worse than that, no one could have ever imagined just how dearly a price he will pay for missing the clues right in front of his face.

About the Author

A. R. Nicole is a North American writer with a background in medicine and a fascination with the written word. Many lazy afternoons are spent either devouring the latest novel, her loyal pup sleeping beside the chair, or writing a new one.

Follow her at:
www.ARNicole.com